Dear Reader,

There's just something about going home again. Returning to our roots can revitalize us, and remind us of who we are and where we came from, but as we learn in these two classic romances from bestselling author Nora Roberts, it can also open our hearts and put us on the path toward an unfolding future....

In *Island of Flowers,* Laine Simmons has traveled halfway across the world to reconcile with her long-estranged father but then finds herself faced with his arrogant, judgmental and *very* handsome business partner. Infuriating as the man is, Laine can't deny that Dillon O'Brian has stirred up something insider her—something she's not sure she's ready for, even if the ghosts of her past have her dreaming about a future with this man she can't seem to forget.

In *Untamed,* lion tamer Jovilette Wilder's career is on the line when her mentor passes on, leaving his circus to estranged son—and no-nonsense lawyer—Keane Prescott. Word is, Keane's looking to sell, which would put Jo's entire way of life in jeopardy, but her resentment wavers the moment she meets her sexy new boss. Jo may tame lions for a living, but facing off against the undeniably charming Keane Prescott could prove to be far more risky....

We hope these sweet stories will evoke that warm, inviting feeling of coming home—and finding someone to share it with.

The Editors

Silhouette Books

CONTENTS

Also available from Silhouette Books
and Harlequin Books by

NORA ROBERTS

FOREVER
When just one night isn't enough…

WHISPERED PROMISES
The most heartfelt promises are often left unspoken

NOT WITHOUT YOU
When being together is the only option

THE MacKADE BROTHERS: RAFE & JARED
THE MacKADE BROTHERS: DEVIN & SHANE
The MacKade brothers all have *one* weakness—
the women they love

WILD AT HEART
When love is meant to be, nothing can stop it

And coming soon:
LOVE COMES ALONG

Be sure to look for more Nora Roberts titles
in your local stores, or contact our
Harlequin Reader Service Center,
U.S.A.: 3010 Walden Avenue
P.O. Box 1325, Buffalo, NY 14269
Canada: P.O. Box 609, Fort Erie, Ontario L2A 5X3
Visit Silhouette Books at www.Harlequin.com

ISLAND OF FLOWERS

For my mother and father

Chapter 1

Laine's arrival at Honolulu International Airport was traditional. She would have preferred to melt through the crowd, but it appeared traveling tourist class categorized her as just that. Golden-skinned girls with ivory smiles and vivid sarongs bestowed brilliant colored leis. Accepting both kiss and floral necklace, Laine wove through the milling crowd and searched for an information desk. The girth of a fellow passenger hampered her journey. His yellow and orange flowered shirt and the twin cameras which joined the lei around his neck attested to his determination to enjoy his vacation. Under different circumstances, his appearance would have nudged at her humor, but the tension in Laine's stomach stifled any amusement. She had not stood on American soil in fifteen years. The ripe land with cliffs and beaches which she had seen as the plane descended brought no sense of homecoming.

The America Laine pictured came in sporadic patches of memory and through the perspective of a child of seven. America was a gnarled elm tree guarding her bedroom window. It was a spread of green grass where buttercups scattered gold. It was a mailbox at the end of a long, winding lane. But most of all, America was the man who had taken her to imaginary African jungles and desert islands. However, there were orchids instead of daisies. The graceful palms and spreading ferns of Honolulu were as foreign to Laine as the father she had traveled half the world to find. It seemed a lifetime ago that divorce had pulled her away from her roots.

Laine felt a quiet desperation that the address she had found among her mother's papers would lead to emptiness. The age of the small, creased piece of paper was unknown to her. Neither did she know if Captain James Simmons still lived on the island of Kauai. There had only been the address tossed in among her mother's bills. There had been no correspondence, nothing to indicate the address was still a vital one. To write to her father was the practical thing to do, and Laine had struggled with indecision for nearly a week. Ultimately, she had rejected a letter in favor of a personal meeting. Her hoard of money would barely see her through a week of food and lodging, and though she knew the trip was impetuous, she had not been able to prevent herself. Threading through her doubts was the shimmering strand of fear that rejection waited for her at the end of her journey.

There was no reason to expect anything else, she

lectured herself. *Why should the man who had left her fatherless during her growing-up years care about the woman she had become?* Relaxing the grip on the handle of her handbag, Laine reasserted her vow to accept whatever waited at her journey's end. She had learned long ago to adjust to whatever life offered. She concealed her feelings with the habit developed during her adolescence.

Quickly, she adjusted the white, soft-brimmed hat over a halo of flaxen curls. She lifted her chin. No one would have guessed her underlying anxiety as she moved with unconscious grace through the crowds. She looked elegantly aloof in her inherited traveling suit of ice blue silk, altered to fit her slight figure rather than her mother's ample curves.

The girl at the information desk was deep in an enjoyable conversation with a man. Standing to one side, Laine watched the encounter with detached interest. The man was dark and intimidatingly tall. Her pupils would undoubtedly have called him *séduisant*. His rugged features were surrounded by black hair in curling disorder, while his bronzed skin proved him no stranger to the Hawaiian sun. There was something rakish in his profile, some basic sensuality which Laine recognized but did not fully comprehend. She thought perhaps his nose had been broken at one time, but rather than spoiling the appeal of the profile, the lack of symmetry added to it. His dress was casual, the jeans well worn and frayed at the cuffs, and a denim work shirt exposed a hard chest and corded arms.

Vaguely irritated, Laine studied him. She observed the easy flow of charm, the indolent stance at the counter, the tease of a smile on his mouth. *I've seen his type before,* she thought with a surge of resentment, *hovering around Vanessa like a crow around carrion.* She remembered, too, that when her mother's beauty had become only a shadow, the flock had left for younger prey. At that moment, Laine could feel only gratitude that her contacts with men had been limited.

He turned and encountered Laine's stare. One dark brow rose as he lingered over his survey of her. She was too unreasonably angry with him to look away. The simplicity of her suit shouted its exclusiveness, revealing the tender elegance of young curves. The hat half shaded a fragile, faintly aristocratic face with well-defined planes, straight nose, unsmiling mouth and morning-sky eyes. Her lashes were thick and gold, and he took them as too long for authenticity. He assessed her as a cool, self-possessed woman, recognizing only the borrowed varnish.

Slowly, and with deliberate insolence, he smiled. Laine kept her gaze steady and struggled to defeat a blush. The clerk, seeing her companion's transfer of attention, shifted her eyes in Laine's direction and banished a scowl.

"May I help you?" Dutifully, she affixed her occupational smile. Ignoring the hovering male, Laine stepped up to the counter.

"Thank you. I need transportation to Kauai. Could you tell me how to arrange it?" A whisper of France lingered in her voice.

"Of course, there's a charter leaving for Kauai in…" The clerk glanced at her watch and smiled again. "Twenty minutes."

"I'm leaving right now." Laine glanced over and gave the loitering man a brief stare. She noted that his eyes were as green as Chinese jade. "No use hanging around the airport, and," he continued as his smile became a grin, "my Cub's not as crowded or expensive as the charter."

Laine's disdainful lift of brow and dismissing survey had been successful before, but did not work this time. "Do you have a plane?" she asked coldly.

"Yeah, I've got a plane." His hands were thrust in his pockets, and in his slouch against the counter, he still managed to tower over her. "I can always use the loose change from picking up island hoppers."

"Dillon," the clerk began, but he interrupted her with another grin and a jerk of his head.

"Rose'll vouch for me. I run for Canyon Airlines on Kauai." He presented Rose with a wide smile. She shuffled papers.

"Dillon…Mr. O'Brian is a fine pilot." Rose cleared her throat and sent Dillon a telling glance. "If you'd rather not wait for the scheduled charter, I can guarantee that your flight will be equally enjoyable with him."

Studying his irreverent smile and amused eyes, Laine was of the opinion that the trip would be something less than enjoyable. However, her funds were low and she knew she must conserve what she had.

"Very well, Mr. O'Brian, I will engage your services." He held out his hand, palm up, and Laine dropped her eyes to it. Infuriated by his rudeness, she brought her eyes back to his. "If you will tell me your rate, Mr. O'Brian, I shall be happy to pay you when we land."

"Your baggage check," he countered, smiling. "Just part of the service, lady."

Bending her head to conceal her blush, Laine fumbled through her purse for the ticket.

"O.K., let's go." He took both the stub and her arm, propelling her away as he called over his shoulder in farewell to the information clerk, "See you next time, Rose."

"Welcome to Hawaii," Rose stated out of habit, then, with a sigh, pouted after Dillon's back.

Unused to being so firmly guided, and hampered by a stride a fraction of his, Laine struggled to maintain her composure while she trotted beside him. "Mr. O'Brian, I hope I don't have to jog to Kauai." He stopped and grinned at her. She tried, and failed, not to pant. His grin, she discovered, was a strange and powerful weapon, and one for which she had not yet developed a defense.

"Thought you were in a hurry, Miss…" He glanced at her ticket, and she watched the grin vanish. When his eyes lifted, all remnants of humor had fled. His mouth was grim. She would have retreated from the waves of hostility had not his grip on her arm prevented her. "Laine Simmons?" It was more accusation than question.

"Yes, you've read it correctly," she said.

Dillon's eyes narrowed. She found her cool façade melting with disconcerting speed. "You're going to see James Simmons?"

Her eyes widened. For an instant, a flash of hope flickered on her face. But his expression remained set and hostile. She smothered the impulse to ask hundreds of questions as she felt his tightening fingers bruise her arm.

"I don't know how that concerns you, Mr. O'Brian,"

she began, "but yes. Do you know my father?" She faltered over the final word, finding the novelty of its use bittersweet.

"Yes, I know him…a great deal better than you do. Well, Duchess—" he released her as if the contact was offensive "—I doubt if fifteen years late is better than never, but we'll see. Canyon Airlines is at your disposal." He inclined his head and gave Laine a half bow. "The trip's on the house. I can hardly charge the owner's prodigal daughter." Dillon retrieved her luggage and stalked from the terminal in thunderous silence. In the wake of the storm, Laine followed, stunned by his hostility and by his information.

Her father owned an airline. She remembered James Simmons only as a pilot, with the dream of his own planes a distant fantasy. When had the dream become reality? Why did this man, who was currently tossing her mother's elegant luggage like so many duffel bags into a small, streamlined plane, turn such hostility on her at the discovery of her name? How did he know fifteen years had spanned her separation from her father? She opened her mouth to question Dillon as he rounded the nose of the plane. She shut it again as he turned and captured her with his angry stare.

"Up you go, Duchess. We've got twenty-eight minutes to endure each other's company." His hands went to her waist, and he hoisted her as if she were no more burden than a feather pillow. He eased his long frame into the seat beside her. She became uncomfortably aware of his virility and attempted to ignore him by giving intense concentration to the buckling of her safety belt. Beneath her lashes, she watched as he flicked at the controls before the engine roared to life.

The sea opened beneath them. Beaches lay white against its verge, dotted with sun worshipers. Mountains rose, jagged and primitive, the eternal rulers of the islands. As they gained height, the colors in the scene below became so intense that they seemed artificial. Soon the shades blended. Browns, greens and blues softened with distance. Flashes of scarlet and yellow merged before fading. The plane soared with a surge of power, then its wings tilted as it made a curving arch and hurtled into the sky.

"Kauai is a natural paradise," Dillon began in the tone of a tour guide. He leaned back in his seat and lit a cigarette. "It offers, on the North Shore, the Wailua River which ends at Fern Grotto. The foliage is exceptional. There are miles of beaches, fields of cane and pineapple. Opeakea Falls, Hanalei Bay and Na Pali Coast are also worth seeing. On the South Shore," he continued, while Laine adopted the air of attentive listener, "we have Kokie State Park and Waimea Canyon. There are tropical trees and flowers at Olopia and Menehune Gardens. Water sports are exceptional almost anywhere around the island. Why the devil did you come?"

The question, so abrupt on the tail of his mechanical recital, caused Laine to jolt in her seat and stare. "To… to see my father."

"Took your own sweet time about it," Dillon muttered and drew hard on his cigarette. He turned again and gave her a slow, intimate survey. "I guess you were pretty busy attending that elegant finishing school."

Laine frowned, thinking of the boarding school which had been both home and refuge for nearly fifteen years. She decided Dillon O'Brian was crazed. There was no use contradicting a lunatic. "I'm glad you approve," she returned coolly. "A pity you missed the experience. It's amazing what can be done with rough edges."

"No thanks, Duchess." He blew out a stream of smoke. "I prefer a bit of honest crudeness."

"You appear to have an adequate supply."

"I get by. Island life can be a bit uncivilized at times." His smile was thin. "I doubt if it's going to suit your tastes."

"I can be very adaptable, Mr. O'Brian." She moved her shoulders with gentle elegance. "I can also overlook a certain amount of discourtesy for short periods of time. Twenty-eight minutes is just under my limit."

"Terrific. Tell me, Miss Simmons," he continued with exaggerated respect, "how is life on the Continent?"

"Marvelous." Deliberately, she tilted her head and looked at him from under the brim of her hat. "The French are so cosmopolitan, so urbane. One feels so…" Attempting to copy her mother's easy polish, she gestured and gave the next word the French expression. "*Chez soi* with people of one's own inclinations."

"Very true." The tone was ironic. Dillon kept his eyes on the open sky as he spoke. "I doubt if you'll find many people of your own inclinations on Kauai."

"Perhaps not." Laine pushed the thought of her father aside and tossed her head. "Then again, I may find the island as agreeable as I find Paris."

"I'm sure you found the men agreeable." Dillon crushed out his cigarette with one quick thrust. Laine found his fresh anger rewarding. The memory of the pitifully few men with whom she had had close contact caused her to force back a laugh. Only a small smile escaped.

"The men of my acquaintance—" she apologized mentally to elderly Father Rennier "—are men of elegance and culture and breeding. They are men of high intellect and discerning tastes who possess the manners and sensitivity which I currently find lacking in their American counterparts."

"Is that so?" Dillon questioned softly.

"That, Mr. O'Brian," said Laine firmly, "is quite so."

"Well, we wouldn't want to spoil our record." Switching over to automatic pilot, he turned in his seat and captured her. Mouth bruised mouth before she realized his intent.

She was locked in his arms, her struggles prevented by his strength and by her own dazed senses. She was overwhelmed by the scent and taste and feel of him. He increased the intimacy, parting her lips with his tongue. To escape from sensations more acute than she had thought possible, she clutched at his shirt.

Dillon lifted his face, and his brows drew straight at her look of stunned, young vulnerability. She could only stare, her eyes filled with confused new knowledge. Pulling away, he switched back to manual control and gave his attention to the sky. "It seems your French lovers haven't prepared you for American technique."

Stung, and furious with the weakness she had just discovered, Laine turned in her seat and faced him. "Your technique, Mr. O'Brian, is as crude as the rest of you."

He grinned and shrugged. "Be grateful, Duchess, that I didn't simply shove you out the door. I've been fighting the inclination for twenty minutes."

"You would be wise to suppress such inclinations," Laine snapped, feeling her temper bubbling at an alarming speed. *I will not lose it,* she told herself. She would not give this detestable man the satisfaction of seeing how thoroughly he had unnerved her.

The plane dipped into an abrupt nosedive. The sea hurtled toward them at a terrifying rate as the small steel bird performed a series of somersaults. The sky and sea were a mass of interchangeable blues with the white of clouds and the white of breakers no longer separate. Laine clutched at her seat, squeezing her eyes shut as the sea and sky whirled in her brain. Protest was impossible. She had lost both her voice and her heart at the first circle. She clung and prayed for her stomach to remain stationary. The plane leveled, then cruised right side up, but inside her head the world still revolved. Laine heard her companion laugh wholeheartedly.

"You can open your eyes now, Miss Simmons. We'll be landing in a minute."

Turning to him, Laine erupted with a long, detailed analysis of his character. At length, she realized she was stating her opinion in French. She took a deep breath. "You, Mr. O'Brian," she finished in frigid English, "are the most detestable man I have ever met."

"Thank you, Duchess." Pleased, he began to hum.

Laine forced herself to keep her eyes open as Dillon began his descent. There was a brief impression of greens and browns melding with blue, and again the swift rise of mountains before they were bouncing on asphalt and gliding to a stop. Dazed, she surveyed the hangars and lines of aircraft, Piper Cubs and cabin planes, twin engines and passenger jets. *There's some mistake,* she thought. *This cannot belong to my father.*

"Don't get any ideas, Duchess," Dillon remarked, noting her astonished stare. His mouth tightened. "You've forfeited your share. And even if the captain was inclined to be generous, his partner would make things very difficult. You're going to have to look someplace else for an easy ride."

He jumped to the ground as Laine stared at him with disbelief. Disengaging her belt, she prepared to lower herself to the ground. His hands gripped her waist before her feet made contact. For a moment, he held her suspended. With their faces only inches apart, Laine found his eyes her jailer. She had never known eyes so green or so compelling.

"Watch your step," he commanded, then dropped her to the ground.

Laine stepped back, retreating from the hostility in his voice. Gathering her courage, she lifted her chin and held her ground. "Mr. O'Brian, would you please tell me where I might find my father?"

He stared for a moment, and she thought he would simply refuse and leave her. Abruptly, he gestured toward a small white building. "His office is in there," he barked before he turned to stride away.

Chapter 2

The building which Laine approached was a midsize hut. Fanning palms and flaming anthurium skirted its entrance. Hands trembling, Laine entered. She felt as though her knees might dissolve under her, as though the pounding of her heart would burst through her head. What would she say to the man who had left her floundering in loneliness for fifteen years? What words were there to bridge the gap and express the need which had never died? Would she need to ask questions, or could she forget the whys and just accept?

Laine's image of James Simmons was as clear and vivid as yesterday. It was not dimmed by the shadows of time. *He would be older,* she reminded herself. *She was older as well.* She was not a child trailing after an idol, but a woman meeting her father. They were neither one the same as they had been. Perhaps that in itself would be an advantage.

The outer room of the hut was deserted. Laine had a vague impression of wicker furnishings and woven mats. She stared around her, feeling alone and unsure. Like a ghost of the past, his voice reached out, booming through an open doorway. Approaching the sound, Laine watched as her father talked on the phone at his desk.

She could see the alterations which age had made on his face, but her memory had been accurate. The sun had darkened his skin and laid its lines upon it, but his features were no stranger to her. His thick brows were gray now, but still prominent over his brown eyes. The nose was still strong and straight over the long, thin mouth. His hair remained full, though as gray as his brows, and she watched as he reached up in a well-remembered gesture and tugged his fingers through it.

She pressed her lips together as he replaced the receiver, then swallowing, Laine spoke in soft memory. "Hello, Cap."

He twisted his head, and she watched surprise flood his face. His eyes ran a quick gamut of emotions, and somewhere between the beginning and the end she saw the pain. He stood, and she noted with a small sense of shock that he was shorter than her child's perspective had made him.

"Laine?" The question was hesitant, colored by a reserve which crushed her impulse to rush toward him. She sensed immediately that his arms would not be open to receive her, and this rejection threatened to destroy her tentative smile.

"It's good to see you." Hating the inanity, she stepped into the room and held out her hand.

After a moment, he accepted it. He held her hand

briefly, then released it. "You've grown up." His survey was slow, his smile touching only his mouth. "You've the look of your mother. No more pigtails?"

The smile illuminated her face with such swift impact, her father's expression warmed. "Not for some time. There was no one to pull them." Reserve settled over him again. Feeling the chill, Laine fumbled for some new line of conversation. "You've got your airport; you must be very happy. I'd like to see more of it."

"We'll arrange it." His tone was polite and impersonal, whipping across her face like the sting of a lash.

Laine wandered to a window and stared out through a mist of tears. "It's very impressive."

"Thank you, we're pretty proud of it." He cleared his throat and studied her back. "How long will you be in Hawaii?"

She gripped the windowsill and tried to match his tone. Even at their worst, her fears had not prepared her for this degree of pain. "A few weeks perhaps, I have no definite plans. I came…I came straight here." Turning, Laine began to fill the void with chatter. "I'm sure there are things I should see since I'm here. The pilot who flew me over said Kauai was beautiful, gardens and…" She tried and failed to remember the specifics of Dillon's speech. "And parks." She settled on a generality, keeping her smile fixed. "Perhaps you could recommend a hotel?"

He was searching her face, and Laine struggled to keep her smile from dissolving. "You're welcome to stay with me while you're here."

Burying her pride, she agreed. She knew she could not afford to stay anywhere else. "That's kind of you. I should like that."

He nodded and shuffled some papers on his desk. "How's your mother?"

"She died," Laine murmured. "Three months ago."

Cap glanced up sharply. Laine watched the pain flicker over his face. He sat down. "I'm sorry, Laine. Was she ill?"

"There was…" She swallowed. "There was a car accident."

"I see." He cleared his throat, and his tone was again impersonal. "If you had written, I would have flown over and helped you."

"Would you?" She shook her head and turned back to the window. She remembered the panic, the numbness, the mountain of debts, the auction of every valuable. "I managed well enough."

"Laine, why did you come?" Though his voice had softened, he remained behind the barrier of his desk.

"To see my father." Her words were devoid of emotion.

"Cap." At the voice Laine turned, watching as Dillon's form filled the doorway. His glance scanned her before returning to Cap. "Chambers is leaving for the mainland. He wants to see you before he takes off."

"All right. Laine," Cap turned and gestured awkwardly, "this is Dillon O'Brian, my partner. Dillon, this is my daughter."

"We've met." Dillon smiled briefly.

Laine managed a nod. "Yes, Mr. O'Brian was kind enough to fly me from Oahu. It was a most…fascinating journey."

"That's fine then." Cap moved to Dillon and clasped a hand to his shoulder. "Run Laine to the house, will you, and see she settles in? I'm sure she must be tired."

Laine watched, excluded from the mystery of masculine understanding as looks were exchanged. Dillon nodded. "My pleasure."

"I'll be home in a couple of hours." Cap turned and regarded Laine in awkward silence.

"All right." Her smile was beginning to hurt her cheeks, so Laine let it die. "Thank you." Cap hesitated, then walked through the door leaving her staring at emptiness. *I will not cry,* she ordered herself. *Not in front of this man.* If she had nothing else left, she had her pride.

"Whenever you're ready, Miss Simmons."

Brushing past Dillon, Laine glanced back over her shoulder. "I hope you drive a car with more discretion than you fly a plane, Mr. O'Brian."

He gave an enigmatic shrug. "Why don't we find out?"

Her bags were sitting outside. She glanced down at them, then up at Dillon. "You seem to have anticipated me."

"I had hoped," he began as he tossed the bags into the rear of a sleek compact, "to pack both them and you back to where you came from, but that is obviously impossible now." He opened his door, slid into the driver's seat and started the engine. Laine slipped in beside him, unaided. Releasing the brake, he shot forward with a speed which jerked her against the cushions.

"What did you say to him?" Dillon demanded, not bothering with preliminaries as he maneuvered skillfully through the airport traffic.

"Being my father's business partner does not entitle you to an account of his personal conversations with me," Laine answered. Her voice was clipped and resentful.

"Listen, Duchess, I'm not about to stand by while you drop into Cap's life and stir up trouble. I didn't like the way he looked when I walked in on you. I gave you ten minutes, and you managed to hurt him. Don't make me stop the car and persuade you to tell me." He paused and lowered his voice. "You'd find my methods unrefined." The threat vibrated in his softly spoken words.

Suddenly Laine found herself too tired to argue. Nights with only patches of sleep, days crowded with pressures and anxiety, and the long, tedious journey had taken their toll. With a weary gesture, she pulled off her hat. Resting her head against the seat, she closed her eyes. "Mr. O'Brian, it was not my intention to hurt my father. In the ten minutes you allowed, we said remarkably little. Perhaps it was the news that my mother had died which upset him, but that is something he would have learned eventually at any rate." Her tone was hollow, and he glanced at her, surprised by the sudden frailty of her unframed face. Her hair was soft and pale against her ivory skin. For the first time, he saw the smudges of mauve haunting her eyes.

"How long ago?"

Laine opened her eyes in confusion as she detected a whisper of sympathy in his voice. "Three months." She sighed and turned to face Dillon more directly. "She ran her car into a telephone pole. They tell me she died instantly." *And painlessly,* she added to herself, *anesthetized with several quarts of vintage champagne.*

Dillon lapsed into silence, and she was grateful that he ignored the need for any trite words of sympathy. She had had enough of those already and found his silence more comforting. She studied his profile, the bronzed chiseled lines and unyielding mouth, before she turned her attention back to the scenery.

The scent of the Pacific lingered in the air. The water was a sparkling blue against the crystal beaches. Screw pines rose from the sand and accepted the lazy breeze, and monkeypods, wide and domelike, spread their shade in invitation. As they drove inland, Laine caught only brief glimpses of the sea. The landscape was a myriad of colors against a rich velvet green. Sun fell in waves of light, offering its warmth so that flowers did not strain to it, but rather basked lazily in its glory.

Dillon turned up a drive which was flanked by two sturdy palms. As they approached the house, Laine felt the first stir of pleasure. It was simple, its lines basic and clean, its walls cool and white. It stood two stories square, sturdy despite its large expanses of glass. Watching the windows wink in the sun, Laine felt her first welcoming.

"It's lovely."

"Not as fancy as you might have expected," Dillon countered as he halted at the end of the drive, "but Cap likes it." The brief truce was obviously at an end. He eased from the car and gave his attention to her luggage.

Without comment, Laine opened her door and slipped out. Shading her eyes from the sun, she stood for a moment and studied her father's home. A set of stairs led to a circling porch. Dillon climbed them, nudged the front door open and strode into the house. Laine entered unescorted.

"Close my door; flies are not welcome."

Laine glanced up and saw, with stunned admiration, an enormous woman step as lightly down the staircase as a young girl. Her girth was wrapped in a colorful, flowing muumuu. Her glossy black hair was pulled tight and secured at the back of her head. Her skin was unlined, the color of dark honey. Her eyes were jet, set deep and widely spaced. Her age might have been anywhere from thirty to sixty. The image of an island priestess, she took a long, uninhibited survey of Laine when she reached the foot of the stairs.

"Who is this?" she asked Dillon as she folded her thick arms over a tumbling bosom.

"This is Cap's daughter." Setting down the bags, he leaned on the banister and watched the exchange.

"Cap Simmons's daughter." Her mouth pursed and her eyes narrowed. "Pretty thing, but too pale and skinny. Don't you eat?" She circled Laine's arm between her thumb and forefinger.

"Why, yes, I…"

"Not enough," she interrupted and fingered a sunlit curl with interest. "Mmm, very nice, very pretty. Why do you wear it so short?"

"I…"

"You should have come years ago, but you are here now." Nodding, she patted Laine's cheek. "You are tired. I will fix your room."

"Thank you. I…"

"Then you eat," she ordered, and hefted Laine's two cases up the stairs.

"That was Miri," Dillon volunteered and tucked his hands in his pockets. "She runs the house."

"Yes, I see." Unable to prevent herself, Laine lifted her hand to her hair and wondered over the length. "Shouldn't you have taken the bags up for her?"

"Miri could carry me up the stairs without breaking

stride. Besides, I know better than to interfere with what she considers her duties. Come on." He grabbed her arm and pulled her down the hall. "I'll fix you a drink."

With casual familiarity, Dillon moved to a double-doored cabinet. Laine flexed her arm and surveyed the cream-walled room. Simplicity reigned here as its outer shell had indicated, and she appreciated Miri's obvious diligence with polish and broom. There was, she noted with a sigh, no room for a woman here. The furnishings shouted with masculinity, a masculinity which was well established and comfortable in its solitary state.

"What'll you have?" Dillon's question brought Laine back from her musings. She shook her head and dropped her hat on a small table. It looked frivolous and totally out of place.

"Nothing, thank you."

"Suit yourself." He poured a measure of liquor into a glass and dropped down on a chair. "We're not given to formalities around here, Duchess. While you're in residence, you'll have to cope with a more basic form of existence."

She inclined her head, laying her purse beside her hat. "Perhaps one may still wash one's hands before dinner?"

"Sure," he returned, ignoring the sarcasm. "We're big on water."

"And where, Mr. O'Brian, do you live?"

"Here." He stretched his legs and gave a satisfied smile at her frown. "For a week or two. I'm having some repairs done to my house."

"How unfortunate," Laine commented and wandered the room. "For both of us."

"You'll survive, Duchess." He toasted her with his

glass. "I'm sure you've had plenty of experience in surviving."

"Yes, I have, Mr. O'Brian, but I have a feeling you know nothing about it."

"You've got guts, lady, I'll give you that." He tossed back his drink and scowled as she turned to face him.

"Your opinion is duly noted and filed."

"Did you come for more money? Is it possible you're that greedy?" He rose in one smooth motion and crossed the room, grabbing her shoulders before she could back away from his mercurial temper. "Haven't you squeezed enough out of him? Never giving anything in return. Never even disturbing yourself to answer one of his letters. Letting the years pile up without any acknowledgment. What the devil do you want from him now?"

Dillon stopped abruptly. The color had drained from her face, leaving it like white marble. Her eyes were dazed with shock. She swayed as though her joints had melted, and he held her upright, staring at her in sudden confusion. "What's the matter with you?"

"I…Mr. O'Brian, I think I would like that drink now, if you don't mind."

His frown deepened, and he led her to a chair before moving off to pour her a drink. Laine accepted with a murmured thanks, then shuddered at the unfamiliar burn of brandy. The room steadied, and she felt the mists clearing.

"Mr. O'Brian, I…am I to understand…" She stopped and shut her eyes a moment. "Are you saying my father wrote to me?"

"You know very well he did." The retort was both swift and annoyed. "He came to the islands right after you and your mother left him, and he wrote you regularly until five years ago when he gave up. He still sent money," Dillon added, flicking on his lighter. "Oh yes, the money kept right on coming until you turned twenty-one last year."

"You're lying!"

Dillon looked over in astonishment as she rose from her chair. Her cheeks were flaming, her eyes flashing. "Well, well, it appears the ice maiden has melted." He blew out a stream of smoke and spoke mildly. "I never lie, Duchess. I find the truth more interesting."

"He never wrote to me. Never!" She walked to where Dillon sat. "Not once in all those years. All the letters I sent came back because he had moved away without even telling me where."

Slowly, Dillon crushed out his cigarette and rose to face her. "Do you expect me to buy that? You're selling to the wrong person, Miss Simmons. I saw the letters Cap sent, *and* the checks every month." He ran a finger down the lapel of her suit. "You seem to have put them to good use."

"I tell you I never received any letters." Laine knocked his hand away and tilted her head back to meet his eyes. "I have not had one word from my father since I was seven years old."

"Miss Simmons, I mailed more than one letter myself, though I was tempted to chuck them into the Pacific. Presents, too; dolls in the early years. You must have quite a collection of porcelain dolls. Then there was the jewelry. I remember the eighteenth birthday present very clearly. Opal earrings shaped like flowers."

"Earrings," Laine whispered. Feeling the room tilt again, she dug her teeth into her lip and shook her head.

"That's right." His voice was rough as he moved to

pour himself another drink. "And they all went to the same place: 17 rue de la Concorde, Paris."

Her color ebbed again, and she lifted a hand to her temple. "My mother's address," she murmured, and turned away to sit before her legs gave way. "I was in school; my mother lived there."

"Yes." Dillon took a quick sip and settled on the sofa again. "Your education was both lengthy and expensive."

Laine thought for a moment of the boarding school with its plain, wholesome food, cotton sheets and leaking roof. She pressed her fingers to her eyes. "I was not aware that my father was paying for my schooling."

"Just who did you think was paying for your French pinafores and art lessons?"

She sighed, stung by the sharpness of his tone. Her hands fluttered briefly before she dropped them into her lap. "Vanessa...my mother said she had an income. I never questioned her. She must have kept my father's letters from me."

Laine's voice was dull, and Dillon moved with sudden impatience. "Is that the tune you're going to play to Cap? You make it very convincing."

"No, Mr. O'Brian. It hardly matters at this point, does it? In any case, I doubt that he would believe me any more than you do. I will keep my visit brief, then return to France." She lifted her brandy and stared into the amber liquid, wondering if it was responsible for her numbness. "I would like a week or two. I would appreciate it if you would not mention this discussion to my father; it would only complicate matters."

Dillon gave a short laugh and sipped from his drink.

"I have no intention of telling him any part of this little fairy tale."

"Your word, Mr. O'Brian." Surprised by the anxiety in her voice, Dillon glanced up. "I want your word." She met his eyes without wavering.

"My word, Miss Simmons," he agreed at length.

Nodding, she rose and lifted her hat and bag from the table. "I would like to go up to my room now. I'm very tired."

He was frowning into his drink. Laine, without a backward glance, walked to her room.

Chapter 3

Laine faced the woman in the mirror. She saw a pale face, dominated by wide, shadowed eyes. Reaching for her rouge, she placed borrowed color in her cheeks.

She had known her mother's faults: the egotism, the shallowness. As a child, it had been easy to overlook the flaws and prize the sporadic, exciting visits with the vibrant, fairy-tale woman. Ice-cream parfaits and party dresses were such a contrast to home-spun uniforms and porridge. As Laine had grown older, the visits had become further spaced and shorter. It became routine for her to spend her vacations from school with the nuns. She had begun to see, through the objectivity of distance, her mother's desperation for youth, her selfish grip on her own beauty. A grown daughter with firm limbs and unlined skin had been more of an obstacle than an accomplishment. A grown daughter was a reminder of one's own mortality.

She was always afraid of losing, Laine thought. Her looks, her youth, her friends, her men. All the creams and potions. She sighed and shut her eyes. All the dyes and lotions. There had been a collection of porcelain dolls, Laine remembered. Vanessa's dolls, or so she had thought. Twelve porcelain dolls, each from a different country. She thought of how beautiful the Spanish doll had been with its high comb and mantilla. And the earrings...Laine tossed down her brush and whirled around the room. Those lovely opal earrings that looked so fragile in Vanessa's ears. I remember seeing her wear them, just as I remember listing them and the twelve porcelain dolls for auction. *How much more that was mine did she keep from me?* Blindly, Laine stared out her window. The incredible array of island blossoms might not have existed.

What kind of woman was she to keep what was mine for her own pleasure? To let me think, year after year, that my father had forgotten me? She kept me from him, even from his words on paper. I resent her for that, how I resent her for that. Not for the money, but for the lies and the loss. She must have used the checks to keep her apartment in Paris, and for all those clothes and all those parties. Laine shut her eyes tight on waves of outrage. At least I know now why she took me with her to France: as an insurance policy. She lived off me for nearly fifteen years, and even then it wasn't enough. Laine felt tears squeezing through her closed lids. Oh, how Cap must hate me. How he must hate me for the ingratitude and the coldness. He would never believe me. She sighed, remembering her father's reaction to her appearance. *"You've the look of your mother."* Opening her eyes, she walked back and studied her face in the mirror.

It was true, she decided as she ran her fingertips along her cheeks. The resemblance was there in the bone structure, in the coloring. Laine frowned, finding no pleasure in her inheritance. He's only to look at me to see her. He's only to look at me to remember. He'll think as Dillon O'Brian thinks. How could I expect anything else? For a few moments, Laine and her reflection merely stared at one another. But perhaps, she mused, her bottom lip thrust forward in thought, with a week or two I might salvage something of what used to be, some portion of the friendship. I would be content with that. But he must not think I've come for money, so I must be careful he not find out how little I have left. More than anything, I shall have to be careful around Mr. O'Brian.

Detestable man, she thought on a fresh flurry of anger. He is surely the most ill-bred, mannerless man I have ever met. He's worse, much worse, than any of Vanessa's hangers-on. At least they managed to wear a light coat of respectability. Cap probably picked him up off the beach out of pity and made him his partner. He has insolent eyes, she added, lifting her brush and tugging it through her hair. Always looking at you as if he knew how you would feel in his arms. He's nothing but a womanizer. Tossing down the brush, she glared at the woman in the glass. He's just an unrefined, arrogant womanizer. Look at the way he behaved on the plane.

The glare faded as she lifted a finger to rub it over her lips. The memory of their turbulent capture flooded back. You've been kissed before, she lectured, shaking her head against the echoing sensations. *Not like that,* a small voice insisted. *Never like that.*

"Oh, the devil with Dillon O'Brian!" she muttered aloud, and just barely resisted the urge to slam her bedroom door on her way out.

Laine hesitated at the sound of masculine voices. It was a new sound for one generally accustomed to female company, and she found it pleasant. There was a mixture of deep blends, her father's booming drum tones and Dillon's laconic drawl. She heard a laugh, an appealing, uninhibited rumble, and she frowned as she recognized it as Dillon's. Quietly, she came down the rest of the steps and moved to the doorway.

"Then, when I took out the carburetor, he stared at it, muttered a stream of incantations and shook his head. I ended up fixing it myself."

"And a lot quicker than the Maui mechanic or any other would have." Cap's rich chuckle reached Laine as she stepped into the doorway.

They were seated easily. Dillon was sprawled on the sofa, her father in a chair. Pipe smoke rose from the tray beside him. Both were relaxed and so content in each other's company that Laine felt the urge to back away and leave them undisturbed. She felt an intruder into some long established routine. With a swift pang of envy, she took a step in retreat.

Her movement caught Dillon's attention. Before she could leave, his eyes held her motionless just as effectively as if his arms had reached out to capture her. She had changed from the sophisticated suit she had worn for the flight into a simple white dress from her own wardrobe. Unadorned and ingenue, it emphasized her youth and her slender innocence. Following the direction of Dillon's unsmiling survey, Cap saw Laine and rose. As he stood, his ease transformed into awkwardness.

"Hello, Laine. Have you settled in all right?"

Laine forced herself to shift her attention from Dillon to her father. "Yes, thank you." The moistening of her lips was the first outward sign of nerves. "The room is lovely. I'm sorry. Did I interrupt?" Her hands fluttered once, then were joined loosely as if to keep them still.

"No…ah, come in and sit down. Just a little shop-talk."

She hesitated again before stepping into the room.

"Would you like a drink?" Cap moved to the bar and jiggled glasses. Dillon remained silent and seated.

"No, nothing, thank you." Laine tried a smile. "Your home is beautiful. I can see the beach from my window." Taking the remaining seat on the sofa, Laine kept as much distance between herself and Dillon as possible. "It must be marvelous being close enough to swim when the mood strikes you."

"I don't get to the water as much as I used to." Cap settled down again, tapping his pipe against the tray. "Used to scuba some. Now, Dillon's the one for it." Laine heard the affection in his voice, and caught it again in his smiling glance at the man beside her.

"I find the sea and the sky have a lot in common," Dillon commented, reaching forward to lift his drink from the table. "Freedom and challenge." He sent Cap an easy smile. "I taught Cap to explore the fathoms; he taught me to fly."

"I suppose I'm more of a land creature," Laine replied, forcing herself to meet his gaze levelly. "I haven't much experience in the air or on the sea."

Dillon swirled his drink idly, but his eyes held challenge. "You do swim, don't you?"

"I manage."

"Fine." He took another swallow of his drink. "I'll teach you to snorkel." Setting down the glass, he resumed his relaxed position. "Tomorrow. We'll get an early start."

His arrogance shot up Laine's spine like a rod. Her tone became cool and dismissive. "I wouldn't presume to impose on your time, Mr. O'Brian."

Unaffected by the frost in her voice, Dillon continued. "No trouble. I've got nothing scheduled until the afternoon. You've got some extra gear around, haven't you, Cap?"

"Sure, in the back room." Hurt by the apparent relief in his voice, Laine shut her eyes briefly. "You'll enjoy yourself, Laine. Dillon's a fine teacher, and he knows these waters."

Laine gave Dillon a polite smile, hoping he could read between the lines. "I'm sure you know how much I appreciate your time, Mr. O'Brian."

The lifting of his brows indicated that their silent communication was proceeding with perfect understanding. "No more than I your company, Miss Simmons."

"Dinner." Miri's abrupt announcement startled Laine. "You." She pointed an accusing finger at Laine, then crooked it in a commanding gesture. "Come eat, and don't pick at your food. Too skinny," she muttered and whisked away in a flurry of brilliant colors.

Laine's arm was captured as they followed in the wake of Miri's waves. Dillon slowed her progress until they were alone in the corridor. "My compliments on

your entrance. You were the picture of the pure young
virgin."

"I have no doubt you would like to offer me to the
nearest volcano god, Mr. O'Brian, but perhaps you
would allow me to have my last meal in peace."

"Miss Simmons." He bowed with exaggerated gal-
lantry and increased his hold on her arm. "Even I can
stir myself on occasion to escort a lady into dinner."

"Perhaps with a great deal of concentration, you
could accomplish this spectacular feat without breaking my arm."

Laine gritted her teeth as they entered the glass-
enclosed dining room. Dillon pulled out her chair. She
glanced coldly up at him. "Thank you, Mr. O'Brian,"
she murmured as she slid into her seat. Detestable man!

Inclining his head politely, Dillon rounded the table
and dropped into a chair. "Hey, Cap, that little cabin
plane we've been using on the Maui run is running a
bit rough. I want to have a look at it before it goes up
again."

"Hmm. What do you think's the problem?"

There began a technical, and to Laine unintelligible, discussion. Miri entered, placing a steaming tray
of fish in front of Laine with a meaningful thump. To
assure she had not been misunderstood, Miri pointed a
finger at the platter, then at Laine's empty plate before
she swirled from the room.

The conversation had turned to the intricacies of fuel
systems by the time Laine had eaten all she could of
Miri's fish. Her silence during the meal had been almost
complete as the men enjoyed their mutual interest. She
saw, as she watched him, that her father's lack of courtesy was not deliberate, but rather the result of years of

living alone. He was, she decided, a man comfortable with men and out of his depth with feminine company. Though she felt Dillon's rudeness was intentional, it was her father's unconscious slight which stung.

"You will excuse me?" Laine rose during a brief lull in the conversation. She felt a fresh surge of regret as she read the discomfort in her father's eyes. "I'm a bit tired. Please." She managed a smile as she started to rise. "Don't disturb yourself, I know the way." As she turned to go, she could almost hear the room sigh with relief at her exit.

Later that evening, Laine felt stifled in her room. The house was quiet. The tropical moon had risen and she could see the curtains flutter with the gentle whispers of perfumed air. Unable to bear the loneliness of the four walls any longer, she stole quietly downstairs and into the night. As she wandered without regard for destination, she could hear the night birds call to each other, piercing the stillness with a strange, foreign music. She listened to the sea's murmur and slipped off her shoes to walk across the fine layer of sand to meet it.

The water fringed in a wide arch, frothing against the sands and lapping back into the womb of midnight blue. Its surface winked with mirrored stars. Laine breathed deeply of its scent, mingling with the flowered air.

But this paradise was not for her. Dillon and her father had banished her. It was the same story all over again. She remembered how often she had been excluded on her visits to her mother's home in Paris. *Again an intruder,* Laine decided, and wondered if she had either the strength or the will to pursue the smiling masquerade for even a week of her father's company. Her place was not with him any more than it had been with Vanessa. Dropping to the sand, Laine brought her knees to her chest and wept for the years of loss.

"I don't have a handkerchief, so you'll have to cope without one."

At the sound of Dillon's voice, Laine shuddered and hugged her knees tighter. "Please, go away."

"What's the problem, Duchess?" His voice was rough and impatient. If she had had more experience, Laine might have recognized a masculine discomfort with feminine tears. "If things aren't going as planned, sitting on the beach and crying isn't going to help. Especially if there's no one around to sympathize."

"Go away," she repeated, keeping her face buried. "I want you to leave me alone. I want to be alone."

"You might as well get used to it," he returned carelessly. "I intend to keep a close eye on you until you're back in Europe. Cap's too soft to hold out against the sweet, innocent routine for long."

Laine sprang up and launched herself at him. He staggered a moment as the small missile caught him off guard. "He's my father, do you understand? My *father*. I have a right to be with him. I have a right to know him." With useless fury, she beat her fists against his chest. He weathered the attack with some surprise before he caught her arms and dragged her, still swinging, against him.

"There's quite a temper under the ice! You can always try the routine about not getting his letters—that should further your campaign."

"I don't want his pity, do you hear?" She pushed and shoved and struck out while Dillon held her with minimum effort. "I would rather have his hate than his disinterest, but I would rather have his disinterest than his pity."

"Hold still, blast it," he ordered, losing patience with the battle. "You're not going to get hurt."

"I will not hold still," Laine flung back. "I am not a puppy who washed up on his doorstep and needs to be dried off and given a corner and a pat on the head. I *will* have my two weeks, and I won't let you spoil it for me." She tossed back her head. Tears fell freely, but her eyes now held fury rather than sorrow. "Let me go! I don't want you to touch me." She began to battle with new enthusiasm, kicking and nearly throwing them both onto the sand.

"All right, that's enough." Swiftly, he used his arms to band, his mouth to silence.

He was drawing her into a whirlpool, spinning and spinning, until all sense of time and existence was lost in the current. She would taste the salt of her own tears mixed with some tangy, vital flavor which belonged to him. She felt a swift heat rise to her skin and fought against it as desperately as she fought against his imprisoning arms. His mouth took hers once more, enticing her to give what she did not yet understand. All at once she lost all resistance, all sense of self. She went limp in his arms, her lips softening in surrender. Dillon drew her away and without even being aware of what she was doing, Laine dropped her head to his chest. She trembled as she felt his hand brush lightly through her hair, and nestled closer to him. Suddenly warm and no longer alone, she shut her eyes and let the gamut of emotions run its course.

"Just who are you, Laine Simmons?" Dillon drew her away again. He closed a firm hand under her chin as she stubbornly fought to keep her head lowered. "Look at me," he commanded. The order was absolute. With his eyes narrowed, he examined her without mercy.

Her eyes were wide and brimming, the tears trembling down her cheeks and clinging to her lashes. All layers of her borrowed sophistication had been stripped away, leaving only the vulnerability. His search ended on an impatient oath. "Ice, then fire, now tears. No, don't," he commanded as she struggled to lower her head again. "I'm not in the mood to test my resistance." He let out a deep breath and shook his head. "You're going to be nothing but trouble, I should have seen that from the first look. But you're here, and we're going to have to come to terms."

"Mr. O'Brian…"

"Dillon, for pity's sake. Let's not be any more ridiculous than necessary."

"Dillon," Laine repeated, sniffling and despising herself. "I don't think I can discuss terms with any coherence tonight. If you would just let me go, we could draw up a contract tomorrow."

"No, the terms are simple because they're all mine."

"That sounds exceedingly reasonable." She was pleased that irony replaced tears.

"While you're here," Dillon continued mildly, "we're going to be together like shadow and shade. I'm your guardian angel until you go back to the Left Bank. If you make a wrong move with Cap, I'm coming down on you so fast you won't be able to blink those little-girl eyes."

"Is my father so helpless he needs protection from his own daughter?" She brushed furiously at her lingering tears.

"There isn't a man alive who doesn't need protection from you, Duchess." Tilting his head, he studied her damp, glowing face. "If you're an operator, you're a good one. If you're not, I'll apologize when the time comes."

"You may keep your apology and have it for breakfast. With any luck, you'll strangle on it."

Dillon threw back his head and laughed, the same appealing rumble Laine had heard earlier. Outraged both with the laughter and its effect on her, she swung back her hand to slap his face.

"Oh, no." Dillon grabbed her wrist. "Don't spoil it. I'd just have to hit you back, and you look fabulous when you're spitting fire. It's much more to my taste than the cool mademoiselle from Paris. Listen, Laine." He took an exaggerated breath to control his laughter, and she found herself struggling to deal with the stir caused by the way her name sounded on his lips. "Let's try a truce, at least in public. Privately, we can have a round a night, with or without gloves."

"That should suit you well enough." Laine wriggled out of his loosened hold and tossed her head. "You have a considerable advantage—given your weight and strength."

"Yeah." Dillon grinned and moved his shoulders. "Learn to live with it. Come on." He took her hand in a friendly gesture which nonplussed her. "Into bed; you've got to get up early tomorrow. I don't like to lose the morning."

"I'm not going with you tomorrow." She tugged her hand away and planted her bare heels in the sand. "You'll probably attempt to drown me, then hide my body in some cove."

Dillon sighed in mock exasperation. "Laine, if I have to drag you out of bed in the morning, you're going to find yourself learning a great deal more than snorkeling. Now, are you going to walk back to the house, or do I carry you?"

"If they could bottle your arrogance, Dillon O'Brian, there would be no shortage of fuel in this country!"

With this, Laine turned and fled. Dillon watched until the darkness shrouded her white figure. Then he bent down to retrieve her shoes.

Chapter 4

The morning was golden. As usual, Laine woke early. For a moment, she blinked in puzzlement. Cool green walls had replaced her white ones, louvered shades hung where she expected faded striped curtains. Instead of her desk stood a plain mahogany bureau topped with a vase of scarlet blossoms. But it was the silence which most confused her. There were no giggles, no rushing feet outside her door. The quiet was broken only by a bird who sang his morning song outside her window. Memory flooded back. With a sigh, Laine lay back against the pillow and wished she could go to sleep again. The habit of early rising was too ingrained. She rose, showered and dressed.

A friend had persuaded her to accept the loan of a swimsuit, and Laine studied the two tiny pieces. She slipped on what had been described as a modified bikini. The silvery blue was flattering, highlighting her subtle curves, but no amount of adjustment could result in a more substantial coverage. There was definitely too much of her and too little suit.

"Silly," Laine muttered and adjusted the halter strings a last time. "Women wear these things all the time, and I've hardly the shape for drawing attention."

Skinny. With a grimace, she recalled Miri's judgment. Laine gave the top a last, hopeless tug. *I don't think all the fish in the Pacific are going to change this inadequacy.* Pulling on white jeans and a scarlet scoopnecked top, she reminded herself that cleavage was not what she needed for dealing with Dillon O'Brian.

As she wandered downstairs, Laine heard the stirrings which accompany an awakening house. She moved quietly, half afraid she would disturb the routine. In the dining room, the sun poured like liquid gold through the windows. Standing in its pool, Laine stared out at soft ferns and brilliant poppies. Charmed by the scene, she decided she would let nothing spoil the perfection of the day. There would be time enough later, on some drizzling French morning, to think of rejections and humiliations, but today the sun was bright and filled with promise.

"So, you are ready for breakfast." Miri glided in from the adjoining kitchen. She managed to look graceful despite her size, and regal despite the glaring flowered muumuu.

"Good morning, Miri." Laine gave her the first smile of the day and gestured toward the sky. "It's beautiful."

"It will bring some color to your skin." Miri sniffed and ran a finger down Laine's arm. "Red if you aren't careful. Now, sit and I will put flesh on your skinny bones." Imperiously, she tapped the back of a chair, and Laine obeyed.

"Miri, have you worked for my father long?"

"Ten years." Miri shook her head and poured steaming coffee into a cup. "Too long a time for a man not to have a wife. Your mother," she continued, narrowing her dark eyes, "she was skinny too?"

"Well, no, I wouldn't say… That is…" Laine hesitated in an attempt to gauge Miri's estimation of a suitable shape.

Rich laughter shot out. Miri's bosom trembled under pink and orange flowers. "You don't want to say she was not as much woman as Miri." She ran her hands over her well-padded hips. "You're a pretty girl," she said unexpectedly and patted Laine's flaxen curls. "Your eyes are too young to be sad." As Laine stared up at her, speechless under the unfamiliar affection, Miri sighed. "I will bring your breakfast, and you will eat what I give you."

"Make it two, Miri." Dillon strolled in, bronzed and confident in cutoff denims and a plain white T-shirt. "Morning, Duchess. Sleep well?" He dropped into the chair opposite Laine and poured himself a cup of coffee. His movements were easy, without any early-morning lethargy, and his eyes were completely alert. Laine concluded that Dillon O'Brian was one of those rare creatures who moved from sleep to wakefulness instantly. It also occurred to her, in one insistent flash, that he was not only the most attractive man she had ever known, but the most compelling. Struggling against an unexplained longing, Laine tried to mirror his casualness.

"Good morning, Dillon. It appears it's going to be another lovely day."

"We've a large supply of them on this side of the island."

"On this side?" Laine watched as he ran a hand through his hair, sending it into a state of appealing confusion.

"Mmm. On the windward slopes it rains almost every day." He downed half his coffee in one movement, and Laine found herself staring at his long, brown fingers. They looked strong and competent against the cream-colored earthenware. Suddenly, she remembered the feel of them on her chin. "Something wrong?"

"What?" Blinking, she brought her attention back to his face. "No, I was just thinking…I'll have to tour the island while I'm here," she improvised, rushing through the words. "Is your…is your home near here?"

"Not far." Dillon lifted his cup again, studying her over its rim. Laine began to stir her own coffee as if the task required enormous concentration. She had no intention of drinking it, having had her first—and, she vowed, last—encounter with American coffee aboard the plane.

"Breakfast," Miri announced, gliding into the room with a heaping tray. "You will eat." With brows drawn, she began piling portions onto Laine's plate. "And then you go out so I can clean my house. You!" She shook a large spoon at Dillon who was filling his own plate with obvious appreciation. "Don't bring any sand back with you to dirty my floors."

He responded with a quick Hawaiian phrase and a cocky grin. Miri's laughter echoed after her as she moved from the room and into the kitchen.

"Dillon," Laine began, staring at the amount of food on her plate, "I could never eat all of this."

He forked a mouthful of eggs and shrugged. "Better make a stab at it. Miri's decided to fatten you up, and even if you couldn't use it—and you can," he added as he buttered a piece of toast, "Miri is not a lady to cross. Pretend it's bouillabaisse or escargots."

The last was stated with a tangible edge, and Laine stiffened. Instinctively, she put up her defenses. "I have no complaints on the quality of the food, but on the quantity."

Dillon shrugged. Annoyed, Laine attacked her breakfast. The meal progressed without conversation. Fifteen minutes later, she searched for the power to lift yet another forkful of eggs. With a sound of impatience, Dillon rose and pulled her from her chair.

"You look like you'll keel over if you shovel in one more bite. I'll give you a break and get you out before Miri comes back."

Laine gritted her teeth, hoping it would help her to be humble. "Thank you."

As Dillon pulled Laine down the hall toward the front door, Cap descended the stairs. All three stopped as he glanced down from man to woman. "Good morning. It should be a fine day for your snorkeling lesson, Laine."

"Yes, I'm looking forward to it." She smiled, straining for a naturalness she was unable to feel in his presence.

"That's good. Dillon's right at home in the water." Cap's smile gained warmth as he turned to the man by her side. "When you come in this afternoon, take a look at the new twin-engine. I think the modifications you specified worked out well."

"Sure. I'm going to do a bit of work on that cabin plane. Keep Tinker away from it, will you?"

Cap chuckled as they enjoyed some personal joke. When he turned to Laine, he had a remnant of his smile and a polite nod. "I'll see you tonight. Have a good time."

"Yes, thank you." She watched him move away and, for a moment, her heart lifted to her eyes. Looking back, she found Dillon studying her. His expression was indrawn and brooding.

"Come on," he said with sudden briskness as he captured her hand. "Let's get started." He lifted a faded, long-stringed bag and tossed it over his shoulder as they passed through the front door. "Where's your suit?"

"I have it on." Preferring to trot alongside rather than be dragged, Laine scrambled to keep pace.

The path he took was a well-worn dirt track. Along its borders, flowers and ferns crept to encroach on the walkway. Laine wondered if there was another place on earth where colors had such clarity or where green had so many shades. The vanilla-scented blossoms of heliotrope added a tang to the moist sea air. With a high call, a skylark streaked across the sky and disappeared. Laine and Dillon walked in silence as the sun poured unfiltered over their heads.

After a ten-minute jog, Laine said breathlessly, "I do hope it isn't much farther. I haven't run the decathlon for years."

Dillon turned, and she braced herself for his irritated retort. Instead, he began to walk at a more moderate pace. Pleased, Laine allowed herself a small smile. She felt even a minor victory in dealing with Dillon

O'Brian was an accomplishment. Moments later, she forgot her triumph.

The bay was secluded, sheltered by palms and laced with satin-petaled hibiscus. In the exotic beauty of Kauai, it was a stunning diamond. The water might have dripped from the sky that morning. It shone and glimmered like a multitude of fresh raindrops.

With a cry of pleasure, Laine began to pull Dillon through the circling palms and into the white heat of sun and sand. "Oh, it's beautiful!" She turned two quick circles as if to insure encompassing all the new wonders. "It's perfect, absolutely perfect."

She watched his smile flash like a brisk wind. It chased away the clouds and, for one precious moment, there was understanding rather than tension between them. It flowed from man to woman with an ease which was as unexpected as it was soothing. His frown returned abruptly, and Dillon crouched to rummage through the bag. He pulled out snorkels and masks.

"Snorkeling's easy once you learn to relax and breathe properly. It's important to be both relaxed and alert." He began to instruct in simple terms, explaining breathing techniques and adjusting Laine's mask.

"There is no need to be quite so didactic," she said at length, irked by his patronizing tone and frowning face. "I assure you, I have a working brain. Most things don't have to be repeated more than four or five times before I grasp the meaning."

"Fine." He handed her both snorkel and mask. "Let's try it in the water." Pulling off his shirt, he dropped it on the canvas bag. He stood above her adjusting the strap on his own mask.

A fine mat of black hair lay against his bronzed

chest. His skin was stretched tight over his rib cage, then tapered down to a narrow waist. The faded denim hung low over his lean hips. With some astonishment, Laine felt an ache start in her stomach and move warmly through her veins. She dropped her eyes to an intense study of the sand.

"Take off your clothes." Laine's eyes widened. She took a quick step in retreat. "Unless you intend to swim in them," Dillon added. His lips twitched before he turned and moved toward the water.

Embarrassed, Laine did her best to emulate his casualness. Shyly, she stripped off her top. Pulling off her jeans, she folded both and followed Dillon toward the bay. He waited for her, water lapping over his thighs. His eyes traveled over every inch of her exposed skin before they rested on her face.

"Stay close," he commanded when she stood beside him. "We'll skim the surface for a bit until you get the hang of it." He pulled the mask down over her eyes and adjusted it.

Easily, they moved along the shallows where sunlight struck the soft bottom and sea lettuce danced and swayed. Forgetting her instructions, Laine breathed water instead of air and surfaced choking.

"What happened?" Dillon demanded, as Laine coughed and sputtered. "You're going to have to pay more attention to what you're doing," he warned. Giving her a sturdy thump on the back, he pulled her mask back over her eyes. "Ready?" he asked.

After three deep breaths, Laine managed to speak. "Yes." She submerged.

Little by little, she explored deeper water, swimming by Dillon's side. He moved through the water as a bird moves through the air, with inherent ease and confidence. Before long, Laine learned to translate his aquatic hand signals and began to improvise her own. They were joined in the liquid world by curious fish. As Laine stared into round, lidless eyes, she wondered who had come to gape at whom.

The sun flickered through with ethereal light. It nurtured the sea grass and caused shells and smooth rocks to glisten. It was a silent world, and although the sea bottom teemed with life, it was somehow private and free. Pale pink fingers of coral grouped together to form a hiding place for vivid blue fish. Laine watched in fascination as a hermit crab slid out of its borrowed shell and scurried away. There was a pair of orange starfish clinging contentedly to a rock, and a sea urchin nestled in spiny solitude.

Laine enjoyed isolation with this strange, moody man. She did not pause to appraise the pleasure she took in sharing her new experiences with him. The change in their relationship had been so smooth and so swift, she had not even been aware of it. They were, for a moment, only man and woman cloaked in a world of water and sunlight. On impulse, she lifted a large cone-shaped shell from its bed, its resident long since evicted. First holding it out for Dillon to view, she swam toward the dancing light on the surface.

Shaking her head as she broke water, Laine splattered Dillon's mask with sundrops. Laughing, she pushed her own mask to the top of her head and stood in the waist-high water. "Oh, that was wonderful! I've never seen anything like it." She pushed damp tendrils behind her ears. "All those colors, and so many shades of blue and green molded together. It feels…it feels as if there were nothing else in the world but yourself and where you are."

Excitement had kissed her cheeks with color, her eyes stealing the blue from the sea. Her hair was dark gold, clinging in a sleek cap to her head. Now, without the softening of curls, her face seemed more delicately sculptured, the planes and hollows more fragile. Dillon watched her in smiling silence, pushing his own mask atop his head.

"I've never done anything like that before. I could have stayed down there forever. There's so much to see, so much to touch. Look what I found. It's beautiful." She held the shell in both hands, tracing a finger over its amber lines. "What is it?"

Dillon took it for a moment, turning it over in his hands before giving it back to her. "A music volute. You'll find scores of shells around the island."

"May I keep it? Does this place belong to anyone?"

Dillon laughed, enjoying her enthusiasm. "This is a private bay, but I know the owner. I don't think he'd mind."

"Will I hear the sea? They say you can." Laine lifted the shell to her ear. At the low, drifting echo, her eyes widened in wonder. *"Oh, c'est incroyable."* In her excitement, she reverted to French, not only in speech, but in mannerisms. Her eyes locked on his as one hand held the shell to her ear and the other gestured with her words. *"On entend le bruit de la mer. C'est merveilleux! Dillon, écoute."*

She offered the shell, wanting to share her discovery. He laughed as she had heard him laugh with her father. "Sorry, Duchess, you lost me a few sentences back."

"Oh, how silly. I wasn't thinking. I haven't spoken

English in so long." She brushed at her damp hair and offered him a smile. "It's marvelous, I can really hear the sea." Her words faltered as his eyes lost their amusement. They were darkened by an emotion which caused her heart to jump and pound furiously against her ribs. Her mind shouted quickly to retreat, but her body and will melted as his arms slid around her. Her mouth lifted of its own accord to surrender to his.

For the first time, she felt a man's hands roam over her naked skin. There was nothing between them but the satin rivulets of water which clung to their bodies. Under the streaming gold sun, her heart opened, and she gave. She accepted the demands of his mouth, moved with the caresses of his hands until she thought they would never become separate. She wanted only for them to remain one until the sun died, and the world was still.

Dillon released her slowly, his arms lingering, as if reluctant to relinquish possession. Her sigh was mixed with pleasure and the despair of losing a newly discovered treasure. "I would swear," he muttered, staring down into her face, "you're either a first-rate actress or one step out of a nunnery."

Immediately, the helpless color rose, and Laine turned to escape to the sand of the beach. "Hold on." Taking her arm, Dillon turned her to face him. His brows drew close as he studied her blush. "That's a feat I haven't seen in years. Duchess, you amaze me. Either way," he continued, and his smile held mockery but lacked its former malice, "calculated or innocent, you amaze me. Again," he said simply and drew her into his arms.

This time the kiss was gentle and teasing. But she had less defense against tenderness than passion, and her body was pliant to his instruction. Her hands tightened on his shoulders, feeling the ripple of muscles under her palms as he drew every drop of response from her mouth. With no knowledge of seduction, she became a temptress by her very innocence. Dillon drew her away and gave her clouded eyes and swollen mouth a long examination.

"You're a powerful lady," he said at length, then let out a quick breath. "Let's sit in the sun awhile." Without waiting for her answer, he took her hand and moved toward the beach.

On the sand, he spread a large beach towel and dropped onto it. When Laine hesitated, he pulled her down to join him. "I don't bite, Laine, I only nibble." Drawing a cigarette from the bag beside them, he lit it, then leaned back on his elbows. His skin gleamed with water and sun.

Feeling awkward, Laine sat very still with the shell in her hands. She tried not only to understand what she had felt in Dillon's arms, but why she had felt it. It had been important, and somehow, she felt certain it would remain important for the rest of her life. It was a gift that did not yet have a name. Suddenly, she felt as happy as when the shell had spoken in her ear. Glancing at it, Laine smiled with unrestrained joy.

"You treat that shell as though it were your firstborn." Twisting her head, she saw Dillon grinning. She decided she had never been happier.

"It is my first souvenir, and I've never dived for sunken treasure before."

"Just think of all the sharks you had to push out of the way to get your hands on it." He blew smoke at the sky as she wrinkled her nose at him.

"Perhaps you're only jealous because you didn't get one of your own. I suppose it was selfish of me not to have gotten one for you."

"I'll survive."

"You don't find shells in Paris," she commented, feeling at ease and strangely fresh. "The children will treasure it as much as they would gold doubloons."

"Children?"

Laine was examining her prize, exploring its smooth surface with her fingers. "My students at school. Most of them have never seen anything like this except in pictures."

"You teach?"

Much too engrossed in discovering every angle of the shell, Laine missed the incredulity in his voice. She answered absently, "Yes, English to the French students and French to the English girls who board there. After I graduated, I stayed on as staff. There was really nowhere else to go, and it had always been home in any case. Dillon, do you suppose I could come back sometime and find one or two others, a different type perhaps? The girls would be fascinated; they get so little entertainment."

"Where was your mother?"

"What?" In the transfer of her attention, she saw he was sitting up and staring at her with hard, probing eyes. "What did you say?" she asked again, confused by his change of tone.

"I said, where was your mother?"

"When…when I was in school? She was in Paris." The sudden anger in his tone threw her into turmoil. She searched for a way to change the topic. "I would like to see the airport again; do you think I…"

"Stop it."

Laine jerked at the harsh command, then quickly tried to slip into her armor. "There's no need to shout. I'm quite capable of hearing you from this distance."

"Don't pull that royal routine on me, Duchess. I want some answers." He flicked away his cigarette. Laine saw both the determination and fury in his face.

"I'm sorry, Dillon." Rising and stepping out of reach, Laine remained outwardly calm. "I'm really not in the mood for a cross-examination."

With a muttered oath, Dillon swung to his feet and captured her arms with a swiftness which left her stunned. "You can be a frosty little number. You switch on and off so fast, I can't make up my mind which is the charade. Just who the devil are you?"

"I'm tired of telling you who I am," she answered quietly. "I don't know what you want me to say; I don't know what you want me to be."

Her answer and her mild tone seemed only to make him more angry. He tightened his hold and gave her a quick shake. "What was this last routine of yours?"

She was yanked against him in a sudden blaze of fury, but before punishment could be meted out, someone called his name. With a soft oath Dillon released her, and turned as a figure emerged from a narrow tunnel of palms.

Laine's first thought was that a spirit from the island was drifting through the shelter and across the sand. Her skin was tawny gold and smooth against a sarong of scarlet and midnight blue. A full ebony carpet of hair fell to her waist, flowing gently with her graceful movements. Almond-shaped amber eyes were fringed with dark velvet. A sultry smile flitted across an exotic and perfect face. She lifted a hand in greeting, and Dillon answered.

"Hello, Orchid."

Her mortality was established in Laine's mind as the beautiful apparition lifted her lips and brushed Dillon's. "Miri said you'd gone snorkeling, so I knew you'd be here." Her voice flowed like soft music.

"Laine Simmons, Orchid King." Dillon's introductions were casual. Laine murmured a response, feeling suddenly as inadequate as a shadow faced with the sun. "Laine's Cap's daughter."

"Oh, I see." Laine was subjected to a more lengthy survey. She saw speculation beneath the practiced smile. "How nice you're visiting at last. Are you staying long?"

"A week or two." Laine regained her poise and met Orchid's eyes. "Do you live on the island?"

"Yes, though I'm off it as often as not. I'm a flight attendant. I'm just back from the mainland, and I've got a few days. I wanted to trade the sky for the sea. I hope you're going back in." She smiled up at Dillon and tucked a hand through his arm. "I would love some company."

Laine watched his charm flow. It seemed he need do nothing but smile to work his own particular magic. "Sure, I've got a couple of hours."

"I think I'll just go back to the house," Laine said quickly, feeling like an intruder. "I don't think I should get too much sun at one time." Lifting her shirt, Laine tugged it on. "Thank you, Dillon, for your time." She bent down and retrieved the rest of her things before speaking again. "It's nice to have met you, Miss King."

"I'm sure we'll see each other again." Undraping

her sarong, Orchid revealed an inadequate bikini and a stunning body. "We're all very friendly on this island, aren't we, cousin?" Though it was the standard island form of address, Orchid's use of the word *cousin* implied a much closer relationship.

"Very friendly." Dillon agreed with such ease that Laine felt he must be quite accustomed to Orchid's charms.

Murmuring a goodbye, Laine moved toward the canopy of palms. Hearing Orchid laugh, then speak in the musical tongue of the island, Laine glanced back before the leaves blocked out the view. She watched the golden arms twine around Dillon's neck, pulling his mouth toward hers in invitation.

Chapter 5

The walk back from the bay gave Laine time to reflect on the varying emotions Dillon O'Brian had managed to arouse in the small amount of time she had known him. Annoyance, resentment and anger had come first. Now, there was a wariness she realized stemmed from her inexperience with men. But somehow, that morning, there had been a few moments of harmony. She had been at ease in his company. And, she admitted ruefully, she had never before been totally at ease in masculine company on a one-to-one basis.

Perhaps it had simply been the novelty of her underwater adventure which had been responsible for her response to him. There had been something natural in their coming together, as if body had been created for body and mouth for mouth. She had felt a freedom in his arms, an awakening. It had been as if walls of glass had shattered and left her open to sensations for the first time.

Stopping, Laine plucked a blush-pink hibiscus, then twirled its stem idly as she wandered up the dirt track. Her tenuous feelings had been dissipated first by Dillon's unexplained anger, then by the appearance of the dark island beauty.

Orchid King, Laine mused. A frown marred her brow as the name of the flirtatious information clerk ran through her brain. *Rose.* Smoothing the frown away, Laine shook off a vague depression. Perhaps Dillon had a predilection for women with flowery names. It was certainly none of her concern. Obviously, she continued, unconsciously tearing off the hibiscus petals, he gave and received kisses as freely as a mouse nibbles cheese. He simply kissed me because I was there. Obviously, she went on doggedly, shredding the wounded blossom without thought, Orchid King has a great deal more to offer than I. She makes me feel like a pale, shapeless wren next to a lush, vibrant flamingo. I would hardly appeal to him as a woman even if he didn't already dislike me. I don't want to appeal to him. Certainly not. The very last thing I want to do is to appeal to that insufferable man. Scowling, she stared down at the mutilated hibiscus. With something between a sigh and a moan, she tossed it aside and increased her pace.

After depositing the shell in her room and changing out of her bathing suit, Laine wandered back downstairs. She felt listless and at loose ends. In the organized system of classes and meals and designated activities, her time had always been carefully budgeted. She found the lack of demand unsettling. She thought of how often during the course of a busy day she had yearned for a free hour to read or simply to sit alone. Now her time was free, and she wished only for occupation. The difference was, she knew, the fear of idle hours and the tendency to think. She found herself avoiding any attempt to sort out her situation or the future.

No one had shown her through the house since her arrival. After a brief hesitation, she allowed curiosity to lead her and gave herself a tour. She discovered that her father lived simply, with no frills or frippery, but with basic masculine comforts. There were books, but it appeared they were little read. She could see by the quantity and ragged appearance of aeronautical magazines where her father's taste in literature lay. Bamboo shades replaced conventional curtains; woven mats took the place of rugs. While far from primitive, the rooms were simply furnished.

Her mind began to draw a picture of a man content with such a basic existence, who lived quietly and routinely; a man whose main outlet was his love of the sky. Now Laine began to understand why her parents' marriage had failed. Her father's lifestyle was as unassuming as her mother's had been pretentious. Her mother would never have been satisfied with her father's modest existence, and he would have been lost in hers. Laine wondered, with a small frown, why she herself did not seem to fit with either one of them.

Laine lifted a black-framed snapshot from a desk. A younger version of Cap Simmons beamed out at her, his arm casually tossed around a Dillon who had not yet reached full manhood. Dillon's smile was the same, however—somewhat cocky and sure. If they had stood in the flesh before her, their affection for each other would have seemed no less real. A shared understanding was revealed in their eyes and their easy stance together. It struck Laine suddenly, with a stab of resentment, that they looked like father and son. The years they had shared could never belong to her.

"It's not fair," she murmured, gripping the picture in both hands. With a faint shudder, she shut her eyes. Who am I blaming? she asked herself. Cap for needing someone? Dillon for being here? Blame won't help, and looking for the past is useless. It's time I looked for something new. Letting out a deep breath, Laine replaced the photograph. She turned away and moved farther down the hall. In a moment, she found herself in the kitchen surrounded by gleaming white appliances and hanging copper kettles. Miri turned from the stove and gave Laine a satisfied smile.

"So you have come for lunch." Miri tilted her head and narrowed her eyes. "You have some color from the sun."

Laine glanced down at her bare arms and was pleased with the light tan. "Why, yes, I do. I didn't actually come for lunch, though." She smiled and made an encompassing gesture. "I was exploring the house."

"Good. Now you eat. Sit here." Miri waved a long knife toward the scrubbed wooden table. "And do not make your bed anymore. That is my job." Miri plopped a glass of milk under Laine's nose, then gave a royal sniff.

"Oh, I'm sorry." Laine glanced from the glass of milk up to Miri's pursed lips. "It's just a habit."

"Don't do it again," Miri commanded as she turned to the refrigerator. She spoke again as she began to remove a variety of contents. "Did you make beds in that fancy school?"

"It isn't actually a fancy school," Laine corrected, watching with growing anxiety as Miri prepared a hefty sandwich. "It's really just a small convent school outside Paris."

"You lived in a convent?" Miri stopped her sandwich-building and looked skeptical.

"Well, no. That is, one might say I lived on the fringes of one. Except, of course, when I visited my mother. Miri…" Daunted by the plate set in front of her, Laine looked up helplessly. "I don't think I can manage all this."

"Just eat, Skinny Bones. Your morning with Dillon, it was nice?"

"Yes, very nice." Laine applied herself to the sandwich as Miri eased herself into the opposite chair. "I never knew there was so much to see underwater. Dillon is an expert guide."

"Ah, that one." Miri shook her head and somehow categorized Dillon as a naughty twelve-year-old boy. "He is always in the water or in the sky. He should keep his feet planted on the ground more often." Leaning back, Miri kept a commanding eye on Laine's progress. "He watches you."

"Yes, I know," Laine murmured. "Like a parole officer. I met Miss King," she continued, lifting her voice. "She came to the bay."

"Orchid King." Miri muttered something in unintelligible Hawaiian.

"She's very lovely…very vibrant and striking. I suppose Dillon has known her for a long time." Laine made the comment casually, surprising herself with the intentional probe.

"Long enough. But her bait has not yet lured the fish into the net." Miri gave a sly smile lost on the woman who stared into her milk. "You think Dillon looks good?"

"Looks good?" Laine repeated and frowned, not understanding the nuance. "Yes, Dillon's a very attractive man. At least, I suppose he is; I haven't known many men."

"You should give him more smiles," Miri advised with a wise nod. "A smart woman uses smiles to show a man her mind."

"He hasn't given me many reasons to smile at him," Laine said between bites. "And," she continued, finding she resented the thought, "I would think he gets an abundance of smiles from other sources."

"Dillon gives his attention to many women. He is a very generous man." Miri chuckled, and Laine blushed as she grasped the innuendo. "He has not yet found a woman who could make him selfish. Now you..." Miri tapped a finger aside her nose as if considering. "You would do well with him. He could teach you, and you could teach him."

"I teach Dillon?" Laine shook her head and gave a small laugh. "One cannot teach what one doesn't know. In the first place, Miri, I only met Dillon yesterday. All he's done so far is confuse me. From one moment to the next, I don't know how he's going to make me feel." She sighed, not realizing the sound was wistful. "I think men are very strange, Miri. I don't understand them at all."

"Understand?" Her bright laugh rattled through the

kitchen. "What need is there to understand? You need only enjoy. I had three husbands, and I never understood one of them. But—" her smile was suddenly young "—I enjoyed. You are very young," she added. "That alone is attractive to a man used to women of knowledge."

"I don't think…I mean, of course, I wouldn't want him to, but…" Laine fumbled and stuttered, finding her thoughts a mass of confusion. "I'm sure Dillon wouldn't be interested in me. He seems to have a very compatible relationship with Miss King. Besides—" Laine shrugged her shoulders as she felt depression growing "—he distrusts me."

"It is a stupid woman who lets what is gone interfere with what is now." Miri placed her fingertips together and leaned back in her chair. "You want your father's love, Skinny Bones? Time and patience will give it to you. You want Dillon?" She held up an imperious hand at Laine's automatic protest. "You will learn to fight as a woman fights." She stood, and the flowers on her muumuu trembled with the movement. "Now, out of my kitchen. I have much work to do."

Obediently, Laine rose and moved to the door. "Miri…" Nibbling her lips, she turned back. "You've been very close to my father for many years. Don't you…" Laine hesitated, then finished in a rush. "Don't you resent me just appearing like this after all these years?"

"Resent?" Miri repeated the word, then ran her tongue along the inside of her mouth. "I do not resent because resent is a waste of time. And the last thing I resent is a child." She picked up a large spoon and tapped it idly against her palm. "When you went away from Cap Simmons, you were a child and you went with

your mother. Now you are not a child, and you are here.
What do I have to resent?" Miri shrugged and moved
back to the stove.

Feeling unexpected tears, Laine shut her eyes on
them and drew a small breath. "Thank you, Miri." With
a murmur, she retreated to her room.

Thoughts swirled inside Laine's mind as she sat
alone in her bedroom. As Dillon's embrace had opened
a door to dormant emotions, so Miri's words had opened
a door to dormant thoughts. *Time and patience,* Laine
repeated silently. Time and patience were Miri's pre-
scription for a daughter's troubled heart. But I have so
little time, and little more patience. How can I win my
father's love in a matter of days? She shook her head,
unable to resolve an answer. *And Dillon,* her heart murmured as she threw herself onto the bed and stared at
the ceiling. Why must he complicate an already impos-
sibly complicated situation? Why must he embrace me,
making me think and feel as a woman one moment, then
push me away and stand as my accuser the next? He can
be so gentle when I'm in his arms, so warm. And then…
Frustrated, she rolled over, laying her cheek against the
pillow. Then he's so cold, and even his eyes are brutal. If only I could stop thinking of him, stop remembering how it feels to be kissed by him. It's only that I
have no experience, and he has so much. It's nothing
more than a physical awakening. There can be nothing
more…nothing more.

The knock on Laine's door brought her up with a
start. Pushing at her tousled hair, she rose to answer.
Dillon had exchanged cutoffs for jeans, and he appeared
as refreshed and alert as she did bemused and heavy-
lidded. Laine stared at him dumbly, unable to bring her

thoughts and words together. With a frown, he surveyed her sleep-flushed cheeks and soft eyes.

"Did I wake you?"

"No, I..." She glanced back at the clock, and her confusion grew as she noted that an hour had passed since she had first stretched out on the bed. "Yes," she amended. "I suppose the flight finally caught up with me." She reached up and ran a hand through her hair, struggling to orient herself. "I didn't even realize I'd been asleep."

"They're real, aren't they?"

"What?" Laine blinked and tried to sort out his meaning.

"The lashes." He was staring so intently into her eyes, Laine had to fight the need to look away.

Nonchalantly, he leaned against the door and completed his survey. "I'm on my way to the airport. I thought you might want to go. You said you wanted to see it again."

"Yes, I would." She was surprised by his courtesy.

"Well," he said dryly, and gestured for her to come along.

"Oh, I'll be right there. It should only take me a minute to get ready."

"You look ready."

"I need to comb my hair."

"It's fine." Dillon grabbed her hand and pulled her from the room before she could resist further.

Outside she found, to her astonishment, a helmet being thrust in her hands as she faced a shining, trim motorcycle. Clearing her throat, she looked from the helmet, to the machine, to Dillon. "We're going to ride on this?"

"That's right. I don't often use the car just to run to the airport."

"You might find this a good time to do so," Laine advised. "I've never ridden on a motorcycle."

"Duchess, all you have to do is to sit down and hang on." Dillon took the helmet from her and dropped it on her head. Securing his own helmet, he straddled the bike, then kicked the starter into life. "Climb on."

With amazement, Laine found herself astride the purring machine and clutching Dillon's waist as the motorcycle shot down the drive. Her death grip eased slightly as she realized that the speed was moderate, and the motorcycle had every intention of staying upright. It purred along the paved road.

Beside them, a river wandered like an unfurled blue ribbon, dividing patterned fields of taro. There was an excitement in being open to the wind, in feeling the hardness of Dillon's muscles beneath her hands. A sense of liberation flooded her. Laine realized that, in one day, Dillon had already given her experiences she might never have touched. I never knew how limited my life was, she thought with a smile. *No matter what happens, when I leave here, nothing will ever be quite the same again.*

When they arrived at the airport, Dillon wove through the main lot, circling to the back and halting in front of a hangar. "Off you go, Duchess. Ride's over."

Laine eased from the bike and struggled with her helmet. "Here." Dillon pulled it off for her, then dropped it to join his on the seat of the bike. "Still in one piece?"

"Actually," she returned, "I think I enjoyed it."

"It has its advantages." He ran his hands down her arms, then captured her waist. Laine stood very still, unwilling to retreat from his touch. He bent down and moved his mouth with teasing lightness over hers. Currents of pleasure ran over her skin. "Later," he said, pulling back. "I intend to finish that in a more satisfactory manner. But at the moment, I've work to do." His thumbs ran in lazy circles over her hips. "Cap's going to take you around; he's expecting you. Can you find your way?"

"Yes." Confused by the urgency of her heartbeat, Laine stepped back. The break in contact did nothing to slow it. "Am I to go to his office?"

"Yeah, the same place you went before. He'll show you whatever you want to see. Watch your step, Laine." His green eyes cooled abruptly, and his voice lost its lightness. "Until I'm sure about you, you can't afford to make any mistakes."

For a moment, she only stared up at him, feeling her skin grow cold, and her pulse slow. "I'm very much afraid," she admitted sadly, "I've already made one."

Turning, she walked away.

Chapter 6

Laine walked toward the small, palm-flanked building. Through her mind ran all which had passed in twenty-four hours. She had met her father, learned of her mother's deception and was now readjusting her wishes.

She had also, in the brief span of time it takes the sun to rise and fall, discovered the pleasures and demands of womanhood. Dillon had released new and magic sensations. Again, her mind argued with her heart that her feelings were only the result of a first physical attraction. It could hardly be anything else, she assured herself. One does not fall in love in a day, and certainly not with a man like Dillon O'Brian. We're total opposites. He's outgoing and confident, and so completely at ease with people. I envy him his honest confidence. There's nothing emotional about that. I've simply never met anyone like him before. That's why I'm confused. It has nothing to do with emotions. Laine felt comforted as she entered her father's office building.

As she stepped into the outer lobby, Cap strode from his office, glancing over his shoulder at a dark girl with a pad in her hand who was following in his wake.

"Check with Dillon on the fuel order before you send that out. He'll be in a meeting for the next hour. If you miss him at his office, try hangar four." As he caught sight of Laine, Cap smiled and slowed his pace. "Hello, Laine. Dillon said you wanted a tour."

"Yes, I'd love one, if you have the time."

"Of course. Sharon, this is my daughter. Laine, this is Sharon Kumocko, my secretary."

Laine observed the curiosity in Sharon's eyes as they exchanged greetings. Her father's tone during the introductions had been somewhat forced. Laine felt him hesitate before he took her arm to lead her outside. She wondered briefly if she had imagined their closeness during her childhood.

"It's not a very big airport," Cap began as they stepped out into the sun and heat. "For the most part, we cater to island hoppers and charters. We also run a flight school. That's essentially Dillon's project."

"Cap." Impulsively, Laine halted his recital and turned to face him. "I know I've put you in an awkward position. I realize now that I should have written and asked if I could come rather than just dropping on your doorstep this way. It was thoughtless of me."

"Laine…"

"Please." She shook her head at his interruption and rushed on. "I realize, too, that you have your own life, your own home, your own friends. You've had fifteen years to settle into a routine. I don't want to interfere with any of that. Believe me, I don't want to be in the way, and I don't want you to feel…" She made a helpless gesture as the impetus ran out of her words. "I would like it if we could be friends."

Cap had studied her during her speech. The smile he gave her at its finish held more warmth than those he had given her before. "You know," he sighed, tugging his fingers through his hair, "it's sort of terrifying to be faced with a grown-up daughter. I missed all the stages, all the changes. I'm afraid I still pictured you as a bad-tempered pigtailed urchin with scraped knees. The elegant woman who walked into my office yesterday and spoke to me with a faint French accent is a stranger. And one," he added, touching her hair a moment, "who brings back memories I thought I'd buried." He sighed again and stuck his hands in his pockets. "I don't know much about women; I don't think I ever did. Your mother was the most beautiful, confusing woman I've ever known. When you were little, and the three of us were still together, I substituted your friendship for the friendship that your mother and I never had. You were the only female I ever understood. I've always wondered if that was why things didn't work."

Tilting her head, Laine gave her father a long, searching look. "Cap, why did you marry her? There seems to be nothing you had in common."

Cap shook his head with a quick laugh. "You didn't know her twenty years ago. She did a lot of changing, Laine. Some people change more than others." He shook his head again, and his eyes focused on some middle distance. "Besides, I loved her. I've always loved her."

"I'm sorry." Laine felt tears burn the back of her

eyes, and she dropped her gaze to the ground. "I don't mean to make things more difficult."

"You're not. We had some good years." He paused until Laine lifted her eyes. "I like to remember them now and again." Taking her arm, he began to walk. "Was your mother happy, Laine?"

"Happy?" She thought a moment, remembering the quicksilver moods, the gay bubbling voice with dissatisfaction always under the surface. "I suppose Vanessa was as happy as she was capable of being. She loved Paris and she lived as she chose."

"Vanessa?" Cap frowned, glancing down at Laine's profile. "Is that how you think of your mother?"

"I always called her by name." Laine lifted her hand to shield her eyes from the sun as she watched the descent of a charter. "She said 'mother' made her feel too old. She hated getting older... I feel better knowing you're happy in the life you've chosen. Do you fly anymore, Cap? I remember how you used to love it."

"I still put in my quota of flight hours. Laine." He took both her arms and turned her to face him. "One question, then we'll leave it alone for a while. Have you been happy?"

The directness of both his questions and his eyes caused her to fumble. She looked away as if fascinated by disembarking passengers. "I've been very busy. The nuns are very serious about education."

"You're not answering my question. Or," he corrected, drawing his thick brows together, "maybe you are."

"I've been content," she said, giving him a smile. "I've learned a great deal, and I'm comfortable with my life. I think that's enough for anyone."

"For someone," Cap returned, "who's reached my age, but not for a very young, very lovely woman." He watched her smile fade into perplexity. "It's not enough, Laine, and I'm surprised you'd settle for it." His voice was stern, laced with a hint of disapproval which put Laine on the defensive.

"Cap, I haven't had the chance..." She stopped, realizing she must guard her words. "I haven't taken the time," she amended, "to chase windmills." She lifted her hands, palms up, in a broad French gesture. "Perhaps I've reached the point in my life when I should begin to do so."

His expression lightened as she smiled up at him. "All right, we'll let it rest for now."

Without any more mention of the past, Cap led Laine through neat rows of planes. He fondled each as if it were a child, explaining their qualities in proud, but to Laine hopelessly technical, terms. She listened, content with his good humor, pleased with the sound of his voice. Occasionally, she made an ignorant comment that made him laugh. She found the laugh very precious.

The buildings were spread out, neat and without pretension; hangars and storage buildings, research and accounting offices, with the high, glass-enclosed control tower dominating all. Cap pointed out each one, but the planes themselves were his consummate interest.

"You said it wasn't big." Laine gazed around the complex and down light-dotted runways. "It looks enormous."

"It's a small, low-activity field, but we do our best to see that it's as well run as Honolulu International."

"What is it that Dillon does here?" Telling herself it

was only idle curiosity, Laine surrendered to the urge to question.

"Oh, Dillon does a bit of everything," Cap answered with frustrating vagueness. "He has a knack for organizing. He can find his way through a problem before it becomes one, and he handles people so well they never realize they've been handled. He can also take a plane apart and put it back together again." Smiling, Cap gave a small shake of his head. "I don't know what I'd have done without Dillon. Without his drive, I might have been content to be a crop duster."

"Drive?" Laine repeated, lingering over the word. "Yes, I suppose he has drive when there is something he wants. But isn't he…" She searched for a label and settled on a generality. "Isn't he a very casual person?"

"Island life breeds a certain casualness, Laine, and Dillon was born here." He steered her toward the communications building. "Just because a man is at ease with himself and avoids pretension doesn't mean he lacks intelligence or ability. Dillon has both; he simply pursues his ambitions in his own way."

Later, as they walked toward the steel-domed hangars, Laine realized she and her father had begun to build a new relationship. He was more relaxed with her, his smiles and speech more spontaneous. She knew her shield was dropped as well, and she was more vulnerable.

"I've an appointment in a few minutes." Cap stopped just inside the building and glanced at his watch. "I'll have to turn you over to Dillon now, unless you want me to have someone take you back to the house."

"No, I'll be fine," she assured him. "Perhaps I can just wander about. I don't want to be a nuisance."

"You haven't been a nuisance. I enjoyed taking you through. You haven't lost the curiosity I remember. You always wanted to know why and how and you always listened. I think you were five when you demanded I explain the entire control panel of a 707." His chuckle was the same quick, appealing sound she remembered from childhood. "Your face would get so serious, I'd swear you had understood everything I'd said." He patted her hand, then smiled over her head. "Dillon, I thought we'd find you here. Take care of Laine, will you? I've got Billet coming in."

"It appears I've got the best of the deal."

Laine turned to see him leaning against a plane, wiping his hand on the loose coveralls he wore.

"Did everything go all right with the union representative?"

"Fine. You can look over the report tomorrow."

"I'll see you tonight, then." Cap turned to Laine, and after a brief hesitation, patted her cheek before he walked away.

Smiling, she turned back to encounter Dillon's brooding stare. "Oh, please," she began, shaking her head. "Don't spoil it. It's such a small thing."

With a shrug, Dillon turned back to the plane. "Did you like your tour?"

"Yes, I did." Laine's footsteps echoed off the high ceiling as she crossed the room to join him. "I'm afraid I didn't understand a fraction of what he told me. He carried on about aprons and funnel systems and became very expansive on wind drag and thrust." She creased her brow for a moment as she searched her memory. "I'm told struts can withstand comprehensive as well as tensile forces. I didn't have the courage to confess I didn't know one force from the other."

"He's happiest when he's talking about planes," Dillon commented absently. "It doesn't matter if you understood as long as you listened. Hand me that torque wrench."

Laine looked down at the assortment of tools, then searched for something resembling a torque wrench. "I enjoyed listening. Is this a wrench?"

Dillon twisted his head and glanced at the ratchet she offered. With reluctant amusement, he brought his eyes to hers, then shook his head. "No, Duchess. This," he stated, finding the tool himself, "is a wrench."

"I haven't spent a great deal of time under cars or under planes," she muttered. Her annoyance spread as she thought how unlikely it was that he would ask Orchid King for a torque wrench. "Cap told me you've added a flight school. Do you do the instructing?"

"Some."

Pumping up her courage, Laine asked in a rush, "Would you teach me?"

"What?" Dillon glanced back over his shoulder.

"Could you teach me to fly a plane?" She wondered if the question sounded as ridiculous to Dillon as it did to her.

"Maybe." He studied the fragile planes of her face, noting the determined light in her eyes. "Maybe," he repeated. "Why do you want to learn?"

"Cap used to talk about teaching me. Of course—" she spread her hands in a Gallic gesture "—I was only a child, but..." Releasing an impatient breath, Laine lifted her chin and was suddenly very American. "Because I think it would be fun."

The change, and the stubborn set to her mouth, touched off Dillon's laughter. "I'll take one of you up tomorrow." Laine frowned, trying to puzzle out his meaning. Turning back to the plane, Dillon held out the wrench for her to put away. She stared at the grease-smeared handle. Taking his head from the bowels of the plane, Dillon turned back and saw her reluctance. He muttered something she did not attempt to translate, then moved away and pulled another pair of coveralls from a hook. "Here, put these on. I'm going to be a while, and you might as well be useful."

"I'm sure you'd manage beautifully without me."

"Undoubtedly, but put them on anyway." Under Dillon's watchful eye, Laine stepped into the coveralls and slipped her arms into the sleeves. "Good grief, you look swallowed." Crouching down, he began to roll up the pants legs while she scowled at the top of his head.

"I'm sure you'll find me more hindrance than help."

"I figured that out some time ago," he replied. His tone was undeniably cheerful as he rolled up her sleeves half a dozen times. "You shouldn't have quit growing so soon; you don't look more than twelve." He pulled the zipper up to her throat in one swift motion, then looked into her face. She saw his expresion alter. For an instant, she thought she observed a flash of tenderness before he let out an impatient breath. Cursing softly, he submerged into the belly of the plane. "All right," he began briskly, "hand me a screwdriver. The one with the red handle."

Having made the acquaintance of this particular tool, Laine foraged and found it. She placed it in Dillon's outstretched hand. He worked for some time, his conversation limited almost exclusively to the request and description of tools. As time passed, the hum of planes outside became only a backdrop for his voice.

Laine began to ask him questions about the job he was performing. She felt no need to follow his answers, finding pleasure only in the tone and texture of his voice. He was absorbed and she was able to study him unobserved. She surveyed the odd intensity of his eyes, the firm line of his chin and jaw, the bronzed skin which rippled along his arm as he worked. She saw that his chin was shadowed with a day-old beard, that his hair was curling loosely over his collar, that his right brow was lifted slightly higher than his left as he concentrated.

Dillon turned to her with some request, but she could only stare. She was lost in his eyes, blanketed by a fierce and trembling realization.

"What's wrong?" Dillon drew his brows together.

Like a diver breaking water, Laine shook her head and swallowed. "Nothing, I... What did you want? I wasn't paying attention." She bent over the box of tools as if it contained the focus of her world. Silently, Dillon lifted out the one he required and turned back to the engine. Grateful for his preoccupation, Laine closed her eyes. She felt bemused and defenseless.

Love, she thought, *should not come with such quick intensity. It should flow slowly, with tenderness and gentle feelings. It shouldn't stab like a sword, striking without warning, without mercy. How could one love what one could not understand?* Dillon O'Brian was an enigma, a man whose moods seemed to flow without rhyme or reason. And what did she know of him? He was her father's partner, but his position was unclear. He was a man who knew both the sky and the sea, and found it easy to move with their freedom. She knew too that he was a man who knew women and could give them pleasure.

And how, Laine wondered, does one fight love when one has no knowledge of it? Perhaps it was a matter of balance. She deliberately released the tension in her shoulders. I have to find the way to walk the wire without leaning over either side and tumbling off.

"It seems you've taken a side trip," Dillon commented, pulling a rag from his pocket. He grinned as Laine gave a start of alarm. "You're a miserable mechanic, Duchess, and a sloppy one." He rubbed the rag over her cheek until a black smudge disappeared. "There's a sink over there; you'd better go wash your hands. I'll finish these adjustments later. The fuel system is giving me fits."

Laine moved off as he instructed, taking her time in removing traces of grime. She used the opportunity to regain her composure. Hanging up the borrowed overalls, she wandered about the empty hangar while Dillon packed away tools and completed his own washing up. She was surprised to see that it had grown late during the time she had inexpertly assisted Dillon. A soft dusk masked the day's brilliance. Along the runways, lights twinkled like small red eyes. As she turned back, Laine found Dillon's gaze on her. She moistened her lips, then attempted casualness.

"Are you finished?"

"Not quite. Come here." Something in his tone caused her to retreat a step rather than obey. He lifted his brows, then repeated the order with a soft, underlying threat. "I said come here."

Deciding voluntary agreement was the wisest choice,

Laine crossed the floor. Her echoing footsteps seemed to bounce off the walls like thunder. She prayed the sound masked the furious booming of her heart as she stopped in front of him, and that its beating was in her ears only. She stood in silence as he studied her face, wishing desperately she knew what he was looking for, and if she possessed it. Dillon said nothing, but placed his hands on her hips, drawing her a step closer. Their thighs brushed. His grip was firm, and all the while his eyes kept hers a prisoner.

"Kiss me," he said simply. She shook her head in quick protest, unable to look or break away. "Laine, I said kiss me." Dillon pressed her hips closer, molding her shape to his. His eyes were demanding, his mouth tempting. Tentatively, she lifted her arms, letting her hands rest on his shoulders as she rose to her toes. Her eyes remained open and locked on his as their faces drew nearer, as their breaths began to mingle. Softly, she touched her lips to his.

He waited until her mouth lost its shyness and became mobile on his, waited until her arms found their way around his neck to urge him closer. He increased the pressure, drawing out her sigh as he slid his hands under her blouse to the smooth skin of her back. His explorations were slow and achingly gentle. The hands that caressed her taught rather than demanded. Murmuring his name against the taste of his mouth, Laine strained against him, wanting him, needing him. The swift heat of passion was all-consuming. Her lips seemed to learn more quickly than her brain. They began to seek and demand pleasures she could not yet understand. The rest of the world faded like a whisper. At that moment, there was nothing in her life but Dillon and her need for him.

He drew her away. Neither spoke, each staring into the other's eyes as if to read a message not yet written. Dillon brushed a stray curl from her cheek. "I'd better take you home."

"Dillon," Laine began, completely at a loss as to what could be said. Unable to continue, she closed her eyes on her own inadequacy.

"Come on, Duchess, you've had a long day." Dillon circled her neck with his hand and massaged briefly. "We're not dealing on equal footing at the moment, and I like to fight fair under most circumstances."

"Fight?" Laine managed, struggling to keep her eyes open and steady on his. "Is that what this is, Dillon? A fight?"

"The oldest kind," he returned with a small lift to his mouth. His smile faded before it was truly formed, and suddenly his hand was firm on her chin. "It's not over, Laine, and when we have the next round, I might say the devil with the rules."

Chapter 7

When Laine came down for breakfast the next morning, she found only her father. "Hello, Skinny Bones," Miri called out before Cap could greet her. "Sit and eat. I will fix you tea since you do not like my coffee."

Unsure whether to be embarrassed or amused, Laine obeyed. "Thank you, Miri," she said to the retreating back.

"She's quite taken with you." Looking over, Laine saw the light of mirth in Cap's eyes. "Since you've come, she's been so wrapped up with putting pounds on you, she hasn't made one comment about me needing a wife."

With a wry smile, Laine watched her father pour his coffee. "Glad to help. I showed myself around a bit yesterday. I hope you don't mind."

"No, of course not." His smile was rueful. "I guess I

should've taken you around the house myself. My manners are a little rusty."

"I didn't mind. Actually," she tilted her head and returned his smile, "wandering around alone gave me a sort of fresh perspective. You said you'd missed all the stages and still thought of me as a child. I think…" Her fingers spread as she tried to clarify her thoughts. "I think I missed them too—that is, I still had my childhood image of you. Yesterday, I began to see James Simmons in flesh and blood."

"Disappointed?" There was more ease in his tone and a lurking humor in his eyes.

"Impressed," Laine corrected. "I saw a man content with himself and his life, who has the love and respect of those close to him. I think my father must be a very nice man."

He gave her an odd smile which spoke both of surprise and pleasure. "That's quite a compliment coming from a grown daughter." He added more coffee to his cup, and Laine let the silence drift.

Her gaze lingered on Dillon's empty seat a moment. "Ah…is Dillon not here?"

"Hmm? Oh, Dillon had a breakfast meeting. As a matter of fact, he has quite a few things to see to this morning." Cap drank his coffee black, and with an enjoyment Laine could not understand.

"I see," she responded, trying not to sound disappointed. "I suppose the airport keeps both of you very busy."

"That it does." Cap glanced at his watch and tilted his head in regret. "Actually, I have an appointment myself very shortly. I'm sorry to leave you alone this way, but…"

"Please," Laine interrupted. "I don't need to be entertained, and I meant what I said yesterday about not wanting to interfere. I'm sure I'll find plenty of things to keep me occupied."

"All right then. I'll see you this evening." Cap rose, then paused at the doorway with sudden inspiration. "Miri can arrange a ride for you if you'd like to do some shopping in town."

"Thank you." Laine smiled, thinking of her limited funds. "Perhaps I will." She watched him stroll away, then sighed, as her gaze fell again on Dillon's empty chair.

Laine's morning was spent lazily. She soon found out that Miri would not accept or tolerate any help around the house. Following the native woman's strong suggestion that she go out, Laine gathered her stationery and set out for the bay. She found it every bit as perfect as she had the day before—the water clear as crystal, the sand white and pure. Spreading out a blanket, Laine sat down and tried to describe her surroundings with words on paper. The letters she wrote to France were long and detailed, though she omitted any mention of her troubled situation.

As she wrote, the sun rose high overhead. The air was moist and ripe. Lulled by the peace and the rays of the sun, she curled up on the blanket and slept.

Her limbs were languid, and behind closed lids was a dull red mist. She wondered hazily how the reverend mother had urged so much heat out of the ancient furnace. Reluctantly, she struggled to toss off sleep as a hand shook her shoulder. *"Un moment, ma soeur,"* she murmured, and sighed with the effort. *"J'arrive."*

Forcing open her leaden lids, she found Dillon's face inches above hers.

"I seem to have a habit of waking you up." He leaned back on his heels and studied her cloudy eyes. "Don't you know better than to sleep in the sun with that complexion? You're lucky you didn't burn."

"Oh." At last realizing where she was, Laine pushed herself into a sitting position. She felt the odd sense of guilt of the napper caught napping. "I don't know why I fell asleep like that. It must have been the quiet."

"Another reason might be exhaustion," Dillon countered, then frowned. "You're losing the shadows under your eyes."

"Cap said you were very busy this morning." Laine found his continued survey disconcerting and shuffled her writing gear.

"Hmm, yes, I was. Writing letters?"

She glanced up at him, then tapped the tip of her pen against her mouth. "Hmm, yes, I was."

"Very cute." His mouth twitched slightly as he hauled her to her feet. "I thought you wanted to learn how to fly a plane."

"Oh!" Her face lit up with pleasure. "I thought you'd forgotten. Are you sure you're not too busy? Cap said…"

"No, I hadn't forgotten, and no, I'm not too busy." He cut her off as he leaned down to gather her blanket. "Stop babbling as if you were twelve and I were taking you to the circus for cotton candy."

"Of course," she replied, amused by his reaction.

Dillon let out an exasperated breath before grabbing her hand and pulling her across the sand. She heard him mutter something uncomplimentary about women in general.

Less than an hour later, Laine found herself seated in Dillon's plane. "Now, this is a single prop monoplane with a reciprocating engine. Another time, I'll take you up in the jet, but…"

"You have another plane?" Laine interrupted.

"Some people collect hats," Dillon countered dryly, then pointed to the variety of gauges. "Basically, flying a plane is no more difficult than driving a car. The first thing you have to do is understand your instruments and learn how to read them."

"There are quite a few, aren't there?" Dubiously, Laine scanned numbers and needles.

"Not really. This isn't exactly an X-15." He let out a long breath at her blank expression, then started the engine. "O.K., as we climb, I want you to watch this gauge. It's the altimeter. It…"

"It indicates the height of the plane above sea level or above ground," Laine finished for him.

"Very good." Dillon cleared his takeoff with the tower, and the plane began its roll down the runway. "What did you do, grab one of Cap's magazines last night?"

"No. I remember some of my early lessons. I suppose I stored away all the things Cap used to ramble about when I was a child. This is a compass, and this…" Her brow furrowed in her memory search. "This is a turn and bank indicator, but I'm not sure I remember quite what that means."

"I'm impressed, but you're supposed to be watching the altimeter."

"Oh, yes." Wrinkling her nose at the chastisement, she obeyed.

"All right." Dillon gave her profile a quick grin, then

turned his attention to the sky. "The larger needle's going to make one turn of the dial for every thousand feet we climb. The smaller one makes a turn for every ten thousand. Once you learn your gauges, and how to use each one of them, your job's less difficult than driving, and there's generally a lot less traffic."

"Perhaps you'll teach me to drive a car next," Laine suggested as she watched the large needle round the dial for the second time.

"You don't know how to drive?" Dillon demanded. His voice was incredulous.

"No. Is that a crime in this country? I assure you, there are some people who believe me to be marginally intelligent. I'm certain I can learn to fly this machine in the same amount of time it takes any of your other students."

"It's possible," Dillon muttered. "How come you never learned to drive a car?"

"Because I never had one. How did you break your nose?" At his puzzled expression, Laine merely gave him a bland smile. "My question is just as irrelevant as yours."

Laine felt quite pleased when he laughed, almost as though she had won a small victory.

"Which time?" he asked, and it was her turn to look puzzled. "I broke it twice. The first time I was about ten and tried to fly a cardboard plane I had designed off the roof of the garage. I didn't have the propulsion system perfected. I only broke my nose and my arm, though I was told it should've been my neck."

"Very likely," Laine agreed. "And the second time?"

"The second time, I was a bit older. There was a disagreement over a certain girl. My nose suffered another insult, and the other guy lost two teeth."

"Older perhaps, but little wiser," Laine commented. "And who got the girl?"

Dillon flashed his quick grin. "Neither of us. We decided she wasn't worth it after all and went off to nurse our wounds with a beer."

"How gallant."

"Yeah, I'm sure you've noticed that trait in me. I can't seem to shake it. Now, watch your famous turn and bank indicator, and I'll explain its function."

For the next thirty minutes, he became the quintessential teacher, surprising Laine with his knowledge and patience. He answered the dozens of questions she tossed out as flashes of her early lessons skipped through her memory. He seemed to accept her sudden thirst to know as if it were not only natural, but expected. They cruised through a sky touched with puffy clouds and mountain peaks and skimmed the gaping mouth of the multihued Waimea Canyon. They circled above the endless, whitecapped ocean. Laine began to see the similarity between the freedom of the sky and the freedom of the sea. She began to feel the fascination Dillon had spoken of, the need to meet the challenge, the need to explore. She listened with every ounce of her concentration, determined to understand and remember.

"There's a little storm behind us," Dillon announced casually. "We're not going to beat it back." He turned to Laine with a faint smile on his lips. "We're going to get tossed around a bit, Duchess."

"Oh?" Trying to mirror his mood, Laine shifted in her seat and studied the dark clouds in their wake. "Can you fly through that?" she asked, keeping her voice light while her stomach tightened.

"Oh, maybe," he returned. She jerked her head around swiftly. When she saw the laughter in his eyes, she let out a long breath.

"You have an odd sense of humor, Dillon. Very unique," she added, then sucked in her breath as the clouds overtook them. All at once, they were shrouded in darkness, rain pelting furiously on all sides. As the plane rocked, Laine felt a surge of panic.

"You know, it always fascinates me to be in a cloud. Nothing much to them, just vapor and moisture, but they're fabulous." His voice was calm and composed. Laine felt her heartbeat steadying. "Storm clouds are the most interesting, but you really need lightning."

"I think I could live without it," Laine murmured.

"That's because you haven't seen it from up here. When you fly above lightning, you can watch it kicking up inside the clouds. The colors are incredible."

"Have you flown through many storms?" Laine looked out her windows, but saw nothing but swirling black clouds.

"I've done my share. The front of this one'll be waiting for us when we land. Won't last long, though." The plane bucked again, and Laine looked on in bewilderment as Dillon grinned.

"You enjoy this sort of thing, don't you? The excitement, the sense of danger?"

"It keeps the reflexes in tune, Laine." Turning, he smiled at her without a trace of cynicism. "And it keeps life from being boring." The look held for a moment, and Laine's heart did a series of jumping jacks. "There's plenty of stability in life," he continued, making adjustments to compensate for the wind. "Jobs, bills, insurance policies, that's what gives you balance. But sometimes, you've got to ride a roller coaster, run a race, ride a wave. That's what makes life fun. The trick is to keep one end of the scope from overbalancing the other."

Yes, Laine thought. Vanessa never learned the trick. She was always looking for a new game and never enjoyed the one she was playing. And perhaps I've overcompensated by thinking too much of the stability. Too many books, and not enough doing. Laine felt her muscles relax and she turned to Dillon with a hint of a smile. "I haven't ridden a roller coaster for a great many years. One could say that I'm due. Look!" She pressed her face against the side window and peered downward. "It's like something out of *Macbeth,* all misty and sinister. I'd like to see the lightning, Dillon. I really would."

He laughed at the eager anticipation on her face as he began his descent. "I'll see if I can arrange it."

The clouds seemed to swirl and dissolve as the plane lost altitude. Their thickness became pale gray cobwebs to be dusted out of the way. Below, the landscape came into view as they dropped below the mist. The earth was rain-drenched and vivid with color. As they landed, Laine felt her pleasure fade into a vague sense of loss. She felt like a child who had just blown out her last birthday candle.

"I'll take you back up in a couple days if you want," said Dillon, taxiing to a halt.

"Yes, please, I'd like that very much. I don't know how to thank you for…"

"Do your homework," he said as he shut off the engine. "I'll give you some books and you can read up on instrumentation."

"Yes, sir," Laine said with suspicious humility. Dillon glared at her briefly before swinging from the plane. Laine's lack of experience caused her to take more time with her exit. She found herself swooped down before she could complete the journey on her own.

In the pounding rain they stood close, Dillon's hands light on her waist. She could feel the heat of his body through the dampness of her blouse. Dark tendrils of hair fell over his forehead, and without thought, Laine lifted her hand to smooth them back. There was something sweetly ordinary about being in his arms, as if it were a place she had been countless times before and would come back to countless times again. She felt her love bursting to be free.

"You're getting wet," she murmured, dropping her hand to his cheek.

"So are you." Though his fingers tightened on her waist, he drew her no closer.

"I don't mind."

With a sigh, Dillon rested his chin on the top of her head. "Miri'll punch me out if I let you catch a chill."

"I'm not cold," she murmured, finding indescribable pleasure in their closeness.

"You're shivering." Abruptly, Dillon brought her to his side and began to walk. "We'll go into my office, and you can dry out before I take you home."

As they walked, the rain slowed to a mist. Fingers of sunlight began to strain through, brushing away the last stubborn drops. Laine surveyed the complex. She remembered the building which housed Dillon's office from the tour she had taken with her father. With a grin, she pushed damp hair from her eyes and pulled away from Dillon. "Race you," she challenged, and scrambled over wet pavement.

He caught her, laughing and breathless, at the door. With a new ease, Laine circled his neck as they laughed together. She felt young and foolish and desperately in love.

"You're quick, aren't you?" Dillon observed, and she tilted her head back to meet his smile.

"You learn to be quick when you live in a dormitory. Competition for the bath is brutal." Laine thought she saw his smile begin to fade before they were interrupted.

"Dillon, I'm sorry to disturb you."

Glancing over, Laine saw a young woman with classic bone structure, her raven hair pulled taut at the nape of a slender neck. The woman returned Laine's survey with undisguised curiosity. Blushing, Laine struggled out of Dillon's arms.

"It's all right, Fran. This is Laine Simmons, Cap's daughter. Fran's my calculator."

"He means secretary," Fran returned with an exasperated sigh. "But this afternoon I feel more like an answering service. You have a dozen phone messages on your desk."

"Anything urgent?" As he asked, he moved into an adjoining room.

"No." Fran gave Laine a friendly smile. "Just several people who didn't want to make a decision until they heard from Mount Olympus. I told them all you were out for the day and would get back to them tomorrow."

"Good." Walking back into the room, Dillon carried

a handful of papers and a towel. He tossed the towel at Laine before he studied the papers.

"I thought you were supposed to be taking a few days off," Fran stated while Dillon muttered over his messages.

"Um-hum. There doesn't seem to be anything here that can't wait."

"I've already told you that." Fran snatched the papers out of his hand.

"So you did." Unabashed, Dillon grinned and patted her cheek. "Did you ask Orchid what she wanted?"

Across the room, Laine stopped rubbing the towel against her hair, then began again with increased speed.

"No, though after the *third* call, I'm afraid I became a bit abrupt with her."

"She can handle it," Dillon returned easily, then switched his attention to Laine. "Ready?"

"Yes." Feeling curiously deflated, Laine crossed the room and handed Dillon the towel. "Thank you."

"Sure." Casually, he tossed the damp towel to Fran. "See you tomorrow, cousin."

"Yes, master." Fran shot Laine a friendly wave before Dillon hustled her from the building.

With a great deal of effort, Laine managed to thrust Orchid King from her mind during the drive home and throughout the evening meal. The sun was just setting when she settled on the porch with Dillon and her father.

The sky's light was enchanting. The intense, tropical blue was breaking into hues of gold and crimson, the low, misted clouds streaked with pinks and mauves. There was something dreamlike and soothing in the dusk. Laine sat quietly in a wicker chair, thinking over her day as the men's conversation washed over her.

Even had she understood their exchange, she was too lazily content to join in. She knew that for the first time in her adult life, she was both physically and mentally relaxed. Perhaps, she mused, it was the adventures of the past few days, the testing of so many untried feelings and emotions.

Mumbling about coffee, Cap rose and slipped inside the house. Laine gave him an absent smile as he passed her, then curled her legs under her and watched the first stars blink into life.

"You're quiet tonight." As Dillon leaned back in his chair, Laine heard the soft click of his lighter.

"I was just thinking how lovely it is here." Her sigh drifted with contentment. "I think it must be the loveliest place on earth."

"Lovelier than Paris?"

Hearing the edge in his voice, Laine turned to look at him questioningly. The first light of the moon fell gently over her face. "It's very different from Paris," she answered. "Parts of Paris are beautiful, mellowed and gentled with age. Other parts are elegant or dignified. She is like a woman who has been often told she is enchanting. But the beauty here is more primitive. The island is ageless and innocent at the same time."

"Many people tire of innocence." Dillon shrugged and drew deeply on his cigarette.

"I suppose that's true," she agreed, unsure why he seemed so distant and so cynical.

"In this light, you look a great deal like your mother," he said suddenly, and Laine felt her skin ice over.

"How do you know? You never met my mother."

"Cap has a picture." Dillon turned toward her, but his face was in shadows. "You resemble her a great deal."

"She certainly does." Cap sauntered out with a tray of coffee in his hands. Setting it on a round glass table, he straightened and studied Laine. "It's amazing. The light will catch you a certain way, or you'll get a certain expression on your face. Suddenly, it's your mother twenty years ago."

"I'm not Vanessa." Laine sprang up from her seat, and her voice trembled with rage. "I'm nothing like Vanessa." To her distress, tears began to gather in her eyes. Her father looked on in astonishment. "I'm nothing like her. I won't be compared to her." Furious with both the men and herself, Laine turned and slammed through the screen door. On her dash for the stairs, she collided with Miri's substantial form. Stuttering an apology, she streaked up the stairs and into her room.

Laine was pacing around her room for the third time when Miri strolled in.

"What is all this running and slamming in my house?" Miri asked, folding her arms across her ample chest.

Shaking her head, Laine lowered herself to the bed, then, despising herself, burst into tears. Clucking her tongue and muttering in Hawaiian, Miri crossed the room. Soon Laine found her head cradled against a soft, pillowing bosom. "That Dillon," Miri muttered as she rocked Laine to and fro.

"It wasn't Dillon," Laine managed, finding the maternal comfort new and overwhelming. "Yes, it was…it was both of them." Laine had a sudden desperate need for reassurance. "I'm nothing like her, Miri. I'm nothing like her at all."

"Of course you are not." Miri patted Laine's blond curls. "Who is it you are not like?"

"Vanessa." Laine brushed away tears with the back of her hand. "My mother. Both of them were looking at me, saying how much I look like her."

"What is this? What is this? All these tears because you look like someone?" Miri pulled Laine away by the shoulders and shook her. "Why do you waste your tears on this? I think you're a smart girl, then you act stupid."

"You don't understand." Laine drew up her knees and rested her chin on them. "I won't be compared to her, not to her. Vanessa was selfish and self-centered and dishonest."

"She was your mother," Miri stated with such authority that Laine's mouth dropped open. "You will speak with respect of your mother. She is dead, and whatever she did is over now. You must bury it," Miri commanded, giving Laine another shake, "or you will never be happy. Did they say you were selfish and self-centered and dishonest?"

"No, but…"

"What did Cap Simmons say to you?" Miri demanded.

Laine let out a long breath. "He said I looked like my mother."

"And do you, or does he lie?"

"Yes, I suppose I do, but…"

"So, your mother was a pretty woman, you are a pretty woman." Miri lifted Laine's chin with her thick fingers. "Do you know who you are, Laine Simmons?"

"Yes, I think I do."

"Then you have no problem." Miri patted her cheek and rose.

"Oh, Miri." Laine laughed and wiped her eyes again. "You make me feel very foolish."

"You make yourself feel foolish," Miri corrected. "I did not slam doors."

Laine sighed over Miri's logic. "I suppose I'll have to go down and apologize."

As Laine stood, Miri folded her arms and blocked her way. "You will do no such thing."

Staring at her, Laine let out a frustrated breath. "But you just said…"

"I said you were stupid, and you were. Cap Simmons and Dillon were also stupid. No woman should be compared to another woman. You are special, you are unique. Sometimes men see only the face." Miri tapped a finger against each of her cheeks. "It takes them longer to see what is inside. So—" she gave Laine a white-toothed smile "—you will not apologize, you will let them apologize. It is the best way."

"I see," Laine said, not seeing at all. Suddenly, she laughed and sat back on the bed. "Thank you, Miri, I feel much better."

"Good. Now go to bed. I will go lecture Cap Simmons and Dillon." There was an unmistakable note of anticipation in her voice.

Chapter 8

The following morning Laine descended the stairs, her Nile-green sundress floating around her, leaving her arms and shoulders bare. Feeling awkward after the previous evening's incident, Laine paused at the doorway of the dining room. Her father and Dillon were already at breakfast and deep in discussion.

"If Bob needs next week off, I can easily take his shift on the charters." Dillon poured coffee as he spoke.

"You've got enough to do at your own place without taking that on, too. Whatever happened to those few days off you were going to take?" Cap accepted the coffee and gave Dillon a stern look.

"I haven't exactly been chained to my desk the past week." Dillon grinned, then shrugged as Cap's expression remained unchanged. "I'll take some time off next month."

"Where have I heard that before?" Cap asked the ceiling. Dillon's grin flashed again.

"I didn't tell you I was retiring next year, did I?" Dillon sipped coffee casually, but Laine recognized the mischief in his voice. "I'm going to take up hang gliding while you slave away behind a desk. Who are you going to nag if I'm not around every day?"

"When you can stay away for more than a week at a time," Cap countered, "that's when *I'm* going to retire. The trouble with you—" he wagged a spoon at Dillon in admonishment "—is that your mind's too good and you've let too many people find it out. Now you're stuck because nobody wants to make a move without checking with you first. You should've kept that aeronautical-engineering degree a secret. Hang gliding." Cap chuckled and lifted his cup. "Oh, hello, Laine."

Laine jolted at the sound of her name. "Good morning," she replied, hoping that her outburst the evening before had not cost her the slight progress she had made with her father.

"Is it safe to ask you in?" His smile was sheepish, but he beckoned her forward. "As I recall, your explosions were frequent, fierce, but short-lived."

Relieved he had not offered her a stilted apology, Laine took her place at the table. "Your memory is accurate, though I assure you, I explode at very infrequent intervals these days." She offered Dillon a tentative smile, determined to treat the matter lightly. "Good morning, Dillon."

"Morning, Duchess. Coffee?" Before she could refuse, he was filling her cup.

"Thank you," she murmured. "It's hard to believe,

but I think today is more beautiful than yesterday. I don't believe I'd ever grow used to living in paradise."

"You've barely seen any of it yet," Cap commented. "You should go up to the mountains, or to the center. You know, the center of Kauai is one of the wettest spots in the world. The rain forest is something to see."

"The island seems to have a lot of variety." Laine toyed with her coffee. "I can't imagine any of it is more beautiful than right here."

"I'll take you around a bit today," Dillon announced. Laine glanced sharply at him.

"I don't want to interfere with your routine. I've already taken up a great deal of your time." Laine had not yet regained her balance with Dillon. Her eyes were both wary and unsure.

"I've a bit more to spare." He rose abruptly. "I'll have things cleared up and be back around eleven. See you later, Cap." He strode out without waiting for her assent.

Miri entered with a full plate and placed it in front of Laine. She scowled at the coffee. "Why do you pour coffee when you aren't going to drink it?" With a regal sniff, she picked up the cup and swooped from the room. With a sigh, Laine attacked her breakfast and wondered how the day would pass. She was to find the morning passed quickly.

As if granting a royal boon, Miri agreed to allow Laine to refresh the vases of flowers which were scattered throughout the house. Laine spent her morning hours in the garden. It was not a garden as Laine remembered from her early American years or from her later French ones. It was a spreading, sprawling, wild tangle of greens and tempestuous hues. The plants would not be organized or dictated to by plot or plan.

Inside again, Laine took special care in the arranging of the vases. Her mind drifted to the daffodils which would be blooming outside her window at school. She found it odd that she felt no trace of homesickness, no longing for the soft French voices of the sisters or the high, eager ones of her students. She knew that she was dangerously close to thinking of Kauai as home. The thought of returning to France and the life she led there filled her with a cold, dull ache.

In her father's den, Laine placed the vase of frangipani on his desk and glanced at the photograph of Cap and Dillon. *How strange,* she thought, *that I should need both of them so badly.* With a sigh, she buried her face in the blossoms.

"Do flowers make you unhappy?"

She whirled, nearly upsetting the vase. For a moment, she and Dillon stared at each other without speaking. Laine felt the tension between them, though its cause and meaning were unclear to her. "Hello. Is it eleven already?'"

"It's nearly noon. I'm late." Dillon thrust his hands in his pockets and watched her. Behind her, the sun poured through the window to halo her hair. "Do you want some lunch?"

"No, thank you," she said with conviction. She saw his eyes smile briefly.

"Are you ready?"

"Yes, I'll just tell Miri I'm going."

"She knows." Crossing the room, Dillon slid open the glass door and waited for Laine to precede him outside.

Laine found Dillon in a silent mood as they drove from the house. She gave his thoughts their privacy and concentrated on the view. Ridges of green mountains

loomed on either side. Dillon drove along a sheer precipice where the earth surrendered abruptly to the sky to
fall into an azure sea.

"They used to toss Kukui oil torches over the cliffs
to entertain royalty," Dillon said suddenly, after miles
of silence. "Legend has it that the menehune lived here.
The pixie people," he elaborated at her blank expression. "You see there?" After halting the car, he pointed
to a black precipice lined with grooves. "That's their
staircase. They built fishponds by moonlight."

"Where are they now?" Laine smiled at him.

Dillon reached across to open her door. "Oh, they're
still here. They're hiding."

Laine joined him to walk to the edge of the cliff. Her
heart flew to her throat as she stared from the dizzying
height down to the frothing power of waves on rock.
For an instant, she could feel herself tumbling helplessly
through miles of space.

Unaffected by vertigo, Dillon looked out to sea.
The breeze teased his hair, tossing it into confusion.
"You have the remarkable capacity of knowing when
to be quiet and making the silence comfortable," he
remarked.

"You seemed preoccupied." The wind tossed curls
in her eyes, and Laine brushed them away. "I thought
perhaps you were working out a problem."

"Did you?" he returned, and his expression seemed
both amused and annoyed. "I want to talk to you about
your mother."

The statement was so unexpected that it took Laine
a moment to react. "No." She turned away, but he took
her arm and held her still.

"You were furious last night. I want to know why."

"I overreacted." She tossed her head as her curls continued to dance around her face. "It was foolish of me, but sometimes my temper gets the better of me." She saw by his expression that her explanation would not placate him. She wanted badly to tell him how she had been hurt, but the memory of their first discussion in her father's house, and his cold judgment of her, prevented her. "Dillon, all my life I've been accepted for who I am." Speaking slowly, she chose her words carefully. "It annoys me to find that changing now. I do not want to be compared with Vanessa because we share certain physical traits."

"Is that what you think Cap was doing?"

"Perhaps, perhaps not." She tilted her chin yet further. "But that's what you were doing."

"Was I?" It was a question which asked for no answer, and Laine gave none. "Why are you so bitter about your mother, Laine?"

She moved her shoulders and turned back toward the sea. "I'm not bitter, Dillon, not any longer. Vanessa's dead, and that part of my life is over. I don't want to talk about her until I understand my feelings better."

"All right." They stood silent for a moment, wrapped in the wind.

"I'm having a lot more trouble with you than I anticipated," Dillon muttered.

"I don't know what you mean."

"No," he agreed, looking at her so intently she felt he read her soul. "I'm sure you don't." He walked away, then stopped. After a hesitation too brief to measure, he turned toward her again and held out his hand. Laine stared at it, unsure what he was offering. Finding it did not matter, she accepted.

During the ensuing drive, Dillon spoke easily. His mood had altered, and Laine moved with it. The world was lush with ripe blossoms. Moss clung, green and vibrant, to cliffs—a carpet on stone. They passed elephant ears whose leaves were large enough to use as a canopy against rain or sun. The frangipani became more varied and more brilliant. When Dillon stopped the car again, Laine did not hesitate to take his hand.

He led her along a path that was sheltered by palms, moving down it as though he knew the way well. Laine heard the rush of water before they entered the clearing. Her breath caught at the sight of the secluded pool circled by thick trees and fed by a shimmering waterfall.

"Oh, Dillon, what a glorious place! There can't be another like it in the world!" Laine ran to the edge of the pool, then dropped down to feel the texture of the water. It was warm silk. "If I could, I would come here to swim in the moonlight." With a laugh, she rose and tossed water to the sky. "With flowers in my hair and nothing else."

"That's the only permissible way to swim in a moonlit pool. Island law."

Laughing again, she turned to a bush and plucked a scarlet hibiscus. "I suppose I'd need long black hair and honey skin to look the part."

Taking the bloom from her, Dillon tucked it behind her ear. After studying the effect, he smiled and ran a finger down her cheek. "Ivory and gold work very nicely. There was a time you'd have been worshiped with all pomp and ceremony, then tossed off a cliff as an offering to jealous gods."

"I don't believe that would suit me." Utterly enchanted, Laine twirled away. "Is this a secret place?

It feels like a secret place." Stepping out of her shoes, she sat on the edge of the pool and dangled her feet in the water.

"If you want it to be." Dropping down beside her, Dillon sat Indian-fashion. "It's not on the tourist route, at any rate."

"It feels magic, the same way that little bay feels magic. Do you feel it, Dillon? Do you realize how lovely this all is, how fresh, or are you immune to it by now?"

"I'm not immune to beauty." He lifted her hand, brushing his lips over her fingertips. Her eyes grew wide as currents of pleasure jolted up her arm. Smiling, Dillon turned her hand over and kissed her palm. "You can't have lived in Paris for fifteen years and not have had your hand kissed. I've seen movies."

The lightness of his tone helped her regain her balance. "Actually, everyone's always kissing my left hand. You threw me off when you kissed my right." She kicked water in the air and watched the drops catch the sun before they were swallowed by the pool. "Sometimes, when the rain drizzles in the fall, and the dampness creeps through the windows, I'll remember this." Her voice had changed, and there was something wistful, something yearning in her tone. "Then when spring comes, and the buds flower, and the air smells of them, I'll remember the fragrance here. And when the sun shines on a Sunday, I'll walk near the Seine and think of a waterfall."

Rain came without warning, a shower drenched in sun. Dillon scrambled up, pulling Laine under a sheltering cluster of palms.

"Oh, it's warm." She leaned out from the green ceiling to catch rain in her palm. "It's as if it's dropping from the sun."

"Islanders call it liquid sunshine." Dillon gave an easy tug on her hand to pull her back as she inched forward. "You're getting soaked. I think you must enjoy getting drenched in your clothes." He ruffled her hair and splattered the air with shimmering drops.

"Yes, I suppose I do." She stared out, absorbed with the deepening colors. Blossoms trembled under their shower. "There's so much on the island that remains unspoiled, as if no one had ever touched it. When we stood on the cliff and looked down at the sea, I was frightened. I've always been a coward. But still, it was beautiful, so terrifyingly beautiful I couldn't look away."

"A coward?" Dillon sat on the soft ground and pulled her down to join him. Her head naturally found the curve of his shoulder. "I would have said you were remarkably intrepid. You didn't panic during the storm yesterday."

"No, I just skirted around the edges of panic."

His laugh was full of pleasure. "You also survived the little show in the plane on the way from Oahu without a scream or a faint."

"That's because I was angry." She pushed at her damp hair and watched the thin curtain of rain. "It was unkind of you."

"Yes, I suppose it was. I'm often unkind."

"I think you're kind more often than not. Though I also think you don't like being labeled a kind man."

"That's a very odd opinion for a short acquaintance." Her answering shrug was eloquent and intensely Gallic. A frown moved across his brow. "This school of yours," he began, "what kind is it?"

"Just a school, the same as any other, with giggling girls and rules which must be broken."

"A boarding school?" he probed, and she moved her shoulders again.

"Yes, a boarding school. Dillon, this is not the place to think of schedules and classes. I shall have to deal with them again soon enough. This is a magic place, and for now I want to pretend I belong here. *Ah, regarde!*" Laine shifted, gesturing in wonder. *"Un arc-en-ciel."*

"I guess that means rainbow." He glanced at the sky, then back at her glowing face.

"There are two! How can there be two?"

They stretched, high and perfect, in curving arches from one mountain ridge to another. The second's shimmering colors were the reverse of the first's. As the sun glistened on raindrops, the colors grew in intensity, streaking across the cerulean sky like a trail from an artist's many-tinted brush.

"Double bows are common here," Dillon explained, relaxing against the base of the palm. "The trade winds blow against the mountains and form a rain boundary. It rains on one side while the sun shines on the other. Then, the sun strikes the raindrops, and…"

"No, don't tell me," Laine interrupted with a shake of her head. "It would spoil it if I knew." She smiled with the sudden knowledge that all things precious should be left unexplained. "I don't want to understand," she murmured, accepting both her love and the rainbows without question, without logic. "I just want to enjoy." Tilting back her head, Laine offered her mouth. "Will you kiss me, Dillon?"

His eyes never left hers. He brought his hands to her face, and gently, his fingers stroked the fragile line of her cheek. In silence, he explored the planes and hollows of her face with his fingertips, learning the texture of fine bones and satin skin. His mouth followed the trail of his fingers, and Laine closed her eyes, knowing nothing had ever been sweeter than his lips on her skin. Still moving slowly, still moving gently, Dillon brushed his mouth over hers in a whisperlike kiss which drugged her senses. He seemed content to taste, seemed happy to sample rather than devour. His mouth moved on, lingering on the curve of her neck, nibbling at the lobe of her ear before coming back to join hers. His tongue teased her lips apart as her heartbeat began to roar in her ears. He took her to the edge of reason with a tender, sensitive touch. As her need grew, Laine drew him closer, her body moving against his in innocent temptation.

Dillon swore suddenly before pulling her back. She kept her arms around his neck, her fingers tangled in his hair as he stared down at her. Her eyes were deep and cloudy with growing passion. Unaware of her own seductive powers, Laine sighed his name and placed a soft kiss on both of his cheeks.

"I want you," Dillon stated in a savage murmur before his mouth crushed hers. She yielded to him as a young willow yields to the wind.

His hands moved over her as if desperate to learn every aspect, every secret, and she who had never known a man's intimate touch delighted in the seeking. Her body was limber under his touch, responsive and eager. She was the student, and he the teacher. Her skin grew hot as her veins swelled with pounding blood. As the low, smoldering fire burst into quick flame, her demands rose with his. She trembled and murmured

his name, as frightened of the new sensation as she had
been at the edge of the cliff.

Dillon lifted his mouth from hers, resting it on her
hair before she could search for the joining again. He
held her close, cradling her head against his chest. His
heart drummed against her ear, and Laine closed her
eyes with the pleasure. Drawing her away, he stood.
He moved his hands to his pockets as he turned his
back on her.

"It's stopped raining." She thought his voice sounded
strange and heard him take a long breath before he
turned back to her. "We'd better go."

His expression was unfathomable. Though she
searched, Laine could find no words to fill the sudden
gap and close the distance which had sprung between
them. Her eyes met his, asking questions her lips could
not. Dillon opened his mouth as if to speak, then closed
it again before he reached down to pull her to her feet.
Her eyes faltered. Dillon lifted her chin with his fingertips, then traced the lips still soft from his. Briskly,
he shook his head. Without a word, he lay his mouth
gently on hers before he led her away from the palms.

Chapter 9

A generous golden ball, the sun dominated the sky as the car moved along the highway. Dillon made easy conversation, as if passion belonged only to a rain-curtained pool. While her brain fidgeted, Laine tried to match his mood.

Men, she decided, must be better able to deal with the demands of the body than women are with those of the heart. He had wanted her; even if he had not said it, she would have known. The urgency, the power of his claim had been unmistakable. Laine felt her color rise as she remembered her unprotesting response. Averting her head as if absorbed in the view, she tried to decide what course lay open to her.

She would leave Kauai in a week's time. Now, she would not only have to abandon the father whom she had longed for all of her life, but the man who held all claim to her heart. Perhaps, she reflected with a small sigh, I'm always destined to love what can never be mine. Miri said I should fight as a woman fights, but I don't know where to begin. Perhaps with honesty. I should find the place and time to tell Dillon of my feelings. If he knew I wanted nothing from him but his affection, we might make a beginning. I could find a way to stay here at least awhile longer. I could take a job. In time, he might learn to really care for me. Laine's mood lightened at the thought. She focused again on her surroundings.

"Dillon, what is growing there? Is it bamboo?" Acres upon acres of towering stalks bordered the road. Clumps of cylindrical gold stretched out on either side.

"Sugarcane," he answered, without glancing at the fields.

"It's like a jungle." Fascinated, Laine leaned out the window, and the wind buffeted her face. "I had no idea it grew so tall."

"Gets to be a bit over twenty feet, but it doesn't grow as fast as a jungle in this part of the world. It takes a year and a half to two years to reach full growth."

"There's so much." Laine turned to face him, absently brushing curls from her cheeks. "It's a plantation, I suppose, though it's hard to conceive of one person owning so much. It must take tremendous manpower to harvest."

"A bit." Dillon swerved off the highway and onto a hard-packed road. "The undergrowth is burned off, then machines cut the plants. Hand cutting is time consuming so machinery lowers production costs even when labor costs are low. Besides, it's one miserable job."

"Have you ever done it?" She watched a quick grin light his face.

"A time or two, which is why I prefer flying a plane."

Laine glanced around at the infinity of fields, wondering when the harvest began, trying to picture the machines slicing through the towering stalks. Her musings halted as the brilliant white of a house shone in the distance. Tall, with graceful colonial lines and pillars, it stood on lush lawns. Vines dripped from scrolled balconies; the high and narrow windows were shuttered in soft gray. The house looked comfortably old and lived in. Had it not been for South Sea foliage, Laine might have been seeing a plantation house in old Louisiana.

"What a beautiful home. One could see for miles from the balcony." Laine glanced at Dillon in surprise as he halted the car and again leaned over to open her door. "This is a private home, is it not? Are we allowed to walk around?"

"Sure." Opening his own door, Dillon slid out. "It's mine." He leaned against the car and looked down at her. "Are you going to sit there with your mouth open or are you going to come inside?" Quickly, Laine slid out and stood beside him. "I gather you expected a grass hut and hammock?"

"Why, no, I don't precisely know what I expected, but…" With a helpless gesture of her hands, she gazed about. A tremor of alarm trickled through her. "The cane fields," she began, praying she was mistaken. "Are they yours?"

"They go with the house."

Finding her throat closed, Laine said nothing as Dillon led her up stone steps and through a wide mahogany door. Inside, the staircase dominated the hall. Wide and arching in a deep half circle, its wood gleamed. Laine had a quick, confused impression of watercolors and wood carvings as Dillon strode straight down the hall and led her into a parlor.

The walls were like rich cream; the furnishings were dark and old. The carpet was a delicately faded needle-point over a glistening wood floor. Nutmeg sheers were drawn back from the windows to allow the view of a manicured lawn.

"Sit down." Dillon gestured to a chair. "I'll see about something cold to drink." Laine nodded, grateful for the time alone to organize her scattered thoughts. She listened until Dillon's footsteps echoed into silence.

Her survey of the room was slow. She seated herself in a high-backed chair and let her eyes roam. The room had an undeniable air of muted wealth. Laine had not associated wealth with Dillon O'Brian. Now she found it an insurmountable obstacle. Her protestations of love would never be accepted as pure. He would think his money had been her enticement. She closed her eyes on a small moan of desperation. Rising, she moved to a window and tried to deal with dashed hopes.

What was it he called me once? *An operator.* With a short laugh, she rested her brow against the cool glass. I'm afraid I make a very poor one. I wish I'd never come here, never seen what he has. At least then I could have hung on to hope a bit longer. Hearing Dillon's approach, Laine struggled for composure. As he entered, she gave him a careful smile.

"Dillon, your home is very lovely." After accepting the tall glass he offered, Laine moved back to her chair.

"It serves." He sat opposite her. His brow lifted frac-tionally at the formality of her tone.

"Did you build it yourself?"

"No, my grandfather." With his customary ease, Dillon leaned back and watched her. "He was a sailor and decided Kauai was the next best thing to the sea."

"So. I thought it looked as if it had known generations." Laine sipped at her drink without tasting it. "But you found planes more enticing than the sea or the fields."

"The fields serve their purpose." Dillon frowned momentarily at her polite, impersonal interest. "They yield a marketable product, assist in local employment and make use of the land. It's a profitable crop and its management takes only a portion of my time." As Dillon set down his glass, Laine thought he appeared to come to some decision. "My father died a couple of months before I met Cap. We were both floundering, but I was angry, and he was…" Dillon hesitated, then shrugged. "He was as he always is. We suited each other. He had a cabin plane and used to pick up island hoppers. I couldn't learn about flying fast enough, and Cap needed to teach. I needed balance, and he needed to give it. A couple of years later, we began planning the airport."

Laine dropped her eyes to her glass. "And it was the money from your fields which built the airport?"

"As I said, the cane has its uses."

"And the bay where we swam?" On a sudden flash of intuition, she lifted her eyes to his. "That's yours, too, isn't it?"

"That's right." She could see no change of expression in his eyes.

"And my father's house?" Laine swallowed the dryness building in her throat. "Is that also on your property?"

She saw annoyance cross his face before he smoothed it away. His answer was mild. "Cap had a fondness for that strip of land, so he bought it."

"From you?"

"Yes, from me. Is that a problem?"

"No," she replied. "It's simply that I begin to see things more clearly. Much more clearly." Laine set down her drink and folded her empty hands. "It appears that you are more my father's son than I shall ever be his daughter."

"Laine…" Dillon let out a short breath, then rose and paced the room with a sudden restlessness. "Cap and I understand each other. We've known each other for nearly fifteen years. He's been part of my life for almost half of it."

"I'm not asking you for justifications, Dillon. I'm sorry if it seemed as if I were." Laine stood, trying to keep her voice steady. "When I return to France next week, it will be good to know that my father has you to rely on."

"Next week?" Dillon stopped pacing. "You're planning to leave next week?"

"Yes." Laine tried not to think of how quickly seven days could pass. "We agreed I would stay for two weeks. It's time I got back to my own life."

"You're hurt because Cap hasn't responded to you the way you'd hoped."

Surprised both by his words and the gentleness of his tone, Laine felt the thin thread of her control straining. She struggled to keep her eyes calm and level with his. "I have changed my mind…on a great many matters. Please don't, Dillon." She shook her head as he started to speak. "I would rather not talk of this; it's only more difficult."

"Laine." He placed his hands on her shoulders to prevent her from turning away. "There are a lot of things that you and I have to talk about, whether they're difficult or not. You can't keep shutting away little parts of yourself. I want…" The ringing of the doorbell interrupted his words. With a quick, impatient oath, he dropped his hands and strode away to answer.

A light, musical voice drifted into the room. When Orchid King entered the parlor on Dillon's arm, Laine met her with a polite smile.

It struck Laine that Orchid and Dillon were a perfectly matched couple. Orchid's tawny, exotic beauty suited his ruggedness, and her fully rounded curves were all the more stunning against his leanness. Her hair fell in an ebony waterfall, cascading down a smooth bare back to the waist of close-fitting pumpkin-colored shorts. Seeing her, Laine felt dowdy and provincial.

"Hello, Miss Simmons." Orchid tightened her hand on Dillon's arm. "How nice to see you again so soon."

"Hello, Miss King." Annoyed by her own insecurities, Laine met Orchid's amusement with eyes of a cool spring morning. "You did say the island was small."

"Yes, I did." She smiled, and Laine was reminded of a tawny cat. "I hope you've been able to see something of it."

"I took Laine around a bit this morning." Watching Laine, Dillon missed the flash of fire in Orchid's amber eyes.

"I'm sure she couldn't find a better guide." Orchid's expression melted into soft appeal. "I'm so glad you were home, Dillon. I wanted to make certain you'd be at the luau tomorrow night." Turning more directly to face him, she subtly but effectively excluded Laine from the conversation. "It wouldn't be any fun without you."

"I'll be there." Laine watched a smile lift one corner of his mouth. "Are you going to dance?"

"Of course." The soft purr of her voice added to Laine's image of a lithesome feline. "Tommy expects it."

Dillon's smile flashed into a grin. He lifted his eyes over Orchid's head to meet Laine's. "Tommy is Miri's nephew. He's having his annual luau tomorrow. You should find both the food and the entertainment interesting."

"Oh, yes," Orchid agreed. "No tourist should leave the islands without attending a luau. Do you plan to see the other islands during your vacation?"

"I'm afraid that will have to wait for another time. I'm sorry to say I haven't lived up to my obligations as a tourist. The purpose of my visit has been to see my father and his home."

Somewhat impatiently, Dillon disengaged his arm from Orchid's grasp. "I have to see my foreman. Why don't you keep Laine company for a few minutes?"

"Certainly." Orchid tossed a lock of rain-straight hair behind her back. "How are the repairs coming?"

"Fine. I should be able to move back in a couple of days without being in the way." With an inclination of his head for Laine, he turned and strode from the room.

"Miss Simmons, do make yourself at home." Assuming the role of hostess with a graceful wave of her hand, Orchid glided farther into the room. "Would you care for anything? A cold drink perhaps?"

Infuriated at being placed in the position of being

Orchid's guest, Laine forced down her temper. "Thank you, no. Dillon has already seen to it."

"It seems you spend a great deal of time in Dillon's company," Orchid commented as she dropped into a chair. She crossed long, slender legs, looking like an advertisement for Hawaii's lush attractions. "Especially for one who comes to visit her father."

"Dillon has been very generous with his time." Laine copied Orchid's action and hoped she was equipped for a feminine battle of words.

"Oh, yes, Dillon's a generous man." Her smile was indulgent and possessive. "It's quite easy to misinterpret his generosity unless one knows him as well as I do. He can be so charming."

"Charming?" Laine repeated, and looked faintly skeptical. "How odd. Charming is not the adjective which comes to my mind. But then," she paused and smiled, "you know him better than I do."

Orchid placed the tips of her fingers together, then regarded Laine over the tips. "Miss Simmons, maybe we can dispense with the polite small talk while we have this time alone."

Wondering if she was sinking over her head, Laine nodded. "Your option, Miss King."

"I intend to marry Dillon."

"A formidable intention," Laine managed as her heart constricted. "I assume Dillon is aware of your goal."

"Dillon knows I want him." Irritation flickered over the exotic face at Laine's easy answer. "I don't appreciate all the time you've been spending with him."

"That's a pity, Miss King." Laine picked up her long-abandoned glass and sipped. "But don't you think you're discussing this with the wrong person? I'm sure speaking to Dillon would be more productive."

"I don't believe that's necessary." Orchid gave Laine a companionable smile, showing just a hint of white teeth. "I'm sure we can settle this between us. Don't you think telling Dillon you wanted to learn to fly a plane was a little trite?"

Laine felt a flush of fury that Dillon had discussed her with Orchid. "Trite?"

Orchid made an impatient gesture. "Dillon's diverted by you at the moment, perhaps because you're such a contrast to the type of woman he's always preferred. But the milk-and-honey looks won't keep Dillon interested for long." The musical voice hardened. "Cool sophistication doesn't keep a man warm, and Dillon is very much a man."

"Yes, he's made that very clear," Laine could not resist interjecting.

"I'm warning you...once," Orchid hissed. "Keep your distance. I can make things very uncomfortable for you."

"I'm sure you can," Laine acknowledged. She shrugged. "I've been uncomfortable before."

"Dillon can be very vindictive when he thinks he's being deceived. You're going to end up losing more than you bargained for."

"Nom de Dieu!" Laine rose. "Is this how the game is played?" She made a contemptuous gesture with the back of her hand. "I want none of it. Snarling and hissing like two cats over a mouse. This isn't worthy of Dillon."

"We haven't started to play yet." Orchid sat back, pleased by Laine's agitation. "If you don't like the rules, you'd better leave. I don't intend to put up with you any longer."

"Put up with me?" Laine stopped, her voice trembling with rage. "No one, Miss King, no one *puts up* with me. You hardly need concern yourself with a woman who will be gone in a week's time. Your lack of confidence is as pitiful as your threats." Orchid rose at that, her fists clenched by her sides.

"What do you want from me?" Laine demanded. "Do you want my assurance that I won't interfere with your plans? Very well, I give it freely and with pleasure. Dillon is yours."

"That's generous of you." Spinning, Laine saw Dillon leaning against the doorway. His arms were crossed, his eyes dangerously dark.

"Oh, Dillon, how quick you were." Orchid's voice was faint.

"Apparently not quick enough." His eyes were locked on Laine's. "What's the problem?"

"Just a little feminine talk, Dillon." Recovered, Orchid glided to his side. "Laine and I were just getting to know each other."

"Laine, what's going on?"

"Nothing important. If it's convenient, I should like to go back now." Without waiting for a reply, Laine picked up her bag and moved to the doorway.

Dillon halted her by a hand on her arm. "I asked you a question."

"And I have given you the only answer I intend to give." She wrenched free and faced him. "I will not be questioned any longer. You have no right to question me; I am nothing to you. You have no right to criticize me as you have done from the first moment. You have no right to judge." The anger in her tone was now laced with despair. "You have no right to make love to me just because it amuses you."

She ran in a flurry of flying skirts, and he watched the door slam behind her.

Chapter 10

Laine spent the rest of the day in her room. She attempted not to dwell on the scene in Dillon's home, or on the silent drive which followed it. She was not sure which had been more draining. It occurred to her that she and Dillon never seemed to enjoy a cordial relationship for more than a few hours at a time. It was definitely time to leave. She began to plan for her return to France. Upon a review of her finances, she discovered that she had barely enough for a return ticket.

It would, she realized with a sigh, leave her virtually penniless. Her own savings had been sorely dented in dealing with her mother's debts, and plane fare had eaten at what remained. She could not, she determined, return to France without a franc in her pocket. If there was a complication of any kind, she would be helpless to deal with it. *Why didn't I stop to think before I came here?* she demanded of herself. *Now I've placed myself in an impossible situation.*

Sitting on the bed, Laine rubbed an aching temple and tried to think. She didn't want to ask her father for money. Pride prevented her from wiring to any friends to ask for a loan. She stared down at the small pile of bills in frustration. They won't proliferate of their own accord, she reflected, so I must plan how to increase their number.

She moved to her dresser and opened a small box. For some minutes, she studied the gold locket it contained. It had been a gift from her father to her mother, and Vanessa had given it to her on her sixteenth birthday. She remembered the pleasure she had felt upon receiving something, however indirectly, from her father. She had worn it habitually until she had dressed for her flight to Hawaii. Feeling it might cause her father pain, Laine had placed it in its box, hoping that unhappy memories would be buried. It was the only thing of value she owned, and now she had to sell it.

Her door swung open. Laine held the box behind her back. Miri glided in, a swirling mountain of color. She regarded Laine's flushed face with raised brows.

"Did you mess something up?"

"No."

"Then don't look guilty. Here." She laid a sheath of brilliant blue and sparkling white on the bedspread. "It's for you. You wear this to the luau tomorrow."

"Oh." Laine stared at the exquisite length of silk, already feeling its magic against her skin. "It's beautiful. I couldn't." She raised her eyes to Miri's with a mixture of desire and regret. "I couldn't take it."

"You don't like my present?" Miri demanded imperiously. "You are very rude."

"Oh, no." Struck with alarm at the unintentional offense, Laine fumbled with an explanation. "It's beautiful…really. It's only that…"

"You should learn to say thank-you and not argue. This will suit your skinny bones." Miri gave a nod of satisfaction encompassing both the woman and the silk. "Tomorrow, I will show you how to wrap it."

Unable to prevent herself, Laine moved over to feel the cool material under her fingers. The combination of longing and Miri's dark, arched brows proved too formidable for pride. She surrendered with a sigh. "Thank you, Miri. It's very good of you."

"That's much better," Miri approved and patted Laine's halo of curls. "You are a pretty child. You should smile more. When you smile, the sadness goes away."

Feeling the small box weighing like a stone in her hand, Laine held it up and opened it. "Miri, I wonder if you might tell me where I could sell this."

One large brown finger traced the gold before Miri's jet eyes lifted. Laine saw the now familiar pucker between her brows. "Why do you want to sell a pretty thing like this? You don't like it?"

"No, no, I like it very much." Helpless under the direct stare, Laine moved her shoulders. "I need the money."

"Money? Why do you need money?"

"For my passage and expenses…to return to France."

"You don't like Kauai?" Her indignant tone caused Laine to smile and shake her head.

"Kauai is wonderful; I'd like nothing better than to stay here forever. But I must get back to my job."

"What do you do in that place?" Miri dismissed France with a regal gesture and settled her large frame into a chair. She folded her hands across the mound of her belly.

"I teach." Laine sat on the bed and closed the lid on the face of the locket.

"Don't they pay you to teach?" Miri pursed her lips in disapproval. "What did you do with your money?"

Laine flushed, feeling like a child who had been discovered spending her allowance on candy. "There... there were debts, and I..."

"You have debts?"

"Well, no, I...not precisely." Laine's shoulders drooped with frustration. Seeing Miri was prepared to remain a permanent fixture of her room until she received an explanation, Laine surrendered. Slowly, she began to explain the financial mountain which she had faced at her mother's death, the necessity to liquidate assets, the continuing drain on her own resources. In the telling, Laine felt the final layers of her resentment fading. Miri did not interrupt the recital, and Laine found that confession had purged her of bitterness.

"Then, when I found my father's address among her personal papers, I took what I had left and came here. I'm afraid I didn't plan things well, and in order to go back..." She shrugged again and trailed off. Miri nodded.

"Why have you not told Cap Simmons? He would not have his daughter selling her baubles. He's a good man, he would not have you in a strange country counting your pennies."

"He doesn't owe me anything."

"He is your father," Miri stated, lifting her chin and peering down her nose at Laine.

"But he's not responsible for a situation brought on by Vanessa's carelessness and my own impulsiveness. He would think… No." She shook her head. "I don't want him to know. It's very important to me that he *not* know. You must promise not to speak of this to him."

"You are a very stubborn girl." Miri crossed her arms and glared at Laine. Laine kept her eyes level. "Very well." Miri's bosom lifted and fell with her sigh. "You must do what you must do. Tomorrow, you will meet my nephew, Tommy. Ask him to come look at your bauble. He is a jeweler and will give you a fair price."

"Thank you, Miri." Laine smiled, feeling a portion of her burden ease.

Miri rose, her muumuu trembling at the movement. "You had a nice day with Dillon?"

"We went by his home," Laine returned evasively. "It's very impressive."

"Very nice place," Miri agreed and brushed an infinitesimal speck of dust from the chair's back. "My cousin cooks there, but not so well as Miri."

"Miss King dropped by." Laine strove for a casual tone, but Miri's brows rose.

"Hmph." Miri stroked the tentlike lines of her flowered silk.

"We had a rather unpleasant discussion when Dillon left us alone. When he came back…" Laine paused and drew her brows together. "I shouted at him."

Miri laughed, holding her middle as if it would split from the effort. For several moments, her mirth rolled comfortably around the room. "So you can shout, Skinny Bones? I would like to have seen that."

"I don't think Dillon found it that amusing." In spite of herself, Laine smiled.

"Oh, that one." She wiped her eyes and shook her head. "He is too used to having his own way with women. He is too good-looking and has too much money." She placed a comforting hand over the barrel of her belly. "He's a fair boss, and he works in the fields when he's needed. He has big degrees and many brains." She tapped her finger on her temple, but looked unimpressed. "He was a very bad boy, with many pranks." Laine saw her lips tremble as she tried not to show amusement at the memories. "He is still a bad boy," she said firmly, regaining her dignity. "He is very smart and *very* important." She made a circling movement with both hands to indicate Dillon's importance, but her voice was full of maternal criticism. "But no matter what he thinks, he does not know women. He only knows planes." She patted Laine's head and pointed to the length of silk. "Tomorrow, you wear that and put a flower in your hair. The moon will be full."

It was a night of silver and velvet. From her window, Laine could see the dancing diamonds of moonlight on the sea. Allowing the breeze to caress her bare shoulders, Laine reflected that the night was perfect for a luau under the stars.

She had not seen Dillon since the previous day. He had returned to the house long after she had retired, and had left again before she had awakened. She was determined, however, not to permit their last meeting to spoil the beauty of the evening. If she had only a few days left in his company, she would make every effort to see that they were pleasant.

Turning from her window, Laine gave one final look at the woman in the mirror. Her bare shoulders rose like marble from the brilliant blue of the sarong. She stared at the woman in the glass, recognizing some change, but unable to discern its cause. She was not aware that over the past few days she had moved from girlhood to womanhood. After a final touch of the brush to her hair, Laine left the room. Dillon's voice rose up the staircase, and she moved to meet it. All at once, it seemed years since she had last heard him speak.

"We'll be harvesting next month, but if I know the schedule of meetings far enough in advance, I can…"

His voice trailed away as Laine moved into the doorway. Pausing in the act of pouring a drink, he made a slow survey. Laine felt her pulse triple its rate as his eyes lingered along their route before meeting hers.

Glancing up from filling his pipe, Cap noted Dillon's absorption. He followed his gaze. "Well, Laine." He rose, surprising her by crossing the room and taking both her hands in his. "What a beautiful sight."

"Do you like it?" Smiling first at him, she glanced down at the sarong. "I'm not quite used to the way it feels."

"I like it very much, but I was talking about you. My daughter is a very beautiful woman, isn't she, Dillon?" His eyes were soft and smiled into Laine's.

"Yes." Dillon's voice came from behind him. "Very beautiful."

"I'm glad she's here." He pressed her fingers between the warmth of his hands. "I've missed her." He bent and kissed her cheek, then turned to Dillon. "You two run along. I'll see if Miri's ready, which she won't be. We'll be along later."

Laine watched him stride away. She lifted one hand to her cheek, unable to believe she could be so deeply affected by one small gesture.

"Are you ready?" She nodded, unable to speak, then felt Dillon's hands descend to her shoulders. "It isn't easy to bridge a fifteen-year gap, but you've made a start."

Surprised by the support in his voice, Laine blinked back tears and turned to face him. "Thank you. It means a great deal to me for you to say that. Dillon, yesterday, I…"

"Let's not worry about yesterday right now." His smile was both an apology and an acceptance of hers. It was easy to smile back. He studied her a moment before lifting her hand to his lips. "You are incredibly beautiful, like a blossom hanging on a branch just out of reach." Laine wanted to blurt out that she was not out of reach, but a thick blanket of shyness covered her tongue. She could do no more than stare at him.

"Come on." Keeping her hand in his, Dillon moved to the door. "You should try everything once." His tone was light again as they slid into his car. "You know, you're a very small lady."

"Only because you look from an intimidating height," she returned, feeling pleased with the ease of their relationship. "What does one do at a luau, Dillon? I'm very much afraid I'll insult a local tradition if I refuse to eat raw fish. But—" resting her head against the seat, she smiled at the stars "—I shall refuse to do so."

"We don't hurl mainlanders into the sea anymore for minor offenses. You haven't much hip," he commented, dropping his eyes for a moment. "But you could have a stab at a hula."

"I'm sure my hips are adequate and will no doubt be more so if Miri has her way." Laine sent him a teasing glance. "Do you dance, Dillon?"

He grinned and met her look. "I prefer to watch. Dancing the hula properly takes years of practice. These dancers are very good."

"I see." She shifted in her seat to smile at him. "Will there be many people at the luau?"

"Mmm." Dillon tapped his finger absently against the wheel. "About a hundred, give or take a few."

"A hundred," Laine echoed. She fought off unhappy memories of her mother's overcrowded, overelegant parties. So many people, so many demands, so many measuring eyes.

"Tommy has a lot of relatives."

"How nice for him," she murmured and considered the advantages of small families.

Chapter 11

The hollow, primitive sound of drums vibrated through air pungent with roasting meat. Torches were set on high stakes, their orange flames shooting flickering light against a black sky. To Laine it was like stepping back in time. The lawn was crowded with guests—some in traditional attire and others, like Dillon, in the casual comfort of jeans. Laughter rose from a myriad of tones and mixed languages. Laine gazed around, enthralled by the scene and the scents.

Set on a huge, woven mat were an infinite variety of mysterious dishes in wooden bowls and trays. Ebony-haired girls in native dress knelt to spoon food onto the plates and serving dishes. Diverse aromas lifted on the night air and lingered to entice. Men, swathed at the waist and bare-chested, beat out pulsating rhythms on high, conical drums.

Introduced to an impossible blur of faces, Laine merely floated with the mood of the crowd. There seemed to be a universal friendliness, an uncomplicated joy in simply being.

Soon sandwiched between her father and Dillon, Laine sat on the grass and watched her plate being heaped with unknown wonders. A roar of approval rose over the music as the pig was unearthed from the *imu* and carved. Dutifully, she dipped her fingers in poi and sampled. She shrugged her shoulders as Dillon laughed at her wrinkled nose.

"Perhaps it's an acquired taste," she suggested as she wiped her fingers on a napkin.

"Here." Dillon lifted a fork and urged its contents into Laine's reluctant mouth.

With some surprise, she found the taste delightful. "That's very good. What is it?"

"Laulau."

"This is not illuminating."

"If it's good, what else do you have to know?" His logic caused her to arch her brows. "It's pork and butterfish steamed in *ti* leaves," he explained, shaking his head. "Try this." Dillon offered the fork again, and Laine accepted without hesitation.

"Oh, what is it? I've never tasted anything like it."

"Squid," he answered, then roared with laughter at her gasp of alarm.

"I believe," Laine stated with dignity, "I shall limit myself to pork and pineapple."

"You'll never grow hips that way."

"I shall learn to live without them. What is this drink…? No," she decided, smiling as she heard her father's chuckle. "I believe I'm better off not knowing."

Avoiding the squid, Laine found herself enjoying the informal meal. Occasionally, someone stopped and crouched beside them, exchanging quick greetings or a long story. Laine was treated with a natural friendliness which soon put her at her ease. Her father seemed comfortable with her, and though he and Dillon enjoyed an entente which eluded her, she no longer felt like an intruder. Music and laughter and the heady perfume of night swam around her. Laine thought she had never felt so intensely aware of her surroundings.

Suddenly, the drummers beat a rapid tempo, reaching a peak, then halting. Their echo fell into silence as Orchid stepped into view. She stood in a circle of torchlight, her skin glowing under its touch. Her eyes were gold and arrogant. Tantalizing and perfect, her body was adorned only in a brief top and a slight swatch of scarlet silk draped low over her hips. She stood completely still, allowing the silence to build before she began slowly circling her hips. A single drum began to follow the rhythm she set.

Her hair, crowned with a circlet of buds, fell down her bare back. Her hands and lithesome curves moved with a hypnotic power as the bare draping of silk flowed against her thighs. Sensuous and tempting, her gestures moved with the beat, and Laine saw that her golden eyes were locked on Dillon's. The faint smile she gave him was knowledgeable. Almost imperceptibly, her dance grew in speed. As the drum became more insistent, her movements became more abandoned. Her face remained calm and smiling above her undulating body. Then, abruptly, sound and movement halted into stunning silence.

Applause broke out. Orchid threw Laine a look of

triumph before she lifted the flower crown from her head and tossed it into Dillon's lap. With a soft, sultry laugh, she retreated to the shadows.

"Looks like you've got yourself an invitation," Cap commented, then pursed his lips in thought. "Amazing. I wonder how many RPMs we could clock her at."

Shrugging, Dillon lifted his glass.

"You like to move like that, Skinny Bones?" Laine turned to where Miri sat in the background. She looked more regal than ever in a high-backed rattan chair. "You eat so you don't rattle, and Miri will teach you."

Flushed with a mixture of embarrassment and the longing to move with such free abandonment, Laine avoided Dillon's eyes. "I don't rattle now, but I think Miss King's ability is natural."

"You might pick it up, Duchess." Dillon grinned at Laine's lowered lashes. "I'd like to sit in on the lessons, Miri. As you well know, I've got a very discerning eye." He dropped his gaze to her bare legs, moving it up the length of blue and white silk, before meeting her eyes.

Miri muttered something in Hawaiian, and Dillon chuckled and tossed back a retort in the same tongue. "Come with me," Miri commanded. Rising, she pulled Laine to her feet.

"What did you say to him?" Laine moved in the wake of Miri's flowing gown.

"I said he is a big hungry cat cornering a small mouse."

"I am not a mouse," Laine returned indignantly.

Miri laughed without breaking stride. "Dillon says no, too. He says you are a bird whose beak is sometimes sharp under soft feathers."

"Oh." Unsure whether to be pleased or annoyed with the description, Laine lapsed into silence.

"I have told Tommy you have a bauble to sell," Miri announced. "You will talk to him now."

"Yes, of course," Laine murmured, having forgotten the locket in the enchantment of the night.

Miri paused in front of the luau's host. He was a spare, dark-haired man with an easy smile and friendly eyes. Laine judged him to be in the later part of his thirties, and she had seen him handle his guests with a practiced charm. "You will talk to Cap Simmons's daughter," Miri commanded as she placed a protective hand on Laine's shoulder. "You do right by her, or I will box your ears."

"Yes, Miri," he agreed, but his subservient nod was not reflected in his laughing eyes. He watched the graceful mountain move off before he tossed an arm around Laine's shoulders. He moved her gently toward the privacy of trees. "Miri is the matriarch of our family," he said with a laugh. "She rules with an iron hand."

"Yes, I've noticed. It's impossible to say no to her, isn't it?" The celebrating sounds of the luau drifted into a murmur as they walked.

"I've never tried. I'm a coward."

"I appreciate your time, Mr. Kinimoko," Laine began.

"Tommy, please, then I can call you Laine." She smiled, and as they walked on, she heard the whisper of the sea. "Miri said you had a bauble to sell. I'm afraid she wasn't any more specific."

"A gold locket," Laine explained, finding his friendly manner had put her at ease. "It's heart-shaped and has a braided chain. I have no idea of its value." She paused, wishing there was another way. "I need the money."

Tommy glanced at the delicate profile, then patted her shoulder. "I take it you don't want Cap to know? Okay," he continued as she shook her head. "I have some free time in the morning. Why don't I come by and have a look around ten? You'll find it more comfortable than coming into the shop."

Laine heard leaves rustle and saw Tommy glance idly toward the sound. "It's very good of you." He turned back to her and she smiled, relieved that the first hurdle was over. "I hope I'm not putting you to any trouble."

"I enjoy troubling for beautiful wahines." He kept his arm over her shoulders as he led her back toward the sound of drums and guitars. "You heard Miri. You don't want me to get my ears boxed, do you?"

"I would never forgive myself if I were responsible for that. I'll tell Miri you've done right by Cap Simmons's daughter, and your ears will be left in peace." Laughing, Laine tilted her face to his as they broke through the curtain of trees.

"Your sister's looking for you, Tommy." At Dillon's voice, Laine gave a guilty start.

"Thanks, Dillon. I'll just turn Laine over to you. Take good care of her," he advised gravely. "She's under Miri's protection."

"I'll keep that in mind." Dillon watched in silence as Tommy merged back into the crowd, then he turned back to study Laine. "There's an old Hawaiian custom," he began slowly, and she heard annoyance color his tone, "which I have just invented. When a woman comes to a luau with a man, she doesn't walk in monkeypod trees with anyone else."

"Will I be tossed to the sharks if I break the rules?" Her teasing smile faded as Dillon took a step closer.

"Don't, Laine." He circled her neck with his hand. "I haven't had much practice in restraint."

She swayed toward him, giving in to the sudden surging need. "Dillon," she murmured, offering her mouth in simple invitation. She felt the strength of his fingers as they tightened on her neck. She rested her hands against his chest and felt his heartbeat under her palms. The knowledge of his power over her, and her own longing, caused her to tremble. Dillon made a soft sound, a lingering expulsion of breath. Laine watched him struggle with some emotion, watched something flicker in his eyes and fade before his fingers relaxed again.

"A wahine who stands in the shadows under a full moon must be kissed."

"Is this another old Hawaiian tradition?" Laine felt his arms slip around her waist and melted against him.

"Yes, about ten seconds old."

With unexpected gentleness, his mouth met hers. At the first touch, her body went fluid, mists of pleasure shrouding her. As from a distant shore, Laine heard the call of the drums, their rhythm building to a crescendo as did her heartbeat. Feeling the tenseness of Dillon's shoulders under her hands, she stroked, then circled his neck to bring his face closer to hers. Too soon, he lifted his mouth, and his arms relinquished his hold of her.

"More," Laine murmured, unsatisfied, and pulled his face back to hers.

She was swept against him. The power of his kiss drove all but the need from her mind. She could taste the hunger on his lips, feel the heat growing on his flesh.

The air seemed to tremble around them. In that moment, her body belonged more to him than to her. If there was a world apart from seeking lips and caressing hands it held no meaning for her. Again, Dillon drew her away, but his voice was low and uneven.

"We'll go back before another tradition occurs to me."

In the morning, Laine lingered under the sun's streaming light, unwilling to leave her bed and the warm pleasure which still clung from the evening before. The taste of Dillon's mouth still lingered on hers, and his scent remained fresh and vital on her senses. She relived the memory of being in his arms. Finally, with a sigh, she abandoned the luxury of her bed and rose to face the day. Just as she was securing the belt of her robe, Miri glided into the room.

"So, you have decided to get up. The morning is half gone while you lay in your bed." Miri's voice was stern, but her eyes twinkled with indulgence.

"It made the night last longer," Laine replied, smiling at the affectionate scold.

"You liked the roast pig and poi?" Miri asked with a wise nod and a whisper of a smile.

"It was wonderful."

With her lilting laugh floating through the room, Miri turned to leave. "I am going to the market. My nephew is here to see your bauble. Do you want him to wait?"

"Oh." Forcing herself back down to earth, Laine ran her fingers through her hair. "I didn't realize it was that late. I don't want to inconvenience him. I…is anyone else at home?"

"No, they are gone."

Glancing down at her robe, Laine decided it was adequate coverage. "Perhaps he could come up and look at it. I don't want to keep him waiting."

"He will give you a fair price," Miri stated as she drifted through the doorway. "Or, you will tell me."

Laine took the small box from her drawer and opened the lid. The locket glinted under a ray of sunshine. There were no pictures to remove but, nonetheless, she opened it and stared at its emptiness.

"Laine."

Turning, she managed to smile at Tommy as he stood in the doorway. "Hello. It was good of you to come. Forgive me, I slept rather late this morning."

"A compliment to the host of the luau." He made a small, rather dapper bow as she approached him.

"It was my first, and I have no doubt it will remain my favorite." Laine handed him the box, then gripped her hands together as he made his examination.

"It's a nice piece," he said at length. Lifting his eyes, Tommy studied her. "Laine, you don't want to sell this—it's written all over your face."

"No." She saw from his manner she need not hedge. "It's necessary that I do."

Detecting the firmness in her voice, Tommy shrugged and placed the locket back in its box. "I can give you a hundred for it, though I think it's worth a great deal more to you."

Laine nodded and closed the lid as he handed the box back to her. "That will be fine. Perhaps you'd take it now. I would rather you kept it."

"If that's what you want." Tommy drew out his wallet

and counted out bills. "I brought some cash. I thought you'd find it easier than a check."

"Thank you." After accepting the money, Laine stared down at it until he rested a hand on her shoulder.

"Laine, I've known Cap a long time. Would you take this as a loan?"

"No." She shook her head, then smiled to ease the sharpness of the word. "No. It's very kind of you, but I must do it this way."

"Okay." He took the offered box and pocketed it. "I will, however, hold this for a while in case you have second thoughts."

"Thank you. Thank you for not asking questions."

"I'll see myself out." He took her hand and gave it a small squeeze. "Just tell Miri to get in touch with me if you change your mind."

"Yes, I will."

After he had gone, Laine sat heavily on the bed and stared at the money she held clutched in her hand. There was nothing else I could do, she told herself. It was only a piece of metal. Now, it's done, I can't dwell on it.

"Well, Duchess, it seems you've had a profitable morning."

Laine's head snapped up. Dillon's eyes were frosted like an ice-crusted lake, and she stared at him, unable to clear her thoughts. His gaze raked her scantily clad body, and she reached a hand to the throat of her robe in an automatic gesture. Moving toward her, he pulled the bills from her hand and dropped the money on the nightstand.

"You've got class, Duchess." Dillon pinned her with his eyes. "I'd say that's pretty good for a morning's work."

"What are you talking about?" Her thoughts were

scattered as she searched for a way to avoid telling him about the locket.

"Oh, I think that's clear enough. I guess I owe Orchid an apology." He thrust his hands in his pockets and rocked back on his heels. The easy gesture belied the burning temper in his eyes. "When she told me about this little arrangement, I came down on her pretty hard. You're a fast worker, Laine. You couldn't have been with Tommy for more than ten minutes last night; you must have made quite a sales pitch."

"I don't know why you're so angry," she began, confused as to why the sale of her locket would bring on such fury. "I suppose Miss King listened to our conversation last night." Suddenly, Laine remembered the quick rustle of leaves. "But why she should feel it necessary to report to you on my business…"

"How'd you manage to get rid of Miri while you conducted your little business transaction?" Dillon demanded. "She has a rather strict moral code, you know. If she finds out how you're earning your pin money, she's liable to toss you out on your ear."

"What do you…" Realization dawned slowly. *Not my locket,* Laine thought dumbly, *but myself.* All trace of color fled from her face. "You don't really believe that I…" Her voice broke as she read the condemnation in his eyes. "This is despicable of you, Dillon. Nothing you've accused me of, nothing you've said to me since we first met compares with this." The words trembled with emotion as she felt a viselike pressure around her heart. "I won't be insulted this way by you."

"Oh, won't you?" Taking her arm, Dillon dragged Laine to her feet. "Have you a more plausible explanation up your sleeve for Tommy's visit and the wad you're fondling? Go ahead, run it by me. I'm listening."

"Oh, yes, I can see you are. Forgive me for refusing, but Tommy's visit and my money are my business. I owe you no explanation, Dillon. Your conclusions aren't worthy of my words. The fact that you gave enough credence to whatever lie Orchid told you to come check on me, means we have nothing more to say to each other."

"I didn't come here to check on you." He was towering menacingly over her, but Laine met his eyes without flinching. "I came by because I thought you'd want to go up again. You said you wanted to learn to fly, and I said I'd teach you. If you want an apology, all you have to do is give me a reasonable explanation."

"I've spent enough time explaining myself to you. More than you deserve. Questions, always questions. Never *trust*." Her eyes smoldered with blue fire. "I want you to leave my room. I want you to leave me alone for the rest of the time I have in my father's house."

"You had me going." His fingers tightened on her arms, and she caught her breath at the pressure. "I bought it all. The big, innocent eyes, the virginal frailty, the pictures you painted of a woman looking for her father's affection and nothing else. *Trust?*" he flung back at her. "You'd taken me to the point where I trusted you more than myself. You knew I wanted you, and you worked on me. All those trembles and melting bones and artless looks. You played it perfectly, right down to the blushes." He pulled her against him, nearly lifting her off her feet.

"Dillon, you're hurting me." She faltered.

"I wanted you," he went on, as if she had not spoken. "Last night I was aching for you, but I treated you with a restraint and respect I've never shown another woman. You slip on that innocent aura that drives a man crazy. You shouldn't have used it on me, Duchess."

Terror shivered along her skin. Her breath was rapid and aching in her lungs.

"Game's over. I'm going to collect." He silenced her protest with a hard, punishing kiss. Though she struggled against his imprisoning arms, she made no more ripple than a leaf battling a whirlpool. The room tilted, and she was crushed beneath him on the mattress. She fought against the intimacy as his mouth and hands bruised her. He was claiming her in fury, disposing of the barrier of her robe and possessing her flesh with angry demand.

Slowly, his movements altered in texture. Punishment became seduction as his hands began to caress rather than bruise. His mouth left hers to trail down her throat. With a sob ending on a moan, Laine surrendered. Her body became pliant under his, her will snapping with the weight of sensations never tasted. Tears gathered, but she made no more effort to halt them than she did the man who urged them from her soul.

All movement stopped abruptly, and Dillon lay still. The room was thrown into a tortured silence, broken only by the sound of quick breathing. Lifting his head, Dillon studied the journey of a tear down Laine's cheek. He swore with sudden eloquence, then rose. He tugged a hand through his hair as he turned his back on her.

"This is the first time I've been driven to nearly forcing myself on a woman." His voice was low and harsh as he swung around and stared at her. Laine lay still, emotionally drained. She made no effort to cover herself, but merely stared up at him with the eyes of a wounded child. "I can't deal with what you do to me, Laine."

Turning on his heel, he strode from the room. Laine thought the slamming of her door the loneliest sound she had ever heard.

Chapter 12

It was raining on the new spring grass. From her dormitory window Laine watched the green brighten with its morning bath. Outside her door, she heard girls trooping down the hall toward breakfast, but she did not smile at their gay chattering in French and English. She found smiles still difficult.

It had not yet been two weeks since Miri had met Laine's packed cases with a frown and drawn brows. She had met Laine's sketchy explanations with crossed arms and further questions. Laine had remained firm, refusing to postpone her departure or to give specific answers. The note she had left for her father had contained no more details, only an apology for her abrupt leave-taking and a promise to write once she had settled back in France. As of yet, Laine had not found the courage to put pen to paper.

Memories of her last moments with Dillon continued to haunt her. She could still smell the perfume of island blossoms, still feel the warm, moist air rise from the sea to move over her skin. Watching the moon wane, she could remember its lush fullness over the heads of palms. She had hoped her memories would fade with time. She reminded herself that Kauai and its promises were behind her.

It's better this way, she told herself, picking up her brush and preparing herself for the day's work. *Better for everyone.* Her father was settled in his life and would be content to exchange occasional letters. One day, perhaps, he would visit her. Laine knew she could never go back. She, too, had her own life, a job, the comfort of familiar surroundings. Here, she knew what was expected of her. Her existence would be tranquil and unmarred by storms of emotions. She closed her eyes on Dillon's image.

It's too soon, she told herself. Too soon to test her ability to think of him without pain. Later, when the memory had dulled, she would open the door. When she allowed herself to think of him again, it would be to remember the beauty.

It was easier to forget if she followed a routine. Laine scheduled each day to allow for a minimum of idle time. Classes claimed her mornings and early afternoons, and she spent the remainder of her days with chores designed to keep her mind and hands busy.

Throughout the day, the rain continued. With a musical plop, the inevitable leak dripped into the basin on Laine's classroom floor. The school building was old and rambling. Repairs were always either just completed, slated to be done or in vague consideration for the future. The windows were shut against the damp, but the gloom crept into the room. The students were languid and inattentive. Her final class of the day was made up of English girls just entering adolescence. They were thoroughly bored by their hour lesson on French grammar. As it was Saturday, there was only a half day of classes, but the hours dragged. Hugging her navy blazer closer, Laine reflected that the afternoon would be better employed with a good book and a cheerful fire than by conjugating verbs in a rain-dreary classroom.

"Eloise," Laine said, recalling her duty. "One must postpone naps until after class."

The girl's eyes blinked open. She gave a groggy, self-conscious smile as her classmates giggled. "Yes, Mademoiselle Simmons."

Laine bit back a sigh. "You will have your freedom in ten minutes," she reminded them as she perched on the edge of her desk. "If you have forgotten, it is Saturday. Sunday follows."

This information brought murmurs of approval and a few straightened shoulders. Seeing she had at least momentarily captured their attention, Laine went on. *"Maintenant,* the verb *chanter.* To sing. *Attendez, ensuite répétez. Je chante, tu chantes, il chante, nous chantons, vous..."* Her voice faded as she saw the man leaning against the open door in the rear of the classroom.

"Vous chantez."

Laine forced her attention back to young Eloise. *"Oui, vous chantez, et ils chantent. Répétez."*

Obediently, the music of high girlish voices repeated the lesson. Laine retreated behind her desk while Dillon stood calmly and watched. As the voices faded into silence, Laine wracked her brain for the assignment she had planned.

"Bien. You will write, for Monday, sentences using this verb in all its forms. Eloise, we will not consider *'Il chante'* an imaginative sentence."

"Yes, Mademoiselle Simmons."

The bell rang signaling the end of class.

"You will not run," she called over the furious clatter of shuffling desks and scurrying feet. Gripping her hands in her lap, Laine prepared herself for the encounter.

She watched the girls giggle and whisper as they passed by Dillon, and saw, as her heart spun circles, his familiar, easy grin. Crossing the room with his long stride, he stood before her.

"Hello, Dillon." She spoke quickly to cover her confusion. "You seem to have quite an effect on my students."

He studied her face in silence as she fought to keep her smile in place. The flood of emotion threatened to drown her.

"You haven't changed," he said at length. "I don't know why I was afraid you would." Reaching in his pocket, he pulled out the locket and placed it on her desk. Unable to speak, Laine stared at it. As her eyes filled, her hand closed convulsively over the gold heart. "Not a very eloquent apology, but I haven't had a lot of practice. For pity's sake, Laine." His tone shifted into anger so quickly, she lifted her head in shock. "If you needed money, why didn't you tell me?"

"And confirm your opinion of my character?" she retorted.

Turning away, Dillon moved to a window and looked into the insistent mist of rain. "I had that one coming," he murmured, then rested his hands on the sill and lapsed into silence.

She was moved by the flicker of pain that had crossed his face. "There's no purpose in recriminations now, Dillon. It's best to leave all that in the past." Rising, she kept the desk between them. "I'm very grateful to you for taking the time and the trouble to return my locket. It's more important to me than I can tell you. I don't know when I'll be able to pay you. I…"

Dillon whirled, and Laine stepped away from the fury on his face. She watched him struggle for control. "No, don't say anything, just give me a minute." His hands retreated to his pockets. For several long moments, he paced the room. Gradually, his movements grew calmer. "The roof leaks," he said idly.

"Only when it rains."

He gave a short laugh and turned back to her. "Maybe it doesn't mean much, but I'm sorry. No." He shook his head to ward her off as she began to answer. "Don't be so blasted generous. It'll only make me feel more guilty." He started to light a cigarette, remembered where he was and let out a long breath. "After my exhibition of stupidity, I went up for a while. I find that I think more clearly a few thousand feet off the ground. You might find this hard to believe, and I suppose it's even more ridiculous to expect you to forgive me, but I did manage to get a grip on reality. I didn't even believe the things I was saying to you when I was saying them." He rubbed his hands over his face, and Laine noticed for the first time that he looked tired and drawn. "I only know that I went a little crazy from the first minute I saw you.

"I went back to the house with the intention of offering a series of inadequate apologies. I tried to rationalize that all the accusations I tossed at you about Cap were made for his sake." He shook his head, and a faint smile touched his mouth. "It didn't help."

"Dillon…"

"Laine, don't interrupt. I haven't the patience as it is." He paced again, and she stood silent. "I'm not very good at this, so just don't say anything until I'm finished." Restless, he continued to roam around the room as he spoke. "When I got back, Miri was waiting for me. I couldn't get anything out of her at first but a detailed lecture on my character. Finally, she told me you'd gone. I didn't take that news very well, but it's no use going into that now. After a lot of glaring and ancient curses, she told me about the locket. I had to swear a blood oath not to tell Cap. It seems you had her word on that. I've been in France for ten days trying to find you." Turning back, he gestured in frustration. "Ten days," he repeated as if it were a lifetime. "It wasn't until this morning that I traced the maid who worked for your mother. She was very expansive once I settled her into broken English. I got an earful about debts and auctions and the little mademoiselle who stayed in school over Christmas vacations while Madame went to Saint

Moritz. She gave me the name of your school." Dillon paused. For a moment there was only the sound of water dripping from the ceiling into the basin. "There's nothing you can say to me that I haven't already said to myself, in more graphic terms. But I figured you should have the chance."

Seeing he was finished, Laine drew a deep breath and prepared to speak. "Dillon, I've thought carefully on how my position would have looked to you. You knew only one side, and your heart was with my father. I find it difficult, when I'm calm, to resent that loyalty or your protection of his welfare. As for what happened on the last morning—" Laine swallowed, striving to keep her voice composed. "I think it was as difficult for you as it was for me, perhaps more difficult."

"You'd make it a whole lot easier on my conscience if you'd yell or toss a few things at me."

"I'm sorry." She managed a smile and lifted her shoulders with the apology. "I'd have to be very angry to do that, especially here. The nuns frown on displays of temper."

"Cap wants you to come home."

Laine's smile faded at his quiet words. He watched her eyes go bleak before she shook her head and moved to the window. "This is my home."

"Your home's in Kauai. Cap wants you back. Is it fair to him to lose you twice?"

"Is it fair to ask me to turn my back on my own life and return?" she countered, trying to block out the pain his words were causing. "Don't talk to me about fair, Dillon."

"Look, be as bitter as you want about me. I deserve

it. Cap doesn't. How do you think he feels knowing what your childhood was like?"

"You told him?" She whirled around, and for the first time since he had come into the room, Dillon saw her mask of control slip. "You had no right…"

"I had every right," he interrupted. "Just as Cap had every right to know. Laine, listen to me." She had started to turn away, but his words and quiet tone halted her. "He loves you. He never stopped, not all those years. I guess that's why I reacted to you the way I did." With an impatient sound, he ran his hands through his hair again. "For fifteen years, loving you hurt him."

"Don't you think I know that?" she tossed back. "Why must he be hurt more?"

"Laine, the few days you were with him gave him back his daughter. He didn't ask why you never answered his letters, he never accused you of any of the things I did." He shut his eyes briefly, and again she noticed fatigue. "He loved you without needing explanations or apologies. It would have been wrong to prolong the lies. When he found you'd left, he wanted to come to France himself to bring you back. I asked him to let me come alone because I knew it was my fault that you left."

"There's no blame, Dillon." With a sigh, Laine slipped the locket into her blazer pocket. "Perhaps you were right to tell Cap. Perhaps it's cleaner. I'll write him myself tonight; it was wrong of me to leave without seeing him. Knowing that he is really my father again is the greatest gift I've ever had. I don't want either one of you to think that my living in France means I hold any resentment. I very much hope that Cap visits me soon. Perhaps you'd carry a note back for me."

Dillon's eyes darkened. His voice was tight with anger when he spoke. "He isn't going to like knowing you're buried in this school."

Laine turned away from him and faced the window.

"I'm not buried, Dillon. The school is my home and my job."

"And your escape?" he demanded impatiently, then swore as he saw her stiffen. He began to pace again. "I'm sorry, that was a cheap shot."

"No more apologies, Dillon. I don't believe the floors can stand the wear."

He stopped his pacing and studied her. Her back was still to him, but he could just see the line of her chin against the pale cap of curls. In the trim navy blazer and white pleated skirt, she looked more student than teacher. He began to speak in a lighter tone. "Listen, Duchess, I'm going to stay around for a couple of days, play tourist. How about showing me around? I could use someone who speaks the language."

Laine shut her eyes, thinking of what a few days in his company would mean. There was no point in prolonging the pain. "I'm sorry, Dillon, I'd love to take you around, but I haven't the time at the moment. My work here has backed up since I took the time off to visit Kauai."

"You're going to make this difficult, aren't you?"

"I'm not trying to do that, Dillon." Laine turned, with an apologetic smile. "Another time, perhaps."

"I haven't got another time. I'm trying my best to do this right, but I'm not sure of my moves. I've never dealt with a woman like you before. All the rules are different." She saw, with curiosity, that his usual confidence had vanished. He took a step toward her, stopped, then walked to the blackboard. For some moments, he studied the conjugation of several French verbs. "Have dinner with me tonight."

"No, Dillon, I..." He whirled around so swiftly, Laine swallowed the rest of her words.

"If you won't even have dinner with me, how the devil am I supposed to talk you into coming home so I can struggle through this courting routine? Any fool could see I'm no good at this sort of thing. I've already made a mess of it. I don't know how much longer I can stand here and be reasonably coherent. I love you, Laine, and it's driving me crazy. Come back to Kauai so we can be married."

Stunned into speechlessness, Laine stared at him. "Dillon," she began, "did you say you love me?"

"Yes, I said I love you. Do you want to hear it again?" His hands descended to her shoulders, his lips to her hair. "I love you so much I'm barely able to do simple things like eat and sleep for thinking of you. I keep remembering how you looked with a shell held to your ear. You stood there with the water running from your hair, and your eyes the color of the sky and the sea, and I fell completely in love with you. I tried not to believe it, but I lost ground every time you got near me. When you left, it was like losing part of myself. I'm not complete anymore without you."

"Dillon." His name was only a whisper.

"I swore I wasn't going to put any pressure on you." She felt his brow lower to the crown of her head. "I wasn't going to say all these things to you at once like this. I'll give you whatever you need, the flowers, the candlelight. You'd be surprised how conventional I can be when it's necessary. Just come back with me, Laine. I'll give you some time before I start pressuring you to marry me."

"No." She shook her head, then took a deep breath. "I won't come back with you unless you marry me first."

"Listen." Dillon tightened his grip, then with a groan of pleasure lowered his mouth to hers. "You drive a hard bargain," he murmured as he tasted her lips. As if starved for the flavor, he lingered over the kiss.

"I'm not going to give you the opportunity to change your mind." Lifting her arms, Laine circled his neck, then laid her cheek against his. "You can give me the flowers and candlelight after we're married."

"Duchess, you've got a deal. I'll have you married to me before you realize what you're getting into. Some people might tell you I have a few faults—such as, I occasionally lose my temper—"

"Really?" Laine lifted an incredulous face. "I've never known anyone more mild and even-tempered. However—" she trailed her finger down his throat and toyed with the top button of his shirt "—I suppose I should confess that I am by nature very jealous. It's just something I can't control. And if I ever see another woman dance the hula especially for you, I shall probably throw her off the nearest cliff!"

"Would you?" Dillon gave a self-satisfied masculine grin as he framed her face in his hands. "Then I think Miri should start teaching you as soon as we get back. I warn you, I plan to sit in on every lesson."

"I'm sure I'll be a quick learner." Rising to her toes, Laine pulled him closer. "But right now there are things I would rather learn. Kiss me again, Dillon!"

* * * * *

UNTAMED

For my sons,
Life's a circus.
Go for it!

Chapter 1

At the crack of the whip, twelve lions stood on their haunches and pawed the air. On command, they began to leap from pedestal to pedestal in a quick, close-formation, figure-eight pattern. This required split-second timing. With voice and hand commands the trainer kept the tawny, springing bodies moving.

"Well done, Pandora."

At her name and the signal, the muscular lioness leaped to the ground and lay down on her side. One by one the others followed suit, until, snarling and baring their teeth, they stretched across the tanbark. A male was positioned beside each female; at a sharp reproof from the trainer, Merlin ceased nibbling on Ophelia's ear.

"Heads up!" They obeyed as the trainer walked briskly in front of them. The whip was tossed aside with a flourish, then, with apparent nonchalance, the trainer reclined lengthwise across the warm bodies. The center cat, a full-maned African, let out a great, echoing bellow. As a reward for his response to the cue, his ear was given a good scratching. The trainer rose from the feline couch, clapped hands and brought the lions to their feet. Then, with a hand signal, each was called by name and sent through the chute and into their cages. One stayed behind, a huge, black-maned cat who, like an ordinary tabby, circled and rubbed up against his trainer's legs.

Deftly, a rope was attached to a chain that was hidden under his mane. Then, with swift agility, the trainer mounted the lion's back. As the door of the big cage opened, lion and rider passed through for a tour of the practice ring. When they reached the back door of the ring barn, Merlin, the obliging lion, was transferred to a wheel cage.

"Well, Duffy." Jo turned after the cage was secured. "Are we ready for the road?"

Duffy was a small, round man with a monk's fringe of chestnut hair and a face that exploded with ginger freckles. His open smile and Irish blue eyes gave him the look of an aging choirboy. His mind was sharp, shrewd and scrappy. He was the best manager Prescott's Circus Colossus could have had.

"Since we open in Ocala tomorrow," he replied in a raspy voice, "you'd better be ready." He shifted his fat cigar stump from the right side of his mouth to the left.

Jo merely smiled, then stretched to loosen muscles grown taut during the thirty minutes in the cage. "My cats are ready, Duffy. It's been a long winter. They need to get back on the road as much as the rest of us."

Duffy frowned. As circumstances had it, he stood only inches higher than his animal trainer. Widely spaced, almond-shaped eyes stared back at him. They were as sharp and green as emeralds, surrounded by thick, inky lashes. At the moment they were fearless and amused, but Duffy had seen them frightened, vulnerable and lost. He shifted his cigar again and took two quick puffs as Jo gave a cage hand instructions.

He remembered Steve Wilder, Jo's father. He had been one of the best cat men in the business. Jo was as good with the cats as Wilder had been. In some ways, Duffy acknowledged, even better. But she had the traits of her mother: delicate build; dark, passionate looks. Jolivette Wilder was as slender as her aerialist mother had been, with bold green eyes and straight, raven black hair that fell to just below her waist. Her brows were delicately arched, her nose small and straight, her cheekbones high and elegant, while her mouth was full and soft. Her skin was tawny from the Florida sun; it added to her gypsy-like appearance. Confidence added spark to the beauty.

Finishing her instructions, Jo tucked her arm through Duffy's. She had seen that frown before. "Somebody quit?" she asked as they began to walk toward Duffy's office.

"Nope."

His monosyllabic reply caused Jo to lift a brow. It was not often Duffy answered any question briefly. Years of experience told her to hold her tongue as they moved across the compound.

Rehearsals were going on everywhere. Vito the wire walker informally sharpened his act on a cable stretched between two trees. The Mendalsons called out to each other as they tossed their juggling pins high in the air, while the equestrian act led their horses into the ring barn. She saw one of the Stevenson girls walking on stilts. She'd be six now, Jo mused, tossing the hair from her eyes as she watched the young girl's wavering progress. Jo remembered the year she had been born. It had been that same year that she had been allowed to work the big cage alone. She had been sixteen, and it had been another full year before she had been permitted to work an audience.

For Jo, there had never been any home but the circus. She had been born during the winter break, had been tucked into her parents' trailer the following spring to spend her first year and each subsequent one of her life thereafter on the road. She had inherited both her fascination and her flair with animals from her father, her style and grace of movement from her mother. Though she had lost both parents fifteen years before, they continued to influence her. Their legacy to her had been a world of restlessness, a world of fantasies. She had grown up playing with lion cubs, riding elephants, wearing spangles and traveling like a gypsy.

Jo glanced down at a cluster of daffodils growing by the side of Prescott's winter office and smiled. She remembered planting them when she had been thirteen and in love with a tumbler. She remembered, too, the man who had stooped beside her, offering advice on bulb planting and broken hearts. As Jo thought of Frank Prescott, her smile grew sad.

"I still can't believe he's gone," she murmured as she and Duffy moved inside.

Duffy's office was sparsely furnished with a wooden desk, metal filing cabinets and two spindly chairs. A collage of posters adorned the walls. They promised the amazing, the astounding, the incredible: elephants that danced, men who flew through the air, beautiful girls who spun by their teeth, raging tigers that rode horseback. Tumblers, clowns, lions, strong men, fat ladies, boys who could balance on their forefingers; they brought the magic of the circus into the drab little room.

As Jo glanced over at a narrow pine door, Duffy followed her gaze. "I keep expecting him to come busting through there with some crazy new idea," he mumbled as he began to fiddle with his prize possession, an automatic coffee maker.

"Do you?" With a sigh Jo straddled a chair, then rested her chin on its back. "We all miss him. It's not going to seem the same without him this year." She looked up suddenly, and her eyes were angry. "He wasn't an old man, Duffy. Heart attacks should be for old men." She brooded into space, touched again with the injustice of Frank Prescott's death.

He had been barely into his fifties and full of laughter and simple kindness. Jo had loved him and trusted him without reservation. At his death she had grieved for him more acutely than she had for her own parents. In her longest memory he had been the core of her life.

"It's been nearly six months," Duffy said gruffly as he studied her face. When Jo glanced up, he stuck out a mug of coffee.

"I know." She took the mug, letting it warm her hands in the chilly March morning. Resolutely, she shook off the mood. Frank would not have wanted to leave sadness behind. Jo studied the coffee, then sipped. It was predictably dreadful. "Rumor has it we're following last year's route to the letter. Thirteen states." Jo smiled, watching Duffy wince over his coffee before he downed it. "Not superstitious, are you?" She grinned, knowing he kept a four-leaf clover in his billfold.

"Pah!" he said indignantly, coloring under his freckles. He set down his empty cup, then moved around his desk and sat behind it. When he folded his hands on the yellow blotter, Jo knew he was getting down to business. Through the open window she could hear the band rehearsing. "We should be in Ocala by six tomorrow," he began. Dutifully, Jo nodded. "Should have the tents up before nine."

"The parade should be over by ten, and the matinee will start at two," Jo finished with a smile. "Duffy, you're not going to ask me to work the menagerie in the sideshow again, are you?"

"Should be a good crowd," he replied, adroitly skirting her question. "Bonzo predicts clear skies."

"Bonzo should stick with pratfalls and unicycles." She watched as Duffy chewed on the stub of a now dead cigar. "Okay," she said firmly, "let's have it."

"Someone's going to be joining us in Ocala, at least temporarily." He pursed his lips as his eyes met Jo's. His were blue, faded with age. "I don't know if he'll finish out the season with us."

"Oh, Duffy, not some first of mayer we have to break in this late?" Jo demanded, using the circus term for novice. "What is he, some energetic writer who wants an epic on the vanishing tent circus? He'll spend a few weeks as a roustabout and swear he knows all there is to know about it."

"I don't think he'll be working as a roustabout," Duffy muttered. Striking a match, he coaxed the cigar back to life. Jo frowned, watching the smoke struggle toward the ceiling.

"It's a bit late to work in a new act now, isn't it?"

"He's not a performer." Duffy swore lightly under his breath, then met Jo's eyes again. "He owns us."

For a moment Jo said nothing. She sat unmoving, as Duffy had seen her from time to time when she trained a young cat. "No!" She rose suddenly, shaking her head. "Not him. Not now. Why does he have to come? What does he want here?"

"It's his circus," Duffy reminded her. His voice was both rough and sympathetic.

"It'll never be his circus," Jo retorted passionately. Her eyes lit and glowed with a temper she rarely let have sway. "It's Frank's circus."

"Frank's dead," Duffy stated in a quiet, final tone. "Now the circus belongs to his son."

"Son?" Jo countered. She lifted her fingers to press them against her temple. Slowly, she moved to the window. Outside, the sun was pouring over the heads of troupers. She watched the members of the trapeze act, in thick robes worn over their tights, head toward the ring barn. The chatter of mixed languages was so familiar she failed to notice it. She placed her palms on the windowsill and with a little sigh, steadied her temper. "What sort of son is it who never bothers to visit his father? In thirty years he never came to see Frank. He never wrote. He didn't even come to the funeral." Jo swallowed the tears of anger that rose to her throat and thickened her voice. "Why should he come now?"

"You've got to learn that life's a two-sided coin, kiddo," Duffy said briskly. "You weren't even alive thirty years ago. You don't know why Frank's wife up and left him or why the boy never visited."

"He's not a boy, Duffy, he's a man." Jo turned back, and he saw that she again had herself under control. "He's thirty-one, thirty-two years old now, a very successful attorney with a fancy Chicago office. He's very wealthy, did you know?" A small smile played on her lips but failed to reach her eyes. "And not just from court cases and legal fees; there's quite a lot of money on his mother's side. Nice, quiet, old money. I can't understand what a rich city lawyer would want with a tent circus."

Duffy shrugged his broad, round shoulders. "Could be he wants a tax shelter. Could be he wants to ride an elephant. Could be anything. He might want to take inventory and sell us off, piece by piece."

"Oh, Duffy, no!" Emotion flew back into Jo's face. "He couldn't do that."

"The heck he couldn't," Duffy muttered as he stubbed out his cigar. "He can do as he pleases. If he wants to liquidate, he liquidates."

"But we have contracts through October...."

"You're too smart for that, Jo." Duffy frowned, scratching his rim of hair. "He can buy them off or let them play through. He's a lawyer. He can figure the way out of a contract if he wants to. He can wait till August when we start to negotiate again and let them all lapse." Seeing Jo's distress, he backpedaled. "Listen, kiddo, I didn't say he was going to sell, I said he *could*."

Jo ran a hand through her hair. "There must be something we can do."

"We can show a profit by the end of the season," Duffy said wryly. "We can show the new owner what we have to offer. I think it's important that he sees we're not just a mud show but a profitable three-ring circus with class acts. He should see what Frank built, how he lived, what he wanted to do. I think," Duffy added, watching Jo's face, "that you should be in charge of his education."

"Me?" Jo was too incredulous to be angry. "Why? You're better qualified in the public relations department than I am. I train lions, not lawyers." She could not keep the hint of scorn from her voice.

"You were closer to Frank than anyone. And there isn't anyone here who knows this circus better than you." Again he frowned. "And you've got brains. Never thought much use would come of all those fancy books you read, but maybe I was wrong."

"Duffy." Her lips curved into a smile. "Just because I like to read Shakespeare doesn't mean I can deal with Keane Prescott. Even thinking about him makes me furious. How will I act when I meet him face to face?"

"Well." Duffy shrugged before he pursed his lips. "If you don't think you can handle it..."

"I didn't say I *couldn't* handle it," Jo muttered.

"Of course, if you're afraid..."

"I'm not afraid of anything, and I'm certainly not afraid of some Chicago lawyer who doesn't know sawdust from tanbark." Sticking her hands in her pockets, she paced the length of the small room. "If Keane Prescott, attorney-at-law, wants to spend his summer with the circus, I'll do my best to make it a memorable one."

"Nicely," Duffy cautioned as Jo moved to the door.

"Duffy," she paused and gave him an innocent smile.

"You know what a gentle touch I have." To prove it, Jo slammed the door behind her.

Dawn was hovering over the horizon as the circus caravan drew up in a large, grassy field. Colors were just a promise in a pale gray sky. In the distance was grove upon grove of orange trees. As Jo stepped from the cab of her truck, the fragrance met her. It's a perfect day, she decided, then took a long, greedy breath. To her, there was no more beautiful sight than dawn struggling to life.

The air was vaguely chilly. She zipped up her gray sweat jacket as she watched the rest of the circus troupe pouring out of their trucks and cars and trailers. The morning quiet was soon shattered by voices. Work began immediately. As the Big Top canvas was being unrolled out of the spool truck, Jo went to see how her lions had fared the fifty-mile journey.

Three handlers unloaded the traveling cages. Buck had been with Jo the longest. He had worked for her father, and during the interim between his death and Jo's professional debut, he had worked up a small act with four male lions. His shyness had made his retirement from performing a relief. To Buck, two people were a crowd. He stood six-feet-four, and his build was powerful enough for him to pad the sideshow from time to time as Hercules the Strong Man. He had an impressive head of wild blond hair and a full, curling beard. His hands were wide, with thick, strong fingers, but Jo remembered their gentleness when the two of them had delivered a lioness of a pair of cubs.

Pete's small frame seemed puny beside Buck's. He was of indeterminable age. Jo guessed between forty and fifty, but she was never certain. He was a quiet man with skin like polished mahogany and a rich, low-pitched voice. He had come to Jo five years before, asking for a job. She had never asked where he had come from, and he had never told her. He wore a fielder's cap and was never seen without a wad of gum moving gently in his teeth. He read Jo's books and was the undisputed king of the poker table.

Gerry was nineteen and eager. He was nearly six feet and still carried the lankiness of his youth. His mother sewed, and his father was a souvenir salesman, or a candy butcher, as circus jargon had it. Working the big cage was Gerry's dream, and because it had been hers, Jo had finally agreed to tutor him.

"How are my babies?" she demanded as she approached. At each cage she paused and soothed a nervous cat, calling each by name until they had settled. "They've traveled well. Hamlet's still edgy, but it's his first year on the road."

"He's a mean one," Buck muttered, watching Jo move from cage to cage.

"Yes, I know," she replied absently. "He's smart, too." She had twisted her hair into one thick braid and now tossed it to her back. "Look, here come some towners." A few cars and a smattering of bikes drew into the field.

These were the people from the outlying towns who wanted to see a Big Top raised, who wanted to see the circus, if only for a moment, from the other side. Some would watch while others would lend a hand with tent poles, stretching canvas and rigging. They would earn a show pass and an unforgettable experience.

"Keep them clear of the cages," Jo ordered, nodding

to Pete before she moved toward the still flaccid canvas. Buck lumbered beside her.

The field was alive with ropes and wire and people. Six elephants were harnessed but idle, with their handlers standing by the stake line. As workers pulled on guy ropes, the dusky brown canvas billowed up like a giant mushroom.

The poles were positioned—side, quarter, center—while the canvas muffled the sounds of scrambling workers. In the east the sun was rising fast, streaking the sky with pink. There were shouted instructions from the head canvas man, laughter from adventuresome boys and an occasional oath. As the quarter poles were driven into the sag of canvas, Jo signaled Maggie, the large African elephant. Obligingly, Maggie lowered her trunk. Jo stepped nimbly into the *u,* then scrambled onto the wide, gray back.

The sun grew higher by the second, shooting the first streams of light onto the field. The scent of orange blossoms mingled with the odor of leather harnesses. Jo had watched the canvas rise under a lightening sky countless times. Each time it was special, and the first raising each season was the most special of all. Maggie lifted her head and trumpeted as if pleased to be around for another season. With a laugh Jo reached back and swatted her rough, wrinkled rump. She felt free and fresh and incredibly alive. If there were a moment, she thought suddenly, that I could capture and bottle, it would be this one. Then, when I'm very old, I could take it out and feel young again. Smiling, she glanced down at the people swarming below her.

Her attention was caught by a man who stood by a coil of cable. Typically, she noted his build first. A well-proportioned body was essential to a performer. He was lean and stood straight. She noted he had good shoulders but doubted if there was much muscle in his arms. Though he was dressed casually in jeans, *city* stood out all over him. His hair was a dark, rich blond, and the early breeze had disturbed it so that it teased his forehead. He was clean-shaven, with a narrow, firm-jawed face. It was an attractive face. It was not, Jo mused, smoothly handsome like Vito the wire walker's but more aware, more demanding. Jo liked the face, liked the shape of the long, unsmiling mouth, liked the hint of bone beneath his tawny skin. Most of all she liked the directness of the amber eyes that stared back at her. They're like Ari's, she observed, thinking of her favorite lion. She was certain that he had been watching her long before she had looked down. Knowing this, Jo was impressed with his unselfconsciousness. He continued to stare, making no effort to camouflage his interest. She laughed, unperturbed, and tossed her braid from her shoulder.

"Want a ride?" she called out. Too many strangers had walked in and out of her world for her to be aloof. She watched his brow lift in acknowledgment of her offer. She would see if it was only his eyes that were like Ari's. "Maggie won't hurt you. She's gentle as a lamb, just bigger." Instantly, she saw he had understood the challenge. He walked across the grass until he stood beside her. He moved well, she noted. Jo tapped Maggie's side with the bull hook she carried. Wearily, the elephant knelt down on her trunklike front legs. Jo held out her hand. With an agility that surprised her, the man mounted the elephant and slid into place behind her.

For a moment she said nothing, a bit stunned by the

trembling that had coursed up her arm as her palm had met his. The contact had been brief. Jo decided she had imagined it. "Up, Maggie," she said, giving her mount another tap. With an elephantine sigh, Maggie obeyed, rocking her passengers gently from side to side.

"Do you always pick up strange men?" the voice behind her inquired. It was a smooth, well-keyed voice, a good pitchman's voice.

Jo grinned over her shoulder. "Maggie's doing the picking up."

"So she is. Are you aware that she's remarkably uncomfortable?"

Jo laughed with genuine enjoyment. "You should try riding her a few miles in a street parade while keeping a smile on your face."

"I'll pass. Are you in charge of her?"

"Maggie? No, but I know how to handle her. You have eyes like one of my cats," she told him. "I like them. And since you seemed to be interested in Maggie and me, I asked you up."

This time it was he who laughed. Jo twisted her head, wanting to see his face. There was humor in his eyes now, and his teeth were white and straight. Liking his smile, she answered with one of her own. "Fascinating. You asked me to take a ride on an elephant because I have eyes like your cat's. And no offense to the lady beneath me, but I was looking at you."

"Oh?" Jo pursed her lips in thought. "Why?"

For several seconds he studied her in silence. "Strange, I believe you really don't know."

"I wouldn't ask if I did," she returned, shifting her weight slightly. "It would be a waste of time to ask a question if I knew the answer." She shifted again and turned away from him. "Hold on now. Maggie's got to earn her bale of hay."

The poles hung between the canvas and the ground at forty-five degree angles. Quickly the elephant's chains were hooked to the metal rings at the base of the quarter poles. Jo urged Maggie forward in unison with her coworkers. Poles skidded along the ground, then up into place, pushing the canvas with it. The Big Top billowed to life under the early morning sky.

Her job done, Maggie moved through the flaps and into the light. "Beautiful, isn't it?" Jo murmured. "It's born fresh every day."

Vito walked by, calling out to Jo in Italian. Sending him a wave, she called back in his own language, then signaled to Maggie to kneel again. Jo waited until her passenger had dismounted before she slid off. It surprised her, when they stood face to face, that he was so tall. Tilting back her head, she judged him to be only two inches shy of Buck.

"You looked shorter when I was up on Maggie," she told him with her usual candor.

"You looked taller."

Jo chuckled, patting Maggie behind the ear. "Will you see the show?" She knew that she wanted him to, knew as well that she wanted to see him again. She found this both strange and intriguing. Men had always taken a second place to her cats, and towners had never interested her.

"Yes, I'm going to see the show." There was a slight smile on his face, but he was studying her thoughtfully. "Do you perform?"

"I have an act with my cats."

"I see. Somehow I pictured you in an aerial act, flying from the trapeze."

She sent him an easy smile. "My mother was an aerialist." Someone called her name, and looking, Jo saw Maggie was needed for raising the sideshow tent. "I have to go. I hope you like the show."

He took her hand before she could lead Maggie away. Jo stood still, again surprised by a trembling up her arm. "I'd like to see you tonight."

Glancing up, she met his eyes. They were direct and unselfconscious. "Why?" The question was sincere. Jo knew she wanted to see him as well but was unsure why.

This time he did not laugh. Gently, he ran a finger down the length of her braid. "Because you're beautiful, and you intrigue me."

"Oh." Jo considered. She had never thought of herself as beautiful. Striking, perhaps, in her costume, surrounded by her cats, but in jeans, without makeup, she doubted it. Still, it was an interesting thought. "All right, if there's no trouble with the cats. Ari hasn't been well."

A smile played at the corners of his mouth. "I'm sorry to hear that."

There was another loud summons for Jo, and both looked toward it. "I see you're needed," he said with a nod. "Perhaps you could point out Bill Duffy for me before you go."

"Duffy?" Jo repeated, surprised. "You can't be looking for a job?" There was incredulity in her voice, and he grinned.

"Why can't I?"

"Because you don't fit any of the types."

"Are there types?" he asked, both interested and amused. Jo shook her head in annoyance.

"Yes, of course, and you don't fit into any of them."

"Actually, I'm not looking for a job, so to speak," he told her, still smiling. "But I am looking for Bill Duffy."

It was against Jo's nature to probe. Privacy was both guarded and respected in the circus. Shielding her eyes with her hand, Jo looked around until she spotted Duffy supervising the raising of the cookhouse tent. "There," she said, pointing. "Duffy's the one with the red checked jacket. He still dresses like an outside talker."

"A what?"

"You'd call it a barker, I imagine." With easy grace she mounted the patient Maggie. "That's a towner's term, not a circus one." She smiled at him, then urged Maggie into a walk. "Tell Duffy Jo said to give you a pass," she called over her shoulder, then waved and turned away.

Dawn was over, and it was morning.

Chapter 2

Jo stood at the back door of the Big Top waiting for her cue. Beside her was Jamie Carter, alias Topo. He was a third generation clown and wore his bright face and orange wig naturally. He was young and limber and used these traits as well as his makeup to bring enthusiasm to his craft. To Jo, Jamie was more brother than friend. He was tall and thin, and under his greasepaint his face was mobile and pleasant. He and Jo had grown up together.

"Did she say anything?" Jamie demanded for the third time. With a sigh, Jo tossed closed the flap of the tent. Inside, clowns were performing around the hippodrome track while hands set up the big cage.

"Carmen said nothing. I don't know why you waste your time." Her voice was sharp, and Jamie bristled.

"I don't expect you to understand," he said with great dignity. His thin shoulders drew straight under his red polka dot shirt. "After all, Ari's the closest you've come to being involved with the opposite sex."

"That's very cute," Jo replied, unoffended by the jibe. Her annoyance stemmed from seeing Jamie make a fool of himself over Carmen Gribalti, the middle sister of the flying Gribaltis. She was darkly beautiful, graceful, talented, selfish and sublimely indifferent to Jamie. Looking into his happy, painted face and moody eyes, Jo's irritation dissipated. "She probably hasn't had a chance to answer the note you sent her," she soothed. "The first day of a new season's always wild."

"I suppose," Jamie muttered with a grudging shrug. "I don't know what she sees in Vito."

Jo thought of the wire walker's dark, cocky looks and rippling muscles. Wisely, she refrained from mentioning them. "Who can account for taste?" She gave him a smacking kiss on his round, red nose. "Personally, I get all wobbly when I see a man with thick, orange hair."

Jamie grinned. "Proves you know what to look for in a man."

Turning, Jo lifted the flap again, noting Jamie's cue was nearly upon them. "Did you happen to notice a towner hanging around today?"

"Only a couple dozen of them," Jamie answered dryly as he lifted the pail of confetti he used to finish the gag now being performed inside.

Jo shot him a half-hearted glare. "Not the usual type. About thirty, I think," she continued. "Wearing jeans and a T-shirt. He was tall, six-one, six-two," she went on as laughter poured out of the open flap to drown out her words. "He had dark blond straight hair."

"Yeah, I saw him." Jamie nudged her out of his way and prepared to make his entrance. "He was going into the red wagon with Duffy." With a wild, high-pitched scream, Topo the clown bounded into the Big Top in size fifteen tennis shoes, brandishing his bucket of confetti.

Thoughtfully, Jo watched Jamie chase three other clowns around the track. It was odd, she thought, for Duffy to take a towner into the administration trailer. He had said he wasn't looking for a job. He wasn't a drifter; there was an unmistakable air of stability about him. He wasn't a circus hand from another show, either. His palm had been too smooth. And, her mind added as she vaulted onto Babette, a pure white mare, there had been an undeniable aura of urbanity about him. Success, as well, she thought. And authority. No, he had not been looking for a job.

Jo shrugged, annoyed that a stranger was crowding into her thoughts. It irritated her further that she had scanned the crowds for him during the parade and that even now she wondered if he sat somewhere in the circular arena. He hadn't been at the matinee. Jo patted the mare's neck absently, then straightened as she heard the ringmaster's whistle.

"Ladies and gentlemen," he called in deep, musical tones. "Presenting the most spectacular exhibition of animal subjugation under the Big Top. Jovilette, Queen of the Jungle Cats!"

Jo nudged Babette with her heels and raced into the arena. The applause rose to meet her as the audience appreciated the dashing figure she cut. Swathed in a black cape, raven hair flying free under a glittering tiara, she galloped bareback on the snow white mare. In each hand she held a long, thin whip, which she cracked alternately overhead. At the entrance to the big cage she leaped from the still racing horse. While Babette galloped out of the back door and into the care of a handler, Jo shifted both whips into one hand, then removed the cape with a flourish. Her costume was a close-fitting, one-piece jumpsuit, dazzling in white and spangled with gold sequins. In dramatic contrast, her hair hung straight and severe down her back.

Make an entrance, Frank had always said. And Jovilette made an entrance.

The twelve cats were already in the cage, banding its inside edge as they perched on blue and white pedestals. Entering the main cage appeared routine to the audience, but Jo knew it was one of the most dangerous moments of the act. To enter, she had to pass directly between two cats as she moved from the safety cage to the main arena. She always stationed her best behaved cats there, but if one was irritated, or even playful, he could easily strike out with a powerful paw. Even with sharp claws retracted, the damage could be deadly.

She entered swiftly and was surrounded by cats on all sides. Her spangles and tiara caught the lights and played with them as she began to move around the cage, cracking the whip for showmanship while using her voice to command the cats to rise on their haunches. She moved them through their routine, adjusting the timing to compensate for any feline reluctance, letting one trick begin where the last ended.

Jo disliked overdone propping, preferring action and movement. The contrast of the big, tawny cats and the small white and gold woman were the best props available to her. She used them well. Hers was a *picture act,* relying on style and flash, rather than a *fighting act,* which emphasized the ferocity of the big cats by employing blank-bulleted guns and rehearsed charges, or *bounces*. Her confidence transmitted itself to the audience, making her handling of the cats appear effortless. In truth, her body was coiled for any danger, and her mind was focused so intently on her cats, there might have been no audience at all.

She stood between two high pedestals as the cats leaped over her head from both directions. They set up a light breeze, which stirred her hair. They roared when she cued them, setting up an echoing din. Now and then one reached out to paw at the stock of her whip, and she stopped him with a quick command. She sent her best leaper through a hoop of flame and coaxed her best balancer to walk on a glistening silver ball. She ended to waves of applause by trotting Merlin around the hippodrome track.

At the back door Merlin jumped into a wheel cage and was turned over to Pete. "Nice show," he said as he handed her a long chenille robe. "Smooth as silk."

"Thanks." Cold, she bundled into the robe. The spring night was frigid in contrast to the hot lights and heat in the big cage. "Listen, Pete, tell Gerry he can feed the cats tonight. They're behaving themselves."

Pete snapped his gum and chuckled. "Won't he be riding high tonight." As he moved to the truck that would pull the cage to the cat area, Jo called after him.

"Pete." She bit her lip, then shrugged when he twisted his head. "You'll keep an eye on him, won't you?"

Pete grinned and climbed into the cab of the truck. "Who you worried about, Jo? Those big cats or that skinny boy?"

"Both," she answered. The rhinestones in her tiara sparkled as she tossed her head and laughed. Knowing she had nearly an hour before the finale parade, Jo walked away from the Big Top. She thought of wandering to the cookhouse for some coffee. Mentally, she began replaying every segment of her act. It had gone well, she thought, pleased with the timing and the flow. If Pete had said it had been smooth, Jo knew it had. She had heard his criticisms more than once over the past five years. True, Hamlet had tested her once or twice, but no one knew that but Jo and the cat. She doubted if anyone but Buck would have seen that he had given her trouble. Closing her eyes a moment, Jo rolled her shoulders, loosening tight, tensed muscles.

"That's quite an act you have."

Jo whirled around at the sound of the voice. She could feel her heart rate accelerate. Though she wondered at her interest in a man she barely knew, Jo was aware that she had been waiting for him. There was a quick surge of pleasure as she watched him approach, and she allowed it to show on her face.

"Hello." She saw that he smoked a cigar, but unlike Duffy's, his was long and slim. Again she admired the elegance of his hands. "Did you like the show?"

He stopped in front of her, then studied her face with a thoroughness that made her wonder if her makeup had smeared. Then he gave a small, surprised laugh and shook his head. "Do you know," he began, "when you told me this morning that you did an act with cats, I had Siamese in mind rather than African."

"Siamese?" Jo repeated blankly, then laughed. "House cats?" He brushed her hair behind her back while Jo giggled at the thought of coaxing a Siamese to jump through a flaming hoop.

"From my point of view," he told her as he let a

strand of her hair linger between his fingers, "it made more sense than a little thing like you walking into a cage with a dozen lions."

"I'm not little," Jo corrected good-naturedly. "Besides, size hardly matters to twelve lions."

"No, I suppose it doesn't." He lifted his eyes from her hair and met hers. Jo continued to smile, enjoying looking at him. "Why do you do it?" he asked suddenly.

Jo gave him a curious look. "Why? Because it's my job."

By the way he studied her, Jo could see that he was not satisfied with the simplicity of her answer. "Perhaps I should ask *how* you became a lion tamer."

"Trainer," Jo corrected automatically. To her left, she could hear the audience's muffled applause. "The Beirots are starting," she said with a glance toward the sound. "You shouldn't miss their act. They're first-rate acrobats."

"Don't you want to tell me?" His voice was soft.

She lifted a brow, seeing that he truly wanted to know. "Why, it's not a secret. My father was a trainer, and I have a knack for working with cats. It just followed." Jo had never thought about her career past this point, and she shrugged it aside. "You shouldn't waste your ticket standing out here. You can stand by the back door and watch the rest of the act." Jo turned to lead the way to the performers' entrance but stopped when his hand took hers.

He stepped forward until their bodies were nearly touching. Jo could feel the heat from his as she watched his face. Her heart was thudding in a quick, steady rhythm. She could hear it vibrate through her the same way it did when she approached a new cat for the first time. Here was something new, something untested. She tingled with the excitement of the unknown when he lifted his hand to touch her cheek. She did not move but let the warmth spread while she watched him carefully, gauging him. Her eyes were wide, curious and unafraid.

"Are you going to kiss me?" she asked in a tone that expressed more interest than desire.

His eyes lit with humor and glittered in the dim light. "I had given it some thought," he answered. "Do you have any objections?"

Jo considered a moment, dropping her eyes to his mouth. She liked its shape and wondered how it would feel against hers. He brought her no closer. One hand still held hers while the other slid around to cradle her neck. Jo shifted her gaze until their eyes met again. "No," she decided. "I haven't any objections."

The corners of his mouth twitched as he tightened his hold slightly on the base of her neck. Slowly, he lowered his head toward hers. Curious and a bit wary, Jo kept her eyes open, watching his. She knew from experience that you could tell more about people and about cats from the eyes. To her surprise, his remained open as well, even as their lips met.

It was a gentle kiss, without pressure, only a whisper of a touch. Amazed, Jo thought she felt the ground tremble under her feet. Dimly, she wondered if the elephants were being led by. But it can't be time, she thought in confusion. His lips moved lightly over hers, and his eyes remained steady. Jo's pulse drummed under her skin. They stood, barely touching, as the Big Top throbbed with noise behind them. Lazily, he traced her lips with the tip of his tongue, teasing them open. Still there was no demand in the kiss, only testing. Unhurried, con-

fident, he explored her mouth while Jo felt her breath
accelerating. A soft moan escaped her as her lids fluttered down.

For an instant she surrendered utterly to him, to the
new sensations swimming through her. She leaned
against him, straining toward pleasure, sighing with it
as the kiss lingered.

He drew her away, but their faces remained close.
Dizzily, Jo realized that she had risen to her toes to
compensate for their difference in height. His hand was
still light on the back of her neck. His eyes were gold
in the darkening night.

"What an incredible female you are, Jovilette," he
murmured. "One surprise after another."

Jo felt stunningly alive. Her skin seemed to tingle
with new feelings. She smiled. "I don't know your
name."

He laughed, releasing her neck to take her other hand
in his. Before he could speak, Duffy called out from
the direction of the Big Top. Jo turned to watch as he
moved toward them in his quick, rolling walk.

"Well, well, well," he said in his jolly, rough voice.
"I didn't know you two had met. Has Jo been showing you around already?" Reaching them, he squeezed
Jo's shoulder. "Knew I could count on you, kiddo." Jo
glanced at him in puzzlement, but he continued before
she could form a question. "Yes, sir, this little girl puts
on quite a show, doesn't she? Always a grabber. And she
knows this circus like the back of her hand. Born and
raised to it," he continued. Jo relaxed. She recognized
that Duffy was into one of his spiels, and there was no
stopping him. "Yessiree, any questions you got, you
just ask our Jo, and she'll tell you. 'Course, I'm always

at your disposal, too. Anything I can tell you about the books or accounts or contracts and the like, you just let me know." Duffy puffed twice on his cigar as Jo felt her first hint of unease.

Why was Duffy rambling about books and contracts? Jo glanced at the man who still held her hands in his. He was watching Duffy with an easy, amused smile.

"Are you a bookkeeper?" Jo asked, perplexed. Duffy laughed and patted her head.

"You know Mr. Prescott's a lawyer, Jo. Don't miss your cue." He gave them both a friendly nod and toddled off.

Jo had stiffened almost imperceptibly at Duffy's offhand information, but Keane had felt it. His brows lowered as he studied her. "Now you know my name."

"Yes." All warmth fled from Jo. Her voice was as cool as her blood. "Would you let go of my hands, Mr. Prescott?"

After a brief hesitation Keane inclined his head and obliged. Jo stuffed her hands quickly into the pockets of her robe. "Don't you think we've progressed to the first name stage of our relationship, Jo?"

"I assure you, Mr. Prescott, if I had known who you were, we wouldn't have progressed at all." Jo's words were stiff with dignity. Inside, though she tried to ignore it, she felt betrayal, anger, humiliation. All pleasure had died from the evening. Now the kiss that had left her feeling clean and alive seemed cheap and shabby. No, she would not use his first name, she vowed. She would never use it. "If you'll excuse me, I have some things to do before my cue."

"Why the turnaround?" he asked, halting her with a hand on her arm. "Don't you like lawyers?"

Coldly, Jo studied him. She wondered how it was possible that she had completely misjudged the man she had met that morning. "I don't categorize people, Mr. Prescott."

"I see." Keane's tone became detached, his eyes assessing. "Then it would appear that you have an aversion to my name. Should I assume you hold a grudge against my father?"

Jo's eyes glittered with quick fury. She jerked her arm from his hold. "Frank Prescott was the most generous, the kindest, most unselfish man I've ever known. I don't even associate you with Frank, Mr. Prescott. You have no right to him." Though it was nearly impossible, Jo forced herself to speak in a normal tone of voice. She would not shout and draw anyone's attention. This would be kept strictly between Keane Prescott and herself. "It would have been much better if you had told me who you were right away, then there would have been no mix-up."

"Is that what we've had?" he countered mildly. "A mix-up?"

His cool tone was nearly Jo's undoing. He watched her with a dispassionate curiosity that tempted her to slap him. She fought to keep her fury from spilling over into her voice. "You have no right to Frank's circus, Mr. Prescott," she managed quietly. "Leaving it to you is the only thing I've ever faulted him for." Knowing her control was slipping, Jo whirled, running across the grass until she merged with the darkness.

Chapter 3

The morning was surprisingly warm. There were no trees to block the sun, and the smell of the earth was strong. The circus had moved north in the early hours. All the usual scents merged into the aroma of circus: canvas, leather, sweating horses, greasepaint and powder, coffee and oilcloth. The trailers and trucks sat in the accustomed spots, forming the "backyard" that would always take the same formation each time the circus made a stop along the thousands of miles it traveled. The flag over the cookhouse tent signaled that lunch was being served. The Big Top stood waiting for the matinee.

Rose hurried along the midway toward the animal cages. Her dark hair was pinned neatly in a bun at the back of her neck. Her big brown eyes darted about searchingly, while her mouth sat softly in a pout. She was wrapped in a terry cloth robe and wore tennis shoes over her tights. When she saw Jo standing in front of Ari's cage, she waved and broke into a half-run. Watching her, Jo shifted her attention from Ari. Rose was always a diversion, and Jo felt in need of one.

"Jo!" She waved again as if Jo had not seen her the first time, then came to a breathless halt. "Jo, I only have a few minutes. Hello, Ari," she added out of politeness. "I was looking for Jamie."

"Yes, I gathered." Jo smiled, knowing Rose had set her heart on capturing Topo's alter ego. And if he had any sense, she thought, he'd let himself be caught instead of pining over Carmen. Silly, she decided, dismissing all affairs of the heart. Lions were easier to understand. "I haven't seen him all morning, Rose. Maybe he's rehearsing."

"Drooling over Carmen, more likely," Rose muttered, sending a sulky glare in the direction of the Gribalti trailer. "He makes a fool of himself."

"That's what he's paid for," Jo reminded her, but Rose did not respond to the humor. Jo sighed. She had a true affection for Rose. She was bright and fun and without pretentions. "Rose," she said, keeping her voice both light and kind. "Don't give up on him. He's a little slow, you know," she explained. "He's just a bit dazzled by Carmen right now. It'll pass."

"I don't know why I bother," she grumbled, but Jo saw the dark mood was already passing. Rose was a creature of quick passions that flared and soon died. "He's not so very handsome, you know."

"No," Jo agreed. "But he has a cute nose."

"Lucky for him I like red," Rose returned and

grinned. "Ah, now we're speaking of handsome," she murmured as her eyes drifted from Jo. "Who is this?"

At the question, Jo glanced over her shoulder. The humor fled from her eyes. "That's the owner," she said colorlessly.

"Keane Prescott? No one told me he was so handsome. Or so tall," she added, admiring him openly as he crossed the backyard. Jo noted that Rose always became more Mexican around men. "Such shoulders. Lucky for Jamie I'm a one-man woman."

"Lucky for you your mama can't hear you," Jo muttered, earning an elbow in the ribs.

"But he comes here, *amiga,* and he looks at you. La, la, my papa would have Jamie to the altar *pronto* if he looked at me that way."

"You're an idiot," Jo snapped, annoyed.

"Ah, Jo," Rose said with mock despair. "I am a romantic."

Jo was helpless against the smile that tugged at her lips. Her eyes were laughing when she glanced up and met Keane's. Hastily, she struggled to dampen their brilliance, turning her mouth into a sober line.

"Good morning, Jovilette." He spoke her name too easily, she thought, as if he had been saying it for years.

"Good morning, Mr. Prescott," she returned. Rose gave a loud, none-too-subtle cough. "This is Rose Sanches."

"It's a pleasure, Mr. Prescott." Rose extended a hand, trying out a smile she had been saving for Jamie. "I heard you were traveling with us."

Keane accepted the hand and smiled in return. Jo noticed with annoyance that it was the same easy, disarming smile of the stranger she had met the morning before. "Hello, Rose, it's nice to meet you."

Seeing her friend's Mexican blood heat her cheeks, Jo intervened. She would not permit Keane Prescott to make a conquest here. "Rose, you only have ten minutes to get back and into makeup."

"Holy cow!" she said, forgetting her attempt at sophistication. "I've got to run." She began to do so, then called over her shoulder, "Don't tell Jamie I was looking for him, the pig!" She ran a little further, then turned and ran backwards. "I'll look for him later," she said with a laugh, then turned back and streaked toward the midway.

Keane watched her dart across the compound while holding up the long skirts of her robe in one hand. "Charming."

"She's only eighteen," Jo offered before she could stop herself.

When Keane turned to her, his look was one of amusement. "I see," he said. "I'll take that information under advisement. And what does the eighteen-year-old Rose do?" he asked, slipping his thumbs into the front pockets of his jeans. "Wrestle alligators?"

"No." Jo returned without batting an eye. "Rose is Serpentina, your premier sideshow attraction. The snake charmer." She was pleased with the incredulous look that passed over his face. It was replaced quickly, however, with one of genuine humor.

"Perfect." He brushed Jo's hair from her cheek before she could protest by word or action. "Cobras?" he asked, ignoring the flash in her eyes.

"And boa constrictors," she returned sweetly. Jo

brushed the dust from the knees of her faded jeans. "Now, if you'll excuse me…"

"No, I don't think so." Keane's voice was cool, but she recognized the underlying authority. She did her best not to struggle against it. He *was* the owner, she reminded herself.

"Mr. Prescott," she began, banking down hard on the urge to mutiny. "I'm very busy. I have to get ready for the afternoon show."

"You've got an hour and a half until you're on," he countered smoothly. "I think you might spare me a portion of that time. You've been assigned to show me around. Why don't we start now?" The tone of the question left room for only one answer. Jo's mind fidgeted in search of a way out.

Tilting her head back, she met his eyes. He won't be easy to beat, she concluded, studying his steady, measuring gaze. I'd better study his moves more carefully before I start a battle. "Where would you like to begin?" she asked aloud.

"With you."

Keane's easy answer brought a deep frown to Jo's brows. "I don't understand what you mean."

For a moment Keane watched her. There was no coyness or guile in her eyes as they looked into his. "No, I can see you don't," he agreed with a nod. "Let's start with your cats."

"Oh." Jo's frown cleared instantly. "All right." She watched as he pulled out a thin cigar, waiting until the flame of his lighter licked the tip before speaking. "I have thirteen—seven males, six females. They're all African lions between four-and-a-half and twenty-two years."

"I thought you worked with twelve," Keane commented as he dropped his lighter into his pocket.

"That's right, but Ari's retired." Turning, Jo indicated the large male lion dozing in a cage. "He travels with me because he always has, but I don't work him anymore. He's twenty-two, the oldest. My father kept him, even though he was born in captivity, because he was born the same day I was." Jo sighed, and her voice became softer. "He's the last of my father's stock. I couldn't sell him to a zoo. It seemed like shoving an old relative into a home and abandoning him. He's been with this circus every day of his life, just as I have. His name is Hebrew for *lion*." Jo laughed, forgetting the man beside her as she sifted through memories. "My father always gave his cats names that meant lion somehow or other. Leo, Leonard, Leonara. Ari was a first-class leaper in his prime. He could climb, too; some cats won't. I could teach Ari anything. Smart cat, aren't you, Ari?" The altered tone of her voice caused the big cat to stir. Opening his eyes, he stared back at Jo. The sound he made was more grumble than roar before he dozed again. "He's tired," Jo murmured, fighting a shaft of gloom. "Twenty-two's old for a lion."

"What is it?" Keane demanded, touching her shoulder before she could turn away. Her eyes were drenched with sadness.

"He's dying," she said unsteadily. "And I can't stop it." Stuffing her hands in her pockets, Jo moved away to the main group of cages. To steady herself, she took two deep breaths while waiting for Keane to join her. Regaining her composure, she began again. "I work with these twelve," she told him, making a sweeping gesture. "They're fed once a day, raw meat six days a week and eggs and milk on the seventh. They were all imported directly from Africa and were cage broken when I got them."

The faint sound of a calliope reached them, signaling the opening of the midway. "This is Merlin, the one I ride out on at the finish. He's ten, and the most even-tempered cat I've ever worked with. Heathcliff," she continued as she moved down the line of cages, "he's six, my best leaper. And this is Faust, the baby at four and a half." The lions paced their cages as Jo walked Keane down the line. Unable to prevent herself, Jo gave Faust a signal by raising her hand. Obediently, he sent out a huge, deafening roar. To Jo's disappointment, Keane did not scramble for cover.

"Very impressive," he said mildly. "You put him in the center when you lie down on them, don't you?"

"Yes." She frowned, then spoke her thoughts candidly. "You're very observant—and you've got steady nerves."

"My profession requires them, too, to an extent," he returned.

Jo considered this a moment, then turned back to the lions. "Lazareth, he's twelve and a natural ham. Bolingbroke, he's ten, from the same lioness as Merlin. Hamlet," she said stopping again, "he's five. I bought him to replace Ari in the act." Jo stared into the tawny eyes. "He has potential, but he's arrogant. Patient, too. He's just waiting for me to make a mistake."

"Why?" Keane glanced over at Jo. Her eyes were cool and steady on Hamlet's.

"So he can get a good clean swipe at me," she told him without altering her expression. "It's his first season in the big cage. Pandora," Jo continued, pointing out the females. "A very classy lady. She's six. Hester, at seven, my best all-around. And Portia; it's her first year, too. She's mostly a seat-warmer."

"Seat-warmer?"

"Just what it sounds like," Jo explained. "She hasn't mastered any complicated tricks yet. She evens out the act, does a few basics and warms the seat." Jo moved on. "Dulcinea, the prettiest of the ladies. Ophelia, who had a litter last year; and Abra, eight, a bit bad-tempered but a good balancer."

Hearing her name, the cat rose, stretched her long, golden body, then began to rub it against the bars of the cage. A deep sound rumbled in her throat. Jo scowled and jammed her hands into her pockets. "She likes you," she muttered.

"Oh?" Lifting a brow, Keane studied the three-hundred-pound Abra more carefully. "How do you know?"

"When a lion likes you, it does exactly what a house cat does. It rubs against you. Abra's rubbing against the bars because she can't get any closer."

"I see." Humor touched his mouth. "I must admit, I'm at a loss on how to return the compliment." He drew on his cigar, then regarded Jo through a haze of smoke. "Your choice of names is fascinating."

"I like to read," she stated, leaving it at that. "Is there anything else you'd like to know about the cats?" Jo was determined to keep their conversation on a professional level. His smile had reminded her all too clearly of their encounter the night before.

"Do you drug them before a performance?"

Fury sparked Jo's eyes. "Certainly not."

"Was that an unreasonable question?" Keane countered. He dropped his cigar to the ground, then crushed it out with his heel.

"Not for a first of mayer," Jo decided with a sigh. She tossed her hair carelessly behind her back. "Drugging is not only cruel, it's stupid. A drugged animal won't perform."

"You don't touch the lions with that whip," Keane commented. He watched the light breeze tease a few strands of her hair. "Why do you use it?"

"To get their attention and to keep the audience awake." She smiled reluctantly.

Keane took her arm. Instantly, Jo stiffened. "Let's walk," he suggested. He began to lead her away from the cages. Spotting several people roaming the backyard, Jo refrained from pulling away. The last thing she wanted was the story spreading that she was having a tiff with the owner. "How do you tame them?" he asked her.

"I don't. They're not tame, they're trained." A tall blond woman walked by carrying a tiny white poodle. "Merlin's hungry today," Jo called out with a grin.

The woman bundled the dog closer to her breast in mock alarm and began a rapid scolding in French. Jo laughed, telling her in the same language that Fifi was too tough a mouthful for Merlin.

"Fifi can do a double somersault on the back of a moving horse," Jo explained as they began to walk again. "She's trained just as my cats are trained, but she's also domesticated. The cats are wild." Jo turned her face up to Keane's. The sun cast a sheen over her hair and threw gold flecks into her eyes. "A wild thing can never be tamed, and anyone who tries is foolish. If you take something wild and turn it into a pet, you've stolen its character, blanked out its spark. And still, there's always an essence of the wild that can come back to life. When a dog turns on his master, it's ugly. When a lion turns, it's lethal." She was beginning to become accustomed to his hand on her arm, finding it easy to talk to him because he listened. "A full-grown male stands three feet at the shoulder and weighs over five hundred pounds. One well-directed swipe can break a man's neck, not to mention what teeth and claws can do." Jo gave a smile and a shrug. "Those aren't the virtues of a pet."

"Yet you go into a cage with twelve of them, armed with a whip?"

"The whip's window dressing." Jo discounted it with a gesture of her hand. "It would hardly be a defense against even one cat at full charge. A lion is a very tenacious enemy. A tiger is more bloodthirsty, but it normally strikes only once. If it misses, it takes it philosophically. A lion charges again and again. Do you know the line Byron wrote about a tiger's spring? 'Deadly, quick and crushing.'" Jo had completely forgotten her animosity and began to enjoy her walk and conversation with this handsome stranger. "It's a true description, but a lion is totally fearless when he charges, and stubborn. He's not the razzle-dazzle fighter the tiger is, just accurate. I'd bet on a lion against a tiger any day. And a man simply hasn't a prayer against one."

"Then how do you manage to stay in one piece?"

The calliope music was just a hint in the air now. Jo turned, noting with surprise that they had walked a good distance from camp. She could see the trailers and tents, hear occasional shouts and laughter, but she felt oddly separated from it all. She sat down cross-legged on the grass and plucked a blade. "I'm smarter than they are. At least I make them think so. And I dominate them, partly by a force of will. In training, you have to develop a rapport, a mutual respect, and if you're lucky, a certain affection. But you can't trust them to the point where you grow careless. And above all," she added, glancing over as he sat down beside her, "you have to remember the basic rule of poker. Bluff." Jo grinned, leaning back on her elbows. "Do you play poker?"

"I've been known to." Her hair trailed out along the grass, and he lifted a strand. "Do you?"

"Sometimes. My assistant handler, Pete..." Jo scanned the backyard, then smiled and pointed. "There he is, by the second trailer, sitting with Mac Stevenson, the one with the fielder's cap. Pete organizes a game now and then."

"Who's the little girl on stilts?"

"That's Mac's youngest, Katie. She wants to walk on them in the street parade. She's getting pretty good. There's Jamie," she said, then laughed as he did a pratfall and landed at Katie's wooden stilts.

"Rose's Jamie?" Keane asked, watching the impromptu show in the back yard.

"If she has her way. He's currently dazzled by Carmen Gribalti. Carmen won't give Jamie the time of day. She bats her lashes at Vito, the wire walker. He bats his at everyone."

"A complicated state of affairs," Keane commented. He twisted Jo's hair around his fingers. "Romance seems to be very popular in circus life."

"From what I read," she countered, "it's popular everywhere."

"Who dazzles you, Jovilette?" He gave her hair a tug to bring her face around to his.

Jo hadn't realized he was so close. She need do no more than sway for her mouth to touch his. Her eyes measured his while she waited for her pulse to calm. It was odd, she thought, that he had such an effect on her. With sudden clarity, she could smell the grass, a clean, sweet scent, and feel the sun. The sounds of the circus were muted in the background. She could hear birds call out with an occasional high-pitched trill. She remembered the taste of his mouth and wondered if it would be the same.

"I've been too busy to be dazzled," she replied. Her voice was steady, but her eyes were curious.

For the first time, Jo truly *wanted* to be kissed by a man. She wanted to feel again what she had felt the night before. She wanted to be held, not lightly as he had held her before, but close, with his arms tight around her. She wanted to renew the feeling of weightlessness. She had never experienced a strong physical desire, and for a moment she explored the sensation. There was a quiver in her stomach which was both pleasant and disturbing. Throughout her silent contemplations Keane watched her, intrigued by the intensity of her eyes.

"What are you thinking of?"

"I'm wondering why you make me feel so odd," she told him with simple frankness. He smiled, and she noticed that it grew in his eyes seconds before it grew on his mouth.

"Do I?" He appeared to enjoy the information. "Did you know your hair catches the sunlight?" Keane took a handful, letting it spill from between his fingers. "I've never seen another woman with hair like this. It's a temptation all in itself. In what way do I make you feel odd, Jovilette?" he asked as his eyes trailed back up to hers.

"I'm not sure yet." Jo found her voice husky. Abruptly, she decided it would not do to go on feeling odd or to go on wanting to be kissed by Keane Prescott. She scrambled up and brushed off the seat of her pants.

"Running away?" As Keane rose, Jo's head snapped up.

"I never run away from anything, Mr. Prescott." Ice sharpened her voice. She was annoyed that she had allowed herself to fall under his charm again. "I certainly won't run from a city-bred lawyer." Her words were laced with scorn. "Why don't you go back to Chicago and get someone thrown in jail?"

"I'm a defense attorney," Keane countered easily. "I get people out of jail."

"Fine. Go put a criminal back on the streets, then."

Keane laughed, bringing Jo's temper even closer to the surface. "That covers both sides of the issue, doesn't it? You dazzle me, Jovilette."

"Well, it's strictly unintentional." She took a step back from the amusement in his eyes. She would not tolerate him making fun of her. "You don't belong here," she blurted out. "You have no business here."

"On the contrary," he disagreed in a cool, untroubled voice. "I have every business here. I own this circus."

"Why?" she demanded, throwing out her hands as if to push his words aside. "Because it says so on a piece of paper? That's all lawyers understand, I imagine— pieces of paper with strange little words. Why did you come? To look us over and calculate the profit and loss? What's the liquidation value of a dream, Mr. Prescott?

What price do you put on the human spirit? Look at it!" she demanded, swinging her arm to encompass the lot behind them. "You only see tents and a huddle of trailers. You can't possibly understand what it all means. But Frank understood. He loved it."

"I'm aware of that." Keane's voice was still calm but had taken on a thin edge of steel. Jo saw that his eyes had grown dark and guarded. "He also left it to me."

"I don't understand why." In frustration, Jo stuffed her hands in her pockets and turned away.

"Neither do I, I assure you, but the fact remains that he did."

"Not once in thirty years did you visit him." Jo whirled back around. Her hair followed in a passionate arch. "Not once."

"Quite true," Keane agreed. He stood with his weight even on both legs and watched her. "Of course, some might look at it differently. Not once in thirty years did he visit me."

"Your mother left him and took you to Chicago—"

"I won't discuss my mother," Keane interrupted in a tone of clipped finality.

Jo bit off a retort, spinning away from him again. Still she could not find the reins to her control. "What are you going to do with it?" she demanded.

"That's my business."

"Oh!" Jo spun back, then shut her eyes and muttered in a language he failed to understand. "Can you be so arrogant? Can you be so dispassionate?" Her lashes fluttered up, revealing eyes dark with anger. "Do the lives of all those people mean nothing to you? Does Frank's dream mean nothing? Haven't you enough money already without hurting people to get more? Greed isn't something you inherited from Frank."

"I'll only be pushed so far," Keane warned.

"I'd push you all the way back to Chicago if I could manage it," she snapped.

"I wondered how much of a temper there was behind those sharp green eyes," Keane commented, watching her passion pour color into her cheeks. "It appears it's a full-grown one." Jo started to retort, but Keane cut her off. "Just hold on a minute," he ordered. "With or without your approval, I own this circus. It might be easier for you if you adjusted to that. Be quiet," he added when her mouth opened again. "Legally, I can do with my—" He hesitated a moment, then continued in a mordant tone. "—inheritance as I choose. I have no obligation or intention of justifying my decision to you."

Jo dug her nails into her palms to help keep her voice from shaking. "I never knew I could grow to dislike someone so quickly."

"Jovilette." Keane dipped his hands into his pockets, then rocked back on his heels. "You disliked me before you ever saw me."

"That's true," she replied evenly. "But I've learned to dislike you in person in less than twenty-four hours. I have a show to do," she said, turning back toward the lot. Though he did not follow, she felt his eyes on her until she reached her trailer and closed the door behind her.

Thirty minutes later Jamie sprang through the back door of the Big Top. He was breathless after a lengthy routine and hooked one hand through his purple suspenders as he took in gulps of air. He spotted Jo stand-

ing beside the white mare. Her eyes were dark and
stormy, her shoulders set and rigid. Jamie recognized
the signs. Something or someone had put Jo in a temper, and she had barely ten minutes to work her way
out of it before her cue.

He crossed to her and gave a tug on her hair. "Hey."

"Hello, Jamie." Jo struggled to keep her voice pleasant, but he heard the traces of emotion.

"Hello, Jo," he replied in precisely the same tone.

"Cut it out," she ordered before taking a few steps
away. The mare followed docilely. Jo had been trying
for some time to put her emotions back into some sem-
blance of order. She was not succeeding.

"What happened?" Jamie asked from directly behind her.

"Nothing," Jo snapped, then hated herself for the
short nastiness of the word.

Jamie persisted, knowing her too well to be offended.
"Nothing is one of my favorite topics of conversation."
He put his hands on her shoulders, ignoring her quick,
bad-tempered jerk. "Let's talk about it."

"There's nothing to talk about."

"Exactly." He began massaging the tension in her
shoulders with his white gloved hands.

"Oh, Jamie." His good-heartedness was irresistible.
Sighing, she allowed herself to be soothed. "You're an
idiot."

"I'm not here to be flattered."

"I had an argument with the owner." Jo let out a long
breath and shut her eyes.

"What're you doing having arguments with the
owner?"

"He infuriates me." Jo whirled around. Her cape

whipped and snapped with the movement. "He shouldn't be here. If he were back in Chicago..."

"Hold it." With a slight shake of her shoulders, Jamie halted Jo's outburst. "You know better than to get yourself worked up like this right before a show. You can't afford to have your mind on anything but what you're doing when you're in that cage."

"I'll be all right," she mumbled.

"Jo." There was censure in his voice mixed with affection and exasperation.

Reluctantly, Jo brought her gaze up to his. It was impossible to resist the grave eyes in the brightly painted face. With something between a sigh and a moan, she dropped her forehead to his chest. "Jamie, he makes me so mad! He could ruin everything."

"Let's worry about it when the time comes," Jamie suggested, patting her hair.

"But he doesn't understand us. He doesn't understand anything."

"Well, then it's up to us to make him understand, isn't it?"

Jo looked up and wrinkled her nose. "You're so logical."

"Of course I am," he agreed and struck a pose. As he wiggled his orange eyebrows, Jo laughed. "Okay?" he asked, then picked up his prop bucket.

"Okay," she agreed and smiled.

"Good, 'cause there's my cue."

When he disappeared behind the flap, Jo leaned her cheek against the mare and nuzzled a moment. "I don't think I'm the one to make him understand, though."

I wish he'd never come, she added silently as she vaulted onto the mare's back. I wish I'd never noticed how his eyes are like Ari's and how nice his mouth is when he smiles, she thought. Jo ran the tip of her tongue gingerly over her lips. I wish he'd never kissed me. *Liar.* Her conscience spoke softly in her ear: *Admit it, you're glad he kissed you. You've never felt anything like that before, and no matter what, you're glad he kissed you last night. You even wanted him to kiss you again today.*

She forced her mind clear, taking deep, even breaths until she heard the ringmaster announce her. With a flick of her heels, she sent the mare sprinting into the tent.

It did not go well. The audience cheered her, oblivious to any problem, but Jo was aware that the routine was far from smooth. And the cats sensed her preoccupation. Again and again they tested her, and again and again Jo was forced to alter her timing to compensate. When the act was over, her head throbbed from the strain of concentration. Her hands were clammy as she turned Merlin over to Buck.

The big man came back to her after securing the cage. "What's the matter with you?" he demanded without preamble. By the underlying and very rare anger in his voice, Jo knew he had observed at least a portion of her act. Unlike the audience, Buck would note any deviation. "You go in the cage like that again, one of those cats is going to find out what you taste like."

"My timing was a little off, that's all." Jo fought against the trembling in her stomach and tried to sound casual.

"A little?" Buck glowered, looking formidable behind the mass of blond beard. "Who do you think you're fooling? I've been around these ugly cats since before you were born. When you go in the cage, you've got to take your brain in with you."

Only too aware that he was right, Jo conceded. "I know, Buck. You're right." With a weary hand she pushed back her hair. "It won't happen again. I guess I was tired and a little off-balance." She sent him an apologetic smile.

Buck frowned and shuffled. Never in his forty-five years had he managed to resist feminine smiles. "All right," he muttered, then sniffed and made his voice firm. "But you go take a nap right after the finale. No coffee. I don't want to see you around again until dinner time."

"Okay, Buck." Jo kept her voice humble, though she was tempted to grin. The weakness was going out of her legs, and the dull buzz of fear was fading from between her temples. Still she felt exhausted and agreeable to Buck's uncharacteristic tone of command. A nap, she decided as Buck drove Merlin away, was just what she needed, not to mention that it was as good a way as any to avoid Keane Prescott for the rest of the day. Shooing this thought aside, Jo decided to while away the time until the finale in casual conversation with Vito the wire walker.

Chapter 4

It rained for three days. It was a solid downpour, not heavy but insistent. As the circus wound its way north, the rain followed. Nevertheless, canvas men pitched the tents in soggy fields and muddy lots while straw was laid on the hippodrome track and performers scurried from trailers to tents under dripping umbrellas.

The lot near Waycross, Georgia, was scattered with puddles under a thick, gray sky. Jo could only be grateful that no evening show had been scheduled. By six, it was nearly dark, with a chill teasing the damp air. She hustled from the cookhouse after an early supper. She would check on the cats, she decided, then closet herself in her trailer, draw the curtains against the rain and curl up with a book. Shivering, she concluded that the idea was inspired.

She carried no umbrella but sought questionable shelter under a gray rolled-brimmed hat and thin wind-breaker. Keeping her head lowered, she jogged across the mud, skimming around or hopping over puddles. She hummed lightly, anticipating the simple pleasures of an idle evening. Her humming ended in a muffled gasp as she ran into a solid object. Fingers wrapped around her upper arms. Even before she lifted her head, Jo knew it was Keane who held her. She recognized his touch. Through some clever maneuvering, she had managed to avoid being alone with him since they had walked together and looked back on the circus.

"Excuse me, Mr. Prescott. I'm afraid I wasn't looking where I was going."

"Perhaps the weather's dampened your radar, Jovilette." He made no move to release her. Annoyed, Jo was forced to hold her hat steady with one hand as she tilted her head to meet his eyes. Rain fell cool on her face.

"I don't know what you mean."

"Oh, I think you do," Keane countered. "There's not another soul around. You've been careful to keep yourself in a crowd for days."

Jo blinked rain from her lashes. She admitted ruefully that it had been foolish to suppose he wouldn't notice her ploy. She saw he carried no umbrella either, nor did he bother with a hat. His hair was darkened with rain, much the same color that one of her cats would be if caught in an unexpected shower. It was difficult, in the murky light, to clearly make out his features, but the rain could not disguise his mockery.

"That's an interesting observation, Mr. Prescott," Jo said coolly. "Now, if you don't mind, I'm getting wet." She was surprised when she remained in his hold after a strong attempt on her part to pull away. Frowning, she put both hands against his chest and pushed. She discovered that she had been wrong; under the lean frame was an amazing amount of strength. Infuriated that she had misjudged him and that she was outmatched, Jo raised her eyes again. "Let me go," she demanded between clenched teeth.

"No," Keane returned mildly. "I don't believe I will."

Jo glared at him. "Mr. Prescott, I'm cold and wet and I'd like to go to my trailer. Now, what do you want?"

"First, I want you to stop calling me Mr. Prescott." Jo pouted but she kept silent. "Second, I'd like an hour of your time for going over a list of personnel." He paused. Through her windbreaker Jo could feel his fingers unyielding on her arms.

"Is there anything else?" she demanded, trying to sound bored.

For a moment there was only the sound of rain drumming on the ground and splashing into puddles. "Yes," Keane said quietly. "I think I'll just get this out of my system."

Jo's instincts were swift but they were standing too close for her to evade him. And he was quick. Her protest was muffled against his mouth. Her arms were pinioned to her sides as his locked around her. Jo had felt a man's body against her own before—working out with the tumblers, practicing with the equestrians—but never with such clarity as this. She was aware of Keane in every fiber of her being. His body was whipcord lean and hard, his arms holding the strength she had discounted the first time she had seen him. But more, it was his mouth that mystified her. Now it was not gentle or testing; it took and plundered and demanded more before she could withhold a response.

Jo forgot the rain, though it continued to fall against her face. She forgot the cold. The warmth spread from inside, where her blood flowed fast, as her body was molded to Keane's. She forgot herself, or the woman she had thought herself to be, and discovered another. When he lifted his mouth, Jo kept her eyes closed, savoring the lingering pleasures, inviting fresh ones.

"More?" he murmured as his hand trailed up, then down her spine. Heat raced after it. "Kissing can be a dangerous pastime, Jo." He lowered his mouth again, then nipped at her soft bottom lip. "But you know all about danger, don't you?" He kissed her hard, leaving her breathless. "How courageous are you without your cats?"

Suddenly her heart raced to her throat. Her legs became rubbery, and a tingle sprinted up her spine. Jo recognized the feeling. It was the way she felt when she experienced a close call with the cats. Reaction would set in after the door of the safety cage locked behind her and the crisis had passed. It was then that fear found her. She studied Keane's bold, amber eyes, and her mouth went dry. She shuddered.

"You're cold." His voice was abruptly brisk. "Small wonder. We'll go to my trailer and get you some coffee."

"No!" Jo's protest was sharp and instantaneous. She knew she was vulnerable and she knew as well that she did not yet possess the experience to fight him. To be alone with him now was too great a risk.

Keane drew her away, but his grip remained firm. She could not read his expression as he searched her face. "What happened just now was personal," he told her. "Strictly man to woman. I'm of the opinion that lovemaking should be personal. You're an appealing armful, Jovilette, and I'm accustomed to taking what I want, one way or another."

His words were like a shot of adrenaline. Jo's chin thrust forward, and her eyes flamed. "No one *takes* me, one way or another." She spoke with the deadly calm of fury. "If I make love with anyone, it's only because I want to."

"Of course," Keane agreed with an easy nod. "We're both aware you'll be willing when the time comes. We could make love quite successfully tonight, but I think it best if we know each other better first."

Jo's mouth trembled open and closed twice before she could speak. "Of all the arrogant, outrageous..."

"Truthful," Keane supplied, tossing her into incoherency again. "But for now, we have business, and while I don't mind kissing in the rain, I prefer to conduct business in a drier climate." He held up a hand as Jo started to protest. "I told you, the kiss was between a man and a woman. The business we have now is between the owner of this circus and a performer under contract. Understood?"

Jo took a long, deep breath to bring her voice to a normal level. "Understood," she agreed. Without another word she let him lead her across the slippery lot.

When they reached Keane's trailer, he hustled Jo inside without preliminaries. She blinked against the change in light when he hit the wall switch. "Take off your coat," he said briskly, pulling down her zipper before she could perform the task for herself. Instinctively, her hand reached for it as she took a step backward. Keane merely lifted a brow, then stripped off his own jacket. "I'll get the coffee." He moved down the length of the narrow trailer and disappeared around the corner where the tiny kitchen was set.

Slowly, Jo pulled off her dripping hat, letting her hair tumble free from where it had been piled under its confinement. With automatic movements she hung both her hat and coat on the hooks by the trailer door. It had been almost six months since she had stood in Frank's trailer, and like a woman visiting an old friend, she searched for changes.

The same faded lampshade adorned the maple table lamp that Frank had used for reading. The shade sat straight now, however, not at its usual slightly askew angle. The pillow that Lillie from wardrobe had sewn for him on some long-ago Christmas still sat over the small burn hole in the seat cushion of the couch. Jo doubted that Keane knew of the hole's existence. Frank's pipe stand sat, as always, on the counter by the side window. Unable to resist, Jo crossed over to run her finger over the worn bowl of his favorite pipe.

"Never could pack it right," she murmured to his well-loved ghost. Abruptly, her senses quivered. She twisted her head to see Keane watching her. Jo dropped her hand. A rare blush mantled her cheeks as she found herself caught unguarded.

"How do you take your coffee, Jo?"

She swallowed. "Black," she told him, aware that he was granting her the privacy of her thoughts. "Just black. Thank you."

Keane nodded, then turned to pick up two steaming mugs. "Come, sit down." He moved toward the Formica table that sat directly across from the kitchen. "You'd better take off your shoes. They're wet."

After squeaking her way down the length of the

trailer, Jo sat down and pulled at the damp laces. Keane set both mugs on the table before disappearing into the back of the trailer. When he returned, Jo was already sipping at the coffee.

"Here." He offered her a pair of socks.

Surprised, Jo shook her head. "No, that's all right. I don't need…"

Her polite refusal trailed off as he knelt at her feet. "Your feet are like ice," he commented after cupping them in his palms. Briskly, he rubbed them while Jo sat mute, oddly disarmed by the gesture. The warmth was spreading dangerously past her ankles. "Since I'm responsible for keeping you out in the rain," he went on as he slipped a sock over her foot, "I'd best see to it you don't cough and sneeze your way through tomorrow's show. Such small feet," he murmured, running his thumb over the curve of her ankle as she stared wordlessly at the top of his head.

Raindrops still clung to and glistened in his hair. Jo found herself longing to brush them away and feel the texture of his hair beneath her fingers. She was sharply aware of him and wondered if it would always be this way when she was near him. Keane pulled on the second sock. His fingers lingered on her calf as he lifted his eyes. Hers were darkened with confusion as they met his. The body over which she had always held supreme control was journeying into frontiers her mind had not yet explored.

"Still cold?" Keane asked softly.

Jo moistened her lips and shook her head. "No. No, I'm fine."

He smiled a lazy, masculine smile that said as clearly as words that he was aware of his effect on her. His eyes told her he enjoyed it. Unsmiling, Jo watched him rise to his feet.

"It doesn't mean you'll win," she said aloud in response to their silent communication.

"No, it doesn't." Keane's smile remained as his gaze roamed possessively over her face. "That only makes it more interesting. Open and shut cases are invariably boring, hardly worth the trouble of going on if you've won before you've finished your opening statement."

Jo lifted her coffee and sipped, taking a moment to settle her nerves. "Are we here to discuss the law or circus business, counselor?" she asked, letting her eyes drift to his again as she set the mug back on the table. "If it's law, I'm afraid I'm going to disappoint you. I don't know much about it."

"What do you know about, Jovilette?" Keane slid into the chair beside hers.

"Cats," she said. "And Prescott's Circus Colossus. I'll be glad to let you know whatever I can about either."

"Tell me about you," he countered, and leaning back, pulled a cigar from his pocket.

"Mr. Prescott—" Jo began.

"Keane," he interrupted, flicking on his lighter. He glanced at the tip of his cigar, then back up at her through the thin haze of smoke.

"I was under the impression you wanted to be briefed on the personnel."

"You are a member of this circus, are you not?" Casually, Keane blew smoke at the ceiling. "I have every intention of being briefed on the entire troupe and see no reason why you shouldn't start with yourself." His eyes traveled back to hers. "Humor me."

Jo decided to take the line of least resistance. "It's a

short enough story," she said with a shrug. "I've been with the circus all my life. When I was old enough, I started work as a generally useful."

"A what?" Keane paused in the action of reaching for the coffeepot.

"Generally useful," Jo repeated, letting him freshen her cup. "It's a circus term that means exactly what it says. Rose's parents, for instance, are generally usefuls. We get a lot of drifters who work that way, too. It's also written into every performer's contract, after the specific terms, that they make themselves generally useful. There isn't room in most circuses, and certainly not in a tent circus, for performers with star complexes. You do what's necessary, what's needed. Buck, my handler, fills in during a slump at the sideshow, and he's one of the best canvas men around. Pete is the best mechanic in the troupe. Jamie knows as much about lighting as most shandies—electricians," she supplied as Keane lifted a brow. "He's also a better-than-average tumbler."

"What about you?" Keane interrupted the flow of Jo's words. For a moment she faltered, and the hands that had been gesturing became still. "Besides riding a galloping horse without reins or saddle, giving orders to elephants and facing lions?" He lifted his cup, watching her as he sipped. A smile lurked in his eyes. Jo frowned, studying him.

"Are you making fun of me?"

His smile sobered instantly. "No, Jo, I'm not making fun of you."

She continued. "In a pinch, I run the menagerie in the sideshow or I fill in the aerial act. Not the trap," she explained, relaxing again. "They have to practice together constantly to keep the timing. But sometimes

I fill in on the Spanish Web, the big costume number where the girls hang from ropes and do identical moves. They're using butterfly costumes this year."

"Yes, I know the one." Keane continued to watch her as he drew on his cigar.

"But mostly Duffy likes to use girls who are more curvy. They double as showgirls in the finale."

"I see." A smile tugged at the corners of Keane's mouth. "Tell me, were your parents European?"

"No." Diverted, Jo shook her head. "Why do you ask?"

"Your name. And the ease with which I've heard you speak both French and Italian."

"It's easy to pick up languages in the circus," Jo said.

"Your accent was perfect in both cases."

"What? Oh." She shrugged and absently shifted in her chair, bringing her feet up to sit cross-legged. "We have a wide variety of nationalities here. Frank used to say that the world could take a lesson from the circus. We have French, Italian, Spanish, German, Russian, Mexican, Americans from all parts of the country and more."

"I know. It's like a traveling United Nations." He tipped his cigar ash in a glass tray. "So you picked up some French and Italian along the way. But if you've traveled with the circus all your life, what about the rest of your schooling?"

The hint of censure in his voice brought up her chin. "I went to school during the winter break and had a tutor on the road. I learned my ABC's, counselor, and a bit more, besides. I probably know more about geography and world history than you, and from more interesting sources than textbooks. I imagine I know more about animals than a third-year veterinary student and have more practical experience healing them. I can speak seven languages and—"

"Seven?" Keane interrupted. "Seven languages?"

"Well, five fluently," she corrected grudgingly. "I still have a bit of trouble with Greek and German, unless I can really take my time, and I can't read Greek yet at all."

"What else besides French, Italian and English?"

"Spanish and Russian." Jo scowled into her coffee. "The Russian's handy. I use it for swearing at the cats during the act. Not too many people understand Russian cursing, so it's safe."

Keane's laughter brought Jo's attention from her coffee. He was leaning back in his chair, his eyes gold with their mirth. Jo's scowl deepened. "What's so funny?"

"You are, Jovilette." Stung, she started to scramble up, but his hands on her shoulders stopped her. "No, don't be offended. I can't help but find it amusing that you toss out so offhandedly an accomplishment that any language major would brag about." Carelessly, he ran a finger over her sulky mouth. "You continually amaze me." He brushed a hand through her hair. "You mumbled something at me the other day. Were you swearing at me in Russian?"

"Probably."

Grinning, Keane dropped his hand and settled into his chair again. "When did you start working with the cats?"

"In front of an audience? When I was seventeen. Frank wouldn't let me start any earlier. He was my legal guardian as well as the owner, so he had me both ways. I was ready when I was fifteen."

"How did you lose your parents?"

The question caught her off guard. "In a fire," she said levelly. "When I was seven."

"Here?"

She knew Keane was not referring to their locale but to the circus. Jo sipped her cooling coffee. "Yes."

"Didn't you have any other family?"

"The circus is a family," she countered. "I was never given the chance to be an orphan. And I always had Frank."

"Did you?" Keane's smile was faintly sarcastic. "How was he as a father figure?"

Jo studied him for a moment. Was he bitter? she wondered. Or amused? Or simply curious? "He never took my father's place," she replied quietly. "He never tried to, because neither of us wanted it. We were friends, as close as I think it's possible for friends to be, but I'd already had a father, and he'd already had a child. We weren't looking for substitutes. You look nothing like him, you know."

"No," Keane replied with a shrug. "I know."

"He had a comfortable face, all creases and folds." Jo smiled, thinking of it while she ran a finger absently around the rim of her mug. "He was dark, too, just beginning to gray when…" She trailed off, then brought herself back with a quick shake of her head. "Your voice is rather like his, though; he had a truly beautiful voice. I'll ask you a question now."

Keane's expression became attentive, then he gestured with the back of his hand. "Go ahead."

"Why are you here? I lost my temper when I asked you before, but I do want to know." It was against her nature to probe, and some of her discomfort found its way into her voice. "It must have caused you some difficulty to leave your practice, even for a few weeks."

Keane frowned at the end of his cigar before he slowly crushed it out. "Let's say I wanted to see first-hand what had fascinated my father all these years."

"You never came when he was alive." Jo gripped her hands together under the table. "You didn't even bother to come to his funeral."

"I would've been the worst kind of hypocrite to attend his funeral, don't you think?"

"He was your father." Jo's eyes grew dark and her tone sharp in reproof.

"You're smarter than that, Jo," Keane countered calmly. "It takes more than an accident of birth to make a father. Frank Prescott was a complete stranger to me."

"You resent him." Jo felt suddenly torn between loyalty for Frank and understanding for the man who sat beside her.

"No." Keane shook his head thoughtfully. "No, I believe I actively resented him when I was growing up, but…" He shrugged the thought aside. "I grew rather ambivalent over the years."

"He was a good man," Jo stated, leaning forward as she willed him to understand. "He only wanted to give people pleasure, to show them a little magic. Maybe he wasn't made to be a father—some men aren't—but he was kind and gentle. And he was proud of you."

"Of me?" Keane seemed amused. "How?"

"Oh, you're hateful," Jo whispered, hurt by his careless attitude. She slipped from her chair, but before she could step away, Keane took her arm.

"No, tell me. I'm interested." His hold on her arm was light, but she knew it would tighten if she resisted.

"All right." Jo tossed her head to send her hair behind her back. "He had the Chicago paper delivered to his Florida office. He always looked for any mention of you, any article on a court case you were involved in or a dinner party you attended. Anything. You have to understand that to us a write-up is very important. Frank wasn't a performer, but he was one of us. Sometimes he'd read me an article before he put it away. He kept a scrapbook."

Jo pulled her arm away and strode past Keane into the bedroom. The oversize wooden chest was where it had always been, at the foot of Frank's bed. Kneeling down, Jo tossed up the lid. "This is where he kept all the things that mattered to him." Jo began to shift through papers and mementos quickly; she had not been able to bring herself to sort through the chest before. Keane stood in the doorway and watched her. "He called it his memory box." She pushed at her hair with an annoyed hand, then continued to search. "He said memories were the rewards for growing old. Here it is." Jo pulled out a dark green scrapbook, then sat back on her heels. Silently, she held it out to Keane. After a moment he crossed the room and took it from her. Jo could hear the rain hissing on the ground outside as their eyes held. His expression was unfathomable as he opened the book. The pages rustled to join the quiet sound of the rain.

"What an odd man he must have been," Keane murmured, "to keep a scrapbook on a son he never knew." There was no rancor in his voice. "What was he?" he asked suddenly, shifting his eyes back to Jo.

"A dreamer," she answered. "His watch was always five minutes slow. If he hung a picture on the wall, it was always crooked. He'd never straighten it because he'd never notice. He was always thinking about tomorrow. I guess that's why he kept yesterday in this box." Glancing down, she began to straighten the chaos she had caused while looking for the book. A snatch of red caught her eye. Reaching for it, her fingers found a familiar shape. Jo hesitated, then drew the old doll out of the chest.

It was a sad piece of plastic and faded silk with its face nearly washed away. One arm was broken off, leaving an empty sleeve. The golden hair was straggled but brave under its red cap. Ballet shoes were painted on the dainty feet. Tears backed up behind Jo's eyes as she made a soft sound of joy and despair.

"What is it?" Keane demanded, glancing down to see her clutching the battered ballerina.

"Nothing." Her voice was unsteady as she scrambled quickly to her feet. "I have to go." Though she tried, Jo could not bring herself to drop the doll back into the box. She swallowed. She did not wish to reveal her emotions before his intelligent, gold eyes. Perhaps he would be cynical, or worse, amused. "May I have this, please?" She was careful with the tone of the request.

Slowly, Keane crossed the distance between them, then cradled her chin in his hand. "It appears to be yours already."

"It was." Her fingers tightened on the doll's waist. "I didn't know Frank had kept it. Please," she whispered. Her emotions were already dangerously heightened. She could feel a need to rest her head against his shoulder. The evening had been a roller coaster for her feelings, climaxing now with the discovery of her most prized childhood possession. She knew that if she did not escape, she would seek comfort in his arms. Her own weakness frightened her. "Let me by."

For a moment, Jo read refusal in his eyes. Then he stepped aside. Jo let out a quiet, shaky breath. "I'll walk you back to your trailer."

"No," she said quickly, too quickly. "It isn't necessary," she amended, moving by him and into the kitchen. Sitting down, she pulled on her shoes, too distraught to remember she still wore his socks. "There's no reason for us both to get wet again." She rambled on, knowing he was watching her hurried movement, but unable to stop. "And I'm going to check on my cats before I go in, and..."

She stopped short when he took her shoulders and pulled her to her feet. "And you don't want to take the chance of being alone in your trailer with me in case I change my mind."

A sharp denial trembled on her lips, but the knowledge in his eyes crushed it. "All right," she admitted. "That, too."

Keane brushed her hair from her neck and shook his head. He kissed her nose and moved down to pluck her hat and coat from their hooks. Cautiously, Jo followed him. When he held out her coat, she turned and slipped her arms into the sleeves. Before she could murmur her thanks, he turned her back and pulled up the zipper. For a moment his fingers lingered at her neck, his eyes on hers. Taking her hair into her hand, he piled it atop her head, then dropped on her hat. The gestures were innocent, but Jo was rocked by a feeling of intimacy she had never experienced.

"I'll see you tomorrow," he said, pulling the brim of her hat down further over her eyes.

Jo nodded. Holding the doll against her side, she pushed open the door. The sound of rain was amplified through the trailer. "Good night," she murmured, then moved quickly into the night.

Chapter 5

The morning scent was clean. In the new lot rainbows glistened in puddles. At last the sky was blue with only harmless white puffs of clouds floating over its surface. In the cookhouse a loud, crowded breakfast was being served. Finding herself without appetite, Jo skipped going to the cookhouse altogether. She was restless and tense. No matter how she disciplined her mind, her thoughts wandered back to Keane Prescott and to the evening they had spent together. Jo remembered it all, from the quick passion of the kiss in the rain to the calmness of his voice when he had said good-night. It was odd, she mused, that whenever she began to talk to him, she forgot he was the owner, forgot he was Frank's son. Always she was forced to remind herself of their positions.

Deep in thought, Jo slipped into tights and a leotard.

It was true, she admitted, that she had failed to keep their relationship from becoming personal. She found it difficult to corral her urge to laugh with him, to share a joke, to open for him the doorway to the magic of the circus. If he could feel it, she thought, he would understand. Though she could admit her interest in him privately, she could not find a clear reason for his apparent interest in her.

Why me? she wondered with a shake of her head. Turning, she opened her wardrobe closet and studied herself in the full-length glass on the back of the door. There she saw a woman of slightly less-than-average height with a body lacking the generous curves of Duffy's showgirls. The legs, she decided, were not bad. They were long and well-shaped with slim thighs. The hips were narrow, more, she thought with a pout, like a boy's than a woman's; and the bustline was sadly inadequate. She knew many women in the troupe with more appeal and a dozen with more experience.

Jo could see nothing in the mirror that would attract a sophisticated Chicago attorney. She did not note the honesty that shone from the exotically shaped green eyes or the strength in her chin or the full promise of her mouth. She saw the touch of gypsy in the tawny complexion and raven hair but remained unaware of the appeal that came from the hint of something wild and untamed just under the surface. The plain black leotard showed her firm, lithe body to perfection, but Jo thought nothing of the smooth satiny sheen of her skin. She was frowning as she pulled her hair back and began to braid it.

He must know dozens of women, she thought as her hands worked to confine her thick mane of hair. He probably takes a different one to dinner every night. They wear beautiful clothes and expensive perfume, she mused, torturing herself with the thought. They have names like Laura and Patricia, and they have low, sophisticated laughs. Jo lifted a brow at the reflection in the mirror and gave a light, low laugh. She wrinkled her brow at the hollowness of the sound. They discuss mutual friends, the Wallaces or the Jamesons, over candlelight and Beaujolais. And when he takes the most beautiful one home, they listen to Chopin and drink brandy in front of the fire. Then they make love. Jo felt an odd tightening in her stomach but pursued the fantasy to the finish. The lovely lady is experienced, passionate and worldly. Her skin is soft and white. When he leaves, she is not devastated but mature. She doesn't even care if he loves her or not.

Jo stared at the woman in the glass and saw her cheeks were wet. On a cry of frustration, she slammed the door shut. *What's wrong with me?* she demanded, brushing all traces of tears from her face. I haven't been myself for days! I need to shake myself out of this—this…whatever it is that I'm in. Slipping on gymnastic shoes and tossing a robe over her arm, Jo hustled from the trailer.

She moved carefully, avoiding puddles and any further speculation on Keane Prescott's romantic life. Before she was halfway across the lot, she saw Rose. From the expression on her face, Jo could see she was in a temper.

"Hello, Rose," she said, strategically stepping aside as the snake charmer splashed through a puddle.

"He's hopeless," Rose tossed back. "I tell you," she

continued, stopping and wagging a finger at Jo, "I'm through this time. Why should I waste my time?"

"You've certainly been patient," Jo agreed, deciding that sympathy was the wisest course. "It's more than he deserves."

"Patient?" Rose raised a dramatic hand to her breast. "I have the patience of a saint. Yet even a saint has her limits!" Rose tossed her hair behind her shoulders. She sighed heavily. "*Adios.* I think I hear Mama calling me."

Jo continued her walk toward the Big Top. Jamie walked by, his hands in his pockets. "She's crazy," he muttered. He stopped and spread his arms wide. His look was that of a man ill-used and innocent. Jo shrugged. Shaking his head, Jamie moved away. "She's crazy," he said again.

Jo watched him until he was out of sight, then darted to the Big Top.

Inside, Carmen watched adoringly while Vito practiced a new routine on the incline wire. The tent echoed with the sounds of rehearsals: voices and thumps, the rattle of rigging, the yapping of clown dogs. In the first ring Jo spotted the Six Beirots, an acrobatic act that was just beginning its warm-ups. Pleased with her timing, Jo walked the length of the arena. A raucous whistle sounded over her head, and she glanced up to shake a friendly fist at Vito. He called from fifteen feet above her as he balanced on a slender wire set at a forty-five-degree angle.

"Hey, chickie, you have a nice rear view. You're almost as cute as me."

"No one's as cute as you, Vito," she called back.

"Ah, I know." With a weighty sigh, he executed a neat pivot. "But I have learned to live with it." He sent down a lewd wink. "When you going into town with me, chickie?" he asked as he always did.

"When you teach my cats to walk the wire," Jo answered as she always did. Vito laughed and began a light-footed cha-cha. Carmen fired Jo a glare. She must have it bad, Jo decided, if she takes Vito's harmless flirting seriously. Stopping beside her, Jo leaned close and spoke in a conspirator's whisper. "He'd fall off his wire if I said I'd go."

"I'd go," Carmen said with a lovely pout, "if he'd just ask me."

Jo shook her head, wondering why romances were invariably complicated. She was lucky not to have the problem. Giving Carmen an encouraging pat on the shoulder, Jo set off toward the first ring.

The Six Beirots were brothers. They were all small-statured, dark men who had immigrated from Belgium. Jo worked out with them often to keep herself limber and to keep her reflexes sharp. She liked them all, knew their wives and children, and understood their unique blending of French and English. Raoul was the oldest, and the stockiest of the six brothers. Because of his build and strength, he was the under-stander in their human pyramid. It was he who spotted Jo and first lifted a hand in greeting.

"Halo." He grinned and ran his palm over his receding hairline. "You gonna tumble?"

Jo laughed and did a quick handspring into the ring. She stuck out her tongue when the unanimous critique was "sloppy." "I just need to warm up," she said, assuming an air of injured dignity. "My muscles need tuning."

For the next thirty minutes Jo worked with them,

doing muscle stretches and limbering exercises, rib stretches and lung expanders. Her muscles warmed and loosened, her heart pumped steadily. She was filled with energy. Her mind was clear. Because of her lightened mood, Jo was easily cajoled into a few impromptu acrobatics. Leaving the more complicated feats to the experts, she did simple back flips, handsprings or twists at Raoul's command. She did a brief, semi-successful thirty seconds atop the rolling globe and earned catcalls from her comrades at her dismount.

She stood back as they began the leaps. One after another they lined up to take turns running along a ramp, bounding upon a springboard and flying up to do flips or twists before landing on the mat. There was a constant stream of French as they called out to each other.

"Hokay, Jo." Raoul gestured with his hand. "Your turn."

"Oh, no." She shook her head and reached for her robe. "Uh-uh." There was a chorus of coaxing, teasing French. "I've got to give my cats their vitamins," she told them, still shaking her head.

"Come on, Jo. It's fun." Raoul grinned and wiggled his eyebrows. "Don't you like to fly?" As she glanced at the ramp, Raoul knew she was tempted. "You take a good spring," he told her."Do one forward somersault, then land on my shoulders." He patted them to show their ability to handle the job.

Jo smiled and nibbled pensively on her lower lip. It had been a long while since she had taken the time to go up on the trapeze and really fly. It did look like fun. She gave Raoul a stern look. "You'll catch me?"

"Raoul never misses," he said proudly, then turned to his brothers. *"Ne c'est pas?"* His brothers shrugged and rolled their eyes to the ceiling with indistinguishable mutters. "Ah." He waved them away with the back of his hand.

Knowing Raoul was indeed a top flight understander, Jo approached the ramp. Still she gave him one last narrow-eyed look. "You catch me," she ordered, shaking her finger at him.

"Cherie." He took his position with a stylish movement of his hand. "It's a piece of pie."

"Cake," Jo corrected, took a deep breath, held it and ran. When she came off the springboard, she tucked into the somersault and watched the Big Top turn upside down. She felt good. As the tent began to right itself, she straightened for her landing, keeping herself loose. Her feet connected with Raoul's powerful shoulders, and she tilted only briefly before he took her ankles in a firm grip. Straightening her poor posture, Jo styled elaborately with both arms while she received exaggerated applause and whistles. She leaped down nimbly as Raoul took her waist to give her landing bounce.

"When do you want to join the act?" he asked her, giving her a friendly pat on the bottom. "We'll put you up on the sway pole."

"That's okay." Grinning, Jo again reached for her robe. "I'll stick with the cats." After a cheerful wave, she slipped one arm into a sleeve and started back down the hippodrome track. She pulled up short when she spotted Keane leaning up against the front seat rail.

"Amazing," he said, then straightened to move to her. "But then, the circus is supposed to be amazing, isn't it?" He lifted the forgotten sleeve to her robe, then slipped her other arm into it. "Is there anything here you can't do?"

"Hundreds of things," Jo answered, taking him seriously. "I'm only really proficient with animals. The rest is just show and play."

"You looked amazingly proficient to me for the last half hour or so," he countered as he pulled out her braid from where it was trapped by her robe.

"Have you been here that long?"

"I walked in as Vito was commenting on your rear view."

"Oh." Jo laughed, glancing back to where Vito now stood flirting with Carmen. "He's crazy."

"Perhaps," Keane agreed, taking her arm. "But his eyesight's good enough. Would you like some coffee?"

Jo was reminded instantly of the evening before. Leery of being drawn to his charms again, she shook her head. "I've got to change," she told him, belting her robe. "We've got a show at two. I want to rehearse the cats."

"It's incredible how much time you people devote to your art. Rehearsals seem to run into the beginning of a show, and a show seems to run into more rehearsals."

Jo softened when he referred to circus skills as art. "Performers always look for just a bit more in themselves. It's a constant struggle for perfection. Even when a performance goes beautifully and you know it, you start thinking about the next time. How can I do it better or bigger or higher or faster?"

"Never satisfied?" Keane asked as they stepped out into the sunlight.

"If we were, we wouldn't have much of a reason to come back and do it all over again."

He nodded, but there was something absent in the

gesture, as if his mind was elsewhere. "I have to leave this afternoon," he said almost to himself.

"Leave?" Jo's heart skidded to a stop. Her distress was overwhelming and so unexpected that she was forced to take an extra moment to steady herself. "Back to Chicago?"

"Hmm?" Keane stopped, turning to face her. "Oh, yes."

"And the circus?" Jo asked, thoroughly ashamed that it had not been her first concern. She didn't want him to leave, she suddenly realized.

Keane frowned a moment, then continued to walk. "I see no purpose in disrupting this year's schedule." His voice was brisk now and businesslike.

"This year's?" Jo repeated cautiously.

Keane turned and looked at her. "I haven't decided its ultimate fate, but I won't do anything until the end of the summer."

"I see." She let out a long breath. "So we have a reprieve."

"In a manner of speaking," Keane agreed.

Jo was silent for a moment but could not prevent herself from asking, "Then you won't—I mean, you'll be staying in Chicago now; you won't be traveling with us?"

They negotiated their way around a puddle before Keane answered. "I don't feel I can make a judicious decision about the circus after so brief an exposure. There's a complication in one of my cases that needs my personal attention, but I should be back in a week or two."

Relief flooded through her. He would be back, a voice shouted in her ear. It shouldn't matter to you, another whispered. "We'll be in South Carolina in a couple of weeks," Jo said casually. They had reached her trailer, and she took the handle of her door before she turned to face him. *It's just that I want him to understand what this circus means,* she told herself as she looked up into his eyes. *That's the only reason I want him to come back.* Knowing she was lying to herself made it difficult to keep her gaze steady.

Keane smiled, letting his eyes travel over her face. "Yes, Duffy's given me a route list. I'll find you. Aren't you going to ask me in?"

"In?" Jo repeated. "Oh, no, I told you, I have to change, and…" He stepped forward as she talked. Something in his eyes told her a firm stand was necessary. She had seen a similar look in a lion's eyes while he contemplated taking a dangerous liberty. "I simply don't have time right now. If I don't see you before you go, have a good trip." She turned and opened the door. Aware of a movement, she turned back, but not before he had nudged her through the door and followed. As it closed at his back, Jo bristled with fury. She did not enjoy being outmaneuvered. "Tell me, counselor, do you know anything about a law concerning breaking and entering?"

"Doesn't apply," he returned smoothly. "There was no lock involved." He glanced around at the attractive simplicity of Jo's trailer. The colors were restful earth tones without frills. The beige-and-brown-flecked linoleum floor was spotlessly clean. It was the same basic floorplan as Frank's trailer, but here there were softer touches. There were curtains rather than shades at the windows; large, comfortable pillows tossed onto a forest green sofa; a spray of fresh wildflowers tucked into a thin, glass vase. Without comment Keane wandered to a black lacquer trunk that sat directly opposite the door. On it was a book that he picked up while Jo fumed. *"The Count of Monte Cristo,"* he read aloud and flipped it open. "In French," he stated, lifting a brow.

"It was written in French," Jo muttered, pulling it from his hand. "So I read it in French." Annoyed, she lifted the lid on the trunk, preparing to drop the book inside and out of his reach.

"Good heavens, are those all yours?" Keane stopped the lid on its downswing, then pushed books around with his other hand. "Tolstoy, Cervantes, Voltaire, Steinbeck. When do you have time in this crazy, twenty-four-hour world you live in to read this stuff?"

"I make time," Jo snapped as her eyes sparked. "My *own* time. Just because you're the owner doesn't mean you can barge in here and poke through my things and demand an account of my time. This is my trailer. I own everything in it."

"Hold on." Keane halted her rushing stream of words. "I wasn't demanding an account of your time, I was simply astonished that you could find enough of it to do this type of reading. Since I can't claim to be an expert on your work, it would be remarkably foolish of me to criticize the amount of time you spend on it. Secondly," he said, taking a step toward her—and though Jo stiffened in anticipation, he did not touch her—"I apologize for 'poking through your things,' as you put it. I was interested for several reasons. One being I have quite an extensive library myself. It seems we have a common interest, whether we like it or not. As for barging into your trailer, I can only plead guilty.

If you choose to prosecute, I can recommend a couple of lousy attorneys who overcharge."

His last comment forced a smile onto Jo's reluctant lips. "I'll give it some thought." With more care than she had originally intended, Jo lowered the lid of the trunk. She was reminded that she had not been gracious. "I'm sorry," she said as she turned back to him.

His eyes reflected curiosity. "What for?"

"For snapping at you." She lifted her shoulders, then let them fall. "I thought you were criticizing me. I suppose I'm too sensitive."

Several seconds passed before he spoke. "Unnecessary apology accepted if you answer one question."

Mystified, Jo frowned at him. "What question?"

"Is the Tolstoy in Russian?"

Jo laughed, pushing loose strands of hair from her face. "Yes, it is."

Keane smiled, enjoying the two tiny dimples that flickered in her cheeks when she laughed. "Did you know that though you're lovely in any case, you grow even more so when you smile?"

Jo's laughter stilled. She was unaccustomed to this sort of compliment and studied him without any idea of how to respond. It occurred to her that any of the sophisticated women she had imagined that morning would have known precisely what to say. She would have been able to smile or laugh as she tossed back the appropriate comment. That woman, Jo admitted, was not Jovilette Wilder. Gravely, she kept her eyes on his. "I don't know how to flirt," she said simply.

Keane tilted his head, and an expression came and went in his eyes before she could analyze it. He stepped toward her. "I wasn't flirting with you, Jo, I was making an observation. Hasn't anyone ever told you that you're beautiful?"

He was much too close now, but in the narrow confines of the trailer, Jo had little room to maneuver. She was forced to tilt back her head to keep her eyes level with his. "Not precisely the way you did." Quickly, she put her hand to his chest to keep the slight but important distance between them. She knew she was trapped, but that did not mean she was defeated.

Gently, Keane lifted her protesting hand, turning it palm up as he brought it to his lips. An involuntary breath rushed in and out of Jo's lungs. "Your hands are exquisite," he murmured, tracing the fine line of blue up the back. "Narrow-boned, long-fingered. And the palms show hard work. That makes them more interesting." He lifted his eyes from her hand to her face. "Like you."

Jo's voice had grown husky, but she could do nothing to alter it. "I don't know what I'm supposed to say when you tell me things like that." Beneath her robe her breasts rose and fell with her quickening heart. "I'd rather you didn't."

"Do you really?" Keane ran the back of his hand along her jaw line. "That's a pity, because the more I look at you, the more I find to say. You're a bewitching creature, Jovilette."

"I have to change," she said in the firmest voice she could muster. "You'll have to go."

"That's unfortunately true," he murmured, then cupped her chin. "Come, then, kiss me goodbye."

Jo stiffened. "I hardly think that's necessary...."

"You couldn't be more wrong," he told her as he lowered his mouth. "It's extremely necessary." In a light, teasing whisper, his lips met hers. His arms encircled

her, bringing her closer with only the slightest pressure.
"Kiss me back, Jo," he ordered softly. "Put your arms
around me and kiss me back."

For a moment longer she resisted, but the lure of his
mouth nibbling at hers was too strong. Letting instinct
rule her will, Jo lifted her arms and circled his neck.
Her mouth grew mobile under his, parting and offering.
Her surrender seemed to lick the flames of his passion.
The kiss grew urgent. His arms locked, crushing her
against him. Her quiet moan was not of protest but of
wonder. Her fingers found their way into his hair, tan-
gling in its thickness as they urged him closer. She felt
her robe loosen, then his hands trail up her rib cage. At
his touch, she shivered, feeling her skin grow hot, then
cold, then hot again in rapid succession.

When his hand took her breast, she shied, drawing
in her breath quickly. "Steady," he murmured against
her mouth. His hands stroked gently, coaxing her to
relax again. He kissed the corners of her mouth, waiting until she quieted before he took her deep again.
The thin leotard molded her body. It created no barrier against the warmth of his searching fingers. They
moved slowly, lingering over the peak of her breast, exploring its softness, wandering to her waist, then tracing her hip and thigh.

No man had ever touched her so freely. Jo was helpless to stop him, helpless against her own growing need
for him to touch her again. Was this the passion she had
read of so often? The passion that drove men to war,
to struggle against all reason, to risk everything? She
felt she could understand it now. She clung to him as he
taught her—as she learned—the demands of her own
body. Her mouth grew hungrier for the taste of him.

She was certain she remained in his arms while seasons flew by, while decades passed, while worlds were destroyed and built again.

But when he drew away, Jo saw the same sun spilling through her windows. Eternity had only been moments.

Unable to speak, she merely stared up at him. Her eyes were dark and aware, her cheeks flushed with desire. But somehow, though it still tingled from his, her mouth maintained a youthful innocence. Keane's eyes dropped to it as his hands loitered at the small of her back.

"It's difficult to believe I'm the first man to touch you," he murmured. His eyes roamed to hers. "And quite desperately arousing. Particularly when I find you've passion to match your looks. I think I'd like to make love with you in the daylight first so that I can watch that marvelous control of yours slip away layer by layer. We'll have to discuss it when I get back."

Jo forced strength back into her limbs, knowing she was on the brink of losing her will to him. "Just because I let you kiss me and touch me doesn't mean I'll let you make love to me." She lifted her chin, feeling her confidence surging back. "If I do, it'll be because it's what I want, not because you tell me to."

The expression in Keane's eyes altered. "Fair enough," he agreed and nodded. "It'll simply be my job to make it what you want." He took her chin in his hand and lowered his mouth to hers for a brief kiss. As she had the first time, Jo kept her eyes open and watched him. She felt him grin against her mouth before he raised his head. "You are the most fascinating woman I've ever met." Turning, he crossed to the door.

"I'll be back," he said with a careless wave before it closed behind him. Dumbly, Jo stared into empty space.

Fascinating? she repeated, tracing her still warm lips with her fingertips. Quickly, she ran to the window, and kneeling on the sofa below it, watched Keane stride away.

She realized with a sudden jolt that she missed him already.

Chapter 6

Jo learned that weeks could drag like years. During the second week of Keane's absence she had searched each new lot for a sign of him. She had scanned the crowds of towners who came to watch the raising of the Big Top, and as the days stretched on and on, she balanced between anger and despair at his continued absence. Only in the cage did she manage to isolate her concentration, knowing she could not afford to do otherwise. But after each performance Jo found it more and more difficult to relax. Each morning she felt certain he would be back. Each night she lay restless, waiting for the sun to rise.

Spring was in full bloom. The high grass lots smelled of it. Often there were wildflowers crushed underfoot, leaving their heavy fragrances in the air. Even as the circus caravan traveled north, the days grew warm, sunlight lingering further into evening. While other

troupers enjoyed the balmy air and providentially sunny
skies, Jo lived on nerves.

It occurred to her that after returning to his life in
Chicago, Keane had decided against coming back. In
Chicago he had comfort and wealth and elegant women.
Why should he come back? Jo closed her mind against
the ultimate fate of the circus, unwilling to face the possibility that Keane might close the show at the end of the
season. She told herself the only reason she wanted him
to come back was to convince him to keep the circus
open. But the memory of being in his arms intruded too
often into her thoughts. Gradually, she grew resigned,
filling the strange void she felt with her work.

Several times each week she found time to give the
eager Gerry more training. At first she had only permitted him to work with the two menagerie cubs, allowing
him, with the protection of leather gloves, to play with
them and to feed them. She encouraged him to teach
them simple tricks with the aid of small pieces of raw
meat. Jo was as pleased as he when the cats responded
to his patience and obeyed.

Jo saw potential in Gerry, in his genuine affection
for animals and in his determination. Her primary concern was that he had not yet developed a healthy fear.
He was still too casual, and with casualness, Jo knew,
came carelessness. When she thought he had progressed
far enough, Jo decided to take him to the next step of
his training.

There was no matinee that day, and the Big Top was
scattered with rehearsing troupers. Jo was dressed in
boots and khakis with a long-sleeved blouse tucked
into the waist. She studied Gerry as she ran the stock

of her whip through her hand. They stood together in the safety cage while she issued instructions.

"All right, Buck's going to let Merlin through the chute. He's the most tractable of the cats, except for Ari." She paused a moment while her eyes grew sad. "Ari isn't up to even a short practice session." She pushed away the depression that threatened and continued. "Merlin knows you, he's familiar with your voice and your scent." Gerry nodded and swallowed. "When we go in, you're to be my shadow. You move when I move, and don't speak until I tell you. If you get frightened, don't run." Jo took his arm for emphasis. "That's *important,* understand? Don't run. Tell me if you want out, and I'll get you to the safety cage."

"I won't run, Jo," he promised and wiped hands, damp with excitement, on his jeans.

"Are you ready?"

Gerry grinned and nodded. "Yeah."

Jo opened the door leading to the big cage and let Gerry through behind her before securing it. She walked to the center of the arena in easy, confident strides. "Let him in, Buck," she called and heard the immediate rattle of bars. Merlin entered without hurry, then leaped onto his pedestal. He yawned hugely before looking at Jo. "A solo today, Merlin," she said as she advanced toward him. "And you're the star. Stay with me," she ordered as Gerry merely stood still and stared at the big cat. Merlin gave Gerry a disinterested glance and waited.

With an upward move of her arm, she sent Merlin into a sit-up. "You know," she told the boy behind her, "that teaching a cat to take his seat is the first trick. The audience won't even consider it one. The sit-up," she continued while signaling Merlin to bring his front paws back down, "is usually next and takes quite a bit of time. It's necessary to strengthen the cat's back muscles first." Again she signaled Merlin to sit up, then, with a quick command, she had him pawing the air and roaring. "Marvelous old ham," she said with a grin and brought him back down. "The primary move of each cue is always given from the same position with the same tone of voice. It takes patience and repetition. I'm going to bring him down off the pedestal now."

Jo flicked the whip against the tanbark, and Merlin leaped down. "Now I maneuver him to the spot in the arena where I want him to lie down." As she moved, Jo made certain her student moved with her. "The cage is a circle, forty feet in diameter. You have to know every inch of it inside your head. You have to know precisely how far you are from the bars at all times. If you back up into the bars, you've got no room to maneuver if there's trouble. It's one of the biggest mistakes a trainer can make." At her signal Merlin laid down, then shifted to his side. "Over, Merlin," she said briskly, sending him into a series of rolls. "Use their names often; it keeps them in tune with you. You have to know each cat and their individual tendencies."

Jo moved with Merlin, then signaled him to stop. When he roared, she rubbed the top of his head with the stock of her whip. "They like to be petted just like house cats, but they are not tabbies. It's essential that you never give them your complete trust and that you remember always to maintain your dominance. You subjugate not by poking them or beating or shouting, which is not only cruel but makes for a mean, undependable cat, but with patience, respect and will. Never humiliate them; they have a right to their pride. You bluff them, Gerry," she said as she raised both arms and brought Merlin up on his hind legs. "Man is the unknown factor. That's why we use jungle-bred rather than captivity-bred cats. Ari is the exception. A cat born and raised in captivity is too familiar with man, so you lose your edge." She moved forward, keeping her arms raised. Merlin followed, walking on his hind legs. He spread seven feet into the air and towered over his trainer. "They might have a sense of affection for you, but there's no fear and little respect. Unfortunately, this often happens if a cat's been with a trainer a long time. They don't become more docile the longer they're in an act, but they become more dangerous. They test you constantly. The trick is to make them believe you're indestructible."

She brought Merlin down, and he gave another yawn before she sent him back to his seat. "If one swipes at you, you have to stop it then and there, because they try again and again, getting closer each time. Usually, if a trainer's hurt in the cage, it's because he's made a mistake. The cats are quick to spot them; sometimes they let them pass, sometimes they don't. This one's given me a good smack on the shoulder now and again. He's kept his claws retracted, but there's always the possibility that one time he'll forget he's just playing. Any questions?"

"Hundreds," Gerry answered, wiping his mouth with the back of his hand. "I just can't focus on one right now."

Jo chuckled and again scratched Merlin's head when he roared. "They'll come to you later. It's hard to absorb anything the first time, but it'll come back to you when you're relaxed again. All right, you know the cue. Make him sit up."

"Me?"

Jo stepped to the side, giving Merlin a clear view of her student. "You can be as scared as you like," she said easily. "Just don't let it show in your voice. Watch his eyes."

Gerry rubbed his palm on the thighs of his jeans, then lifted it as he had seen Jo do hundreds of times. "Up," he told the cat in a passably firm voice.

Merlin studied him a moment, then looked at Jo. This, his eyes told her clearly, was an amateur and beneath his notice. Carefully, Jo kept her face expressionless. "He's testing you," she told Gerry. "He's an old hand and a bit harder to bluff. Be firm and use his name this time."

Gerry took a deep breath and repeated the hand signal. "Up, Merlin."

Merlin glanced back at him, then stared with measuring, amber eyes. "Again," Jo instructed and heard Gerry swallow audibly. "Put some authority into your voice. He thinks you're a pushover."

"Up, Merlin!" Gerry repeated, annoyed enough by Jo's description to put some dominance into his voice. Though his reluctance was obvious, Merlin obeyed. "He did it," Gerry whispered on a long, shaky breath. "He really did it."

"Very good," Jo said, pleased with both the lion and her student. "Now bring him down." When this was accomplished, Jo had him bring Merlin from the seat. "Here." She handed Gerry the whip. "Use the stock to scratch his head. He likes it best just behind the ear." She felt the faint tremble in his hand as he took the whip, but he held it steady, even as Merlin closed his eyes and roared.

Because he had performed well, Jo afforded Merlin the liberty of rubbing against her legs before she called for Buck to let him out. The rattle of the bars was the cat's cue to exit, and like a trouper, he took it with his head held high. "You did very well," she told Gerry when they were alone in the cage.

"It was great." He handed her back the whip, the stock damp from his sweaty palms. "It was just great. When can I do it again?"

Jo smiled and patted his shoulder. "Soon," she promised. "Just remember the things I've told you and come to me when you remember all those questions."

"Okay, thanks, Jo." He stepped through the safety cage. "Thanks a lot. I want to go tell the guys."

"Go ahead." Jo watched him scramble away, leaping over the ring and darting through the back door. With a grin, she leaned against the bars. "Was I like that?" she asked Buck, who stood at the opposite end of the cage.

"The first time you got a cat to sit up on your own, we heard about it for a week. Twelve years old and you thought you were ready for the big show."

Jo laughed, and wiping the damp stock of her whip against her pants, turned. It was then she saw him standing behind her. "Keane!" she used the name she had sworn not to use as pleasure flooded through her. It shone on her face. Just as she had given up hope of seeing him again, he was there. She took two steps toward him before she could check herself. "I didn't know you were back." Jo gripped the stock of the whip with both hands to prevent herself from reaching out to touch him.

"I believe you missed me." His voice was as she remembered, low and smooth.

Jo cursed herself for being so naïve and transparent. "Perhaps I did, a little," she admitted cautiously. "I suppose I'd gotten used to you, and you were gone longer than you said you'd be." He looks the same, she thought rapidly, exactly the same. She reminded herself that it had only been a month. It had seemed like years.

"*Mmm,* yes. I had more to see to than I had expected. You look a bit pale," he observed and touched her cheek with his fingertip.

"I suppose I haven't been getting much sun," she said with quick prevarication. "How was Chicago?" Jo needed to turn the conversation away from personal lines until she had an opportunity to gauge her emotions; seeing him suddenly had tossed them into confusion.

"Cool," he told her, making a long, thorough survey of her face. "Have you ever been there?"

"No. We play near there toward the end of the season, but I've never had time to go all the way into the city."

Nodding absently, Keane glanced into the empty cage behind her. "I see you're training Gerry."

"Yes." Relieved that they had lapsed into a professional discussion, Jo let the muscles of her shoulders ease. "This was the first time with an adult cat and no bars between. He did very well."

Keane looked back at her. His eyes were serious and probing. "He was trembling. I could see it from where I stood watching you."

"It was his first time—" she began in Gerry's defense.

"I wasn't criticizing him," Keane interrupted with a

tinge of impatience. "It's just that he stood beside you, shaking from head to foot, and you were totally cool and in complete control."

"It's my job to be in control," Jo reminded him.

"That lion must have stood seven feet tall when he went up on his hind legs, and you walked under him without any protection, not even the traditional chair."

"I do a picture act," she explained, "not a fighting act."

"Jo," he said so sharply she blinked. "Aren't you ever frightened in there?"

"Frightened?" she repeated, lifting a brow. "Of course I'm frightened. More frightened than Gerry was—or than you would be."

"What are you talking about?" Keane demanded. Jo noted with some curiosity that he was angry. "I could see that boy sweat in there."

"That was mostly excitement," Jo told him patiently. "He hasn't the experience to be truly frightened yet." She tossed back her hair and let out a long breath. Jo did not like to talk of her fears with anyone and found it especially difficult with Keane. Only because she felt it necessary that he understand this to understand the circus did she continue. "Real fear comes from knowing them, working with them, understanding them. You can only speculate on what they can do to a man. I *know*. I know exactly what they're capable of. They have an incredible courage, but more, they have an incredible guile. I've seen what they can do." Her eyes were calm and clear as they looked into his. "My father almost lost a leg once. I was about five, but I remember it perfectly. He made a mistake, and a five-hundred-pound Nubian sunk into his thigh and dragged him around the arena. Luckily, the cat was diverted by a female in season. Cats are unpredictable when they have sex on their minds, which is probably one of the reasons he attacked my father in the first place. They're fiercely jealous once they've set their minds on a mate. My father was able to get into the safety cage before any of the other cats took an interest in him. I can't remember how many stitches he had or how long it was before he could walk properly again, but I do remember the look in that cat's eyes. You learn quickly about fear when you're in the cage, but you control it, you channel it or you find another line of work."

"Then why?" Keane demanded. He took her shoulders before she could turn away. "Why do you do it? And don't tell me because it's your job. That's not good enough."

It puzzled Jo why he seemed angry. His eyes were darkened with temper, and his fingers dug into her shoulders. As if wanting to draw out her answer, he gave her one quick shake. "All right," Jo said slowly, ignoring the ache in her flesh. "That is part of it, but not all. It's all I've ever known, that's part of it, too. It's what I'm good at." While she spoke, she searched his face for a clue to his mood. She wondered if perhaps he had felt it wrong of her to take Gerry into the cage. "Gerry's going to be good at it, too," she told him. "I imagine everyone needs to be good—really good—at something. And I enjoy giving the people who come to see me the best show I can. But over all, I suppose it's because I love them. It's difficult for a layman to understand a trainer's feeling for his animals. I love their intelligence, their really awesome beauty, their strength, the unquenchable streak of wildness that separates them from well-trained horses. They're exciting, challenging and terrifying."

Keane was silent for a moment. She saw that his eyes were still angry, but his fingers relaxed on her shoulders. Jo felt a light throbbing where bruises would certainly show in the morning. "I suppose excitement becomes addicting—difficult to live without once it's become a habit."

"I don't know," Jo replied, grateful that his temper was apparently cooling. "I've never thought about it."

"No, I suppose you'd have little reason to." With a nod, he turned to walk away.

Jo took a step after him. "Keane." His name raced through her lips before she could prevent it. When he turned back to her, she realized she could not ask any of the dozens of questions that flew through her mind. There was only one she felt she had any right to ask. "Have you thought any more about what you're going to do with us...with the circus?"

For an instant she saw temper flare again into his eyes. "No." The word was curt and final. As he turned his back on her again, she felt a spurt of anger and reached for his arm.

"How can you be so callous, so unfeeling?" she demanded. "How is it possible to be so casual when you hold the lives of over a hundred people in your hands?"

Carefully, he removed her hand from his arm. "Don't push me, Jo." There was warning in his eyes and in his voice.

"I'm not trying to," she returned, then ran a frustrated hand through her hair. "I'm only asking you to be fair, to be...kind," she finished lamely.

"Don't ask me anything," he ordered in a brisk, authoritative tone. Jo's chin rose in response. "I'm here," he reminded her. "You'll have to be satisfied with that for now."

Jo battled with her temper. She could not deny that in coming back he had proved himself true to his word. She had the rest of the season if nothing else. "I don't suppose I have any choice," she said quietly.

"No," he agreed with a faint nod. "You don't."

Frowning, Jo watched him stride away in a smooth, fluid gait she was forced to admire. She noticed for the first time that her palms were as damp as Gerry's had been. Annoyed, she rubbed them over her hips.

"Want to talk about it?"

Jo turned quickly to find Jamie behind her in full clown gear. She knew her preoccupation had been deep for her to be caught so completely unaware. "Oh, Jamie, I didn't see you."

"You haven't seen anything but Prescott since you stepped out of the cage," Jamie pointed out.

"What are you doing in makeup?" she asked, skirting his comment.

He gestured toward the dog at her feet. "This mutt won't respond to me unless I'm in my face. Do you want to talk about it?"

"Talk about what?"

"About Prescott, about the way you feel about him."

The dog sat patiently at Jamie's heels and thumped his tail. Casually, Jo stopped and ruffled his gray fur.

"I don't know what you're talking about."

"Look, I'm not saying it can't work out, but I don't want to see you get hurt. I know how it is to be nuts about somebody."

"What in the world makes you think I'm nuts about Keane Prescott?" Jo gave the dog her full attention.

"Hey, it's me, remember?" Jamie took her arm and pulled her to her feet. "Not everybody would've noticed, maybe, but not everybody knows you the way I do. You've been miserable since he went back to Chicago, looking for him in every car that drove on the lot. And just now, when you saw him, you lit up like the midway on Saturday night. I'm not saying there's anything wrong with you being in love with him, but—"

"In love with him?" Jo repeated, incredulous.

"Yeah." Jamie spoke patiently. "In love with him."

Jo stared at Jamie as the realization slid over her. "In love with him," she murmured, trying out the words. "Oh, no." She sighed, closing her eyes. "Oh, no."

"Didn't you have enough sense to figure it out for yourself?" Jamie said gently. Seeing Jo's distress, he ran a hand gently up her arm.

"No, I guess I'm pretty stupid about this sort of thing." Jo opened her eyes and looked around, wondering if the world should look any different. "What am I going to do?"

"Heck, I don't know." Jamie kicked sawdust with an oversized shoe. "I'm not exactly getting rave notices myself in that department." He gave Jo a reassuring pat. "I just wanted you to know that you always have a sympathetic ear here." He grinned engagingly before he turned to walk away, leaving Jo distracted and confused.

Jo spent the rest of the afternoon absorbed with the idea of being in love with Keane Prescott. For a short time she allowed herself to enjoy the sensation, the novel experience of loving someone not as a friend but as a lover. She could feel the light and the power spread through her, as if she had caught the sun in her hand. She daydreamed.

Keane was in love with her. He'd told her hundreds of times as he'd held her under a moonlit sky. He wanted to marry her, he couldn't bear to live without her. She was suddenly sophisticated and worldly enough to deal with the country club set on their own ground. She could exchange droll stories with the wives of other attorneys. There would be children and a house in the country. How would it feel to wake up in the same town every morning? She would learn to cook and give dinner parties. There would be long, quiet evenings when they would be alone together. There would be candlelight and music. When they slept together, his arms would stay around her until morning.

Idiot. Jo dragged herself back sternly. As she and Pete fed the cats, she tried to remember that fairy tales were for children. None of those things are ever going to happen, she reminded herself. I have to figure out how to handle this before I get in any deeper.

"Pete," she began, keeping her voice conversational as she put Abra's quota of raw meat on a long stick. "Have you ever been in love?"

Pete chewed his gum gently, watching Jo hoist the meat through the bars. "Well, now, let's see." Thrusting out his lower lip, he considered. "Only 'bout eight or ten times, I guess. Maybe twelve."

Jo laughed, moving down to the next cage. "I'm serious," she told him. "I mean *really* in love."

"I fall in love easy," Pete confessed gravely. "I'm a pushover for a pretty face. Matter of fact, I'm a pushover for an ugly face." He grinned. "Yes sir, the only thing like being in love is drawing an ace-high flush when the pot's ripe."

Jo shook her head and continued down the line. "Okay, since you're such an expert, tell me what you do when you're in love with a person and the person doesn't love you back and you don't want that person to know that you're in love because you don't want to make a fool of yourself."

"Just a minute." Pete squeezed his eyes tight. "I got to think this one through first." For a moment he was silent as his lips moved with his thoughts. "Okay, let's see if I've got this straight." Opening his eyes, he frowned in concentration. "You're in love—"

"I didn't say *I* was in love," Jo interrupted hastily.

Pete lifted his brows and pursed his lips. "Let's just use *you* in the general sense to avoid confusion," he suggested. Jo nodded, pretending to absorb herself with the feeding of the cats. "So, you're in love, but the guy doesn't love you. First off, you've got to be sure he doesn't."

"He doesn't," Jo murmured, then added quickly, "let's say he doesn't."

Pete shot her a look out of the corner of his eye, then shifted his gum to the other side of his mouth. "Okay, then the first thing you should do is change his mind."

"Change his mind?" Jo repeated, frowning at him.

"Sure." Pete gestured with his hand to show the simplicity of the procedure. "You fall in love with him, then he falls in love with you. You play hard to get, or you play easy to get. Or you play flutter and smile." He demonstrated by coyly batting his lashes and giving a winsome smile. Jo giggled and leaned on the feeding pole. Pete in fielder's cap, white T-shirt and faded jeans was the best show she'd seen all day. "You make him jealous," he continued. "Or you flatter his ego. Girl, there're so many ways to get a man, I can't count them, and I've been gotten by them all. Yes, sir, I'm a real pushover." He looked so pleased with his weakness, Jo smiled. How easy it would be, she thought, if I could take love so lightly.

"Suppose I don't want to do any of those things. Suppose I don't really know how and I don't want to humiliate myself by making a mess of it. Suppose the person isn't—well, suppose nothing could ever work between us, anyway. What then?"

"You got too many supposes," Pete concluded, then shook his finger at her. "And I got one for you. Suppose you ain't too smart because you figure you can't win even before you play."

"Sometimes people get hurt when they play," Jo countered quietly. "Especially if they aren't familiar with the game."

"Hurting's nothing," Pete stated with a sweep of his hand. "Winning's the best, but playing's just fine. This whole big life, it's a game, Jo. You know that. And the rules keep changing all the time. You've got nerve," he continued, then laid his rough, brown hand on her shoulder. "More raw nerve than most anybody I've ever known. You've got brains, too, hungry brains. You going to tell me that with all that, you're afraid to take a chance?"

Meeting his eyes, Jo knew hypothetical evasions would not do. "I suppose I only take calculated risks, Pete. I know my turf; I know my moves. And I know exactly what'll happen if I make a mistake. I take a chance that my body might be clawed, not my emotions. I've never rehearsed for anything like this, and I think playing it cold would be suicide."

"I think you've got to believe in Jo Wilder a little more," Pete countered, then gave her cheek a quick pat.

"Hey, Jo." Looking over, Jo saw Rose approaching. She wore straight-leg jeans, a white peasant blouse and a six-foot boa constrictor over her shoulders.

"Hello, Rose." Jo handed Pete the feeding pole. "Taking Baby out for a walk?"

"He needed some air." Rose gave her charge a pat. "I think he got a little carsick this morning. Does he look peaked to you?"

Jo looked down at the shiny, multicolored skin, then studied the tiny black eyes as Rose held Baby's head up for inspection. "I don't think so," she decided.

"Well, it's a warm day," Rose observed, releasing Baby's head. "I'll give him a bath. That might perk him up."

Jo noticed Rose's eyes darting around the compound. "Looking for Jamie?"

"Hmph." Rose tossed her black curls. "I'm not wasting my time on that one." She stroked the latter half of Baby's anatomy. "I'm indifferent."

"That's another way to do it," Pete put in, giving Jo a nudge. "I forgot about that one. It's a zinger."

Rose frowned at Pete, then at Jo. "What's he talking about?"

With a laugh, Jo sat down on a water barrel. "Catching a man," she told her, letting the warm sun play on her face. "Pete's done a study on it from the male point of view."

"Oh." Rose threw Pete her most disdainful look. "You think I'm indifferent so he'll get interested?"

"It's a zinger," Pete repeated, adjusting his cap. "You get him confused so he starts thinking about you. You make him crazy wondering why you don't notice him."

Rose considered the idea. "Does it usually work?"

"It's got an eighty-seven percent success average," Pete assured her, then gave Baby a friendly pat. "It even works with cats." He jerked his thumb behind him and winked at Jo. "The pretty lady cat, she sits there and stares off into space like she's got important things occupying her mind. The boy in the next cage is doing everything but standing on his head to get her attention. She just gives herself a wash, pretending she doesn't even know he's there. Then, maybe after she's got him banging his head against the bars, she looks over, blinks her big yellow eyes and says, 'Oh, were you talking to me?'" Pete laughed and stretched his back muscles. "He's hooked then, brother, just like a fish on a line."

Rose smiled at the image of Jamie dangling from her own personal line. "Maybe I won't put Baby in Carmen's trailer after all," she murmured. "Oh, look, here comes Duffy and the owner." An inherent flirt, Rose instinctively fluffed her hair. "Really, he is the most handsome man. Don't you think so, Jo?"

Jo's eyes had already locked on Keane's. She seemed helpless to release herself from the gaze. Gripping the edge of the water barrel tightly, she reminded herself not to be a fool. "Yes," she agreed with studied casualness. "He's very attractive."

"Your knuckles are turning white, Jo," Pete muttered next to her ear.

Letting out a frustrated breath, Jo relaxed her hands.

Straightening her spine, she determined to show more restraint. Control, she reminded herself, was the basic tool of her trade. If she could train her emotions and outbluff a dozen lions, she could certainly outbluff one man.

"Hello, Duffy." Rose gave the portly man a quick smile, then turned her attention to Keane. "Hello, Mr. Prescott. It's nice to have you back."

"Hello, Rose." He smiled into her upturned face, then lifted a brow as his eyes slid over the reptile around her neck and shoulders. "Who's your friend?"

"Oh, this is Baby." She patted one of the tan-colored saddle marks on Baby's back.

"Of course." Jo noticed how humor enhanced the gold of his eyes. "Hello, Pete." He gave the handler an easy nod before his gaze shifted and then lingered on Jo.

As on the first day they had met, Keane did not bother to camouflage his stare. His look was cool and assessing. He was reaffirming ownership. It shot through Jo that yes, she was in love with him, but she was also afraid of him. She feared his power over her, feared his capacity to hurt her. Still, her face registered none of her thoughts. Fear, she reminded herself as her eyes remained equally cool on his, was something she understood. Love might cause impossible problems, but fear could be dealt with. She would not cower from him, and she would honor the foremost rule of the arena. She would not turn and run.

Silently, they watched each other while the others looked on with varying degrees of curiosity. There was the barest touch of a smile on Keane's lips. The battle of wills continued until Duffy cleared his throat.

"Ah, Jo."

Calmly, without hurry, she shifted her attention. "Yes, Duffy?"

"I just sent one of the web girls into town to see the local dentist. Seems she's got an abscess. I need you to fill in tonight."

"Sure."

"Just for the web and the opening spectacular," he continued. Unable to prevent himself, he cast a quick look at Keane to see if he was still staring at her. He was. Duffy shifted uncomfortably and wondered what the devil was going on. "Take your usual place in the finale. We'll just be one girl shy in the chorus. Wardrobe'll fix you up."

"Okay." Jo smiled at him, though she was very much aware of Keane's eyes on her. "I guess I'd better go practice walking in those three-inch heels. What position do I take?"

"Number four rope."

"Duffy," Rose chimed in and tugged on his sleeve. "When are you going to let me do the web?"

"Rose, how's a pint-sizer like you going to stand up with that heavy costume on?" Duffy shook his head at her, keeping a respectable distance from Baby. After thirty-five years of working carnies, sideshows and circuses, he still was uneasy around snakes.

"I'm pretty strong," Rose claimed, stretching her spine in the hope of looking taller. "And I've been practicing." Anxious to demonstrate her accomplishments, Rose deftly unwound Baby. "Hold him a minute," she requested and dumped several feet of snake into Keane's arms.

"Ah…" Keane shifted the weight in his arms and

looked dubiously into Baby's bored eyes. "I hope he's eaten recently."

"He had a nice breakfast," Rose assured him, going into a fluid backbend to show Duffy her flexibility.

"Baby won't eat owners," Jo told Keane. She did not bother to suppress her grin. It was the first time she had seen him disconcerted. "Just a stray towner, occasionally. Rose keeps him on a strict diet."

"I assume," Keane began as Baby slithered into a more comfortable position, "that he's aware I'm the owner."

Grinning at Keane's uncomfortable expression, Jo turned to Pete. "Gee, I don't know. Did anybody tell Baby about the new owner?"

"Haven't had a chance, myself," Pete drawled, taking out a fresh stick of gum. "Looks a lot like a towner, too. Baby might get confused."

"They're just teasing you, Mr. Prescott," Rose told him as she finished her impromptu audition with a full split. "Baby doesn't eat people at all. He's docile as a lamb. Little kids come up and pet him during a demonstration." She rose and brushed off her jeans. "Now, you take a cobra…"

"No, thank you," Keane declined, unloading the six-foot Baby back into Rose's arms.

Rose slipped the boa back around her neck. "Well, Duffy, I'm off. What do you say?"

"Get one of the girls to teach you the routine," he said with a nod. "Then we'll see." Smiling, he watched Rose saunter away.

"Hey, Duffy!" It was Jamie. "There's a couple of towners looking for you. I sent them over to the red wagon."

"Fine. I'll just go right on along with you." Duffy winked at Jo before turning to catch up with Jamie's long stride.

Keane was standing very close to the barrels. Jo knew getting down from her perch was risky. She knew, too, however, that her pulse was beginning to behave erratically despite her efforts to control it. "I've got to see about my costume." Nimbly, she came down, intending to skirt around him. Even as her boots touched the ground, his hands took her waist. Exercising every atom of willpower, she neither jerked nor struggled but lifted her eyes calmly to his.

His thumbs moved in a lazy arch. She could feel the warmth through the fabric of her blouse. With her entire being she wished he would not hold her. Then, perversely, she wished he would hold her closer. She struggled not to weaken as her lips grew warm under the kiss of his eyes. Her heart began to hammer in her ears.

Keane ran a hand down the length of her long, thick braid. Slowly, his eyes drifted back to hers. Abruptly, he released her and backed up to let her pass. "You'd best go have wardrobe take a few tucks in that costume."

Deciding she was not meant to decipher his changing moods, Jo stepped by him and crossed the compound. If she spent enough time working, she could keep her thoughts from dwelling on Keane Prescott. Maybe.

Chapter 7

The Big Top was packed for the evening show. Jo watched the anticipation in the range of faces as she took her temporary position in the opening spectacular. The band played jumpy, upbeat music, leaning heavily on brass as the theme parade marched around the hippodrome track. As the substitute Bo Peep, Jo wore a demure mopcap and a wide crinoline skirt and led a baby lamb on a leash. Because her act came so swiftly on the tail of the opening, she rarely participated in the spectacular. Now she enjoyed a close-up look at the audience. In the cage, she blocked them out almost completely.

They were, she decided, a well-mixed group: young babies, older children, parents, grandparents, teenagers. They gave the pageant enthusiastic applause. Jo smiled and waved as she performed the basic choreography with hardly a thought.

After a quick costume change, she took her cue as Queen of the Jungle Cats. After that followed another costume change that transformed her into one of the Twelve Spinning Butterflies.

"Just heard," Jamie whispered in her ear as she took the customary pose by the rope. "You got the job for the next week. Barbara won't be able to handle the teeth grip."

Jo shifted her shoulders to compensate for the weight of her enormous blue wings. "Rose is going to learn the routine," she mumbled back, smiling in the flood of the sunlight. "Duffy's giving her the job if she can stand up under this blasted costume." She made a quick, annoyed sound and smiled brightly. "It weighs a ton."

Slowly, to the beat of the waltz the band played, Jo climbed hand over hand up the rope. "Ah, showbiz," she heard Jamie sigh. She vowed to poke him in the ribs when she took her bow. Then, hooking her foot in the hoop, she began the routine, imitating the other eleven Spinning Butterflies.

She was able to share a cup of coffee with Rose's mother when she returned the butterfly costume to wardrobe and changed into her own white and gold jumpsuit. Her muscles complained a bit due to the unfamiliar weight of the wings, and she gave a passing thought to a long, luxurious bath. That was a dream for September, she reminded herself. Showers were the order of the day on the road.

Jo's last duty in the show was to stand on the head of Maggie, the key elephant in the finale's long mount. Sturdy and dependable, Maggie stood firm while four elephants on each side of her rose on their hind legs, resting their front legs on the back of the one in front.

Atop Maggie's broad head, Jo stood glittering under the lights with both arms lifted in the air. It was here, more than any other part of the show, that the applause washed over her. It merged with the music, the ringmaster's whistle, the laughter of children. Where she had been weary, she was now filled with energy. She knew the fatigue would return, so she relished the power of the moment all the more. For those few seconds there was no work, no long hours, no predawn drives. There was only magic. Even when it was over and she slid from Maggie's back, she could still feel it.

Outside the tent, troupers and roustabouts and shandies mingled. There were anecdotes to exchange, performances to dissect, observations to be made. Gradually, they drifted away alone, in pairs or in groups. Some would change and help strike the tents, some would sleep, some would worry over their performances. Too energized to sleep, Jo planned to assist in the striking of the Big Top.

She switched on a low light as she entered her trailer, then absently braided her hair as she moved to the tiny bath. With quick moves she creamed off her stage makeup. The exotic exaggeration of her eyes was whisked away, leaving the thick fringe of her lashes and the dark green of her irises unenhanced. The soft bloom of natural rose tinted her cheeks again, and her mouth, unpainted, appeared oddly vulnerable. Accustomed to the change, Jo did not see the sharp contrast between Jovilette the performer and the small, somewhat fragile woman in the glittering jumpsuit. With her face naked and the simple braid hanging down her back, the look of the wild, of the gypsy, was less apparent. It remained in her movements, but her face rinsed of all artifice and unframed, was both delicate and young, part ingenue, part flare. But Jo saw none of this as she reached for her front zipper. Before she could pull it down, a knock sounded on her door.

"Come in," she called out and flicked her braid behind her back as she started down the aisle. She stopped in her tracks as Keane stepped through the door.

"Didn't anyone ever tell you to ask who it is first?" He shut the door behind him and locked it with a careless flick of his wrist. "You might not have to lock your door against the circus people," he continued blandly as she remained still, "but there are several dozen curious towners still hanging around."

"I can handle a curious towner," Jo replied. The offhand quality of his dominance was infuriating. "I never lock my door."

There was stiffness and annoyance in her voice. Keane ignored them both. "I brought you something from Chicago."

The casual statement succeeded in throwing Jo's temper off the mark. For the first time, she noticed the small package he carried. "What is it?" she asked.

Keane smiled and crossed to her. "It's nothing that bites," he assured her, then held it out.

Still cautious, Jo lifted her eyes to his, then dropped her gaze back to the package. "It's not my birthday," she murmured.

"It's not Christmas, either," Keane pointed out.

The easy patience in the tone caused Jo to lift her eyes again. She wondered how it was he understood her hesitation to accept presents. She kept her gazed locked on his. "Thank you," she said solemnly as she took the gift.

"You're welcome," Keane returned in the same tone.

The amenities done, Jo recklessly ripped the paper. "Oh! It's Dante," she exclaimed, tearing off the remaining paper and tossing it on the table. With reverence she ran her palm over the dark leather binding. The rich scent drifted to her. She knew her quota of books would have been limited to one a year had she bought a volume so handsomely bound. She opened it slowly, as if to prolong the pleasure. The pages were heavy and rich cream in color. The text was Italian, and even as she glanced over the first page, the words ran fluidly through her mind.

"It's beautiful," she murmured, overcome. Lifting her eyes to thank him again, Jo found Keane smiling down at her. Shyness enveloped her suddenly, all the more intense because she had so rarely experienced it. A lifetime in front of crowds had given her a natural confidence in almost any situation. Now color began to surge into her cheeks, and her mind was a jumble of words that would not come to order.

"I'm glad you like it." He ran a finger down her cheek. "Do you always blush when someone gives you a present?"

Because she was at a loss as to how to answer his question, Jo maneuvered around it. "It was nice of you to think of me."

"It seems to come naturally," Keane replied, then watched Jo's lashes flutter down.

"I don't know what to say." She was able to meet his eyes again with her usual directness, but he had again touched her emotions. She felt inadequate to deal with her feelings or with his effect on her.

"You've already said it." He took the book from Jo's

hand and paged through it. "Of course, I can't read a word of it. I envy you that." Before Jo could ponder the idea of a man like Keane Prescott envying her anything, he looked back up and smiled. Her thoughts scattered like nervous ants. "Got any coffee?" he asked and set the book back down on the table.

"Coffee?"

"Yes, you know, coffee. They grow it in quantity in Brazil."

Jo gave him a despairing look. "I don't have any made. I'd fix you a cup, but I've got to change before I help strike the tents. The cookhouse will still be serving."

Keane lifted a brow as he let his eyes wander over her face. "Don't you think that between Bo Peep, lions and butterflies, you've done enough work tonight? By the way, you make a very appealing butterfly."

"Thank you, but—"

"Let's put it this way," Keane countered smoothly. He took the tip of her braid in his fingers. "You've got the night off. I'll make the coffee myself if you show me where you keep it."

Though she let out a windy sigh, Jo was more amused than annoyed. Coffee, she decided, was the least she could do after he had brought her such a lovely present. "I'll make it," she told him, "but you'll probably wish you'd gone to the cookhouse." With this dubious invitation, Jo turned and headed toward the kitchen. He made no sound, but she knew he followed her. For the first time, she felt the smallness of her kitchen.

Setting an undersized copper kettle on one of the two burners, Jo flicked on the power. It was a simple matter to keep her back to him while she plucked cups from the cupboard. She was well aware that if she turned around in the compact kitchen, she would all but be in his arms.

"Did you watch the whole show?" she asked conversationally as she pulled out a jar of instant coffee.

"Duffy had me working props," Keane answered. "He seems to be making me generally useful."

Amused, Jo twisted her head to grin at him. Instantly, she discovered her misstep in strategy. Keane's face was only inches from hers, and in his eyes she read his thoughts. He wanted her, and he intended to have her. Before she could shift her position, Keane took her shoulders and turned her completely around. Jo knew she had backed up against the bars.

Leisurely, he began to loosen her hair, working his fingers through it until it pooled over her shoulders. "I've wanted to do that since the first time I saw you. It's hair to get lost in." His voice was soft as he took a generous handful. The gesture itself seemed to stake his claim. "In the sun it shimmers with red lights, but in the dark it's like night itself." It came to her that each time she was close to him, she was less able to resist him. She became more lost in his eyes, more beguiled by his power. Already her mouth tingled with the memory of his kiss, with the longing for a new one. Behind them the kettle began a feverish whistle.

"The water," she managed and tried to move around him. With one hand in her hair, Keane kept her still as he turned off the burner. The whistle sputtered peevishly, then died. The sound echoed in Jo's head.

"Do you want coffee?" he murmured as his fingers trailed to her throat.

Jo's eyes clung to his. Hers were enormous and direct, his quiet and searching. "No," she whispered, knowing she wanted nothing more at that moment than to belong to him. He circled her throat with his hand and pressed his fingers against her pulse. It fluttered wildly.

"You're trembling." He could feel the light tremor of her body as he brought her closer. "Is it fear?" he demanded as his thumbs brushed over her lips. "Or excitement?"

"Both," she answered in a voice thickened with emotion. She made a tiny, confused sound as his palm covered her heart. Its desperate thudding increased. "Are you..." She stopped a moment because her voice was breathless and unsteady. "Are you going to make love to me?" Did his eyes really darken? she wondered dizzily. Or is it my imagination?

"Beautiful Jovilette," he murmured as his mouth lowered to hers. "No pretentions, no evasions...irresistible." The quality of the kiss altered swiftly. His mouth was hungry on hers, and her response leaped past all caution. If loving him was madness, her heart reasoned, could making love take her further beyond sanity? Past wisdom and steeped in sensation, she let her heart rule her will. When her lips parted under his, it was not in surrender but in equal demand.

Keane gentled the kiss. He kept her shimmering on the razor's edge of passion. His mouth teased, promised, then fed her growing need. He found the zipper at the base of her throat and pulled it downward slowly. Her skin was warm, and he sought it, giving a low sound of pleasure as her breast swelled under his hand. He explored without hurry, as if memorizing each curve and plane. Jo no longer trembled but became pliant as her body moved to the rhythm he set. Her sigh was spontaneous, filled with wonder and delight.

With a suddenness that took her breath away, Keane crushed her mouth beneath his in fiery urgency. Jo's instincts responded, thrusting her into a world she had only imagined. His hands grew rougher, more insistent. Jo realized he had relinquished control. They were both riding on the tossing waves of passion. This sea had no horizon and no depth. It was a drowning sea that pulled the unsuspecting under while promising limitless pleasure. Jo did not resist but dove deeper.

At first she thought the knocking was only the sound of her heart against her ribs. When Keane drew away, she murmured in protest and pulled him back. Instantly, his mouth was avid, but as the knocking continued, he swore and pulled back again.

"Someone's persistent," he muttered. Bewildered, Jo stared up at him. "The door," he explained on a long breath.

"Oh." Flustered, Jo ran a hand through her hair and tried to collect her wits.

"You'd better answer it," Keane suggested as he pulled the zipper to her throat in one quick move. Jo broke the surface into reality abruptly. For a moment Keane watched her, taking in her flushed cheeks and tousled hair before he moved aside. Willing her legs to carry her, Jo walked to the front of the trailer. The door handle resisted, then she remembered that Keane had locked it, and she turned the latch.

"Yes, Buck?" she said calmly enough when she opened the door to her handler.

"Jo." His face was in shadows, but she heard the distress in the single syllable. Her chest tightened. "It's Ari."

He had barely finished the name before Jo was out

of the trailer and running across the compound. She found both Pete and Gerry standing near Ari's cage.

"How bad?" she demanded as Pete came to meet her. He took her shoulders. "Really bad this time, Jo."

For a moment she wanted to shake her head, to deny what she read in Pete's eyes. Instead, she nudged him aside and walked to Ari's cage. The old cat lay on his side as his chest lifted and fell with the effort of breathing. "Open it," she ordered Pete in a voice that revealed nothing. There was the jingle of keys, but she did not turn.

"You're not going in there." Jo heard Keane's voice and felt a restraining grip on her shoulders. Her eyes were opaque as she looked up at him.

"Yes, I am. Ari isn't going to hurt me or anyone else. He's just going to die. Now leave me alone." Her voice was low and toneless. "Open it," she ordered again, then pulled out of Keane's loosened hold. The bars rattled as he slid the door open. Hearing it, Jo turned, then hoisted herself into the cage.

Ari barely stirred. Jo saw, as she knelt beside him, that his eyes were open. They were glazed with weariness and pain. "Ari," she sighed, seeing there would be no tomorrow for him. His only answer was a hollow wheezing. Putting a hand to his side, she felt the ragged pace of his breathing. He made an effort to respond to her touch, to his name, but managed only to shift his great head on the floor. The gesture tore at Jo's heart. She lowered her face to his mane, remembering him as he had once been: full of strength and a terrifying beauty. She lifted her face again and took one long, steadying breath. "Buck." She heard him approach but kept her eyes on Ari. "Get the medical kit.

I want a hypo of pentobarbital." She could feel Buck's brief hesitation before he spoke.

"Okay, Jo."

She sat quietly, stroking Ari's head. In the distance were the sounds of the Big Top going down, the call of men, the rattle of rigging, the clang of wood against metal. An elephant trumpeted, and three cages down, Faust roared half-heartedly in response.

"Jo." She turned her head as Buck called her and pushed her hair from her eyes. "Let me do it."

Jo merely shook her head and held out her hand.

"Jo." Keane stepped up to the bars. His voice was gentle, but his eyes were so like the cat's at her knees, Jo nearly sobbed aloud. "You don't have to do this yourself."

"He's my cat," she responded dully. "I said I'd do it when it was time. It's time." Her eyes shifted to Buck. "Give me the hypo, Buck. Let's get it done." When the syringe was in her hand, Jo stared at it, then closed her fingers around it. Swallowing hard, she turned back to Ari. His eyes were on her face. After more than twenty years in captivity there was still something not quite tamed in the dying cat. But she saw trust in his eyes and wanted to weep. "You were the best," she told him as she passed a hand through his mane. "You were always the best." Jo felt a numbing cold settling over her and prayed it would last until she had finished. "You're tired now. I'm going to help you sleep." She pulled the safety from the point of the hypodermic and waited until she was certain her hands were steady. "This won't hurt, nothing is going to hurt you anymore."

Involuntarily, Jo rubbed the back of her hand over her mouth, then, moving quickly, she plunged the needle into Ari's shoulder. A quiet whimper escaped her as she emptied the syringe. Ari made no sound but continued to watch her face. Jo offered no words of comfort but sat with him, methodically stroking his fur as his eyes grew cloudy. Gradually, the effort of his breathing lessened, becoming quieter and quieter until it wasn't there at all. Jo felt him grow still, and her hand balled into a fist inside the mass of his mane. One quick, convulsive shudder escaped her. Steeling herself, she moved from the cage, closing the door behind her. Because her bones felt fragile, she kept them stiff, as though they might shatter. Even as she stepped back to the ground, Keane took her arm and began to lead her away.

"Take care of things," he said to Buck as they moved past.

"No." Jo protested, trying and failing to free her arm. "I'll do it."

"No, you won't." Keane's tone held a quiet finality. "Enough's enough."

"Don't tell me what to do," she said sharply, letting her grief take refuge in anger.

"I *am* telling you," he pointed out. His hand was firm on her arm.

"You *can't* tell me what to do," she insisted as tears rose treacherously in her throat. "I want you to leave me alone."

Keane stopped, then took her by the shoulders. His eyes caught the light of a waning moon. "There's no way I'm going to leave you alone when you're so upset."

"My emotions have nothing to do with you." Even as she spoke, he took her arm again and pulled her toward her trailer. Jo wanted desperately to be alone to weep out her grief in private. The mourning belonged to her, and the tears were personal. As if her protests were nonexistent, he pulled her into the trailer and closed the door behind them. "Will you get out of here?" she demanded, frantically swallowing tears.

"Not until I know you're all right." Keane's answer was calm as he walked back to the kitchen.

"I'm perfectly all right." Her breath shuddered in and out quickly. "Or I will be when you leave me alone. You have no right to poke your nose in my business."

"So you've told me before," Keane answered mildly from the back of the trailer.

"I just did what had to be done." She held her body rigid and fought against her own quick, uneven breathing. "I put a sick animal out of his misery; it's as simple as that." Her voice broke, and she turned away, hugging her arms. "For heaven's sake, Keane, go away!"

Quietly, he walked back to her carrying a glass of water. "Drink this."

"No." She whirled back to him. Tears spilled out of her eyes and trickled down her cheeks despite her efforts to banish them. Hating herself, she pressed the heel of her hand between her brows and closed her eyes. "I don't want you here." Keane set down the glass, then gathered her into his arms. "No, don't. I don't want you to hold me."

"Too bad." He ran a hand gently up and down her back. "You did a very brave thing, Jo. I know you loved Ari. I know how hard it was to let him go. You're hurting, and I'm not leaving you."

"I don't want to cry in front of you." Her fists were tight balls at his shoulders.

"Why not?" The stroking continued up and down her back as he cradled her head in the curve of his shoulder.

"Why won't you let me be?" she sobbed as her control slipped. Her fingers gripped his shirt convulsively. "Why am I always losing what I love?" She let the grief come. She let his arms soothe her. As desperately as she had protested against it, she clung to his offer of comfort.

She made no objection as he carried her to the couch and cradled her in his arms. He stroked her hair, as she had stroked Ari, to ease the pain of what couldn't be changed. Slowly, her sobbing quieted. Still she lay with her cheek against his chest, with her hair curtaining her face.

"Better?" he asked as the silence grew calmer. Jo nodded, not yet trusting her voice. Keane shifted her as he reached for the glass of water. "Drink this now."

Gratefully, Jo relieved her dry throat, then went without resistance back against his chest. She closed her eyes, thinking it had been a very long time since she had been held in anyone's lap and soothed. "Keane," she murmured. She felt his lips brush over the top of her head.

"Hmm?"

"Nothing." Her voice thickened as she drifted toward sleep. "Just Keane."

Chapter 8

Jo felt the sun on her closed lids. There was the summer morning sound of excited birds. Her mind, levitating slowly toward the surface, told her it must be Monday. Only on Monday would she sleep past sunrise. That was the enroute day, the only day in seven the circus held no show. She thought lazily of getting up. She would set aside two hours for reading. Maybe I'll drive into town and see a movie. What town are we in? With a sleepy sigh she rolled onto her stomach.

I'll give the cats a good going over, maybe hose them down if it gets hot enough. Memory flooded back and snapped her awake. *Ari.* Opening her eyes, Jo rolled onto her back and stared at the ceiling. Now she recalled vividly how the old cat had died with his eyes trusting on her face. She sighed again. The sadness was still there, but not the sharp, desperate grief of the night before. Acceptance was settling in. She realized that Keane's insistence on staying with her during the peak of her mourning had helped her. He had given her someone to rail at, then someone to hold on to. She remembered the incredible comfort of being cradled in his lap, the solid dependability of his chest against her cheek. She had fallen asleep with the sound of his heart in her ear.

Turning her head, Jo looked out the window, then at the patch of white light the sun tossed on the floor. But it isn't Monday, she remembered suddenly. It's Thursday. Jo sat up, pushing at her hair, which seemed to tumble everywhere at once. What was she doing in bed on a Thursday when the sun was up? Without giving herself time to work out the answer, she scrambled out of bed and hurried from the room. She gave a soft gasp as she ran headlong into Keane.

His hand ran down the length of her hair before he took her shoulder. "I heard you stirring," he said easily, looking down into her stunned face.

"What are you doing here?"

"Making coffee," he answered as he gave her a critical study. "Or I was a moment ago. How are you?"

"I'm all right." Jo lifted her hand to her temple as if to gain her bearings. "I'm a bit disoriented, I suppose. I overslept. It's never happened before."

"I gave you a sleeping pill," Keane told her matter-of-factly. He slipped an arm around her shoulder as he turned back to the kitchen.

"A pill?" Jo's eyes flew to his. "I don't remember taking a pill."

"It was in the water you drank." On the stove the kettle began its piercing whistle. Moving to it, Keane finished making the coffee. "I had my doubts as to whether you'd take it voluntarily."

"No, I wouldn't have," Jo agreed with some annoyance. "I've never taken a sleeping pill in my life."

"Well, you did last night." He held out a mug of coffee. "I sent Gerry for it while you were in the cage with Ari." Again he gave her a quick, intense study. "It didn't seem to do you any harm. You went out like a light. I carried you to bed, changed your clothes—"

"Changed my..." All at once Jo became aware that she wore only a thin white nightshirt. Her hand reached instinctively for the top button that nestled just above her bosom. Thinking hard, she found she could recall nothing beyond falling asleep in his arms.

"I don't think you'd have spent a very comfortable night in your costume," Keane pointed out. Enjoying his coffee, he smiled at the nervous hand she held between her breasts. "I've had a certain amount of experience undressing women in the dark." Jo dropped her hand. It was an unmistakable movement of pride. Keane's eyes softened. "You needed a good night's sleep, Jo. You were worn out."

Without speaking, Jo lifted her coffee to her lips and turned away. Walking to the window, she could see that the backyard was deserted. Her sleep must indeed have been deep to have kept her unaware of camp breaking.

"Everyone's gone but a couple of roustabouts and a generator truck. They'll take off when you don't need power anymore."

The vulnerability Jo felt was overwhelming. Several times in the course of the evening before, she had lost control, which had always been an essential part of her. Each time, it had been Keane who had been there.

She wanted to be angry with him for intruding on her privacy but found it impossible. She had needed him, and he had known it.

"You didn't have to stay behind," she said, watching a crow swoop low over the ground outside.

"I wasn't certain you'd be in any shape to drive fifty miles this morning. Pete's driving my trailer."

Her shoulders lifted and fell before she turned around. Sunlight streamed through the window at her back and poured through the thin folds of her night-shirt. Her body was a slender shadow. When she spoke, her voice was low with regret. "I was horribly rude to you last night."

Keane shrugged and lifted his coffee. "You were upset."

"Yes." Her eyes were an open reflection of her sorrow. "Ari was very important to me. I suppose he was an ongoing link with my father, with my childhood. I'd known for some time he wouldn't make it through the season, but I didn't want to face it." She looked down at the mug she held gripped in both hands. A faint wisp of steam rose from it and vanished. "Last night was a relief for him. It was selfish of me to wish it otherwise. And I was wrong to strike out at you the way I did. I'm sorry."

"I don't want your apology, Jo." Because he sounded annoyed, she looked up quickly.

"I'd feel better if you'd take it, Keane. You've been very kind."

To her astonishment, he swore under his breath and turned back to the stove. "I don't care for your gratitude any more than your apology." He set down his mug and poured in more coffee. "Neither of them is necessary."

"They are to me," Jo replied, then took a step toward

him. "Keane…" She set down her coffee and touched his arm. When he turned, she let impulse guide her. She rested her head on his shoulder and slipped her arms around his waist. He stiffened, putting his hands to her shoulders as if to draw her away. Then she heard his breath come out in a long sigh as he relaxed. For an instant he brought her closer.

"I never know precisely what to expect from you," he murmured. He lifted her chin with his finger. In automatic response, Jo closed her eyes and offered her mouth. She felt his fingers tighten on her skin before his lips brushed hers lightly. "You'd better go change." His manner was friendly but cool as he stepped away. "We'll stop off in town, and I'll buy you some breakfast."

Puzzled by his attitude but satisfied he was no longer annoyed, Jo nodded. "All right."

Spring became summer as the circus wound its way north. The sun stayed longer, peeking into the Big Top until well after the evening show began. Heavy rain came infrequently, but there were quick summer storms with thunder and lightning. Through June, Prescott's Circus Colossus snaked through North Carolina and into western Tennessee.

During the long weeks while spring tripped over into summer, Jo found Keane's attitude a paradox. His friendliness toward her was offhand. He laughed if she said something amusing, listened if she had a complaint and to her confusion, slipped a thin barrier between them. At times she wondered if the passion that had flared between them the night he had returned from Chicago had truly existed. Had the desire she had tasted on his lips been a fantasy? The closeness she had felt blooming between them had withered and blown away. They were only owner and trouper now.

Keane flew back to Chicago twice more during this period, but he brought no surprise presents back with him. Not once during those long weeks did he come by her trailer. Initially, his altered manner confused her. He was not angry. His mood was neither heated nor icy with temper but fell into an odd middle ground she could not understand. Jo ached with love. As days passed into weeks, she was forced to admit that Keane did not seem to be interested in a close relationship.

On the eve of the July Fourth show, Jo sat sleepless in her bed. In her hand she held the volume of Dante, but the book was only a reminder of the emptiness she felt. She closed it, then stared at the ceiling. It's time to snap out of it, she lectured herself. It's time to stop pretending he was ever really part of my life. Loving someone only makes him a part of your wishes. He never talked about love, he never promised anything, never offered anything but what he gave to me. He's done nothing to hurt me. Jo squeezed her eyes shut and pressed the book between her fingers. How I wish I could hate him for showing me what life could be like and then turning away, she thought.

But I can't. Jo let out a shaky breath and relaxed her grip on the book. Gently, she ran a finger down its smooth, leather binding. I can't hate him, but I can't love him openly, either. How do I stop? I should be grateful he stopped wanting me. I would have made love with him. Then I'd hurt a hundred times more. Could I hurt a hundred times more? For several moments she lay still, trying to quiet her thoughts.

It's best not to know, she told herself sternly. It's best to remember he was kind to me when I needed him and that I haven't a right to make demands. Summer doesn't last forever. I may never see him again when it's over. At least I can keep the time we have pleasant.

The words sounded hollow in her heart.

Chapter 9

The Fourth of July was a full day with a run to a new lot, the tent raising, a street parade and two shows. But it was a holiday. Elephants wore red, white and blue plumes atop their massive heads. The evening performance would be held an hour earlier to allow for the addition of a fireworks display. Traditionally, Prescott's circus arranged to spend the holiday in the same small town in Tennessee. The license and paperwork for the display were seen to in advance, and the fireworks were shipped ahead to be stored in a warehouse. The procedure had been precisely the same for years. It was one of the circus's most profitable nights. Concessions thrived.

Jo moved through the day with determined cheerfulness. She refused to permit the distance between her and Keane to spoil one of the highlights of the summer. Brooding, she decided, would not change things. The mood of the crowd helped to keep her spirits light.

Between shows came the inevitable lull. Some troupers sat outside their trailers exchanging small talk and enjoying the sun. Others got in a bit more practice or worked out a few kinks. Bull hands washed down the elephants, causing a minor flood in the pen area.

Jo watched the bathing process with amusement. She never ceased to enjoy this particular aspect of circus life, especially if there were one or two inexperienced bull hands involved. Invariably, Maggie or one of the other veteran bulls would spray a trunkful of water over the new hands to initiate them. Though Jo knew the other hands encouraged it, they always displayed remarkable innocence.

Spotting Duffy, Jo moved away from the elephant area and wandered toward him. She could see he was deep in discussion with a towner. He was as short as Duffy but wider, with what she had once heard Frank call a successful frame. His stomach started high and barreled out to below his waist. He had a ruddy complexion and pale eyes that squinted hard against the sun. Jo had seen his type before. She wondered what he was selling and how much he wanted for it. Since Duffy was puffing with annoyance, Jo assumed it was quite a lot.

"I'm telling you, Carlson, we've already paid for storage. I've got a signed receipt. And we pay fifteen bucks delivery, not twenty."

Carlson was smoking a small, unfiltered cigarette and dropped it to the ground. "You paid Myers for storage, not me. I bought the place six weeks ago." He shrugged his wide shoulders. "Not my problem you paid in advance."

Looking over, Jo saw Keane approaching with Pete. Pete was talking rapidly, Keane nodding. As Jo watched, Keane glanced up and gave Carlson a quick study. She had seen that look before and knew the older man had been assessed. Keane caught her eye, smiled and began to move past her. "Hello, Jo."

Unashamedly curious, Jo fell into step beside him. "What's going on?"

"Why don't we find out?" he suggested as they stopped in front of Duffy and Carlson. "Gentlemen," Keane said in an easy tone. "Is there a problem?"

"This character," Duffy spouted, jerking a scornful thumb at Carlson's face, "wants us to pay twice for storage on the fireworks. Then he wants twenty for delivery when we agreed on fifteen."

"Myers agreed on fifteen," Carlson pointed out. He smiled without humor. "I didn't agree on anything. You want your fireworks, you gotta pay for them first—cash," he added, then spared Keane a glance. "Who's this guy?"

Duffy began to wheeze with indignation, but Keane laid a restraining hand on his shoulder. "I'm Prescott," he told him in untroubled tones. "Perhaps you'd like to fill me in."

"Prescott, huh?" Carlson stroked both his chins as he studied Keane. Seeing youth and amiable eyes, he felt closer to success. "Well, now we're getting somewhere," he said jovially and stuck out his hand. Keane accepted it without hesitation. "Jim Carlson," he continued as he gave Keane's hand a brisk pump. "Nice circus you got here, Prescott. Me and the missus see it every year. Well, now," he said again and hitched up his belt. "Seeing as you're a businessman, too, I'm sure we can straighten all this out. Problem is, your fireworks've been stored in my warehouse. Now, I gotta make a living, they can't just sit there for free. I bought the place off Myers six weeks ago. I can't be held responsible for a deal you made with him, can I?" Carlson gave a stretched-lip smile, pleased that Keane listened so politely. "And as for delivery, well…" He made a helpless gesture and patted Keane's shoulder. "You know about gas prices these days, son. But we can work that out after we settle this other little problem."

Keane nodded agreeably. "That sounds reasonable." He ignored Duffy's huffing and puffing. "You do seem to have a problem, Mr. Carlson."

"I don't have a problem," Carlson countered. His smile suffered a fractional slip. "You've got the problem, unless you don't want the fireworks."

"Oh, we'll have the fireworks, Mr. Carlson," Keane corrected with a smile Jo thought more wolfish than friendly. "According to paragraph three, section five, of the small business code, the lessor is legally bound by all contracts, agreements, liens and mortgages of the previous lessor until such time as all aforesaid contracts, agreements, liens and mortgages are expired or transferred."

"What the…" Carlson began with no smile at all, but Keane continued blandly.

"Of course, we won't pursue the matter in court as long as we get our merchandise. But that doesn't solve your problem."

"My problem?" Carlson sputtered while Jo looked on in frank admiration. "I haven't got a problem. If you think…"

"Oh, but you do, Mr. Carlson, though I'm sure there was no intent to break the law on your part."

"Break the law?" Carlson wiped damp hands on his slacks.

"Storing explosives without a license," Keane pointed out. "Unless, of course, you obtained one after your purchase of the warehouse."

"Well, no, I..."

"I was afraid of that." Keane lifted his brow in pity. "You see, in paragraph six of section five of the small business code it states that all licenses, permits and warrants shall be nontransferable. Authorization for new licenses, permits or warrants must be requested in writing by the current owner. Notarized, naturally." Keane waited a bit to allow Carlson to wrestle with the idea. "If I'm not mistaken," he continued conversationally, "the fine's pretty hefty in this state. Of course, sentencing depends on—"

"Sentencing?" Carlson paled and mopped the back of his neck with a handkerchief.

"Look, tell you what." Keane gave Carlson a sympathetic smile. "You get the fireworks over here and off your property. We don't have to bring the law in on something like this. Just an oversight, after all. We're both businessmen, aren't we?"

Too overwrought to detect sarcasm, Carlson nodded.

"That was fifteen on delivery, right?"

Carlson didn't hesitate but stuck the damp handkerchief back in his pocket and nodded again.

"Good enough. I'll have the cash for you on delivery. Glad to help you out."

Relieved, Carlson turned and headed for his pickup. Jo managed to keep her features grave until he pulled off the lot. Simultaneously, Pete and Duffy began to hoot with laughter.

"Was it true?" Jo demanded and took Keane's arm.

"Was what true?" Keane countered, merely lifting a brow over the hysterics that surrounded him.

"'Paragraph three, section five, of the small business code,'" Jo quoted.

"Never heard of it," Keane answered mildly, nearly sending Pete into orbit.

"You made it up," Jo said in wonder. "You made it all up!"

"Probably," Keane agreed.

"Smoothest con job I've seen in years," Duffy stated and gave Keane a parental slap on the back. "Son, you could go into business."

"I did," Keane told him and grinned.

"I ever need a lawyer," Pete put in, pushing his cap further back on his head, "I know where to go. You come on by the cookhouse tonight, Captain. We're having ourselves a poker game. Come on, Duffy, Buck's gotta hear about this."

As they moved off, Jo realized that Keane had been officially accepted. Before, he had been the legal owner but an outsider, a towner. Now he was one of them. Turning, she lifted her face to his. "Welcome aboard."

"Thank you." She saw he understood precisely what had been left unsaid.

"I'll see you at the game," she said before her smile became a grin. "Don't forget your money."

She turned away, but Keane touched her arm, bringing her back to him. "Jo," he began, puzzling her by the sudden seriousness of his eyes.

"Yes?"

There was a brief hesitation, then he shook his head. "Nothing, never mind. I'll see you later." He rubbed his knuckles over her cheek, then walked away.

Jo studied her hand impassively. On the deal, she had missed a heart flush by one card and now waited for someone to open. Casually, she moved her glance around the table. Duffy was puffing on a cigar, apparently unconcerned with the dwindling chips in front of him. Pete chewed his gum with equal nonchalance. Amy, the wife of the sword swallower, sat beside him, then Jamie, then Raoul. Directly beside Jo was Keane, who, like Pete, was winning consistently.

The pot grew. Chips clinked on the table. Jo discarded and was pleased to exchange a club for the fifth heart. She slipped it into her hand without blinking. Frank had taught her the game. Before the second round of betting, Jamie folded in disgust. "Should never have taken Buck's seat," he muttered and frowned when Pete raised the bet.

"You got out cheap, kiddo," Duffy told him dolefully as he tossed in chips. "I'm only staying in so I don't change my standard of living. Money'll do that to you," he mumbled obscurely.

"Three kings," Pete announced when called, then spread his cards. Amid a flutter of complaints cards were tossed down.

"Heart flush," Jo said mildly before Pete could rake in the pot. Duffy leaned back and gave a hoot of laughter.

"Atta, girl, Jo. I hate to see him win all my money."

During the next two hours the cookhouse tent grew hot and ripe with the scents of coffee and tobacco and beer. Jamie's luck proved so consistently poor that he called for Buck to relieve him.

Jo found herself with an indifferent pair of fives. Almost immediately the betting grew heavy as Keane raised Raoul's opening. Curiosity kept Jo in one round, but practicality had her folding after the draw. Divorced from the game, she watched it with interest. Leaning on her elbows, she studied each participant. Keane played a good game, she mused. His eyes gave nothing away. They never did. Casually, he nursed the beer beside him while Duffy, Buck and Amy folded. Studying him closely, Pete chewed his gum. Keane returned the look, keeping the stub of his cigar clamped between his teeth. Raoul muttered in French and scowled at his cards.

"Could be bluffing," Pete considered, seeing Keane's raise. "Let's raise it five more and see what's cooking." Raoul swore in French, then again in English, before he tossed in his hand. Taking his time, Keane counted out the necessary chips and tossed them into the pot. It was a plastic mountain of red, white and blue. Then, he counted out more.

"I'll see your five," he said evenly, "and raise it ten."

There was mumbling around the table. Pete looked into his hand and considered. Shifting his eyes, he took in the generous pile of chips in front of him. He could afford to risk another ten. Glancing up, he studied Keane's face while he fondled his chips. Abruptly, he broke into a grin.

"Nope," he said simply, turning his cards face down. "This one's all yours."

Setting down his cards, Keane raked in a very sweet pot. "Gonna show 'em?" Pete asked. His grin was affable.

Keane pushed a stray chip into the pile and shrugged. With his free hand he turned over the cards. The reaction ranged from oaths to laughter.

"Trash," Pete mumbled with a shake of his head. "Nothing but trash. You've got nerve, Captain." His grin grew wide as he turned over his own cards. "Even I had a pair of sevens."

Raoul gnashed his teeth and swore elegantly in two languages. Jo grinned at his imaginative choice of words. She rose on a laugh and snatched off the soft felt hat Jamie wore. Deftly, she scooped her chips into it. "Cash me in later," she requested, then gave him a smacking kiss on the mouth. "But don't play with them."

Duffy scowled over at her. "Aren't you cashing in early?"

"You've always told me to leave 'em wanting more," she reminded him. With a grin and a wave, she swung through the door.

"That Jo," said Raoul, chuckling as he shuffled the cards. "She's one smart cracker."

"Cookie," Pete corrected, opening a fresh stick of gum. He noticed that Keane's gaze had drifted to the door she had closed behind her. "Some looker, too," he commented and watched Keane's eyes wander back to his. "Don't you think, Captain?"

Keane slipped his cards into a pile as they were dealt to him. "Jo's lovely."

"Like her mother," Buck put in, frowning at his cards. "She was a beaut, huh, Duffy?" Duffy grunted in agreement and wondered why Lady Luck refused to smile on him. "Always thought it was a crime for her to die that way. Wilder, too," he added with a shake of his head.

"A fire, wasn't it?" Keane asked as he picked up his cards and spread them.

"Electrical fire." Buck nodded and lifted his beer. "A short in their trailer's wiring. What a waste. If they hadn't been in bed asleep, they'd probably still be alive. The trailer was halfway gone before anybody set up an alarm. Just plain couldn't get to the Wilders. Their side of the trailer was like a furnace. Jo's bedroom was on the other side, and we nearly lost her. Frank busted in the window and pulled her out. Poor little tyke. She was holding onto this old doll like it was the last thing she had left. Kept it with her for I don't know how long. Remember, Duffy?" He glanced into his hand and opened for two. "It only had one arm." Duffy grunted again and folded. "Frank sure knew how to handle that little girl."

"She knew how to handle him, more likely," Duffy mumbled. Raoul bumped the pot five, and Keane folded.

"Deal me out the next hand," he said as he rose and moved to the door. One of the Gribalti brothers took the chair Jo had vacated, and Jamie slipped into Keane's. Curious, he lifted the tip of the cards. He saw a jack-high straight. With a thoughtful frown, he watched the door swing shut.

Outside, Jo moved through the warm night. With a glance at the sky, she thought of the fireworks. They had been wonderful, she mused, stirring up the stars with exploding color. Though it was over and a new day hovered, she felt some magic remained in the night. Far from sleepy, she wandered toward the Big Top.

"Hello, pretty lady."

Jo looked into the shadows and narrowed her eyes. She could just barely make out a form. "Oh, you're

Bob, aren't you?" She stopped and gave him a friendly smile. "You're new."

He stepped toward her. "I've been on for nearly three weeks." He was young, Jo guessed about her own age, with a solid build and sharp-featured face. Just that afternoon she had watched Maggie give him a shower.

Jo pushed her hands into the pockets of her cut-offs and continued to smile. It appeared he thought his tenure made him a veteran. "How do you like working with the elephants?"

"It's okay. I like putting up the tent."

Jo understood his feeling. "So do I. There's a game in the cookhouse," she told him with a gesture of her arm. "You might like to sit in."

"I'd rather be with you." As he moved closer, Jo caught the faint whiff of beer. He's been celebrating, she thought and shook her head.

"It's a good thing tomorrow's Monday," she commented. "No one's going to be in any shape to pitch a tent. You should go to bed," she suggested. "Or get some coffee."

"Let's go to your trailer." Bob weaved a little, then took her arm.

"No." Firmly, Jo turned in the opposite direction. "Let's go to the cookhouse." His advances did not trouble her. She was close enough to the cookhouse tent that if she called out, a dozen able-bodied men would come charging. But that was precisely what Jo wanted to avoid.

"I want to go with you," he said, stumbling over the words as he veered away from the cookhouse again. "You look so pretty in that cage with those lions." He put both arms around her, but Jo felt it was as much for balance as romance. "A fella needs a pretty lady once in a while."

"I'm going to feed you to my lions if you don't let me go," Jo warned.

"Bet you can be a real wildcat," he mumbled and made a fumbling dive for her mouth.

Though her patience was wearing thin, Jo endured the kiss that landed slightly to the left of bull's-eye. His hands, however, had better aim and grabbed the firm roundness of her bottom. Losing her temper, Jo pushed away but found his hold had taken root. In a quick move, she brought up her fist and caught him square on the jaw. With only a faint sound of surprise, Bob sat down hard on the ground.

"Well, so much for rescuing you," Keane commented from behind her.

Turning quickly, Jo pushed at her hair and gave an annoyed sigh. She would have preferred no witnesses. Even in the dim light, she could see he was furious. Instinctively, she stepped between him and the man who sat on the ground fingering his jaw and shaking the buzzing from his ears.

"He—Bob just got a bit overenthusiastic," she said hastily and put a restraining hand on Keane's arm. "He's been celebrating."

"I'm feeling a bit enthusiastic myself," Keane stated. As he made to brush her aside, Jo clung with more fervor.

"No, Keane, please."

Looking down, he fired a glare. "Jo, would you let go so that I can deal with this?"

"Not until you listen." The faint hint of laughter in her eyes only enraged him further, and Jo fought to suppress it. "Keane, please, don't be hard on him. He didn't hurt me."

"He was attacking you," Keane interrupted. He barely resisted the urge to shake her off and drag the still seated Bob by the scruff of the neck.

"No, he was really more just leaning on me. His balance is a trifle impaired. He only tried to kiss me," she pointed out, wisely deleting the wandering hands. "And I hit him much harder than I should have. He's new, Keane, don't fire him."

Exasperated, he stared at her. "Firing was the least of what I had in mind for him."

Jo smiled, unable to keep the gleam from her eyes. "If you were going to avenge my honor, he really didn't do much more than breathe on it. I don't think you should run him through for that. Maybe you could just put him in the stocks for a couple of days."

Keane swore under his breath, but a reluctant smile tugged at his mouth. Seeing it, Jo loosened her hold. "Miss Wilder wants to give you a break," he told the dazed Bob in a tough, no-nonsense voice that Jo decided he used for intimidating witnesses. "She has a softer heart than I do. Therefore, I won't knock you down several more times or kick you off the lot, as I had entertained doing." He paused, allowing Bob time to consider this possibility. "Instead, I'll let you sleep off your—enthusiasm." In one quick jerk, he pulled Bob to his feet. "But if I ever hear of you breathing uninvited on Miss Wilder or any other of my female employees, we'll go back to the first choice. And before I kick you out," he added with low menace, "I'll let it be known that you were decked by one punch from a hundred-pound woman."

"Yes, sir, Mr. Prescott," said Bob as clearly as possible.

"Go to bed," Jo said kindly, seeing him pale. "You'll feel better in the morning."

"Obviously," Keane commented as Bob lurched away, "you haven't done much drinking." He turned to Jo and grinned. "The one thing he's not going to feel in the morning is better." Jo smiled, pleased to have Keane talk to her without the thin shield of politeness. "And where," he asked and took her hand for examination, "did you learn that right jab?"

Jo laughed, allowing Keane's fingers to interlock with hers. "It would hardly have knocked him down if he hadn't already been tilting in that direction." Her face turned up to his and sparkled with starlight. In his eyes an expression she couldn't comprehend came and went. "Is something wrong?"

For a moment he said nothing. In her breast her heart began to hammer as she waited to be kissed. "No, nothing," he said. The moment was shattered. "Come on, I'll walk you back to your trailer."

"I wasn't going there." Wanting to put him back into an easy mood, she linked her arm with his. "If you come with me, I'll show you some magic." Her smile slanted invitingly. "You like magic, don't you, Keane? Even a sober, dedicated lawyer must like magic."

"Is that how I strike you?" Jo almost laughed at the trace of annoyance in his voice. "As a sober, dedicated lawyer?"

"Oh, not entirely, though that's part of you." She enjoyed feeling that for the moment she had him to herself. "You've also got a streak of adventure and a rather nice sense of humor. And," she added with generous emphasis, "there's your temper."

"You seem to have me all figured out."

"Oh, no." Jo stopped and turned to him. "Not at all. I only know how you are here. I can only speculate on how you are in Chicago."

His brow lifted as she caught his attention. "Would I be different there?"

"I don't know." Jo's forehead wrinkled in thought. "Wouldn't you be? Circumstances would. You probably have a house or a big apartment, and there's a housekeeper who comes in once—no, twice—a week." Caught up in the picture, she gazed off into the distance and built it further. "You have an office with a view of the city, a very efficient secretary and a brilliant law clerk. You go to business lunches at the club. In court you're deadly and very successful. You have your own tailor and work out at the gym three times a week. There's the theater on the weekends, along with something physical. Tennis maybe, not golf. No, handball."

Keane shook his head. "Is this the magic?"

"No." Jo shrugged and began to walk again. "Just guesswork. You don't have to have a great deal of money to know how people who do behave. And I know you take the law seriously. You wouldn't choose a career that wasn't very important to you."

Keane walked in silence. When he spoke, his voice was quiet. "I'm not certain I'm comfortable with your little outline of my life."

"It's very sketchy," Jo told him. "I'd have to understand you better to fill in the gaps."

"Don't you?"

"What?" Jo asked, pausing. "Understand you?" She laughed, tickled at the absurdity of his question. "No, I don't understand you. How could I? You live in a different world." With this, she tossed aside the flap of the Big Top and stepped into its darkness. When she hit the switch, two rows of overhead lights flashed on. Shadows haunted the corners and fell over the arena seats.

"It's wonderful, isn't it?" Her clear voice ran the length of the tent and echoed back. "It's not empty, you know. They're always here—the troupers, the audience, the animals." She walked forward until she stood beside the third ring. "Do you know what this is?" she asked Keane, tossing out her arms and turning a full circle. "It's an ageless wonder in a changing world. No matter what happens on the outside, this is here. We're the most fragile of circuses, at the mercy of the elephants, of emotions, of mechanics, of public whims. But six days a week for twenty-nine weeks we perform miracles. We build a world at dawn, then disappear into the dark. That's part of it—the mystery." She waited until Keane moved forward to join her.

"Tents pop up on an empty lot, elephants and lions walk down Main Street. And we never grow old, because each new generation discovers us all over again." She stood slender and exquisite in a circle of light. "Life here's crazy. And it's hard. Muddy lots, insane hours, sore muscles, but when you've finished your act and you get that feeling that tells you it was special, there's nothing else like it in the world."

"Is that why you do it?" Keane asked.

Jo shook her head and moved out of the circle of light into the dark and into another ring. "It's all part of the same thing. We all have our own reasons, I suppose. You've asked me that before; I'm not certain I can explain. Maybe it's that we all believe in miracles." She turned under the light, and it shimmered around her.

"I've been here all my life. I know every trick, every illusion. I know how Jamie's dad gets twenty clowns into a two-seater car. But each time I see it, I laugh and I believe it. It's not just the excitement, Keane, it's the anticipation of the excitement. It's knowing you're going to see the biggest or the smallest or the fastest or the highest." Jo ran to the center ring and threw up her arms.

"Ladies and gentlemen," she announced with a toss of her head. "For your amazement and astonishment, for the first time in America, a superabundance of mountainous, mighty pachyderms led in a stupendous exhibition of choreography by the Great Serena." Jo laughed and shifted her hair to her back with a quick movement of her hand. "Dancing elephants!" she said to Keane, pleased that he was smiling. "Or you listen to the talker in the sideshow when he starts his spiel. Step right up. Come a little closer." She curled her fingers in invitation. "See the Amazing Serpentina and her monstrous, slithering vipers. Watch the beautiful young girl charm a deadly cobra. Watch her accept the reptilian embrace of the gargantuan boa. Don't miss the chance to see the enchantress of the evil serpent!"

"I suppose Baby might sue for slander."

Jo laughed and stepped up on the ring. "But when the crowds see little Rose with a boa constrictor wrapped around her shoulders, they've gotten their money's worth. We give them what they come for: color, fantasy, the unique. Thrills. You've seen the audience when Vito does his high wire act without a net."

"A net seems little enough protection when he's balancing on a wire at two hundred feet." Keane stuck his hands in his pockets and frowned. "He risks his life every day."

"So does a police officer or a firefighter." Jo spoke quietly and rested her hands on his shoulders. It seemed more necessary than ever that she make him understand his father's dream. "I know what you're saying, Keane, but you have to understand us. The element of danger is essential to many of the acts. You can hear the whole audience suck in their breath when Vito does his back somersault on the wire. They'd be impressed if he used a net, but they wouldn't be terrified."

"Do they need to be?"

Jo's sober expression lightened. "Oh, yes! They need to be terrified and fascinated and mesmerized. It's all included in the price of a ticket. This is a world of superlatives. We test the limit of human daring, and every day it changes. Do you know how long it took before the first man accomplished the triple on the trapeze? Now it's nearly a standard." A light of anticipation flared in her eyes. "One day someone will do a quadruple. If a man stands in this ring and juggles three torches today, tomorrow someone will juggle them on horseback and after that there'll be a team tossing them back and forth while swinging on a trap. It's our job to do the incredible, then, when it's done, to do the impossible. It's that simple."

"Simple," Keane murmured, then lifted a hand to caress her hair. "I wonder if you'd think so if you could see it from the outside."

"I don't know." Her fingers tightened on his shoulders as he buried his other hand in her hair. "I never have."

As if his thoughts centered on it, Keane combed his

fingers through her hair. Gradually, he pushed it back until only his hands framed her face. They stood in a pool of light that threw their shadows long behind them. "You are so lovely," he murmured.

Jo neither spoke nor moved. There was something different this time in the way he touched her. There was a gentleness and a hesitation she had not felt before. Though they looked directly into hers, she could not read his eyes. Their faces were close, and his breath fluttered against her mouth. Jo slid her arms around his neck and pressed her mouth to his.

Not until that moment had she realized how empty she had felt, how desperately she had needed to hold him. Her lips were hungry for his. She clung while all gentleness fled from his touch. His hands were greedy. The weeks that he had not touched her were forgotten as her skin warmed and hummed with quickening blood. Passion stripped her of inhibitions, and her tongue sought his, taking the kiss into wilder and darker depths. Their lips parted, only to meet again with sharp new demands. She understood that all needs and all desires were ultimately only one—Keane.

His mouth left hers, and for an instant he rested his cheek against her hair. For that moment Jo felt a contentment more complete than she had ever known. Abruptly, he drew away.

Puzzled, she watched as he drew out a cigar. She lifted a hand to run it through the hair he had just disturbed. He flicked on his lighter. "Keane?" She looked at him, knowing her eyes offered everything.

"You've had a long day," he began in an oddly polite tone. Jo winced as if he had struck her. "I'll walk you back to your trailer."

She stepped off the ring and away from him. Pain seared along her skin. "Why are you doing this?" To her humiliation, tears welled in her eyes and lodged in her throat. The tears acted as a prism, refracting the light and clouding her vision. She blinked them back. Keane's brows drew together at the gesture.

"I'll take you back," he said again. The detached tone of his voice accelerated all Jo's fury and grief.

"How dare you!" she demanded. "How dare you make me…" The word *love* nearly slipped through her lips, and she swallowed it. "How dare you make me want you, then turn away! I was right about you from the beginning. I thought I'd been wrong. You're cold and unfeeling." Her breath came quickly and unevenly, but she refused to retreat until she had said it all. Her face was pale with the passion of her emotions. "I don't know why I thought you'd ever understand what Frank had given you. You need a heart to see the intangible. I'll be glad when the season's over and you do whatever it is you're going to do. I'll be glad when I never have to see you again. I won't let you do this to me anymore!" Her voice wavered, but she made no attempt to steady it. "I don't want you to ever touch me again."

Keane studied her for a long moment, then took a careful drag on his cigar. "All right, Jo."

The very calmness of his answer tore a sob from her before she turned and ran from the Big Top.

Chapter 10

In July the troupe circled through Virginia, touched the tip of West Virginia on their way into Kentucky, then moved into Ohio. Audiences fanned themselves as the temperatures in the Big Top rose, but they still came.

Since the evening of the Fourth, Jo had avoided Keane. It was not as difficult as it might have been, as he spent half the month in Chicago dealing with his business. Jo functioned. She ate because eating was necessary in order to maintain her strength. She slept because rest was essential to remaining alert in the cage. She did not find any enjoyment in food nor was her sleep restful. Because so many in the troupe knew her well, Jo struggled to keep on a mask of normalcy. Above all, she needed to avoid any questions, any advice, any sympathy. It was necessary, because of her profession, to put her emotions on hold a great deal of the time.

After some struggle and some failure, Jo achieved a reasonable success.

Her training of Gerry continued, as did his progress. The additional duty of working with him helped fill her small snatches of spare time. On afternoons when no matinee was scheduled, Jo took him into the big cage. As he grew more proficient, she brought other cats in to join Merlin. By the first week in August they were working together with her full complement of lions.

The only others who were rehearsing in the Big Top were the equestrian act. They ran through the Thread the Needle routine in the first ring. Hooves echoed dully on tanbark. Jo supervised while Gerry sent the cats into a pyramid. At his urging, Lazarus climbed up the wide, arched ladder that topped the grouping. Twice he balked, and twice Gerry was forced to reissue the command.

"Good," Jo commented when the pyramid was complete.

"He wouldn't go." Gerry began to complain, but she cut him off.

"Don't be in too much of a hurry. Bring them down." Her tone was brisk and professional. "Make certain they dismount and take their seats in the right order. It's important to stick to routine."

Hands resting on hips, Jo watched. In her opinion, Gerry had true potential. His nerves were good, he had a feeling for the animals, and he was slowly developing patience. Still she balked at the next step in his training: leaving him alone in the arena. Even with only Merlin, she felt it too risky. He was still too casual. Not yet did he possess enough respect for the lion's guile.

Jo moved around the arena, and the lions, used to

her, were not disturbed. As the cats settled onto their pedestals, she once more moved to stand beside Gerry. "Now we'll walk down the line. You make each do a sit-up before we send them out."

One by one the cats rose on their haunches and pawed the air. Jo and Gerry moved down their ranks. The heat was becoming oppressive, and Jo shifted her shoulders, longing for a cool shower and a change of clothes. When they came to Hamlet, he ignored the command with a rebellious snarl.

Bad-tempered brute, thought Jo absently as she waited for Gerry to reissue the command. He did so but moved forward as if to emphasize the words.

"No, not so close!" Jo warned quickly. Even as she spoke, she saw the change in Hamlet's eyes.

Instinctively, she stepped over, nudging Gerry back and shielding his body with hers. Hamlet struck out, claws extended. There was a moment of blind heat in her shoulder as the skin ripped. Swiftly, she was facing the cat, holding tightly onto Gerry's arm as they stood just out of range.

"Don't run," she ordered, feeling his jerk of panic. Her arm was on fire as the blood began to flow freely. Keeping her movements quick but smooth, she took the whip from Gerry's nerveless hand and cracked it hard, using her left arm. She knew that if Hamlet continued his defiance and attacked, it was hopeless. The other cats were certain to join in a melee. It would be over before anything could be done. Already, Abra shifted restlessly and bared her teeth.

"Open the chute," Jo called out. Her voice was cool as ice. "Back toward the safety cage," she instructed Gerry as she gave the cats their signal to leave the arena.

"I've got to get them out one at a time. Move slow, and if I tell you to stop, you stop dead. Understand?"

She heard him swallow as she watched the cats begin to leap off their pedestals and file into the chute. "He got you. Is it bad?" The words were barely a whisper and drenched in terror.

"I said go." Half the cats were gone, and still Hamlet's eyes were locked on hers. There was no time to waste. One part of her brain heard shouting outside the cage, but she blocked it out and focused all her concentration on the cat. "Go now," she repeated to Gerry. "Do as you're told."

He swallowed again and began to back away. Long seconds dragged until she heard the rattle of the safety cage door. When his turn came, Hamlet made no move to leave his seat. Jo was alone with him. She could smell the heat, the scent of the wild and the fragrance of her own blood. Her arm was alive with pain. Slowly, she tested him by backing up. The safety cage seemed hundreds of miles away. The cat tensed immediately, and she stopped. She knew he would not let her cross the arena. Outrunning him was impossible, as the distance between them could be covered in one spring. She had to outbluff him instead.

"Out," she ordered firmly. "Out, Hamlet." As he continued to watch her, Jo felt a trickle of sweat slide down between her shoulder blades. Her skin was clammy with it in contrast to the warmth of the blood that ran down her arm. There was a sudden, vivid picture inside her head of her father being dragged around the cage. Fear tripped inside her throat. There was a lightness fluttering in the top of her head, and she knew that a moment's terror would cause her to faint. She stiffened her spine and pushed it away.

Speed was important. The longer she allowed the cat to remain in the arena after his cue, the more defiant he would become. And the more dangerous. As yet he was unaware that he held her at such a sharp disadvantage. "Out, Hamlet." Jo repeated the command with a crack of the whip. He leaped from the pedestal. Jo's stomach trembled. She locked every muscle, and as the cat hesitated, she repeated the command. He was confused, and she knew this could work as an advantage or a curse. Confused, he might spring or retreat. Her fingers tightened on the stock of the whip and trembled. The cat paced nervously and watched her.

"Hamlet!" She raised her voice and bit off each syllable. "Go out." To the words she added the hand signal she had used before he was fully trained to voice command.

As if rebuffed, Hamlet relaxed his tail and padded into the chute. Before the door slid completely closed, Jo sank to her knees. Her body began to quake fiercely with the aftershock. No more than five minutes had passed since Hamlet had defied Gerry's command, but her muscles bore the strain of hours. For an instant her vision blurred. Even as she shook her head to clear it, Keane was on the ground beside her.

She heard him swear, ripping the tattered sleeve of her blouse from her arm. He fired questions at her, but she could do no more than shake her head and gulp in air. Focusing on him, she noticed his eyes were unusually dark against his face.

"What?" She followed his voice but not the words. He swore again, sharply enough to penetrate the first layer of her shock. He pulled her to her feet, then continuing the motion smoothly, lifted her into his arms. "Don't." Her mind struggled to break through the fog and function. "I'm all right."

"Shut up," he said harshly as he carried her from the cage. "Just shut up."

Because speaking cost her some effort, Jo obeyed. Closing her eyes, she let the mixture of excited voices whirl around her. Her arm screamed with pain, but the throbbing reassured her. Numbness would have terrified her. Still she kept her eyes shut, not yet having the courage to look at the damage. Being alive was enough.

When she opened her eyes again, Keane was carrying her into the administration wagon. At the sound of the chaos that followed them, Duffy strode through from his office. "What the..." he began, then stopped and paled beneath his freckles. He moved quickly forward as Keane set Jo in a chair. "How bad?"

"I don't know yet," Keane muttered. "Get a towel and the first-aid kit."

Buck had come in behind them and, already having secured the items, handed them to Keane. Then he moved to a cabinet and located a bottle of brandy.

"It's not too bad," Jo managed. Because her voice was tolerably steady, she screwed up her courage and looked down. Keane had fastened a rough bandage from the remains of her sleeve. Though the flow of blood had slowed, there were streaks of it down her arm, and too much spreading from the wound to be certain how extensive the cuts were. Nausea rocked in her stomach.

"How do you know?" Keane demanded between his teeth as he began to clean the wound. He wrung out the towel in the basin Buck set beside him.

"It's not bleeding that badly." Jo swallowed the quea-
siness. As her mind began to clear, she frowned at the
tone of Keane's voice. Feeling her stare, he glanced up.
In his eyes was such fury, she pulled away.

"Be still," he ordered roughly and gave his attention
back to her arm.

The cat had delivered only a glancing blow, but even
so, there were four long slices in her upper arm. Jo set
her jaw as pain ripped through her. Keane's brusqueness
brought more hurt, and she fought to show no reaction
to either. The aftermath of fear was bubbling through
her. She longed to be held, to be soothed by the hands
that tended to her wound.

"She's going to need stitches," Keane said without
looking at her.

"And an antitoxin shot," Buck added, handing Jo a
generous glass of brandy. "Drink this, honey. It'll help
settle you."

The gentleness in his voice nearly undid her. He laid
his big hand against her cheek, and for a moment she
pressed against it.

"Drink now," Buck ordered again. Obediently, Jo
lifted the glass and swallowed. The room whirled, then
snapped into focus. She made a small sound and pressed
the glass to her forehead. "Tell me what happened in
there." Buck crouched down beside her as Keane began
to apply a temporary bandage.

Jo took a moment to draw air in and out of her lungs.
She lowered the glass and spoke steadily. "Hamlet didn't
respond, and Gerry repeated a command, but he stepped
forward. Too close. I saw Hamlet's eyes, and I knew. I
should have moved faster. I should have been watching

him more carefully. It was a stupid mistake." She stared into the brandy as she berated herself.

"She stepped between the boy and the cat." Keane bit off the words as he completed the bandaging. Rising, he moved to the brandy and poured. Not once did he turn to look at Jo. Hurt, she stared at his back before looking back at Buck.

"How's Gerry?"

Buck urged the glass back to her lips. A faint tint of pink was creeping into her cheeks. "Pete's with him. Got his head between his knees. He'll be fine."

Jo nodded. "I guess I'll have to go to town and have this seen to." She handed the glass to Buck and wondered if she dare attempt to rise yet. With another deep breath, she glanced at Duffy. "Make sure he's ready to go in when I get back."

Keane turned from the window. "Go in where?" His face was set in hard lines.

In response, Jo's voice was chilled. "In the cage." She turned her eyes to Buck. "We should be able to have a short run-through before the evening show."

"No." Jo's head snapped up as Keane spoke. For a long moment they stared at each other with odd, unreasonable antagonism. "You're not going back in there today." His voice held curt authority.

"Of course I am," Jo countered, managing to keep the combination of pain and anger from her words. "And if Gerry wants to be a cat man, he's going in, too."

"Jo's right," Buck put in, trying to soothe what he sensed was an explosive situation. "It's like falling off a horse. You can't wait too long before you get back up, or you won't ride again."

Keane never took his eyes from Jo. He continued as if Buck hadn't spoken. "I won't permit it."

"You can't stop me." Indignation forced her to her feet. The brisk movement caused her arm to protest, and her struggle against it showed momentarily in her eyes.

"Yes, I can." Keane took a long swallow of brandy. "I own this circus."

Jo's fists tightened at his tone, at his careless use of his authority. Not once since he had knelt beside her in the cage had he given her any sign of comfort or reassurance. She had needed it from him. To masquerade its trembling, she kept her voice low. "But you don't own me, Mr. Prescott. And if you'll check your papers and the legalities, you'll see you don't own the lions or my equipment. I bought them, and I maintain them out of my salary. My contract doesn't give you the right to tell me when I can or can't rehearse my cats."

Keane's face was granite hard. "Neither does it give you the right to set up in the Big Top without my permission."

"Then I'll set up some place else," she tossed back. "But I *will* set up. That cat will be worked again today. I won't take the risk of losing months of training."

"But you will risk being killed," Keane shot back and slammed down his glass.

"What do you care?" Jo shouted. All control deserted her. The cuts were deep on her emotions as well as her flesh. She had passed through a terror more acute than she had known since the night of her parents' death. More than anything else, she wanted to feel Keane's arms around her. She wanted to know the security she had felt when he had let her weep out her grief for Ari in his arms. "I'm nothing to you!" Her head shook quickly, tossing her hair. There was a bubble of hysteria in her voice, and Buck reached out to lay a hand on her shoulder.

"Jo," he warned in his soft, rumbling voice.

"No!" She shook her head and spoke rapidly. "He hasn't the right. You haven't the right to interfere with my life." She flared at Keane again with eyes vivid with emotion. "I know what I have to do. I know what I *will* do. Why should it matter to you? You aren't legally responsible if I get mauled. No one's going to sue you."

"Hold on, Jo." This time Buck spoke firmly. As he took her uninjured arm, he felt the tremors shooting through her. "She's too upset to know what she's saying," he told Keane.

There was a mask over Keane's face which concealed all emotion. "Oh, I think she knows what she's saying," he disagreed quietly. For a moment there was only the sound of Jo shuddering and the splash of brandy being poured into a glass. "You do what you have to do, Jo," he said after drinking again. "You're perfectly correct that I haven't any rights where you're concerned. Take her into town," he told Buck, then turned back to the window.

"Come on, Jo." Buck urged her to the door, slipping a supportive arm around her waist. Even as they stepped outside, Rose came running from the direction of the midway.

"Jo!" Her face was white with concern. "Jo, I just heard." She glanced at the bandage with wide, terrified eyes. "How bad is it?"

"Just scratches, really," Jo assured her. She added the best smile she could muster. "Buck's going to take me into town for a couple of stitches."

"Are you sure?" She looked up at the tall man for reassurance. "Buck?"

"Several stitches," he corrected but patted Rose's hand. "But it's not too bad."

"Do you want me to come with you?" She fell into step beside them as Buck began to lead Jo again.

"No. Thank you, Rose." Jo smiled with more feeling. "I'll be fine."

Because of the smile, Rose was able to relax. "I thought when I heard…well, I imagined all sorts of terrible things. I'm glad you're not badly hurt." They had reached Buck's truck, and Rose leaned over to kiss Jo's cheek. "We all love you so."

"I know." Squeezing her hand, Jo let Buck help her into the cab of his truck. As he maneuvered from the lot, Jo rested her head against the back of the seat and shut her eyes. Never could she remember feeling more spent, more battered.

"Hurt bad?" Buck asked as they switched to an asphalt road.

"Yes," she answered simply, thinking of her heart as much as her arm.

"You'll feel better when you're patched up."

Jo kept her eyes shut, knowing some wounds never heal. Or if they did, they left scars that ached at unexpected times.

"You shouldn't have gone off on him that way, Jo." There was light censure in Buck's voice.

"He shouldn't have interfered," Jo retorted. "It's none of his business. *I'm* none of his business."

"Jo, it's not like you to be so hard."

"Hard?" She opened her eyes and turned to Buck. "What about him? Couldn't he have been kinder, shown even the barest trace of compassion? Did he have to speak to me as if I were a criminal?"

"Jo, the man was terrified. You're only looking at this from one side." He scratched his beard and gave a gusty sigh. "You can't know what it's like to be outside that cage, helpless when someone you care about is facing down death. I had to all but knock him unconscious to keep him out of there until we got it through his head that he'd just get you killed for sure. He was scared, Jo. We were all scared."

Jo shook her head, certain Buck exaggerated because of his affection for her. Keane's voice had been hard, his eyes angry. "He doesn't care," she corrected quietly. "Not like the rest of you. You didn't swear at me. You weren't cold."

"Jo, people have different ways—" Buck began, but she interrupted.

"I know he wouldn't want to see me hurt, Buck. He's not heartless or cruel." She sighed as all the force of anger and fear washed out of her body and left her empty. "Please, I don't want to talk about him."

Buck heard the weariness in her voice and patted her hand. "Okay, honey, just relax. We'll have you all fixed up in no time."

Not all fixed up, Jo thought. Far from all fixed up.

Chapter 11

As the weeks passed, Jo's arm lost its stiffness. She healed cleanly. The only traces were thin scars that promised to fade but not disappear. She found, however, that some spark had gone out of her life. Constantly, she fought against a vague dissatisfaction. Nothing—not her work, not her friends, not her books—brought about the contentment she had grown up with. She had become a woman, and her needs had shifted. Jo knew the root of her problem was Keane, but the knowledge was not a solution. He had left the circus again on the very night of her accident. Nearly four weeks later he had not returned.

Three times Jo had sat down to write him, needing to assuage her guilt for the harsh things she had said to him. Three times she had torn up the paper in frustration. No matter how she rearranged the words, they were wrong. Instead, she clung to the hope that he would come back one last time. If, she felt, they could part as friends, without bitterness or hard words, she could accept the separation. Willing this to happen, she was able to return to her routine with some tranquility. She rehearsed, performed, joined in the daily duties of circus life. She waited. The caravan moved closer to Chicago.

Jo stood in the steaming Big Top on a late August afternoon. Dressed in a leotard, she worked on ground exercises with the Beirot Brothers. It was this daily regimentation that had aided in keeping her arm limber. She could now move into a back walk-over without feeling any protest in her injured arm.

"I feel good," Jo told Raoul as they worked out. "I feel really good." She did a quick series of pirouettes.

"You don't keep your shoulder in shape by dancing on your feet," Raoul challenged.

"My shoulder's fine," she tossed back, then proved her point by bending into a handstand. Slowly, she lowered her legs to a forty-five degree angle, bringing one foot to rest on the knee of the opposite leg. "It's perfect." She executed a forward roll and sprang to her feet. "I'm strong as an ox," she claimed and did a quick back handspring followed by a back flip.

She landed at Keane's feet.

The cascade of emotions that raced through her reflected briefly in her eyes before she regained her balance. "I didn't—I didn't know you were back." Instantly, she regretted the inanity of the words but could find no others. The longing was raw in her to hurl her-

self into his arms. She wondered that he could not feel
her need through the pores of her skin.

"I just got in." His eyes continued to search her
face after his hands dropped to his sides. "This is my
mother," he added. "Rachael Loring, Jovilette Wilder."

At his words, Jo's gaze moved from his face. She saw
the woman beside him. If she had seen Rachael Loring
in a crowd of two thousand, she would have known her
for Keane's mother. The bone structure was the same,
though hers was more elegant. Her brows were golden
wings, flaring out at the end, as Keane's did. Her hair
was smooth, brushed up and away from her face with
no gray to mar its tawny perfection. But it was the eyes
that sent a jolt through Jo. She had not thought to see
them in anyone's face but Keane's. The woman was
dressed simply in an unpretentiously tailored suit that
bespoke taste and wealth. There was, however, none
of the cool, distant polish that Jo had always attributed
to the woman who had taken her son and left Frank.
There was a charm to the smile that curved in greeting.

"Jovilette, such a lovely name. Keane's told me of
you." She extended her hand, and Jo accepted, intending
a quick, impersonal shake. Rachael Loring, however,
laid her other hand atop their joined ones and added
warmth. "Keane tells me you we're very close to Frank.
Perhaps we could talk."

The affection in her voice confused Jo into a stumbling reply. "I— Yes. I—if you'd like."

"I should like very much." She squeezed Jo's hand
again before releasing it. "Perhaps you have time to
show me around?" She smiled with the question, and
Jo found it increasingly difficult to remain aloof. "I'm
sure there've been some changes since I was here last.

You must have some business to attend to," she said, looking up at Keane. "I'm sure Jovilette will take good care of me. Won't you, dear?" Without waiting for either to respond, Rachael tucked her arm through Jo's and began to walk. "I knew your parents," she said as Keane watched them move away. "Not terribly well, I'm afraid. They came here the same year I left. But I recall they were both thrilling performers. Keane tells me you've followed your father's profession."

"Yes, I..." She hesitated, feeling oddly at a disadvantage. "I did," she finished lamely.

"You're so young." Rachael gave her a gentle smile. "How terribly brave you must be."

"No...no, not really. It's my job."

"Yes, of course." Rachael laughed at some private memory. "I've heard that before."

They were outside now, and she paused to look thoughtfully around her. "I think perhaps I was wrong. It hasn't really changed, not in thirty years. It's a wonderful place, isn't it?"

"Why did you leave?" As soon as the words were spoken, Jo regretted them. "I'm sorry," she said quickly. "I shouldn't have asked."

"Of course you should." Rachael sighed and patted Jo's hand. "It's only natural. Duffy's still here, Keane tells me." At the change in subject, Jo imagined her question had been evaded.

"Yes, I suppose he always will be."

"Could we have some coffee, or some tea, perhaps?" Rachael smiled again. "It's such a long drive from town. Is your trailer nearby?"

"It's just over in the backyard."

"Oh, yes." Rachael laughed and began to walk again.

"The neighborhood that never changes over thousands of miles. Do you know the story of the dog and the bones?" she asked. Though Jo knew it well, she said nothing. "One version is that a roustabout gave his dog a bone every night after dinner. The dog would bury the bone under the trailer, then the next day try to dig it back up. Of course, it was fifty miles behind in an empty lot. He never figured it out." Quietly, she laughed to herself.

Feeling awkward, Jo opened the door to her trailer. How could this woman be the one she had resented all of her life? How could this be the cold, heartless woman who had left Frank? Oddly, Rachael seemed totally at ease in the narrow confines of the trailer.

"How efficient these are." She looked around with interest and approval. "You must barely realize you're on wheels." Casually, she picked up the volume of Thoreau which lay on Jo's counter. "Keane told me you have an avid interest in literature. In language, too," she added, glancing up from the book. Her eyes were golden and direct like her son's. Jo was tossed back suddenly to the first morning of the season when she had looked down and found Keane's eyes on her.

It made her uncomfortable to learn Keane had discussed her with his mother. "I have some tea," Jo told her as she moved toward the kitchen. "It's a better gamble than my coffee."

"That's fine," Rachael said agreeably and followed her. "I'll just sit here while you fix it." She settled herself with apparent ease at the tiny table across from the kitchen.

"I'm afraid I haven't anything else to offer you."

Jo kept her back turned as she routed through her cupboard.

"Tea and conversation," Rachael answered in mild tones, "will be fine."

Jo sighed and turned. "I'm sorry." She shook her head. "I'm being rude. I just don't know what to say to you, Mrs. Loring. I've resented you for as long as I can remember. Now you're here and not at all as I imagined." She managed to smile, albeit ruefully. "You're not cold and hateful, and you look so much like…" She stopped, horrified that she had nearly blurted out Keane's name. For a moment her eyes were utterly naked.

Rachael smoothed over the awkwardness. "I don't wonder you resented me if you were as close to Frank as Keane tells me. Jovilette," she said softly, "did Frank resent me, too?"

Helpless, Jo responded to the hint of sadness. "No. Not while I knew him. I don't think Frank was capable of resentments."

"You understood him well, didn't you?" Rachael watched as Jo poured boiling water into mugs. "I understood him, too," she continued as Jo brought the mugs to the table. "He was a dreamer, a marvelous free spirit." Absently, she stirred her tea.

Consumed with curiosity, Jo sat across from her and waited for the story she sensed was coming.

"I was eighteen when I met him. I had come to the circus with a cousin. The Colossus was a bit smaller in those days," she added with a reminiscent smile, "but it was all the same. Oh, the magic!" She shook her head and sighed. "We tumbled into love so fast, married against all my family's objections and went on the road. It was exciting. I learned the web routine and helped out in wardrobe."

Jo's eyes widened. "You performed?"

"Oh, yes." Rachael's cheeks tinted a bit with pride. "I was quite good. Then I became pregnant. We were both like children waiting for Christmas. I wasn't quite nineteen when I had Keane, and I'd been with the circus for nearly a year. Things became difficult over the next season. I was young and a bit frightened of Keane. I panicked if he sneezed and was constantly dragging Frank into town to see doctors. How patient he was."

Rachael leaned forward and took Jo's hand. "Can you understand how hard this life is for one not meant for it? Can you see that through the magic of it, the excitement and wonder, there are hardships and fears and impossible demands? I was little more than a child myself, with an infant to care for, without the endurance or vocation of a trouper, without the experience or confidence of a mother. I lived on nerves for an entire season." She let out a little rush of breath. "When it was over, I went home to Chicago."

For the first time, Jo imagined the flight from Rachael's point of view. She could see a girl, younger than herself, in a strange, demanding world with a baby to care for. Over the years Jo had seen scores of people try the life she'd led and last only weeks. Still she shook her head in confusion.

"I think I understand how difficult it must have been for you. But if you and Frank loved each other, couldn't you have worked it out somehow?"

"How?" Rachael countered. "Should I have taken a house somewhere and lived with him half a year? I would have hated him. Should he have given up his life here and settled down with me and Keane? It would have destroyed everything I loved about him." Rachael shook her head, giving Jo a soft smile. "We did love each other, Jovilette, but not enough. Compromise isn't always possible, and neither of us were capable of adjusting to the needs of the other. I tried, and Frank would have tried had I asked him. But it was lost before it had really begun. We did the wisest thing under the circumstances." Looking into Jo's eyes, she saw youth and confidence. "It seems cold and hard to you, but it was no use dragging out a painful situation. He gave me Keane and two years I've always treasured. I gave him his freedom without bitterness. Ten years after Frank, I found happiness again." She smiled softly with the memory. "I loved Frank, and that love remains as young and sweet as the day I met him."

Jo swallowed. She searched for some way to apologize for a grudge held for a lifetime. "He—Frank kept a scrapbook on Keane. He followed the Chicago papers."

"Did he?" Rachael beamed, then leaned back in her chair and lifted her mug. "How like him. Was he happy, Jovilette? Did he have what he wanted?"

"Yes," Jo answered without hesitation. "Did you?"

Rachael's eyes came back to Jo's. For a moment the look was speculative, then it grew warm. "What a good heart you have, generous and understanding. Yes, I had what I wanted. And you, Jovilette, what do you want?"

At ease now, Jo shook her head and smiled. "More than I can have."

"You're too smart for that," Rachael observed, studying her. "I think you're a fighter, not a dreamer. When the time comes to make your choice, you won't settle for anything less than all." She smiled at Jo's intent look, then rose. "Will you show me your lions? I can't tell you how I'm looking forward to seeing you perform."

"Yes, of course." Jo stood, then hesitated. She held out her hand. "I'm glad you came."

Rachael accepted the gesture. "So am I."

Throughout the rest of the day Jo looked for Keane without success. After meeting and talking with his mother, it had become even more imperative that she speak with him. Her conscience would have no rest until she made amends. By showtime she had not yet found him.

Each act seemed to run on and on as she fretted for the finish. He would be with his mother in the audience, and undoubtedly she would find him after the show. She strained with impatience as the acts dragged.

After the finale she stood at the back door, unsure whether to wait or to go to his trailer. She was struck with both relief and alarm when she saw him approaching.

"Jovilette." Rachael spoke first, taking Jo's hands in hers. "How marvelous you were, and how stunning. I see why Keane said you had an untamed beauty."

Surprised, Jo glanced up at Keane but met impassive amber eyes. "I'm glad you enjoyed it."

"Oh, I can't tell you how much. The day has brought me some very precious memories. Our talk this afternoon meant a great deal to me." To Jo's surprise, Rachael leaned over and kissed her. "I hope to see you again. I'm going to say goodbye to Duffy before you drive me back, Keane," she continued. "I'll meet you in the car. Goodbye, Jovilette."

"Goodbye, Mrs. Loring." Jo watched her go before

she turned to Keane. "She's a wonderful person. She makes me ashamed."

"There's no need for that." He tucked his hands into his pockets and watched her. "We both had our reasons for resentments, and we were both wrong. How's your arm?"

"Oh." Jo's fingers traveled to the wound automatically. "It's fine. There's barely any scarring."

"Good." The word was short and followed by silence. For a moment Jo felt her courage fail her.

"Keane," she began, then forced herself to meet his eyes directly. "I want to apologize for the horrible way I behaved after the accident."

"I told you once before," he said coolly, "I don't care for apologies."

"Please." Jo swallowed her pride and touched his arm. "I've been saving this one for a very long time. I didn't mean those things I said," she added quickly. "I hope you'll forgive me." It wasn't the eloquent apology she had planned, but it was all she could manage. His expression never altered.

"There's nothing to forgive."

"Keane, please." Jo grabbed his arm again as he turned to go. "Don't leave me feeling as if you don't forgive me. I know I said dreadful things. You have every right to be furious, but couldn't you—can't we be friends again?"

Something flickered over his face. Lifting his hand, he touched the back of it to her cheek. "You have a habit of disconcerting me, Jovilette." He dropped his hand, then thrust it into his pocket. "I've left something for you with Duffy. Be happy." He walked away from her while she dealt with the finality of his tone. He was walking out of her life. She watched him until he disappeared.

Jo had thought she would feel something, but there was nothing; no pain, no tears, no desperation. She had not known a human being could be so empty and still live.

"Jo." Duffy lumbered up to her, then held out a thick envelope. "Keane left this for you." Then he moved past her, anxious to see that all straggling towners were nudged on their way.

Jo felt all emotions had been stripped away. Absently, she glanced at the envelope as she walked to her trailer. Without enthusiasm, she stepped inside, then tore it open. She remained standing as she pulled out the contents. It took her several moments to decipher the legal jargon. She read the group of papers through twice before sitting down.

He's given it to me, she thought. Still she could not comprehend the magnitude of it. *He's given me the circus.*

Chapter 12

O'Hare Airport was an army of people and a cacophony of sound. Nearly losing herself in the chaos of it, Jo struggled through the masses and competed for a cab. At first she had merely gawked at the snow like a towner seeing his first sword swallower. Then, though she shivered inside the corduroy coat she had bought for the trip, she began to enjoy it. It was beautiful as it lay over the city, and it helped to turn her mind from the purpose of her journey. Never had she been north so late in the year. Chicago in November was a sensational sight.

She had learned, after the initial shock had worn off, that Keane had not only given her the circus but a responsibility as well. Almost immediately there had been contracts to negotiate. She had been tossed into a sea of paperwork, forced to rely heavily on Duffy's experience as she tried to regain her balance. As the season had come to a close, Jo had attempted a dozen times to call Chicago. Each time, she had hung up before Keane's number could be dialed. It would be, she had decided, more appropriate to see him in person. Her trip had been postponed a few weeks due to Jamie and Rose's wedding.

It was there, as she had stood as maid of honor, that Jo had realized what she must do. There was only one thing she truly wanted, and that was to be with Keane. Watching Rose's face as their vows had been exchanged, Jo had recalled her unflagging determination to win the man she loved.

And will I stay here? Jo had demanded of herself thousands of miles away from him. No. Her heart had begun to thud as she had mapped out a plan. She would go to Chicago to see him. She would not be turned away. He had wanted her once; she would make him want her again. She would not live out her life without at least some small portion of it being part of his. He didn't have to love her. It was enough that she loved him.

And so, shivering against the unfamiliar cold, Jo scrambled into a cab and headed across town. She brushed her hair free of snow with chilled fingers, thinking how idiotic she had been to forget to buy a hat and gloves. What if he isn't home? she thought suddenly. What if he's gone to Europe or Japan or California? Panic made her giddy, and she pushed it down. He has to be home. It's Sunday, and he's sitting at home reading or going over a brief—or entertaining a woman, she thought, appalled. I should stop and call. I should tell the driver to take me back to the airport. Closing her eyes, Jo fought to regain her calm. She took long, deep breaths and stared at the buildings and sidewalks. Gradually, she felt the tiny gurgle of hysteria dissipate.

I won't be afraid, she told herself and tried to believe it. I won't be afraid. But Jovilette, the woman who reclined on a living rug of lions, was very much afraid. What if he rejected her? I won't let him reject me, she told herself with a confident lift of her chin. *I'll seduce him.* She pressed her fingers to her temples. *I wouldn't know how to begin.* I've got to tell the driver to turn around.

But before she could form the words, the cab pulled up to a curb. With the precision of a robot, Jo paid the fare, overtipping in her agitation, and climbed out.

Long after the cab had pulled away, she stood staring up at the massive glass-girdled building. Snow waltzed around her, sprinkling her hair and shoulders. A jostle from a rushing pedestrian broke the spell. She picked up her suitcases and hurried through the front door of the apartment buildings.

The lobby was enormous, with smoked glass walls and a deep shag carpet. Not knowing she should give her name at the desk, Jo wandered toward the elevators, innocently avoiding detection by merging with a group of tenants. Once inside the car, Jo pushed the button for the penthouse with a nerveless forefinger. The chatter of those in the elevator with her registered only as a distant humming. She never noticed when the car stopped for their departure.

When it stopped a second time and the doors slid open, she stared at the empty space for ten full seconds. Only as the automatic doors began to close did she snap out of her daze. Pushing them open again, she stepped through and into the hall. Her legs were wobbly, but she forced them to move forward in the direction of the penthouse. Panic sped up and down her spine until she set down her bags and leaned her brow against Keane's door. She urged air in and out of her lungs. She remembered that Rachael Loring had called her a fighter. Jo swallowed, lifted her chin and knocked. The wait was mercifully brief before Keane opened the door. She saw surprise light his eyes as he stared at her.

Her hair was dusted with snow as it lay over the shoulders of her coat. Her face glowed with the cold, and her eyes were bright, nearly feverish with her struggle for calm. Only once did her mouth tremble before she spoke.

"Hello, Keane."

He only stared, his eyes running over her in disbelief. He was leaner, she thought as she studied his face. As she filled herself with the sight of him, she saw he wore a sweatshirt and jeans. His feet were bare. He hadn't shaved, and her hand itched to test the roughness of his beard.

"What are you doing here?" Jo felt a resurgence of panic. His tone was harsh, and he had not answered her smile. She strained for poise.

"May I come in?" she asked, her smile cracking.

"What?" He seemed distracted by the question. His brows lowered into a frown.

"May I come in?" she repeated, barely defeating the urge to turn tail and run.

"Oh, yes, of course. I'm sorry." Running a hand through his hair, Keane stepped back and gestured her inside.

Instantly, Jo's shoes sank into the luxurious pile of the buff-colored carpet. For a moment she allowed herself to gaze around the room, using the time for the additional purpose of regaining her composure. It was an open, sweeping room with sharp, contrasting colors. There was a deep brown sectional sofa with a chrome and glass coffee table. There were high-backed chairs in soft creams and vivid slashes of blue in chunky floor pillows. There were paintings, one she thought she recognized as a Picasso, and a sculpture she was certain was a Rodin.

On the far right of the room there was an elevation of two steps. Just beyond was a huge expanse of glass that featured a spreading view of Chicago. Jo moved toward it with undisguised curiosity. Now, unexplicably, fear had lessened. She found that once she had stepped over the threshold she had committed herself. She was no longer afraid.

"It's wonderful," she said, turning back to him. "How marvelous to have a whole city at your feet every day. You must feel like a king."

"I've never thought of it that way." With half the room between them, he studied her. She looked small and fragile with the bustling city at her back.

"I would," she said, and now her smile came easily. "I'd stand at the window and feel regal and pompous."

At last she saw his lips soften and curve. "Jovilette," he said quietly. "What are you doing in my world?"

"I needed to talk to you," she answered simply. "I had to come here to do it."

He moved to her then, but slowly, with his eyes on hers. "It must be important."

"I thought so."

His brow lifted, then he shrugged. "Well, then, we'll talk. But first, let's have your coat."

Jo's cold fingers fumbled with the buttons and caused Keane to frown again. "Good heavens, you're frozen." He captured her hands between his and swore. "Where are your gloves?" he demanded like an irate parent. "It must be all of twelve degrees outside."

"I forgot to buy any," Jo told him as she dealt with the heavenly feeling of his hands restoring warmth to hers.

"Idiot. Don't you know better than to come to Chicago in November without gloves?"

"No." Jo responded to his anger with a cheerful smile. "I've never been to Chicago in November before. It's wonderful."

His eyes lifted from her hands to her face. He watched her for a long moment, then she heard him sigh. "I'd nearly convinced myself I could be cured."

Jo's eyes clouded with concern. "Have you been ill?"

Keane laughed with a shake of his head, then he pushed away the question and became brisk again. "Here, let's have your coat. I'll get you some coffee."

"You needn't bother," she began as he undid the buttons on the coat himself and drew it from her shoulders.

"I'd feel better if I was certain your circulation was restored." He paused and looked down at her as he laid her coat over his arm. She wore a green angora sweater with pearl buttons and a gray skirt in thin wool. The soft fabric draped softly at her breasts and over her hips and thighs. Her shoes were dainty and impractical sling-back heels.

"Is something wrong?"

"I've never seen you wear anything but a costume or jeans."

"Oh." Jo laughed and combed her fingers through her damp hair. "I expect I look different."

"Yes, you do." His voice was low, and there was a frown in his eyes. "Right now you look as if you've come from college for the holidays." He touched the ends of her hair, then turned away. "Sit down. I'll get the coffee."

A bit puzzled by his mercurial moods, Jo wandered about the room, finally ignoring a chair to kneel beside one of the pillows near the picture window. Though the carpet swallowed Keane's footsteps, she sensed his return.

"How wonderful to have a real winter, if just for the snow." She turned a radiant face his way. "I've always wondered what Christmas is like with snow and icicles." Images of snowflakes danced in her eyes. Seeing he carried two mugs of coffee, she rose and took one. "Thank you."

"Are you warm enough?" he asked after a moment.

Jo nodded and sat in one of the two chairs opposite the sofa. The novelty of the city made her mission seem like a grand adventure. Keane sat beside her, and for a moment they drank in companionable silence.

"What did you want to talk to me about, Jo?"

Jo swallowed, ignoring the faint trembling in her chest. "A couple of things. The circus, for one." She shifted in her chair until she faced him. "I didn't write because I felt it too important. I didn't phone for the same reason. Keane…" All her carefully thought-out speeches deserted her. "You can't just give something like that away. I can't take it from you."

"Why not?" He shrugged and sipped his coffee. "We both know it's always been yours. A piece of paper doesn't change that one way or the other."

"Keane, Frank left it to you."

"And I gave it to you."

Jo made a small sound of frustration. "Perhaps if I could pay you for it..."

"Someone asked me once what was the value of a dream or the price of a human spirit." Jo shifted her eyes to his helplessly. "I didn't have an answer then. Do you have one now?"

She sighed and shook her head. "I don't know what to say to you. 'Thank you' is far from adequate."

"It's not necessary, either," Keane told her. "I simply gave back what was yours in any case. What else was there, Jo? You said there were a couple of things."

This was it, Jo's brain told her. Carefully, she set down the coffee and rose. Waiting for her stomach to settle, she walked a few feet out into the room, then turned. She allowed herself a deep breath before she met Keane's eyes.

"I want to be your mistress," she said with absolute calm.

"What?" Both Keane's face and voice registered utter shock.

Jo swallowed and repeated. "I want to be your mistress. That's still the right term, isn't it, or is it antiquated? Is *lover* right? I've never done this before."

Slowly, Keane set his mug beside hers and rose. He did not move toward her but watched her with probing eyes. "Jo, you don't know what you're saying."

"Oh, yes, I do," she cut him off and nodded. "I might not have the terminology exactly right, but I do know what I mean, and I'm sure you do, too. I want to be with you," she continued and took a step toward him. "I want you to make love to me. I want to live with you if you'll let me, or at least close by."

"Jo, you're not talking sensibly." Sharply, Keane broke into her speech. Turning away, he thrusted his hands into his pockets and balled them into fists. "You don't know what you're asking."

"Don't I appeal to you anymore?"

Keane whirled, infuriated with the trace of curiosity in her voice. "How can you ask me that?" he demanded. "Of course you appeal to me! I'm not dead or in the throes of senility!"

She moved closer to him. "Then if I want you, and you want me, why can't we be lovers?"

Keane swore violently and grabbed her shoulders. "Do you think I could have you for a winter and then blithely let you go? Do you think I could untangle myself at the start of the season and watch you stroll out of my life? Haven't you the sense to see what you do to me?" He shook her hard with the question, stealing any breath she might have used to answer him.

"You make me crazy!" Abruptly, he dragged her against him. His mouth bruised hers, his fingers dug into her flesh. Jo's head spun with confusion and pain and ecstasy. It seemed centuries since she had tasted his mouth on hers. She heard him groan as he tore himself away. He turned, leaving her to find her own balance as the room swayed. "What do I have to do to be rid of you?" His words came in furious undertones.

Jo blew out a breath. "I don't think kissing me like that is a very good start."

"I'm aware of that," he murmured. She watched the rise and fall of his shoulders. "I've been trying to avoid doing it since I opened the door."

Quietly, Jo walked to him and put a hand on his arm. "You're tense," she discovered and automatically sought to soothe the muscles. "I'm sorry if I'm going about this the wrong way. I thought telling you outright would be better than trying to seduce you. I don't think I'd be very good at that."

Keane made a sound somewhere between a laugh and a moan. "Jovilette," he murmured before he turned and gathered her into his arms. "How do I resist you? How many times must I pull away before I'm free of you? Even the thought of you drives me mad."

"Keane." She sighed and shut her eyes. "I've wanted you to hold me for so long. I want to belong to you, even for just a little while."

"No." He pulled away, then forced her chin up with his thumb and forefinger. "Don't you see that once would be too much and a lifetime wouldn't be enough? I love you too much to let you go and enough to know I have to." Shock robbed her of speech. She only stared as he continued. "It was different when I didn't know, when I thought I was—how did you put it? 'Dazzled.'" He smiled briefly at the word. "I was certain if I could make love to you, I could get you out of my system. Then, the night Ari died, I held you while you slept. I realized I was in love with you, had been in love with you right from the beginning."

"But you…" Jo shook her head as if to clear it. "You never told me, and you seemed so cold, so distant."

"I couldn't touch you without wanting more." He pulled her close again and for a moment buried his face in her hair. "But I couldn't stay away. I knew if I wanted to have you, to really have you, one of us had to give up what we did, what we were. I wondered if I could give up the law; it was really all I ever wanted to do. I discovered I wanted you more."

"Oh, Keane." She shook her head, but he put her from him suddenly.

"Then I found out that wouldn't work, either." Keane turned, paced to the window and stared out. The snow was falling heavily. "Every time you walked into that cage, I walked into hell. I thought perhaps I'd get used to it, but it only got worse. I tried leaving, coming back here, but I could never shake you loose. I kept coming back. The day you were hurt…" Keane paused. Jo heard him draw in his breath, and when he continued, his voice was deeper. "I watched you step in front of that boy and take the blow. I can't tell you what I felt at that moment; there aren't words for it. All I could think of was getting to you. I wonder if Pete ever told you that I decked him before Buck got to me. He took it very well, considering. Then I had to—to just stand there and watch while that cat stalked you. I've never known that kind of fear before. The kind that empties you out, body and soul."

He lapsed into silence. "Then it was over," he continued, "and I got to you. You were so white, and you were bleeding in my arms." He muttered an oath, then was silent again. He shook his head. "I wanted to burn the place down, get you away, strangle the cats with my bare hands. Anything. I wanted to hold you, but I couldn't get past the fear and the unreasonable anger at having been helpless. Before my hands stopped shaking, you were making plans to go back into that damnable cage. I wanted to kill you myself then and be done with it."

Slowly, Keane turned and walked back to her. "I saw it happen again every time I closed my eyes for weeks afterward. I can show you exactly where the scars are."

He lifted a finger and traced four lines on her upper arm precisely where the claws had ripped her skin. He dropped his hand and shook his head. "I can't watch you go in the cage, Jo." He lifted his hand again and let it linger over her hair. "If I let you stay with me now, I wouldn't be able to let you go back to your own life. And I can't ask you to give it up."

"I wish you would." Solemn-eyed, Jo watched him. "I very much wish you would."

"Jo." Shaking his head, he turned away. "I know what it means to you."

"No more than the law means to you, I imagine," she said briskly. "But you said you were willing to give that up."

"Yes, but..."

"Oh, very well." She pushed back her hair. "If you won't ask me, I'll have to ask you. Will you marry me?"

Keane turned back, giving her his lowered brow frown. "Jo, you can't..."

"Of course I can. This is the twentieth century. If I want to ask you to marry me, then I will. I did," she pointed out.

"Jo, I don't..."

"Yes or no, please, counselor. This isn't an easy question." She stepped forward until they stood toe to toe. "I'm in love with you, and I want to marry you and have several babies. Is that agreeable?"

Keane's mouth opened and closed. He gave her an odd smile and lifted his hands to her shoulders. "This is rather sudden."

Jo felt a wild surge of joy. "Perhaps it is," she admitted. "I'll give you a minute to think about it. But I might as well tell you, I won't take no for an answer."

Keane's fingers traced the curve of her neck. "It seems I have little choice."

"None at all," she corrected. Boldly, she locked her arms around him and pulled his mouth down to hers. The kiss was instantly urgent, instantly searching. Joined, they lowered to the rug and clung. For a long, long moment, their lips were united in a language too complex for words. Then, as if to reassure himself she was real, Keane searched the familiar curves of her body, tasted the longed-for flavor of her skin.

"Why did I think I could live without you?" he whispered. His mouth came desperately back to hers. "Be sure, Jo, be sure." Roughened with emotion, his voice was low while the words were spoken against her lips. "I'll never be able to let you go. I'm asking you for everything."

"No. No, it's not like that. Hold me tighter. Kiss me again," she demanded as his lips roamed her face. "Kiss me." She wondered if the sound of pleasure she heard was his or her own. She had not known a kiss could be so intimate, so terrifyingly exciting. No, she thought as she soared with the knowledge that he loved her. He wasn't asking everything, he was giving it.

"I'm leaving something behind," she told him when their lips parted, "and replacing it with something infinitely more important." She buried her face in the curve of his neck. "When you realize how much I love you, you'll understand."

Keane drew away and stared down at her. At last he spoke, but it was only her name. It was a soft sigh of a sound. She smiled at it and lifted a hand to his cheek. "If there's a way to compromise..."

"No." She shook her head, remembering his mother's words. "Sometimes there can't be a compromise. We love each other enough not to need one. Please, don't think I'm making a sacrifice; I'm not." She smiled a little and rubbed her palm experimentally over the stubble of his neglected beard. "I don't regret one minute of my life in the circus, and I don't regret changing it. You've given me the circus, so I'll always be a part of it." Her smile faded, and her eyes grew serious. "Will you belong to me, Keane?"

He took her hand from his cheek and pressed it to his lips. "I already do. I love you, Jovilette. I'll spend a lifetime loving you."

"That's not long enough," she said as their lips met again. "I want more. I want forever."

With slow, building passion, his hands moved over her. Taking his time, he loosened the buttons on her sweater. "So beautiful," he murmured as his lips trailed down her throat and found the gentle swell. Jo's breath caught at the new intimacy. "You're trembling. I love knowing I can make your skin tremble under my hands." His lips roamed back to hers before he cradled her in his arms. "I've wanted to be with you, to hold you, just hold you, for so long. I can't remember not wanting it."

With a sigh washed with contentment, Jo snuggled against him. "Keane," she murmured.

"Hmm?"

"You never answered me."

"About what?" He kissed her closed lids, then tangled his fingers in her hair.

Jo opened her eyes. Her brows arched over them. "Are you going to marry me or not?"

Keane laughed, rolled her onto her back and planted a long, lingering kiss on her mouth. "Is tomorrow soon enough?"

* * * * *

New York Times and USA TODAY Bestselling Author

KRISTAN HIGGINS

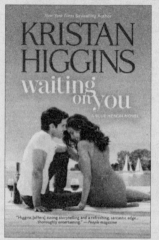

"Higgins [offers] strong storytelling and a refreshing, sarcastic edge... thoroughly entertaining." —*People* magazine

Does being nobody's fool mean that you're nobody's love?

Colleen O'Rourke is in love with love…just not when it comes to herself. Most nights, she can be found behind the bar at the Manningsport, New York, tavern she owns with her twin brother, doling out romantic advice to the lovelorn, mixing martinis and staying more or less happily single. See, ten years ago, Lucas Campbell, her first love, broke her heart…an experience Colleen doesn't want to have again, thanks. Since then, she's been happy with a fling here and there, some elite-level flirting and playing matchmaker to her friends.

But a family emergency has brought Lucas back to town, handsome as ever and still the only man who's ever been able to crack her defenses. Seems like maybe they've got some unfinished business waiting for them—but to find out, Colleen has to let her guard down, or risk losing a second chance with the only man she's ever loved.

Available wherever books are sold!

Be sure to connect with us at:

Harlequin.com/Newsletters
Facebook.com/HarlequinBooks
Twitter.com/HarlequinBooks

www.Harlequin.com

PHKH858

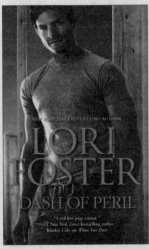

REQUEST YOUR
FREE BOOKS!

2 FREE NOVELS
FROM THE ROMANCE COLLECTION
PLUS 2 FREE GIFTS!

YES! Please send me 2 FREE novels from the Romance Collection and my 2 FREE gifts (gifts are worth about $10). After receiving them, if I don't wish to receive any more books, I can return the shipping statement marked "cancel." If I don't cancel, I will receive 4 brand-new novels every month and be billed just $6.24 per book in the U.S. or $6.74 per book in Canada. That's a savings of at least 22% off the cover price. It's quite a bargain! Shipping and handling is just 50¢ per book in the U.S. and 75¢ per book in Canada.* I understand that accepting the 2 free books and gifts places me under no obligation to buy anything. I can always return a shipment and cancel at any time. Even if I never buy another book, the two free books and gifts are mine to keep forever.

194/394 MDN F4XY

Name	(PLEASE PRINT)

Address	Apt. #

City	State/Prov.	Zip/Postal Code

Signature (if under 18, a parent or guardian must sign)

Mail to the **Harlequin® Reader Service:**
IN U.S.A.: P.O. Box 1867, Buffalo, NY 14240-1867
IN CANADA: P.O. Box 609, Fort Erie, Ontario L2A 5X3

Want to try two free books from another line?
Call 1-800-873-8635 or visit www.ReaderService.com.

* Terms and prices subject to change without notice. Prices do not include applicable taxes. Sales tax applicable in N.Y. Canadian residents will be charged applicable taxes. Offer not valid in Quebec. This offer is limited to one order per household. Not valid for current subscribers to the Romance Collection or the Romance/Suspense Collection. All orders subject to credit approval. Credit or debit balances in a customer's account(s) may be offset by any other outstanding balance owed by or to the customer. Please allow 4 to 6 weeks for delivery. Offer available while quantities last.

Your Privacy—The Harlequin® Reader Service is committed to protecting your privacy. Our Privacy Policy is available online at www.ReaderService.com or upon request from the Harlequin Reader Service.

We make a portion of our mailing list available to reputable third parties that offer products we believe may interest you. If you prefer that we not exchange your name with third parties, or if you wish to clarify or modify your communication preferences, please visit us at www.ReaderService.com/consumerschoice or write to us at Harlequin Reader Service Preference Service, P.O. Box 9062, Buffalo, NY 14269. Include your complete name and address.

ROM13R